Sarah Harvey lives in Leicester and has written four previous novels, *Misbehaving*, *Fly-fishing*, *Split Ends* and *Long Division*, also available from Headline.

# Postcards from Wits End

## Sarah Harvey

**headline**

First published in 2002
by HEADLINE BOOK PUBLISHING

First published in paperback in 2003
by HEADLINE BOOK PUBLISHING

10 9 8 7 6 5 4 3 2

ISBN 0 7472 6524 0

Typeset in Meridien by
Letterpart Limited, Reigate, Surrey

Printed and bound in Great Britain by
Mackays of Chatham plc, Chatham, Kent

HEADLINE BOOK PUBLISHING
A division of Hodder Headline
338 Euston Road
LONDON NW1 3BH

www.headline.co.uk
www.hodderheadline.com

For Terry.

## Acknowledgements

Thanks, as always, to my agent Luigi Bononi without whom this book would not have been written, and to Clare Foss, Sherise Hobbs, and the fantastic team at Headline. To Dave and Jane, and everyone at the Narrowcliff Hotel in Newquay for their wonderful hospitality. And, as ever, to mine and Terry's family and friends whose support is boundless and invaluable.

# *Prologue*

The beginning isn't meant to be the end. You don't launch into the biggest love story of the century only for it to finish when the hero and heroine have just begun. Then again, when you read a book it usually ends just after the lovers have finally sorted out whatever problems there were to keep them apart – because believe me, there are always problems – and they are just starting out on the Happy Ever After part.

I suppose therefore that it was apt for us to end here, after a brief six months of marriage.

Major obstacles supposedly surmounted, Rob and I had come to that wonderful moment – the fairy-tale wedding. There was I, basking in love, radiating happiness as brides are wont to do, even allowing myself to be a little smug for once, just for one day – one glorious, white-dressed, cherry-blossomed, champagne-flowing, spine-tingling, neverending, slow, soul-swapping kiss of a day – that I believed would be one of the happiest days of my life.

My ignorance was truly blissful, for instead of the beginning, Rob and I had somehow reached the final chapter.

The End.

I will not cry. To cry is to heal. I cannot heal. I need the pain to remind me of what I've lost. To keep him fresh in my mind.

1

*My husband.*

The man who is no longer standing beside me, strong, vibrant, and full of life. The man whom I loved with all of my heart and yet cannot cry for. I am like a cactus. I keep my water on the inside and my thorns on the outside to protect me.

Today I will remain hidden. Hidden behind dark glasses and an air of unapproachability that people feel duty-bound to broach.

'I'm so sorry for your loss.'

How can you lose someone? It's a strange way of putting it – as if you've been careless or something. Maybe I was. Maybe if I'd taken more care, not let him out of my sight, then Rob would still be here with me now. On autopilot I take the outstretched hand of the woman standing in front of me, her eyes sorrowful and sympathetic. I open my mouth to say, 'Thank you,' but find I cannot speak.

Then the Reverend Rachael James comes to stand before me. The same woman who, only six months ago, at this very same church, presided over our wedding.

'I know there are few words of comfort I can give you at this time, Natalie. God must seem to you to be very unjust in taking Robert away from us. But I hope that deep in your heart it will give you solace to know that he is in a better place . . .'

Oh, not you as well! How many more times am I going to hear that? What better place could he be in, than here with the people who love him? The people who *need* him.

'I'm sorry, Natalie, I know it's not easy . . .'

Oh, you know, do you?

'. . . I know it's hard to believe at the moment, but people do understand how you feel. There isn't one among us who hasn't been touched by the loss of someone we love. You're not alone.'

Then why do I feel as if I am? Completely alone.

2

She puts a gentle hand on my arm. 'It's probably the last thing you want to hear at the moment, but it will get better, you know, given time.'

Given time.

Time is the one thing I don't have any more. Time to myself, yes, but the only time I really want is more time with Rob. Please, somebody, give me time with him.

My heart feels as if it is still here, beating within my chest, but I know it's not. It was buried today with Rob – but I can still feel it. A phantom limb.

I am aware of my best friend Petra's hand holding mine, and focus on that instead, draw strength from the solidity of her body set against mine, like a sturdy bamboo cane supporting a wilting flower.

To the other side of Petra is my mother Laura. She is watching me, a strange expression on her handsome face, a whole decade and a half of my own unresolved antipathy firmly holding her at arm's length, despite the fact I can see that she desperately longs to be close to me, to comfort me in any way she can.

Beyond her, opposite me, stands Cassie, Rob's fourteen-year-old daughter. My step-daughter. Holding herself stiffly and firmly away from me, as I do with Laura.

Cassie lost her own mother, Eve, many years ago, and now stands silently at her father's graveside, a handkerchief covering the bottom of her face, her chin, her mouth, her nose; above it, only her ice-blue eyes are visible, staring blankly. She catches my eye, and then looks away as quickly.

Cassie has her father's eyes, although whereas his used to look upon me with warmth, love and affection, hers are far colder. She has never accepted me, always pushed me away. Looked upon me as an interloper who stole her father's time and affection. And now, when we need each other the most, she still turns away from me, preferring to stand alone.

Despite the physical and emotional distance between us, we are together now, come what may. I have lost a husband, and yet now I officially have a daughter. More so even than if Rob were still alive. I am Cassie's only *legal guardian*. Written down in black and white and presented to me by Rob's solicitors Messrs Freeland, Quinn & Joseph two days ago.

I long to reach out to that solitary figure whose young heart must surely be twisted with the same searing agony that now cripples mine, and yet somehow, I am afraid to go to her. And yet how could I ever forgive myself if I did not?

'Cassie . . .'

She turns with a start at the sound of my voice.

'I . . . I . . .' I falter, the sight of her stony hostile face too much for me. I take a deep breath. 'I just want you to know that I'm here for you, if you ever need anything . . . if you ever need me.'

She looks at me for a moment, icy and still. Her voice when she replies is as cold as her eyes. 'I don't need *you*.' And she turns away from me again.

Cassie's only other surviving relative is her grandmother, Louisa-May, Eve's mother. She is standing between Cas and me, her frail body shaking like a leaf in the wind, leaning heavily on a walking stick, determined not to use the wheelchair on which her multiple sclerosis has now made her semi-reliant. I feel something cold touch my other hand and realise that it is Louisa's thin hand, seeking to comfort and be comforted.

'Forgive her,' she whispers to me, her soft voice catching on the tears she is suppressing. 'She doesn't mean it. It's a difficult day. A black day.' She clings on to my hand, her worn eyes awash with tears and sadness.

I think that's the most apt thing anyone has said to me today.

*It's a black day.*

Black as an endless night with no moon or stars. Black

4

as the coldest heart. Black as the ice that will send car wheels skidding to a final, shattering impact.

When I get home, I close the door behind me and lean back against it, suddenly conscious of the way that I breathe. The way that I still inhale and exhale. Amazed by the fact that somehow I have managed to live on in this world, even though Rob has gone from it.

I am alone.

Cas has returned to her boarding-school, refusing point blank to come back to the house; her grand-mother, desperately torn, accompanying her on the drive back at my quiet insistence.

Those who wanted to come with me – Petra, my mother, friends – I have sent away. I couldn't do it. Even though some people expected it, even though a few spoke about my failure to conform in hushed and sometimes disapproving tones, I just couldn't do it. I couldn't hold a wake for him. I couldn't sit in our home and watch people drink tea, and eat sandwiches; listen to the hum of hushed voices, smile stoically at the well-meant platitudes.

My legs heavy and leaden, I slowly climb the stairs to our room, and push open the door, stand on the thresh-old, looking in.

This is our room. It is here, and yet it feels like it belongs to another life. Like I am watching it from a distance, and any minute now the picture will go hazy and fade, and it will simply cease to be there any more. Like Rob.

Yet when I take a tentative step forward the room remains, the floor feels firm and very real beneath my feet. It is still here. *I* am still here. This is my new reality.

I sit down on the bed but it doesn't feel right. I move to the chair by the window but can't settle here either. I open the door of the wardrobe and see Rob's clothes in neat ranks within. The smell of him hits me like a physical wave, threatening to knock me to the wooden floor.

Hesitantly I reach towards a cashmere jumper and pull a sleeve to my face, at first holding it two inches away from my nose, inhaling tentatively, and then thrusting the soft warmth against my face, rubbing it almost violently into my skin, into my eyes, tearing the fibre across the chapped and broken skin of my lips.

Slowly I sink to the floor, curling into a ball like a child in the womb, cushioning my head within my arms, the inside of my wrists pressed to my cheekbones, my hands covering my ears, fingers twisted into my hair, tugging so hard it hurts. But I can't feel the physical pain. The only pain I am conscious of is the tearing, searing, grinding ache inside of me.

I don't know how long I crouch there, a kind of buzzing silence filling a head that is empty of everything except a long and anguished silent scream, but finally my dry, staring eyes find a focus.

There is a photograph of Rob beside the bed. My favourite photograph: I took it. And although he is looking into the camera, he is also looking beyond it, at me. And his eyes are so full of love, and laughter, and life.

I see his face smiling out at me and realise that I am balanced on the edge waiting to fall either way; realise that the one thing I do have left is a choice. I can either let myself slide into this quicksand of soul-destroying loss, or I can haul myself out by my broken nails and survive.

Rob would want me to survive.

# Chapter One

**Twenty Months Later**

Magna the American publishing giant, with offices in New York, London, Paris and Hong Kong, owns an entire, impressively modern building on the Euston Road. It is one of those buildings that is designed to reflect the natural light around it, and therefore appears to be unobtrusive despite the fact that it is twenty-two floors of very solid glass and steel. It is also a building that has been more of a home to me since Rob's death, than the house that we once shared together.

I have worked for one of Magna's major publications, *Naked*, a women's magazine, for the past six years. My job has always been extremely important to me, not least because it was through the magazine that I met the two people who have been the most influential in my life over the past few years. Firstly Petra, who took me under her wing from the very start, and then Rob.

I met Rob whilst writing an assignment on men in the mainly female world of ballet; he, an up-and-coming theatre director, was one of my last interviews. We almost didn't meet at all. He'd cancelled our first meeting; I, the second.

By the third I had enough for my piece without his interview, and was keen to get to work putting everything together. I almost cancelled completely, but something stopped me. Looking back I'd like to think it was the hand of fate, but if I'm being completely honest it was probably more to do with manners.

Then, when we finally agreed on a time for this third appointment, the Esoteric Theatre lived up to its name, being very securely closed when I arrived. The Theatre Director, however, couldn't have been more open. He turned up ten minutes late, full of apologies for making me wait, with a smile that was so endearing it stayed in my mind for the whole three weeks it took him to find the courage to call me to suggest meeting up for dinner.

It was through *Naked* that I met a man who taught me how to give and accept love again, and for that I will always be eternally thankful. Now the magazine means more than ever to me. *Naked* represents something far more than a pile of print; it represents a lifeline.

For the last twenty months I have done practically nothing except work.

*Twenty months.*

I can't believe this much time has passed. Time that has seemed somehow to contradict all laws of Physics; that has run faster than the swiftest athlete, whilst standing quietly still. Our wedding anniversary, Christmas, Rob's birthday, the anniversary of the accident . . . all have come and gone in a kind of self-induced dislocation from reality.

I picked myself up, dusted myself down and have been sleepwalking my way through life ever since. I could not cope with what had happened and therefore I found other occupations for my broken mind. I have worked harder than ever before in my entire life – from when I get up, to when I fall into bed exhausted, but still unable to sleep, in the early hours of the morning. I have crammed so many other thoughts into my head that I don't have time to feel. And I don't have time to think about Rob . . . too much.

Another lifesaver has been Petra.

Petra James is a high flyer, an art expert, whose opinion is as sought after as Centre Court tickets at

Wimbledon. Her position as Associate Art Director for the magazine is a profile thing for us more than her. She is a name that is splashed across our front pages on a regular basis in order to entice a wider reader base. More importantly, to me at least, Petra is also my best friend.

A six-foot Amazon with hair the colour of copper-beech leaves, and a loud American confidence, she can come across as intimidating, but underneath the hard-as-a-conker-soaked-in-vinegar exterior, she is the kindest, most thoughtful person I have ever met. She has been my strength when I had none since Rob's accident.

Petra usually divides her time between London and New York, flying back and forth on a regular basis. For the times when she is in London she leases a beautiful apartment in an old listed building in Regent's Park, but she could have saved herself the expense, because since the accident, she has practically moved in with me.

I arrive home late again from work tonight to find her waiting for me with a Chinese takeaway and a perfectly chilled bottle of white wine. Greeting me at the door she takes the files I am carrying and replaces them with a large glass full of Chardonnay, before I've even had a chance to kick off my shoes or hang up my coat.

'No work tonight, Nat,' she tells me, putting the files down on the telephone table. 'We're having the evening off to relax – do you remember that word, honey? *Relaaaax.*'

I open my mouth to protest that I have reading to do, but Petra holds up her hands to silence me.

'Elaine does *not* pay you enough to justify you working twenty-four seven, so no argument – go upstairs and slip into something more comfortable . . . and don't be long. I've got you a surprise.'

I take a large grateful gulp from my drink, hand it back to Petra, and head upstairs to change as bid. When I come back down, Petra is in the kitchen. She is shielding something behind her back, and grinning like an idiot.

'What's going on?' I ask, trying to peer round her.

'I bought you a present.' Slowly and carefully, she moves to one side, revealing a large glass bowl filled with water set on the work surface; in it swims a lone goldfish.

'A fish,' I state stupidly.

'No, it's a parrot,' she drawls. 'Her name's Meryl.' Petra grins at me.

'How do you know it's a girl?'

'Well, if it was a boy it would be called Bob or something instead, wouldn't it?' she teases. She thrusts the bowl closer to me and I take it, albeit a little reluctantly.

'Thank you.'

'You think I'm crazy, don't you?'

'Yes, but that's nothing to do with the fish,' I reply, watching Meryl dart underneath a small blue bridge, before hiding in some fronds of weed as she spots me peering into her bowl. The little fish watches me for a moment, then swims out to thrust a small black nose against the glass where I am looking in, staring back at me with two bulbous black eyes.

'See? She likes you!' Petra exclaims happily.

And I feel a smile pulling at the corners of my mouth. One of the many things I love about Petra is her unfailing ability to make me laugh, no matter how bad I'm feeling. I would never have survived without her. She has this almost telepathic knack of knowing when I need her, and when I want to be on my own for a while. Slipping in and out of my life with practised ease, she remembers the things that I forget to do, like stocking my fridge, picking up the suits I leave at the dry cleaners for weeks on end, even turning up with a pint of milk, just as I have used the last drop in yet another cup of coffee. And she is always ready to listen, no matter that she's heard it all a thousand times before.

.We collapse on the sofa in the sitting room after dinner, our second bottle of wine on the coffee-table in front of us, Meryl beside it in her bowl swimming endlessly round in circles.

I watch the little goldfish, a curious feeling of empathy flooding me. I sometimes feel as though I too am swimming round in endless circles, scared that if I stop for just one second, I'll never get moving again, simply sink to the bottom and drown. And so I keep on moving through my life at breakneck speed, shutting it all away deep within me, so deep I cannot touch it and it cannot touch me. It's hardly the healthiest way of dealing with things, I know, moving forward and yet never moving on, too scared to feel the pain enough · to purge it. Scared of what will happen if I lose this fierce control, over my emotions and my life, I have become locked in a constant motor of *doing*.

I know Petra sees the harm in it. She's always trying to get me to talk about Rob, to open up, to heal. I try not to talk about Rob as much as I try not to think about him, but as always the fourth glass of wine loosens my inhibitions as well as my tongue, and a conversation she has been angling to start all evening – hell, all year – finally begins to happen.

'I miss him so much.'

'I know you do.'

'Do you know what always brings it home to me?'

Petra says nothing, silently encouraging me to speak. I pause for a moment, draining the last of the wine from my glass, then turn to her with a half-smile.

'Cold feet.'

'Cold feet?' She frowns.

'Yes.' I reach for the bottle and refill our glasses. 'I always had cold feet in bed until I met Rob. He used to keep them warm for me. Wrap his feet around mine. It

11

was like sleeping with an electric blanket. A horny electric blanket.'

Memories.

We'd made love that day, the day he died, in the dim grey light of a cold February morning, half-asleep, slow, languorous and leisurely. Woken by kisses on the back of my neck, a gentle hand curling its way down my stomach to dip between the soft warm hollows of my thighs, awakening me and my senses with an insistent rhythmic pressure that brought slow gasping pleasure . . .

The next morning I woke at the same time; I must have been asleep for only a few minutes, but it was long enough to forget the car crash, to forget that when I reached out for him, he wouldn't be there. He'd never be there again.

Sometimes I feel as if I'm looking back on myself, as if I was a different person then. I know I've changed in the past twenty months: I've had to. They say that with time comes healing. It's true to some degree: the pain lessens but only from a constant full-pitched crescendo to a roller-coaster of emotion. Sometimes you can slide into a cool valley of respite, maybe even laugh and feel a little happy, but then you can guarantee to go swooping back up to that same pain peak you keep hitting with guaranteed regularity.

'Do you miss sex?' Petra's voice breaks into my head.

I blink my eyes open, and look at her for a moment before answering. 'I miss sex with Rob. I haven't thought beyond that.'

'Not at all?'

'No,' I reply honestly. 'You know, it's so odd, I was giving myself a good talking-to the other day, the "pull yourself together" thing, and I was trying to think of something that could help me through this – anything – and I realised that the only person who could see me through was the one person who . . .' I stumble to a halt, unable to find the right words.

'It's okay, I know exactly what you mean.'

'If Rob were here he'd sort me out.'

'If he were here, what would he say to you?'

'To pull myself together, not to get upset, not to mope, I must start to live again, enjoy life to the full.'

'And he'd be right, Nattie. He'd hate to see you so unhappy.'

'I want to be happy, Pet, I really do. There was a time to start off with when I didn't. I never wanted to be happy again. I just wanted to curl up in a ball and disappear, cease to exist. I just wanted to be with Rob, wherever that may be. I still want to be with him, but I don't yearn for oblivion any more.'

'Not unless it's found at the bottom of a wine bottle, eh?' Petra smiles anxiously at me as I refill my glass yet again.

'A bit of temporary oblivion now and then is a good thing.'

'As long as you don't come to depend on it.' She gently moves the wine bottle away from me.

'I miss music,' I tell her, changing the subject. 'I can't listen to it any more. Not old stuff anyway, not music that we shared. I can listen to new CDs, but I can't listen to love songs, which just about rules out seventy-five per cent of what's out at the moment.'

'I'll buy you some Heavy Metal.' Petra's mouth curls up into a smile on the right-hand side of her face only. A tentative smile, like a woodland animal, a little unsure as to whether it's safe to come out of the undergrowth.

'It must be hard being my friend at the moment,' I tell her.

'It's always hard being your friend,' she retorts, poking her tongue out at me. 'You can hit me if it makes you feel better,' she offers when I don't laugh at her joke. I hug her instead.

The television is on although we are not watching it;

the sound is turned down low. One of the leading supermarkets is advertising their Christmas Fayre, a beaming red velvet-clad mother and child loading their dining table with far too much food for one nuclear family.

Petra looks from me to the television screen and then back to me again. 'What are you going to do for Christmas, Nat? Have you thought about it?'

'Christmas?' I reply as though it's a totally new concept. Although it's hard to believe, I've almost managed not to notice that Christmas is only a few weeks away. I've managed to miss the endless advertising, the decorations that have steadily been hung in shops and streets since the end of September, the coloured-light-covered trees that wink at you from every house window that you wander past at night, the cards that have been building up in an unopened pile on the telephone table by the front door.

'It's only five weeks away now.'

'I think ignore it is my best option at the moment.' I smile weakly.

'You can't ignore Christmas!'

'Why not? I managed to last year.'

'I know. I can't *believe* you worked over Christmas.' She shakes her head.

'Lots of people work on Christmas Day.'

'Sure – if you work in a hospital or a something, not on a bloody magazine.'

'Well, you were in New York . . .'

'And I asked you to come with me,' she cuts in quickly.

'Cassie was skiing, and Louisa-May was so poorly last winter, it just didn't feel right.'

'Your mother asked you down as well.'

I don't answer.

'And this year? What about Cassie? It's her birthday soon, isn't it?'

'Yeah,' I nod, 'but I didn't see her for it last year. She chose to go to her friends' instead.'

'Will she be coming home for Christmas?'

'I doubt it. She's hardly spent any time here since . . .' I sigh and push my hair out of my face. 'I honestly don't think she classifies this as home any more. She'll probably go to a friend's, that's what she's chosen to do so far. I can't see her suddenly deciding she wants to spend Christmas with me, can you? I swear she only went skiing with a friend last year so she didn't have to come back here.'

Petra doesn't answer. She doesn't need to. We both know that Cas will do everything she can to avoid spending any time with me, despite the fact that whether she likes it or not, with me is where she should now be until she is eighteen.

I have barely seen my step-daughter in the past twenty months. I am sure she wishes that her grandmother could have been granted guardianship of her, but Louisa-May, although only sixty-two and fiercely independent, is badly affected by multiple sclerosis, and has no choice other than to live in sheltered accommodation, where she can receive the care she needs. She couldn't possibly care for Cassie in her position, but I fear I have fared little better.

I have tried so hard to see my guardianship as a positive thing. To be there for her if she ever wants or needs me, and yet she still rejects me. It was hard enough being Cassie's step-mother when Rob was alive. The times that she was at home, I felt as if I had all the crap of being a parent without any of the things that make the slog of parenthood worth while: the affection, the hugs and kisses, the bond, the pride, the feeling of belonging to a family.

Cas would do anything she could to make me feel that I didn't belong. She was very good at building a wall around herself and her father, an impenetrable wall, suggesting things that they could do together that would alienate me – a favourite being trips to funfairs or theme parks where the inevitable two-seat rides would see me standing on my own waiting for them to come back to earth, laughing, smiling and holding hands.

I always tried not to take it personally and remember that having lost her mother, she would inevitably resent any other call on her father's affection, my mantra being *she's just a child*. In time she would get used to me, I hoped. I didn't expect her to see me as a replacement for her mother, but I hoped that one day we could be friends. She is nearly sixteen now, and still as far away from me as ever, despite the fact that I am responsible for her, and she is responsible to me.

And still she hates me. Even more so now than she ever used to. Her hatred is almost palpable. Where I cling to work to keep me going, Cassie feeds off her loathing for me. She seeks to blame, and for some reason she blames *me* for her loss, not the drunk on the wrong side of the road who made Rob swerve so violently, nor the black ice that made the skid uncontrollable.

Just me.

It's all my fault.

We have seen each other five times exactly in the last twenty months, one of those times being the funeral, and another the meeting at the solicitor's. I get regular reports on her welfare from her school, and updates from when I visit or speak with Louisa-May, but if Cassie can find any alternative, she will *not* come home. The loathing she so obviously felt for me when I first started seeing her father has increased beyond measure since Rob's death.

I am certain Cas feels in some way that if I hadn't come into her father's life then he would probably still be here. What makes this worse is that sometimes I feel this myself as well.

Was it something I did that made this happen?

Could I have done something to stop it?
*If only he'd . . .*
*If only I'd . . .*
*If only . . .*

I've always loved my job. Passionately. I feel I've really had to fight every step of the way to get where I am today, and that gives me a sense of satisfaction that I don't think I would have had if everything had been easy.

*Naked* is a slightly more serious magazine than some; every other article isn't about how to spice up your sex-life or change your boyfriend from slob to sex god in four easy steps. We deal with real issues – world situations, poverty, hunger, disease – with the arts thrown in for a recreational point of view. Our main thrust is how the modern woman copes with the flak thrown at her by the modern world.

The people who work there are like family to me. Some of them I love, others I wish I only had to see at Christmas.

Dora is one of the ones that I like immensely. She has the colouring and round face of a Matrioshka doll, with dark raven curls, pale skin and pink cheeks. Flushed and pretty. Short and curvy. She always smells of Pears soap and Pears shampoo. You never see *her* eating junk food – her only foray into what the majority of people would consider snacking being the occasional bag of Kettle crisps. To Dora, snacking is eating an apple or munching her way through a stack of raw vegetables. She has the glowing velvet skin of someone who keeps a fresh two-litre bottle of water at the side of her chair every day, and actually drinks it. When people admire her willpower she simply laughs and states that you don't need willpower to stop you eating garbage.

I wish I had her philosophy on eating. Her garbage is my soul food. When I actually remember to eat, it's always something that I shouldn't. In the top left-hand drawer of my desk I currently have two jam doughnuts and a bag of fun-sized Mars Bars. It is amazing therefore that I have lost over a stone in weight. I reach for one of the doughnuts, take a huge bite.

'Call for you, Nat.'

'Who is it?' I mouth, licking jam from my chin, and sugar from my lips. 'Sorry, she did say but I've forgotten. Asked to speak with Mrs Forester though.'

'Really?' My heart dips down to the pit of my stomach where it begins to pulse a little faster.

'Uhuh.' She nods and takes another bite of her apple. 'I think that's why I forgot her name because it was so odd hearing her ask for you like that.'

When I married Rob, I was fiercely possessive of my own surname. Why should I give up my name? I wasn't suddenly a subordinate to him because we'd signed a marriage licence. Rob and I were a team. We did discuss going double-barrelled, but only for a brief drunken moment, which had us laughing at the prospect of becoming the Dunne-Foresters, which Rob said made us sound like a merry band of retired tree fellers.

And so we decided that neither of us should change at all. He would remain Mr Robert Alexander Forester, and I would stay Natalie Dunne. No middle name, because my mother and father never gave one to me, and no Ms, because I've always thought that was a bit of an aggressive title. More of a statement than I wanted to make.

Now I wish I hadn't been so emancipated. Now I need the recognition that the name 'Mrs Forester' would give me. It is another link, another connection to an identity that I'm now trying desperately to hang on to.

Dora pushes the hold button, and replacing the receiver on her phone, dials the number to pass the call through to me.

'Mrs Forester?' The voice is articulate, and unfamiliar.

'Speaking.'

'It's Eleanor Brice from Cheal.'

It takes me a moment to place her, my mind hunting through a bunch of hazy memories that hang like shadows at the back of my mind, and then I realise why the name is familiar to me. Eleanor Brice is the headmistress from Cassie's school. I've never met the woman, but it's a name I've heard often in discussions with Rob, and then the solicitors; a name signed with a neat cultured hand at the end of letters and school reports. Her voice is soft and steady, but with an underlying strength that I would imagine from her reputation is echoed in her personality.

'I'm so sorry to disturb you at work, but I'm afraid there's been a rather unfortunate incident.'

'Is Cassie okay?' I cut in quickly, breathlessly.

'I can assure you that *physically* Cassandra is in perfectly good health,' she says slowly after a brief pause, 'but I'm afraid I do have a problem with her behaviour.'

'You do?'

'A rather serious one, I'm afraid.'

*Join the club*, I sigh in silent sympathy. Join the club.

The next day, I drive down to Cheal. I have an appointment with Eleanor Brice at eleven. She was decidedly uninformative on the telephone, stating that she would prefer to give me the precise details of 'Cassandra's misdemeanour' in person.

At least I know the problem with Cassie is her behaviour rather than her health, which whilst extremely reassuring in one way – I am used to bad behaviour from Cas – leaves me wondering exactly what she has been up to. I haven't seen Cassie since the last school summer holiday when she managed to spend almost a whole week with me in Hampstead. A record amount of time, made possible and tolerable only by the presence of her grandmother Louisa-May, who is the dearest sweetest person in the world, the frailest yet most forceful referee. But she was, as always, a whirlwind of discord.

Her school reports, once impeccable, have steadily deteriorated, and I have watched her decline with a mixture of frustration, fear and guilt, knowing that I should do *something*, yet failing to see what, watching from a distance as she sinks ever deeper into trouble.

I'm not surprised to have been called here today, just disappointed, but only in myself, for allowing my fear of doing something that would make Cassie hate me more, stop me from doing anything at all.

Once the country home of a well-known eighteenth-century Minister for Foreign Affairs who was far more renowned for his local ones, Highdown House has been home to Cheal, a private girls' school, for the last two hundred years, and prides itself on an excellent academic reputation. It also has unrivalled dance and drama facilities, which is one of the main reasons that Cassie attends.

Her almost obsessive aim in life is to follow in her mother's footsteps. Rob's first wife Eve was a dancer, a prima ballerina. When I first started seeing him, he had a painting of her above the fireplace in the sitting room of the house in Hampstead. It was one of the first things you noticed when you walked into the room. Eve Forester was the possessor of an almost ethereal beauty that I am assured was not a case of artistic largesse; she looked like a mythical creature who had been captured in that frame by some form of sorcery. The painting was entitled *Eve as Titania, A Midsummer Night's Dream, Act III.* A hard act to follow.

Eve died when Cassie was only two, almost as dramatically as she had lived, not quite on stage, but waiting in the wings. An aneurysm. A congenital weakness made fatal by her punishing schedule. Of course Cassie worships the memory of her mother far more than she would have ever adored the reality. Eve, I have been informed, was difficult and rather egocentric – but of course to Cas she would always be beautiful, and just, and angelic.

Unlike me, the wicked step-mother.

Set in the heart of the Sussex countryside, Highdown is reached via a long straight drive that leads through gently undulating fields of grazing cattle who glance up as my car slowly motors past them. Pasture gives way to parkland, oak trees to acacia, countryside to cultivation, with beautifully tended lawns stepping their way up like exam grades toward the main body of the huge Georgian house.

Beyond perfectly clipped, human-height hedges, unused grass tennis courts give way to hard courts and the first signs of human life; two young girls in perfect whites are making the most of the winter sunshine in an amazingly athletic and powerful display of the game. Volleys as hard as gunshots crack back and forth with frightening rapidity.

I park my car on a gravel area where a movable wooden sign states *Visitors' Parking*, and then follow another sign to the main entrance of the house. Stepping from the sunlight into the shadow cast by the huge stone-columned portico entrance, I shiver, and pause to collect myself before heading up the steps and into the building.

Cassie has kept me away from her school as effectively as she has kept me out of her life. I think this must be the first time I've stepped inside a school since I left college when I was eighteen. Not that my college was anything like this place. It was a rather drab 1970s concrete Open College disaster, whereas Highdown House is elitist with a capital P for Posh.

The air is filled with a sort of soft silence, broken by the gentle hum of a hundred voices murmuring as if in unison, the distant sound of a piano repeating the same chord over and over as the unknown fingers playing it stumble each time on the same stanza. Then the sounding of a bell vibrates through the still air, and the almost-silence is cracked like an egg against a frying pan; there is a bursting sizzle of noise, as girls spill out from doors to either side of the long wide corridor.

A pretty girl with long straight blonde hair, and cut-glass cheekbones pauses as she passes me, her smile and her violet eyes friendly yet slightly guarded. A badge on her neat royal-blue jumper tells me that she is a prefect.

'May I help you?'

'Er, I have an appointment with Eleanor Brice. Your head mistress,' I add somewhat unnecessarily, as I'm certain that the girl is more than aware who Eleanor Brice is.

She smiles again and points to a sign beside the door that I missed when I came in. *Please ring for assistance.* Beside the notice a small brass bell is set into the wall.

'Oh, right. I didn't see that – thank you.'

The girl nods and makes to move away, then changes her mind, and turns back to me.

'You're supposed to ring the bell, but if you wait for Potty Price to come and fetch you, you'll be here for ever. I can show you up, if you like. I've got to go past Miss Brice's office to get to English.'

I stumble over my thank you, amazed that at thirty-two, I can be made tongue-tied by the poise of a sixteen-year-old girl.

Eleanor Brice's office is neat and cool, with dark oak panelling on the walls. Rich winter-green velvet curtains frame a huge sash window that overlooks the gardens and sweeping parkland. The walls are hung with several rather good watercolours, presumably of the house and gardens. The carpet is a soft fern green that feels springy to the step, like treading on a bouncy castle. Coming from the continuous buzz of noise in the corridors outside, the silence inside this one small room is almost deafening.

I am shown in by the Headmistress's secretary, an austere-looking woman with a hawk-like nose, and greying hair swept back from her head into a severe bun. The wooden name-plate on her desk tells me that she is Miss Price – or should that be Potty Price? The similarity in surnames could make things a little confusing. Price, Brice, Brice, Price. Like a tongue-twister, I can't stop repeating the words in my head. Miss Price's pale grey face is completely devoid of make-up, and she appears to be as nervy and highly-strung as a rabbit that's just caught the scent of the local fox in its twitching nostrils.

When my youthful companion shows me into her office and announces my name, she responds by almost dropping the pile of papers she is carrying from her cluttered desk to a nearby steel filing cabinet, and with a flurry and fluster of 'oh my goodness' and 'yes indeed' bothers me through a nearby door like an insect-phobic trying to get a wasp out of an open window.

Eleanor Brice, in contrast, is as neat and cool as her office. She is waiting for me, behind an oak desk bound with green leather, her neat Windsmoor-suited bottom perched upon the studded, padded green leather seat of an old secretary's chair made of oak almost blackened with age and use. She is leaning back in a quiet, observant manner, studying me as curiously as I am studying her surroundings. She gestures for me to sit across from her.

'Mrs Forester? Eleanor Brice.' Lifting slightly from her seat, she holds out a small slender hand, which I take and shake nervously, hoping that my own isn't too damp with nerves or trembling too obviously.

'Thank you for responding to my phone call so promptly. I do hope your journey here wasn't too

arduous? Can Miss Price fetch you some refreshment –
coffee, perhaps?'

I nod gratefully, my throat suddenly very dry at the
thought of seeing Cassie once more.

Miss Brice smiles at Miss Price, who nods her
acknowledgement.

Eleanor Brice has silvery-yellow blonde hair cut into a
neat, fringed bob, which falls in soft waves to just above
her shoulders. Her face is not unattractive, symmetrical,
as though mirror-imaged. Her figure is trim and petite,
yet oozing calm authority from every pore. I can see her
being iron-willed but fair, and on first impression I think
I like her. She's certainly far removed from the Gorgon
who ran my own high school with the whip of a very
sharp tongue.

When Miss Price returns with coffee on a tray, she
hands the first cup to her employer before giving me the
second and retreating silently from the room. Eleanor
Brice waits until she has closed the door behind her,
before she continues to speak.

'I'm very sorry we had to call you down here at such
short notice.'

'What's happened? Is Cassie okay?'

'I think we should wait until Cassandra joins us before
I give you the full details of this rather . . . *unfortunate*
incident.'

'Actually I think I'd rather like a few details first. You
know, forewarned is forearmed.'

Eleanor Brice pauses for a moment to consider, pressing her fingertips together and pursing her lips. Before
she can answer me, however, there is a knock at the
door.

The girl who enters the room is at first glance almost
unrecognisable as the sour-faced fifteen year old I last
saw nearly four months ago. Her once long, pale-gold
hair has undergone the most amazing transformation.
Shorn to within two inches of her head, it is now dyed

the palest platinum blonde, with traces of shocking pink on the ends. The urchin cut makes her face look more fragile and elfin still. Her fierce blue eyes burn with an outraged and embarrassed intensity – the same colour as her father's, but hers are like the churning angry ocean, to his still calm waters. She has grown, and she has lost weight, although she may look thinner because she is now a good inch and a half taller. The wedding ring that belonged to her mother, which she used to wear upon a chain around her neck, now fits the middle finger of her right hand. The look of hatred she throws my way is still the same, however.

What's *she* doing here? Cas doesn't say it, clearly having enough respect for Eleanor Brice to remain silent, but I can see it in her eyes.

'Sit down, Cassandra.' Eleanor Brice throws a steely glance in Cas's direction, which has her folding her knees and sinking to her backside faster than a collapsed deckchair.

The head mistress turns back to face me. 'I'm afraid I've had to call you here today because there has been a very er . . . *disappointing* incident. Very disappointing indeed.'

Eleanor Brice looks across at Cassandra again. I do the same.

Cas is looking down at her hands, picking at the skin beside her thumbnail. She refuses to look up, so Eleanor Brice returns her steady gaze to me.

'I'll come straight to the point, Mrs Forester. Cassandra posted a fellow student's photograph, e-mail address and mobile telephone number on a website of, shall we say, a somewhat *insalubrious* nature.' Reaching into one of the desk drawers, Eleanor Brice pulls out a buff folder and, removing a piece of paper, passes it across the desk to me with a look of extreme distaste on her pale beige face.

I reach for the paper, trying to hide the fact that my hands are now shaking, and turn my attention to its

25

contents. It's an advertisement. A printed-off version of an internet 'sex for sale' advert. A girl's head, with a blonde crop, freckles and mean eyes, is perched a little obviously atop a body that blatantly doesn't belong to her. A body of Pamela Anderson-esque proportions. Legs wide apart, modesty covered only by a strategically and somewhat suggestively placed hand. *Libby Labia, Queen of Cock*, shouts the title above the arrogant face, followed by a list of sexual acts from the sublime to the seriously sordid, and the corresponding price for each one.

I know my mouth has fallen open in shock, but instead of outrage, I can feel this awful bubble of laughter begin to well up in my throat. I swallow hard, but it doesn't work, and I have to turn the giggle that escapes into a cough instead, covering my mouth and half of my face with my hand, until I've regained enough composure to look at Eleanor Brice and Cassie with a straight face. Eleanor Brice is watching me, clearly expecting an admonition of some kind from me toward Cassie. A sane, sensible, grown-up parental kind of admonition that is quite clearly appropriate at this moment.

'Why did you do this, Cassie?'

Cassie throws me another look that clearly states, 'What the hell has anything I do got to do with you?' but as both Eleanor Brice and I continue to watch her, waiting for an answer, she finally replies in tones so dry they're brittle.

'Because she pissed me off.'

I make a mental note to check out the web for my own photofit. I'm probably Nasty Natalie No Knickers from North London who's willing to snog a dog for six quid.

What makes the whole thing ten times worse is that I'm still finding it really hard not to laugh. I know it's probably awful for the girl concerned, but I came across enough school bitches in my time to feel a certain sympathy with Cas – more than that really; in a way I want to congratulate her for getting her own back in such spectacular fashion. It reminds me of the things that I used to get up to when I was Cas's age, but I was never brave or bold enough to be quite so high-profile about it.

'This is a very serious matter, Mrs Forester.' Eleanor Brice obviously feels from my demeanour that I need to be reminded of the gravity of the occasion.

I take a breath and attempt to put on a straight face and listen as she continues solemnly.

'. . . endangering the personal safety of a fellow student in such a manner. We have no choice other than to suspend Cassandra for the remainder of the term.'

'Suspension!' I find myself exclaiming. Thank you for pre-warning me!

I know to those assembled I sound outraged at the punishment being given to my step-daughter, but I'm not. Not really, anyway. Although I find what Cas did amusing, I do see that it was wrong. What concerns me most, however, are the implications of Cas being suspended. If Cassie is suspended, then she will be coming home. My step-daughter and I will be living in the same house together for the first time since Rob . . . since . . .

'She is lucky we are not talking of expulsion, Mrs Forester.' Eleanor Brice leans towards me. 'But we are taking into account the difficulties that Cassandra has experienced over the past year . . .'

'*Difficulties?*' I repeat in disbelief, my selfish panic subsiding instantly. The loss of her father described as a mere *difficulty*?

I find my previous warmth toward Eleanor Brice sliding down the thermometer somewhat, and am instantly angry at myself for looking upon Cas as a problem instead of a person. I cannot imagine what it has been like for Cassandra in this place since Rob's death.

This school. An old school in every sense of the word. Stiff upper lip. Your whole world has just fallen apart, but there – dry your eyes, blow your nose and carry on as normal. Worse things happen at sea.

They cannot even begin to imagine what she has been through. I am ashamed to admit that I have been trying not to imagine what she has been through. It has been too convenient for me to let her drift away. I have let her down. I have let Rob down.

I no longer feel the urge to giggle like an adolescent. I sit upright in my seat and try to exude the same calm air of authority that Eleanor Brice is blessed with.

'I cannot imagine Cassandra carrying out something so . . . er, *drastic*, without severe provocation,' I tell her. I am lying. From my own experience of Cassie's behaviour, I can imagine her doing something far worse than this for no reason quite easily, but I'm telling myself I don't really know her that well. 'I hope you have done all that you can to look into every aspect of this incident, not just Cassie's involvement.'

'We have spoken with Miss Lansford regarding alleged bullying, yes.'

'And have you suspended her as well?' I ask.

'I'm afraid in this instance we only have Cassandra's word against hers, whereas with Cassandra we have very – let's say very *public* evidence of a serious transgression.'

Eleanor Brice mouths *serious transgression* with a gravity of tone that indicates her level of disapproval, and I can't help but take another glance at the piece of paper onto which I'm still holding. I can't help it. The mocked-up photograph is just so ridiculously funny. I just about manage to suppress another giggle, making me sound like I've got hiccups, and try to look disapproving instead.

'We have no choice other than to suspend Cassie from school. We are hoping that this will give her the time to reflect on the gravity of her behaviour, and on the effect such behaviour and a possible expulsion could have, not only on her future at Cheal, but her future in the outside world. We would be very sorry to lose Cassie, she is normally an excellent pupil, but we cannot and will not tolerate this kind of behaviour.'

Although she is talking to me about Cas, she is actually looking at Cas as she says this, making sure that her words are hitting home. Cassie's face remains cold and impassive.

Eleanor Brice returns her steady gaze to me. 'We are hoping that she will return to us after the Christmas holiday with an improved attitude. The suspension is immediate. Cassie, will you go with Miss Price to collect your belongings. Mrs Forester, if you would care to wait in Miss Price's office, you may take Cassie home with you today.'

'And what if that isn't convenient?' I burst out indignantly. 'You haven't given me any notice. What if I *can't* take her with me today?'

Eleanor Brice's gaze remains steadfast. 'And is that the case, Mrs Forester?' she replies reasonably.

I have no reason not to take Cas with me. I'm just angry that an assumption was made, and so I bluster about lack of procedure and notification, and then go to Miss Price's austere little office to await Cassie's return.

Cas hasn't spoken a word to me since my arrival; this doesn't change as we head out to my car, her trunk carried between us, the only thing connecting us.

'Libby Lansford sounds like she deserves everything she got,' I mutter, as we head back down the long drive which leads from the Estate to the main road. 'If it's any consolation, I'd have done exactly the same thing. Well, not exactly the same thing. We didn't have access to the internet when I was at school.'

Cas gives me a look that quite clearly says that if I'm trying to score brownie points by making out that I'm on her side, then it's not going to work. She then looks away from me again, to stare morosely out of the car window. We lapse back into the far from comfortable silence that lasts the entire journey, getting tenser even, the closer we get to the house in Hampstead. I am highly relieved to find Petra waiting for us there, front door flung open as she peers down the road looking out for my car.

Cas doesn't look as pleased to see her as I do though, throwing her a look that clearly states, 'What the hell are *you* doing here?' The same look she gave me in Eleanor Brice's office. She then thumps up the two flights of stairs to her bedroom without saying a word, and without taking her bags either, which are now dumped at the foot of the stairs in an untidy heap that is more of an angry statement than the furious slamming of her bedroom door.

'She's been suspended.' I answer Petra's unspoken query.

'Really?' My friend's eyes are wide with awe. 'So what was it all about then? She looks too angelic to do anything too awful, apart from the hair. What on earth has happened to the *hair*?'

'The same thing that's happened to the mind. Totally fucked-up.' I bite my bottom lip, watching the empty staircase where Cassie's feet have just burned an imprint with their misery.

'So what did she do that was terrible enough to get kicked out then, albeit temporarily?'

I am unable to keep the smile from my lips.

'She posted another student's head on top of a page three model's body, and stuck it on the *Pussypinboard* with all of her contact details, and a price list.'

Petra snorts with laughter. 'Oh Nat, I'm sorry! It's not really funny, is it?'

'Don't worry, that was my reaction as well. I was finding it hard not to burst out laughing in front of Cas's headmistress. Good example, eh?'

'It's a shame that Cas doesn't realise how alike you two actually are. You might get on a bit better then.'

I shrug, acknowledging Petra's reasoning and the logic behind it, but despairing of Cas ever seeing things this way.

'Come and have a drink.' Petra holds out a hand, and tows me down the corridor toward the back of the house and the kitchen. A bottle of wine is open on the table, along with two glasses and a plastic tray of ready-made party sandwiches from Marks. Petra shrugs as I look at them.

'I was going to make something in case you were hungry, but you know me.'

'Never cook unless you absolutely have to,' I answer her.

'Are you hungry? How about Cas?'

I shake my head. 'I'm not, and I think we should leave Cas alone for a while.'

'How about a glass of wine?'

'Please. I probably shouldn't but I really need one. Well, I really need two – bottles preferably – but I think I have a duty to stay sober now there's a minor in the house.'

'How long have you got her for?'

'Heavens, I hadn't really thought about that one. Not sure. She can't go back to school until after Christmas, and only then when she's convinced her headmistress of a little contrition.'

'Never, then,' Petra jokes weakly.

'Probably. As to whether she'll want to stay here though is another question.' Absentmindedly I pick up a ham and rocket sandwich and chew. I didn't realise how hungry I was until the food hit my tongue. My stomach's been too tied up in knots all day to even think about eating.

'I thought you said you weren't hungry?' Petra teases

as I pick up a second sandwich before I've even finished the first.

'I wasn't.' I sigh heavily.

'Are you okay?'

I shrug. 'I don't know. I feel weird.'

'Seeing Cassie after so long? It's bound to be difficult.'

'Yeah. But it's not just that. She just looks so like . . . so like him, Petra. It's a really strange feeling.'

'Do you want me to stay over?'

I look up at her gratefully. 'Oh, would you?'

'Of course.' Petra hugs me with one arm, the other balancing her glass of wine.

Cassie slams into the kitchen, eyeing us sourly. Without comment she heads for the fridge, and pulls open the door so clumsily that an egg falls from the door and smashes on the tile floor. Ignoring the egg, she pulls a face at the contents of the fridge, which obviously fail to please her, and then turns about the room, scanning for something that is more appealing.

Her eyes stop on the bottle of wine on the table. Turning, she takes a glass from the cupboard, walks to the table, picks up the bottle of wine and pours herself a glass. I'm torn between admonishing her, and turning a blind eye for the sake of peace and my own sanity. Cowardice wins. I say nothing. And hate myself for it as well.

Petra has none of my qualms, however.

'You're fifteen,' she tells her, striding up and pulling the glass from her hands just as it's raised to her lips. 'And you have precious few brain cells already. You start drinking now, you'll be a vegetable by the time you hit puberty.'

Cassie's mouth, which was opening to take the rim of the glass, falls wide open in outrage, but fortunately instead of staying to argue, she simply scorches Petra with a burning look, and marches angrily from the room. I hear the creak of protesting springs as she throws herself on a sofa in the sitting room, and then we're drowned out by the mournful sound of Marilyn Manson blaring out of the hifi speakers.

I get out of my chair and push the kitchen door to, muffling at least some of the noise. 'Thanks for that.'

'Do I detect a note of sarcasm?'

'No, it needed saying.'

'Just not in my oh so subtle way, eh? Don't be scared to put your foot down, Nat. If she's going to be staying for a while you can't have her behaving like a delinquent. The more you let her get away with things, the more she'll try it on. Kids need boundaries if only for something to kick against.'

'I know, but it's so difficult. It's like the only thing she wants to kick against is me. You know the people she goes to stay with in the holidays, her best friend's family? Well, I've spoken with the mother a few times, sorting out money and thank yous and practicalities, and she simply raves about her, tells me what a little angel she is, and how it's always such a pleasure to have her to stay.'

'You're doing your best in very difficult circumstances, Nat.'

'Am I? Am I really doing my best? I don't know that I am, Pet. I've just left her to get on with things. Abandoned her, almost. I know she doesn't want me around, so I've kept away from her, but that's not the right thing, is it? Oh, I don't know . . . I don't know if what I'm doing is right or wrong for her. I'm not old enough to have a fifteen-year-old daughter.'

'Technically speaking you are, darling.'

'Okay, so I am, but I would have been a child bride. What I'm trying to say is maybe I've just been taking the easy option. I'm her legal guardian – maybe I should insist she comes home to me for the holidays. How are we going to build up any kind of relationship if we never see each other? She wants to stay away, and I never fight her over it because to be honest it makes life easier for me not to have her here. But this is her home. Do you know, it feels completely weird for me that she's here, and yet this was her home long before it was ever mine. If I feel this odd, how on earth must she be feeling right now? What stability has the poor child got left? I can't have her humping her bags from friend to friend every holiday like a gypsy.'

'Don't be too hard on yourself, Nattie,' Petra is quick to reassure me. 'You've had enough responsibilities of your own to deal with.'

'That's the thing though, Petra. Cassie *is* my responsibility. I've just been completely ignoring the fact.'

An hour later, Cassie pushes back into the kitchen and, ignoring us both, sticks her head in the fridge, gathers together a huge tub of Greek yoghurt and a carton of fresh orange juice, grabs a tube of salt and vinegar Pringles from the cupboard above, and stomps back out again. I can hear her heavy-footing it up the wooden stairs, then the slam of her bedroom door.

Petra's face is set in a hard, disapproving expression. 'She acts like she owns the place.'

'Technically speaking, she does.'

Petra raises her eyebrows inviting further explanation.

'It's held in trust until she's thirty. I get to live here, if I want to, until then, when she can have me out on my ear with a snap of her fingers if she so pleases. Assuming I've made it that far.'

'Bet she can't wait.'

'I did try moving back to my place, before I let it out.'

'I didn't know that.'

'It lasted two days, that's why. I was torn between wanting to be here, and not wanting to be here. I couldn't decide which was worse – everything reminding me of Rob, or hardly anything reminding me of Rob. I decided that here would be the right place, for now anyway. And easier as well if Cas decided she ever wanted to come home in the school holidays. Not that she has – until now, of course – but then being here now is hardly her choice, is it?'

'Is she staying?'

'You mean is she sodding off to one of her friends' houses as usual? I don't think so. Apparently the people that she normally stays with are visiting family in Geneva for Christmas, although of course Emily will still be at school until the end of term.'

'So you've got her for Christmas then?'

'It certainly looks that way. She hasn't mentioned it and I haven't mentioned it either. It's a hard subject to bring up anyway, even aside from the fact that we barely communicate.'

'What are you going to do about work?'

'Cas is old enough to be left on her own during the day, but I'm not sure that's a good idea. It's Saturday tomorrow. I'll see how she settles in over the weekend and then decide, but perhaps I could take some leave. I think I should be here for her.'

'Saint Natalie,' Petra mocks, but not unpleasantly. 'How can you be so bloody understanding? She's a nightmare.'

'I don't mean to sound patronising, but I feel sorry for her.' I shrug. 'Losing Rob . . . well, I know how it made *me* feel.'

I also know how it feels to lose your dad when you're a kid. It's the end of the world. My own father died when I was six, as unexpectedly as Rob. An outwardly healthy man, he dropped dead of heart failure just days short of his thirty-seventh birthday. I was devastated by his death, and my mother was left too broken to comfort me.

'She's lost both of her parents, Petra. Admittedly she was too young to really remember her mother, but can you imagine what's going on inside that head? How much hurt there is in there?'

Petra nods thoughtfully.

'What are you doing for Christmas?' I ask her.

'The Old Git's taking Evil Edna away,' she replies, with pretend nonchalance, referring to her married lover and his wife. 'Somewhere in the Mexican Gulf, where hopefully she'll either fry or sink – whichever, I really don't mind.' Petra pulls a somewhat squashed packet of Marlboro from her handbag, and lighting a cigarette with telltale hands, inhales deeply. 'So I shall probably ask Santa for a Toyboy, and spend the entire holiday tied up in a four-poster having sordid sex.'

She takes another drag on her cigarette and visibly relaxes a little. 'In order to placate me he's offered to send me to some fabulously expensive health spa some-where fabulously hot. Well, it's either to placate me or get me out of the way – I'm not sure which at the moment.' Although she's trying to keep her tone light and jovial, I can hear some genuine grievance in there still.

'How's it going?' I ask her.

Petra shrugs noncommittally.

'I often wonder what you see in him.' I sigh, picking up my wine glass.

'I really wonder sometimes too, but we're still chug-ging along together, despite everything. He has his good points you know.'

'Like what?'

'Well, he may take up two seats on Concorde, but his investment portfolio's larger than life too.' She winks at me.

I know she doesn't mean this. Petra is very money-minded, but her aim in life is to make plenty of her own, not spend other people's. I have my own theory as to why she maintains what could be seen as a pretty pointless relationship. It gives her a sense of being wanted whilst allowing her a lot of freedom, and most of all she doesn't have to give anything away, especially her heart – something she guards with vigour.

'I know you don't mean that,' I tell her.

'Don't I?'

'Not at all. Try again.'

'Okay.' She replies slowly, 'He's taller than me, and that's very difficult to find. I mean, do you know what it's like being six foot four in heels? And I'm not wearing flats for anybody, not even Tom Cruise, although I could always balance my plate on his head at parties, you know that old problem of holding your food and your drink at the same time . . .'

A gasp of laughter escapes my mouth, a big hiccuping bubble that has a lot to do with the wine I have as usual been drinking far too quickly, as well as what Petra just said. Petra's mouth too begins to curl up at the corners and we are both laughing. The only problem is, I find that once I start, I simply cannot stop. It's hysterical laughter. A release of all the pressure that has been building up inside of me.

Suddenly the laughter stops as abruptly as it started.

Cassie is standing in the doorway. Her face and eyes are glowing with indignation, and she is visibly shaking.

'What the hell do you think you're doing?' she demands like an adult telling off an errant child. 'You sit here laughing your head off and drinking Daddy's wine cellar dry as if nothing has happened. You didn't care about him at all, did you? Well – did you!'

I put down my wine glass as though it's incriminating evidence. 'Of course I did,' I counter. 'More than anything.'

'Then how can you carry on like this? How can you just act like everything's normal?'

It takes me a moment to find the right words to answer, and when I say them to Cas, it's as if I'm hearing them for the first time myself.

'Don't you understand? I either carry on as normal or

37

I don't carry on at all. It's as simple as that. When your father died I wished I had too.'

'Yeah, well that makes two of us,' she spits, and turning back into the hallway, slams the door behind her so hard the glasses on the table shake. Petra and I blink at each other for a moment in horrified silence.

'How can someone who looks so ethereal be such a complete and utter bitch?' Petra finally says quietly. She comes to stand behind me, leaning down to wrap her arms around my neck so that her hands are resting on my shoulders, and her cheek is resting against my head.

'Don't be too down on her, Petra, she's had a hard time,' I mutter, leaning back against her welcome comforting warmth, and closing my eyes.

'And you haven't?' Petra exclaims in protective outrage.

'She's just a kid.'

'She's hardly a kid any more but she's certainly acting like one.'

'She's got to blame someone. Heaven knows *I* wanted to. It's just easy for her to blame me. I can't take it personally.'

'Maybe.' Petra lets go and comes round to sit beside me again, filling my wine glass to the very top. 'But I know you, and you *will* take it personally, every last bloody word. And you don't need this at the moment, Nat.'

She pushes the glass across the coffee-table towards me, but instead of taking what is normally a welcome panacea, I find myself reluctant to drink any more.

'Look, do you want me to have a chat with her?'

I shake my head. 'I know you mean well, but she doesn't need that at the moment either.'

'She needs a bloody good kick up the backside, that's what she needs,' Petra huffs.

'No, she doesn't. She needs what you just gave me.'

'Alcohol?' Petra looks in puzzlement at my full wine glass.

'No. Although it might help her to relax a little.' I laugh dryly.

'Then what?'

'What she really needs,' I reply, 'and what I know for a fact she won't let me give her, is a great big hug.'

The frightening thing is that what I said to Cassie about wishing I had died with Rob was true. I not only thought it, but really felt it. *Really* felt like putting a pistol in my mouth and pulling the trigger, and the only thing that stopped me was my cowardice. Fear of what, I'm not quite sure. Not death, I know that much. Judgement? Maybe. Pain? No, not fear of pain either; nothing could have hurt more than the knot of agony that slowly pulsed and grew inside me like a canker, fuelled by the knowledge that I'm never going to see him again, never going to touch him, to feel his skin against mine, to smell him, to smell the comforting, erotic, delicious fragrance of his skin.

And yet I quelled these feelings as best I could and carried on. I had to carry on as normal, even though for me there was no normal any more.

Cassie spends the whole of Saturday avoiding me. She doesn't come down to breakfast or lunch, and only emerges from her room in the evening, when I force myself to go out and get the papers from the twenty-four shop. When I get back, the sitting-room door is closed and I can hear a music programme on the television.

The plate of lunch I left her has been taken from the fridge, and put in the microwave. I know this, because the microwave door is open, the light inside blinking at me in the semi-darkness of the kitchen, and the inside is covered in an explosion of carrot and roast potato where she hasn't covered the plate before attempting to heat it. What is left of the food has been pushed around the plate with a fork, before being abandoned on the table, where she sat.

There is an empty orange-juice carton left on the side, only two feet from the swing bin, a glass stained with juice and pith standing partially empty next to it. I clear up the kitchen, then sit down at the kitchen table, cross with myself that I'm too much of a coward to open that door and go into the sitting room and join her. It's only a door, but it may as well be the Berlin Wall, patrolled by soldiers with rifles and bad-tempered Alsatian dogs.

'Coward,' I chide myself, opening the fridge and reaching for the half-bottle of chilled white that's nestled in the shelf inside.

It takes me an hour and a half to read my way through the newspapers. I sit alone in the kitchen in silence for a further three hours. Just me and my half-bottle of wine, which is quickly replaced with another. When the clock on the kitchen wall tells me that it is nearly eleven I finally summon the courage to push open the sitting-room door.

The only light in the room is coming from the flickering images on the television screen. The sound is turned down low, the control gripped in Cassie's small slender hand. She is fast asleep on the sofa, long dark eyelashes fluttering against pale tear-stained cheeks, a large velvet cushion hugged to her chest like a comforter.

For a long time I sit and watch her sleeping, listening to the soft sigh of her breathing, the low murmur of the TV, and the occasional growl of a passing car. When she shows no sign of stirring, I turn off the TV, and not wanting to enter her bedroom uninvited, fetch the duvet from the guest room to cover her.

When I wake up the next morning, Cassie has gone from the sofa, and her bedroom door is once again firmly locked.

Monday morning, I phone Elaine, tell her that I'll be

working from home for a couple of days, and then drive to the local supermarket.

You can't escape Christmas when you're food shopping. Despite the fact that it's not even quite December yet, my vision is assaulted by a thirty-foot Christmas tree as soon as I hit the car park. Of course it makes me think of Rob.

*Another Christmas without you. I only ever had two Christmases with you.*

I feel robbed. There's a hollow ache in the pit of my stomach that has nothing to do with the fact that I haven't eaten since yesterday morning.

We made an attempt at a family Christmas after we were married. Rob and I, Cassie and Louisa-May. I even asked my mother, Laura, whom I hadn't seen on a Christmas Day for years, although admittedly I left it rather late to call her. She had, of course, already made other plans, but her obvious upset that she couldn't break them at such short notice left me feeling slightly regretful.

My attempts at conciliation with Cas made me think of Laura with a less critical heart. In a misguided attempt to win Cas over I had put time and effort into finding things that I thought she'd really love. Things that on Christmas Day were discarded by my step-daughter with a contemptuous sneer, or a cold look of pure disinterest.

I remember Rob pulling me into an embrace in the kitchen and thanking me for trying. 'It'll be better next year,' he murmured, his lips brushing a kiss across the top of my head.

I think of Cas, thin almost to the point of emaciation, eyes dull. She must feel as lost and frightened as I do. I am suddenly overcome by a desire to try to make some sort of Christmas for her. Heading back to the aisles that I previously ignored, I chuck a box of crackers into the trolley. I even buy a small fibre-optic tree that has flashing coloured lights at the end of each synthetic branch. I hate it almost as much as I hate myself for buying it.

I also find myself looking for things that might encourage Cas to eat. I don't even know what she likes. The usual teenage choice of chips, crisps and microwave pizzas might not be her thing. Instead I load the cart with yoghurt and fruit juice, both of which I know she eats in vast quantities, with pasta, salad, and more chocolate. Hell, if she doesn't eat it, I know that it won't go to waste.

My final destination is the aisles where alcohol is piled, shelf upon shelf. I seem to have spent a lot of my shopping time over the past few months in these aisles. I know the location of every single bottle of my favourite types of wine, but for some reason today, I find myself pushing straight through without pause to the check-out.

On the way home, unsure that my take on her desire for junk food is right, I pull into a McDonald's, and with a small sense of delight at the irony, buy her a Happy Meal.

Cas has emerged from her room when I get back, lured like a wild animal by the scent of food. At first when I hand her the McDonald's bag, she looks at me as if I'm an IRA terrorist handing her something that's ticking. But then she reaches out a thin hand.

'Oh, thanks.'

I watch in surprise as she takes the bag and heads back upstairs, small feet thumping as though they are attached to something that weighs eight hundred pounds, not eighty, followed by the inevitable click of the lock on her bedroom door.

It's evening, and as usual I'm at home on the sofa, wearing a comfy grey tracksuit and some slipper socks. My mobile phone rings. It's Petra.

'What are you doing?'

'Drinking wine and watching TV.'

'Where's Satan's daughter?'

'Don't call her that, Petra. She's in her room, playing loud music.' I open the door and hold the telephone receiver up so that Petra can get the full effect of the Eminem CD that's currently on full volume on Cas's CD player.

'That's loud,' Petra agrees when I put the receiver back to my ear, kicking the door to again with my foot. Then: 'What are you watching?'

'A repeat of *Morse*.'

'What sort of wine are you drinking?'

'A very good bottle of Châteauneuf du Pape.'

'Is there any left?'

I pick up the bottle and gaze into the depths. 'Oh, about a third.'

'I'd better bring another one with me then.' She puts down the receiver.

Half an hour later I hear a key in the front door as Petra lets herself in. The music is back on high volume in Cas's room. The sitting-room door opens, letting the noise flood in, then closes to once more muffle the worst of it, although I can still feel the bass throbbing through the walls like the tremors of a minor earthquake.

Petra grins tersely at me as she takes off her coat and throws it across the back of the sofa. She's wearing a glittering gold backless Joseph dress that clings to her sensational figure in all the right places, accentuating her long brown back, her endless toned legs, and the enviable deep valley of her cleavage.

'You look very glam.'

'Been out with Peter,' she replies, kicking off a pair of strappy shoes and sitting down next to me.

'And you're home by ten?'

'We had an early dinner,' she announces bluntly, her

43

beautiful face soured by petulance. 'We were going to have an early night as well but we were interrupted by a phone call and he had to go.'

'Oh. Right.'

Petra pulls a face. 'I know. The perils of being a bit on the side.'

We're companionably silent for a moment, Petra's attention captured by something on the TV.

'I've been thinking,' I tell her. 'About Christmas.'

'What about it?' she replies without looking at me.

'I'm definitely going to keep her with me for Christmas.'

'Who – Cas?'

'Yeah.'

'I thought you were going to cancel Christmas.'

'Well, I've just reinstated it.'

'Don't tell me you've been visited by Marley's Ghost – oh my goodness!' Her head snaps round to me, face mortified. 'I'm so sorry, darling. I can't believe I just said that.'

'Don't worry,' I hasten to reassure her. 'One of the things I love about you is that you still speak to me as if I'm normal.'

The smile returns. 'Darling, I can assure you I've *never* spoken to you as if you're normal.' She squeezes my hand. 'So what are you going to do then – about Christmas?'

'I'm going to make sure that Cas has a good one, preferably with her family, instead of being a waif and stray taken in at someone else's table.'

'That's all very laudable, but remember – this particular stray has a rather nasty bite. I can just see the two of you sitting happily across a large stuffed turkey.'

'Yeah, Cassie reaching for the knife and asking "shall I carve", before making a lunge for my throat,' I joke. 'Why don't you ditch the health spa and spend the day with us?' I plead.

Petra almost chokes on her drink. 'Oh wow. I can't

believe I forgot to tell you,' she splutters, emerging from her glass. 'That's my news. Huge change of plan. I'm not going to Barbados any more.'

'You're not?'

'No. There's something much better on offer. Peter's wife, Evil Edna, is flying out to her sister in Florida on the nineteenth. You should see her sister; she's had so much plastic surgery and sunshine she looks like an old chamois leather stretched out to dry after mopping down a very dirty Porsche. Anyway, she's found herself another husband, number six I think, someone rich enough to pay for her to have her tits lifted again anyway... and they're getting married on New Year's Eve, so the whole family is decamping to the good old US of A for two weeks.'

'This is good news?' I query.

'Well yes, because the Old Git can't make the flight on the twenty-third due to work commitments, so he's arranged to follow her out there on Christmas Eve instead, but – big but – he's promised to make some kind of excuse and spend Christmas Day with me instead. Isn't that wonderful? He's going to fly out on Boxing Day and swear blind the plane caught fire or the pilot spontaneously combusted or something, so I actually get to spend a whole Christmas Day with him. Isn't that wonderful?' she repeats as though she almost can't believe this 'good fortune' herself.

'Yeah, that's great,' I reply dubiously, all too aware of the butterfly-like fragility of Peter England's promises.

'Oh, but I would have loved to spend the day with you.' Petra puts a consoling hand on mine, mistaking the look on my face for one of disappointment.

'Don't worry about it, I'll sort something out.'

Three days later I'm woken late after a fitful night where I finally dropped off just as everyone else in the world was waking up, by the sound of the telephone at the side of the bed. This shouldn't be unusual, apart from the fact that one of the things I've noticed since Rob died is that the phone hardly ever rings any more. This probably stems from the fact that after Rob's death I simply ceased to answer it. I went through this awful period of being convinced that when I picked up the phone it would be him, and of course it never was. It was so weird: I knew in my head that it couldn't possibly be Rob calling, but my heart still plummeted every time it wasn't his voice on the end of the line.

Friends, aware of my new habit of vetting or simply ignoring calls, tend to ring me on my mobile so that I can see who it is that's calling before I answer. Hence the fact that the house phone hardly ever rings.

I slide a hand out from under my duvet and grope around the table for the receiver.

''Lo?' I cough.

'Natalie?'

I sit bolt upright, suddenly wide awake. It's my mother. I haven't seen her since the funeral. We've spoken a few stilted times, her not quite knowing what to say to me, and vice versa. She did try to help, but I'm afraid to say I shut her out as always. She asked me down to stay several times and I refused. She offered to come up and I put her off. We've never shared confidences, we've never really had that sort of relationship. To be honest, after my father died, we never had any sort of relationship to speak of.

I felt as if I had lost both my parents; she changed so radically. She was always there, but I never felt that she was *with* me.

At this moment in time, however, her voice sounds so calm and reassuring as she asks me how I am and gently probes deeper, not accepting my usual monosyllabic answers, that I suddenly find myself blurting out all of my woes. She gets the whole Cassie tale from beginning to current situation. The sound of my mother's laughter when I tell her about the internet incident is oddly comforting.

'That was my initial reaction as well,' I tell her. 'I'm glad I'm not the only one who found it funny.'

'So now you're stuck playing the step-mother from hell for the entire holiday,' she replies. 'I bet you're both absolutely delighted about that, aren't you?'

'I think Cassie's upstairs as we speak, ringing round all of her schoolfriends to see if anyone wants an extra guest for Christmas Dinner. I think she'd rather share turkey with Libby Labia, Queen of Cock, than Nasty Natalie, sickly step-mother.'

Laura laughs again. 'And you, what do you want?'

'I want to keep her with me over Christmas. I'm the closest thing she has left to family, apart from Louisa-May, and even she's supposed to be going away. She's promised to spend Christmas with her sister. They're going on a cruise round the Med. It was booked ages ago. She's tried everything she can to get out of it. I think Louisa was hoping to persuade her sister to go on her own, but her sister was widowed last year and she's relying on Louisa for company – not to mention the fact that her sister paid a fortune, is desperate to go, and is actually being rather unfair, pressuring her, making her feel guilty.'

'Families, eh?' Laura laughs.

'Yeah,' I sigh, missing her irony. 'Louisa offered to take Cas with her, but when I suggested it to her, Cas didn't seem too keen on that idea either.'

'What did she say?'

'Something about no way was she going to spend two weeks on a boat full of geriatrics, and Louisa should be spending Christmas at home anyway. She got into such a sulk about it I haven't dared to bring the subject up since.'

'Look, Nat, I want to suggest something, but I want you to be honest with me. If you'd rather not then just say okay, and I promise I won't be offended.'

'What is it?'

'Why don't you both come down to me?'

'Come down? For Christmas?'

'For Christmas – yes, definitely. I'd love to have you. But why wait? Why not come now? You were wondering what you could do with Cassie, so bring her here. I'd love to have you both.'

'You would?'

'Of course,' she replies.

My obvious surprise at this must be a little insulting.

'Come down,' she repeats insistently. 'I wanted to invite you for Christmas anyway, I just wasn't sure that you'd want to come. I'm sure our Christmases here would be dreadfully dull compared with London.'

'Dreadfully dull sounds just what I need at the moment,' I reply without thinking.

'Then it's settled? You'll come to me?'

I'm almost surprised to hear the words coming out of my mouth. 'Yeah. Yes, thank you. I think we will.'

I break the news about our trip to Cornwall over a breakfast that is for once shared, albeit silent, seated opposite each other at the kitchen table. Cassie is slowly peeling an orange. First taking off the thick bitter skin, then minutely stripping every piece of pith from the segments. She then splits them individually before placing them in a pattern around her plate, where they remain uneaten to be thrown dried and shrivelled into the swing bin when I clear up.

I must admit I'm not very hungry either. I've been pushing the same spoonful of muesli round and round my dish for ten minutes, trying to pluck up the courage to talk to her. It's so hard to find the right words.

My best approach, I decide, is to sound reluctant myself. I know if Cas thinks that it's something I'm keen to do, then she's more likely to say no, just to spite me.

'My mother wants us to stay with her for Christmas,' I

48

offer, sounding as hesitant about this as I can.

Cas ignores me, simply rearranges her orange segments into something that vaguely resembles a fruit swastika. I think maybe she's trying to send me subliminal messages.

'Of course, it's far from ideal. I've been trying to think of an excuse for us not to go. What do you think? Got any ideas why we shouldn't go?'

Cas shrugs.

'No?'

She shrugs again.

'Do you want to go?'

'Don't know.'

'Would you rather stay here?'

At this point she actually looks across at me. '*No,*' she says adamantly, before returning her concentration to her plate.

'So should I say yes then? We'll go down to Cornwall?'

'Whatever.'

I phone my mother with Cas still in the kitchen, half expecting her to interject halfway through my acceptance of the invitation with an angry denial that she isn't going anywhere with me. But although I expect resistance, instead I get a weary sort of resignation. I think this is mainly due to the fact that to argue about it means that Cas has to actually speak to me, and this is something she's been trying very hard not to do.

Phone call finished, I turn to face her. 'So that's all settled then. We're going down at the weekend.'

She stares at me with her unsettling, hurt, resentful eyes, and simply shrugs again, before looking back down at her orange artwork and rearranging the swastika into a hand that's throwing a determined 'V' sign in my direction.

I take a leave of absence from work. My editor Elaine is

surprisingly willing to let this happen. Still stunned I think by my more than rapid return to work straight after the funeral, she either feels it's wise to give me some time off in case she has a restrained mental patient in the making in her employ, or she has someone else in mind for the job, but at the moment I don't really care.

I feel interminably weary, and to be honest the prospect of a lengthy holiday from work is actually far more attractive than I ever thought it would be. Besides, I can still write down in Cornwall, maybe do some freelance pieces. It'll be nice to have total jurisdiction over my work for a change. Elaine's a good boss, but she's a self-confessed control freak, who is never happy with a piece unless she has changed at least some part of it, even if it's only the title or your punctuation.

Christmas is still three and a half weeks away, so this means that by the time I return to work in the New Year I shall have had five weeks off. This is the longest time I have spent away from work in one go since I started my very first job. Considering work has been my oxygen for the past year or so, I am surprised that I'm actually looking forward to getting away, to getting out of London and away from everything that is familiar to me.

Whitsunday, although the last place I ever lived with my mother, is one of a series of childhood homes. Is 'home' the right word? It's one of the places that my mother and I moved to after my father died. The last in a long line, a place I never really took the trouble to explore.

It's funny. Whenever I think of home, I think of the house that we lived in before Dad died. The three of us. A place where my mother was always laughing and happy and dancing and singing, and generally being so upbeat she was pleasantly exhausting.

I don't know how my mother and my father got together. It was always meant to be the prince and the showgirl, not the accountant and the showgirl. He, small, unassuming, shy almost – she, larger than life and twice as beautiful. They were very much in love and very tactile, always kissing each other. I used to be embarrassed of them in a nice kind of way. We were a tactile family, every hug turning into a group hug.

I always used to join them in bed every Sunday morning when I was little. Sandwiched between them, warm, cosy and safe, whilst my father read the Sunday papers, and my mother re-read a fashion magazine for the umpteenth time.

When my father died it was like they had both gone. My father altogether; my mother as I knew her.

We moved not long after my father's death, something Laura rushed into somewhat. To be honest, I think she regretted it for a long time. She was running away from the memories that the house brought her, I suppose, but the initial relief soon gave way to a greater sense of loss at not being in a home they had built together.

That's one of the reasons I moved back into Rob's house. Our house. Although it was his family home long before he ever met me, he always made sure I felt as if it was our home too. To be here is at once heart-rending, yet comforting, like being wrapped in an old pullover that still smells of his aftershave.

I try hard to remember the good things about our life together. This is one of the few things that brings me strength.

In a sense, my mother went back to her Vaudeville roots after Dad's death; she returned to the days when she was a happy wanderer. It's funny, her favourite group has always been the Rolling Stones, and in the years after my father's death that is what she became, never stopping in one place for long enough to gather moss, roots or sadly, many friends.

From the impersonal little flat my mother first moved us to in Brighton when I was seven, we made a southerly journey, like winged birds seeking warmer climates. From Brighton to Portsmouth, from Portsmouth to Bournemouth, from Bournemouth to Exmouth, from Exmouth to Plymouth, from Plymouth to Falmouth, until she finally reached Land's End, and couldn't go any further without crossing the ocean. Moving so many times, further and further away from London, until we ended up at Whitsunday.

I think I was there for almost a year before I moved back to London on my own. I only ever remember spending one Christmas there anyway. A Christmas where we were snowbound from Boxing Day to two days after New Year. I think it was then, stuck in the house, just my mother and me, that I decided that as soon as my exams were over, I'd leave. Go back to the place that I remembered as a proper home.

London.

Sweet sixteen, with about two hundred pounds to my name, no job, nowhere to stay, but a determination that overrode any fear of the unknown. I was lucky. I found myself a bunk in a YWCA, and spent three weeks trudging the entire length and width of London on foot, searching newspapers from the *Guardian* to the *Islington Christian Times* for a job, any job to get my foot on the first rung of the publishing ladder.

Refusing to take no for an answer despite the fact that this was the answer most frequently given due to my total lack of experience, I ended up putting myself through journalism college by working at three jobs. Up at six every day, waitressing in a greasy spoon in Watford first thing in the morning serving breakfast to starving truckers, heading off to College for nine, finishing around four, lying about my age to get a cash-in-hand bar job in the local spit and sawdust five nights a week, then cleaning offices on a Saturday and Sunday morning.

It must have been one of the hardest times of my life,

but it was also one of the most fulfilling. I had a goal, an aim, something to work toward. I don't know if I could do it again now, even though I am twice the age I was then. I think I was tougher at sixteen than I am at thirty-two. A hard little thing, a shiny horse chestnut, still firmly wedged in its prickly green casing.

The years have softened me.

Rob softened me.

Not always good for a hard-as-nails journalist, but although I admittedly lost an edge when I met him, I also gained perspective, which I think made my writing better. Rob taught me to slow down and listen more. I have a keen ear. I have to have a keen ear to do the job I do, to get the stories, but if an eye can be blinkered then so can an ear. Before Rob, whenever I interviewed someone, I was always looking for a particular angle, based on what I already knew about them, and I would listen only for certain things. Rob taught me to go in with an open mind and look at the whole picture; that way you often learn more than you ever thought you could about somebody.

Rob taught me so many things; even in death I am still learning from him. Most importantly, I am learning that I should be building bridges instead of burning them.

# *Chapter Two*

We leave for Whitsunday on the last day of November. To my relief, Cassie spends the majority of the journey asleep, waking only as we pass over Bodmin Moor, taking in the bleak rain-soaked landscape with a noticeable shudder, before closing her eyes again, not to sleep, but to avoid conversation.

It's tiring trying to drive through an endless shower of grey rain that almost completely obscures your vision. It's not actually falling that heavily. The majority of the water is being thrown up from the road by the cars in front of me, to be wiped away by the monotonous double metronome of the windscreen wipers.

I pull over at a Little Chef on the A30 for a caffeine break, to endure another endlessly silent moment together, which seems worse in that we are facing each other, and not side by side in a car where I can concentrate on driving, and she can pretend to sleep or stare relentlessly out at the passing scenery.

Perched on red plastic seats, looking out across the brown bracken landscape of the moor through windows flanked by faded candy-stripe curtains, I drink my way through three cups of too-milky coffee, whilst Cas nibbles the edges of a burger, working it round and round in her mouth with her fingers like a cog rotating in a very complicated piece of machinery. Bite, bite, bite with her small perfect white teeth.

I don't know whether she's simply not hungry or if

she's doing it to irritate me. In the end, I leave her at the grey Formica table and join the queue of wet and weary travellers waiting to pay their bills. I smile indulgently at the old couple in matching rain macs waiting in the queue in front of me. They have been holding hands throughout their brunch of a shared cherry pancake. They are holding hands now; even as the man struggles with his one free hand to search in his pocket for his wallet, he does not let go his grip on his wife's thin wrinkled fingers.

Abandoning her barely eaten burger, Cas heads for the loo to reapply a vicious circle of black kohl around her ice-blue eyes, and attempt to coax her hair back into the spikes she was sporting when I first collected her from Cheal. It has grown a little since then and now only wants to flop around her face Meg Ryan-style. For a home-made haircut, and one that's grown out at that, it is absurdly flattering. To my relief it's also faded a little from violent fuchsia pink, to a softer pastel hue, so that whilst still making people turn to stare, it actually looks rather pretty in a retro-punk kind of way. She hasn't as yet made any attempt to re-colour, and I think she might be regretting the loss of her beautiful long golden hair a little, although of course she would never admit this to me.

I stand outside waiting for her to emerge from the lav, trying to clear my head of the fug that has settled around it after three hours of constant driving. After five minutes I duck back into the car to avoid the rain which has turned from a persistent drizzle into a heavier shower, and phone my mother to let her know that we are nearly there. She sounds pleased that we are close by, almost excited. I don't know why I find this so unexpected; the fact that she might be looking forward to having us stay hadn't really occurred to me. I must confess that now we're nearly here, I wish we were safely back in Hampstead in our cosy head-to-head enmity. To throw my mother into this equation, to turn the terrible two into a tempestuous trio, could just make things worse than they already are.

Although I am an adult, and I tell myself that my life is now in my own hands, and what I make of it or don't make of it is down to me, and me alone, if I was being totally honest with myself I'd have to admit that there are still emotional problems with my mother that have never been resolved.

Firmly swept under the carpet, yes, but never actually resolved.

As we approach Land's End, the rain finally begins to break, the dark grey clouds above us parting to let through a weak ray of sunshine which falls like a long golden path across the expanse of countryside before us.

Whitsunday is sited between Land's End and Cape Cornwall, a twenty-acre patchwork quilt of pocket-handkerchief fields, bordered on the north-west by the Atlantic sea. Once I reach the great white spinning windmills that catch the winds coming in from the Atlantic to generate electricity, I know we're nearly there. Just the sight of them is enough to tighten the knot of anxiety I already have in my empty stomach.

I haven't been back very often since I left here almost sixteen years ago. I think I've dared to venture here about five times altogether – duty visits, instigated by my mother and complicated by me. Not bad – averaging just under once every three years, I realise with a slight pang of guilt. Still, this place never felt like home.

I feel tired and drawn and very weary. Cas is either asleep again, or doing a very good job of pretending to be, her mouth slightly open, her breathing heavy and even, her head lolling forward like a nodding dog in the back of a car with less than effective suspension. She remains asleep until I finally turn the car from the narrow main road, where the trees grow so close that in summer their leaves join to form a canopy above your head, onto the bumpy track that winds down from the main road to Whitsunday.

My front wheel immediately dives straight down into a deep pothole, and Cas is jerked awake none too gently. She looks around her in disgruntled agitation.

'Where are we?' she rasps, peeling her tongue from the roof of her mouth.

'We're here.'

'Where's here?'

'Wits End,' I reply dryly.

My mother is waiting for us by the five-bar wooden gate that guards the entrance into the farmyard. No matter how great a time elapses between our meeting, she never seems to change. I used to think my mother was the most beautiful woman in the world. I was a young child in the 1970s, where flares and kaftans abounded in hideous plenty, but my mother ignored all of this, choosing to dress, in my eyes anyway, just like a film star. Like Ava Gardner, or Katharine Hepburn, she wore womanly clothes with nipped-in waists and flattering skirts, and shoes that belonged to our life in London, not in a farmyard. Classic and elegant. Tan court shoes made of the softest leather, with tapered heels, and softly rounded toes. Or open toes through which you could always see her immaculately manicured and painted toenails.

She was apparently considered quite a catch in her day. I always remember my father boasting of this, in a kind of wonderment that it was he who had managed to hook such a universally coveted fish – a cross between Honor Blackman and Lauren Bacall, with her tiny waist, full bust, and long elegant legs that she used to like to show off in fitted skirts that sat just above her knee.

She's softer at the edges now, her figure blossomed from a size ten to a curvaceous fourteen, but she still looks as glamorous as ever. Caramel-coloured waves cascade to just below her jawline in a distinctly 1950s style, the long fringe held out of her face by a small diamanté pin. Despite the fact that she spends her time either up to her elbows in farmyard, or up to her knees in mud, she always looks totally immaculate. At the moment she looks as if she's just stepped out of the film *Landgirls*, with her belted grey wool slacks tucked into Wellington boots, a crimson polo-neck sweater hugging her torso like a glove, a cigarette poised between the perfectly painted crimson lips, her hands protected by a pair of leather riding gloves. A pretty black and white Collie is seemingly attached to her left ankle, moving silently wherever she goes.

When she spots the car, she waves excitedly, her mouth breaking into a huge smile. She throws the cigarette to the ground, extinguishing it with the heel of her boot, and unlatching the gate, lifts it back to allow us through. I pull up near to the house, which sits to the right of the cobbled yard.

Whitsunday is a long, low, crumbling slate-grey stone farmhouse, with a central door. Like a house in a child's drawing, its first-floor windows sit under a roof that slopes so low, they look like square eyes blinking out of a long fringe.

Despite the fact that it is winter, the yard is full of flowers. Anything that has a cavity has been planted – from an old square sink balanced on bricks, through great wooden tubs bursting at the seams with the yellow and white of winter jasmine, to more conventional window boxes, and unconventional hanging containers made from what look like old wicker baskets.

Next to the front door, pink and white Vibernum jostle for space within the confines of an old tin bucket suspended by its handle from a nail in the wall. A winter clematis is climbing the walls around the door and the kitchen window, its freckled cream flowers knocking gently at the glass panes as they are buffeted by a breeze. The only thing that hasn't been planted is the water trough at the end of the stable block, upon whose slightly muddied waters sits a lone, wild duck – a handsome mallard with his vicar's dog-collar of dark green. The hens are locked behind chicken netting just beyond a compound that contains three very large, fat geese.

'Well, hello there!' Laura is on Cassie's side of the car, her greeting resounding and friendly. 'How was your journey? I hope it wasn't too awful on the A30. There was a nasty accident there yesterday and it seemed to take them forever to get the road clear again.'

She opens Cas's door for her. 'Hi, Cassie. Welcome to Whitsunday.'

Cas steps out of the car carefully, looking around her at the wet muddy cobbles, and the motley crew of damp animals with a slight sneer on her pretty face. She ignores my mother, but fortunately Laura is too preoccupied to notice, coming round to my side of the car, and offering a tentative, 'Welcome home, darling,' as I step out into the slight drizzle.

I smile half-heartedly at this. I don't really know where home is at the moment.

Laura steps forward and hugs me, enveloping me in a soft cashmere embrace. She smells of cigarette smoke and Chanel. When she steps back, my black jumper is flecked with crimson hairs.

My mother's smile has slipped a little. I can see from the look in her eyes that she is shocked at how much weight I have lost since I saw her last, disguised by the bulk of my clothing, until her hug met bone instead of flesh. She now looks more closely at my face, noting the more prominent cheekbones, the new hollows beneath them and my eyes.

'I would imagine you're both gasping for a cup of tea and something to eat maybe,' she finally ventures, as though determined to start fattening us up straight away.

I shake my head. 'We stopped on the way.'

'Well, in that case why don't we take your things inside and then show Cas round? Just pop your bags in the kitchen, and then we can introduce her to the gang.' We pull our bags from the boot of the car and follow her silently into the house. The kitchen smells of hot sweet tea, a slight tang of tobacco, cinnamon, oranges, and warmth. It is a large room with a low ceiling, lit and warmed by the red glow of a fire burning slowly in the huge grate.

I duck under the low lintel of the door, even though I know it clears my head by at least three inches. Maybe I thought I'd grown as well as grown up since I lived here myself.

It's so strange being back. Almost eerie to step into this room once more, as if déjà vu is suddenly tangible and constant instead of emotional and fleeting. Oddly, I feel almost tearful. But that's how I am at the moment anyway. Tender. More vulnerable than I ever used to be, and hating myself for this weakness. I take a deep breath and look around me, try to find reassurance instead of rejection in the familiarity of the room.

The kitchen is dominated by a huge open fireplace, a scrubbed pine table large enough to seat ten people, and a heavy Welsh dresser that is a Tardis for everything you may ever need in a lifetime, from safety pins to plasters, Sellotape to envelopes, fashion magazines to fruit cake.

There are photographs on the tobacco-coloured walls. Black and whites. Lots of them. I don't remember them being here the last time I was down, although as I said, that was about two and half years ago.

My mother follows my gaze. 'I had a clear-out in the attic. Found all of those in a dusty album at the bottom of a trunk. Thought they'd be better where I could see them, than stuck in the dark in a drawer somewhere.'

Cas is looking at a shot of a group on stage in a theatre, arms linked, pancaked faces all beaming broadly as if it's a celebration of something. It's the first sign of interest she has shown. I can see her moving closer to look at a particular part of the photograph.

'Is this you?'

It is also the first time she has spoken since our arrival.

Laura turns at the sound of Cassie's voice, her eyes narrowing as she struggles to see what Cassie is looking at. She steps forward and looks more closely, beaming as she recognises a shot of herself in fishnet tights, black dance pants, and a white wrap jumper.

'Yes, that's me. I was only nineteen then.'

'And the guy next to you, the one who's got his arm around you, he looks like Freddie Davies.'

Laura's smile broadens. 'That's because it *is* Freddie Davies.'

Cas turns to us, her eyes wide with astonishment. 'But he was *the* best jazz dancer in the world.'

'I know, and he was such a nice man too.'

'You actually *knew* him?'

'We did a whole season together at the Hammersmith Palais.'

Cassie looks back at the picture, then over at Laura again with a curious expression on her face. 'Were you a dancer?'

'Oh no, not really, not like you. I was an actress, darling.' Laura rolls her eyes and purrs the 'actress, darling' in pretend affectation. 'Although I did fancy myself as a bit of a hoofer – I could high kick with the best of them.'

I almost think she's going to give us a demonstration as she transfers her weight to her left leg and throws her right forward, but she simply gives a tiny kick and beams happily at Cas.

'I can't quite reach the heights that I used to but I

could still give the Moulin Rouge a run for their money if I wanted to.'

Cas's face is hard to read; I can't tell if she's smiling or mocking. She moves on to the picture to the right of the one they were discussing, just as my own eyes fall upon it, drawn to it by a warm sense of recognition.

'Who's this?'

It's a black and white portrait of a small but handsome man, looking straight into the camera.

Laura opens her mouth to reply.

'My father,' I answer, breathing in sharply.

I step closer, my heart quickening as his handsome, happy face comes more clearly into view. His eyes are shining with laughter and a slight hint of embarrassment. He never did like having his photograph taken, whereas Laura revelled in it.

This is the first time I have seen my father's face in sixteen years. I don't keep photographs of him. Didn't want them at the time. Thought it was better not to have a physical reminder. Felt I could keep his face locked securely in my head and my heart; it's so odd, seeing him now. A stranger almost.

I keep a picture of Rob in my wallet, scared that the memories of him will fade like they did of my father. The reality of the print before me brings with it a sharp stab of buried emotion.

I don't know if she can sense how I'm feeling but Laura engineers an abrupt end to the conversation. 'Enough reminiscing.' Reaching out, she takes Cassie's hand.

Cas jumps like a startled colt, looking at my mother's hand as if something offensive has just landed on her. I almost expect her to swat it away like she would an annoying insect. Laura is oblivious, however, and simply sweeps her outside with a levity of attitude that seems to add wings to Cassie's previously shuffling feet. 'I promised to introduce you both to the gang,' she says enthusiastically, as I tail along after them.

By the gang, Laura means her animals.

My mother collects animals like an orphanage seeks out lost children. Each time that I have been back to Whitsunday, I have been greeted by a different motley assortment. In the three years since my last visit, Laura's old German Shepherd Rufus has passed away to be replaced by the pretty rough collie that follows her now as silently as a shadow.

To the rear of the yard are animal pens housing an assortment of feathered friends, or 'feathered fiends' as I used to call them when it was one of my jobs to feed them every morning. The pens have been converted from one long low barn with several doors, the addition of metal gates and chicken wire forming segregated runs for the different birds; in the middle are three huge cantankerous geese, ducks to the left, and in the large end pen closest to the house, about twenty chickens.

To the left of the yard opposite the house frontage is a row of immaculate stables, all empty except for the end one, where a handsome chestnut gelding is leaning out of the top half, head nodding rhythmically as he waits for us to acknowledge him. Laura crosses to him, reaches up to pat his muzzle, but he moves his head so that his nose is buried in the palm of her hand, hunting for treats, blowing through his grey whiskers as he tries to ascertain whether she's brought him anything to eat.

'This is Chance,' she tells us, pushing his nose down with the flat of her hand, and scratching underneath his forelock. 'Last Chance.'

'What a stupid name,' Cassie spits sulkily, still rubbing her wrist where Laura's fingers had been closed about it as though trying to rub away imaginary marks. Although she had brightened perceptibly whilst looking at the photographs, Cassie's mood has slipped again during our guided tour of the farmyard.

'Well, I didn't choose it,' Laura replies cheerfully. 'He

used to be a racehorse. A very good one actually. He's retired now, aren't you, old fella?' My mother pats Chance's neck as he blows his whiskered muzzle about her pockets searching for the treats he feels sure he'll find eventually. 'Living the good life.'

'Cassie rides, don't you, Cas?' I offer, embarrassed that she is being so taciturn, and trying to draw her out of herself and into the conversation a little. Cas grunts something almost unintelligible, which I think is an attempt at an affirmation.

Laura turns to her. 'You can ride him if you want to – he'd enjoy the exercise. I don't get out much myself at the moment, far too busy.'

Cassie shrugs boredly, but when Laura and I move down to the opposite end of the stable block, next to where I have now parked my car, we both note that she remains at the loose box long enough to feed Chance something from her pocket, and scratch his whiskered chestnut muzzle.

Laura opens another door into a stable that I initially thought was empty. In two large pens are two mother goats with an assortment of kids, about five in all.

'These aren't mine,' Laura explains as they too crowd about her hopeful of food. 'They're lodgers. I'm looking after them for a friend who's gone on holiday. She keeps them as pets in her back garden, says they're far more use to her than a lawnmower now she's getting on a bit. They'll be going home at the end of next week.'

'Thank heavens for that!' Cas has followed us into the dimly lit stable. 'They totally *stink*.' She screws up her eyes, her nose wrinkling in offence at the rather pungent smell of warm but slightly damp goat.

'Well, I think they're kind of cute,' I tell Laura, ignoring Cassie's comment and her pained expression.

'I must admit I've always thought they smelt a little . . . now how shall I put it?' Laura rubs her chin in thought.

'Rank?' Cassie offers.

'About as rancid as a month-old Gorgonzola,' Laura agrees with her, eliciting a rare yet brief smile. 'Although they have their uses.'

'Such as?' Cas queries in disbelief.

'They make excellent waste-disposal units: they eat practically anything . . .' Laura's smile turns into a mischievous grin as her eyes avert to my left ankle. I look down in alarm to see one of the larger kids chewing happily on the hem of my expensive wool trousers.

'Why, you little . . .' I growl, side-stepping quickly, my indignation tempered only by the realisation that Cas has for once forgotten to look pained and is actually almost smiling.

I hasten outside, closely followed by the other two who are grinning in the camaraderie built by someone else being the butt of a joke.

The day, which is dull, seems bright after the dim and dust-ridden light of the stables. Laura leads us past the end stable and left down the long passage which runs between two long stone barns. To the right, its end wall providing shelter to the animal pens, is a huge barn with two great wooden doors about ten feet high, housing everything under the sun. Empty cardboard boxes with *Fragile* stamped in red on the sides, tools, two wheelbarrows, an old black ladies' pushbike with a brown wicker basket on the front, and assorted bags of feed. Corn for the ducks and geese, bran and pony nuts for Chance, big pink bricks of salt, and huge sacks of cattle feed for the small herd of cows that live in one of the meadows.

To the left of the long passage is an open-sided barn that sits just behind the stable block. This is home to about fifty bales of hay piled high on top of each other like dusty Lego bricks in a child's playroom, a huge blue tarpaulin pegged down loosely over them. There is also an assortment of farm machinery, an old red tractor that my mother tells us no longer works, and several pieces of metalwork that were probably once attached to it – dangerous-looking objects with spikes and sharp discs.

A gate at the end of the long passage leads into a sloping field beyond. If you turn right and walk its length, it runs for about a mile right down to the very edge of the cliff, and the Atlantic Ocean beyond.

I remember Mile Meadow. I used to walk down there sometimes in the evening, on my own, and watch the sun sinking over the sea, glorying in the rich vivacity of the colours and the overwhelming clarity the sights and sounds induced in my senses. It is the only part of this place that I remember really liking. I would sit on the edge of the cliff and dare the waves and the wind to pull me over, and plot my escape from a place that I thought was the end of the world.

Wits End. A place that when I left it, seemed to signify the end of my unhappy childhood.

There is another collie half asleep in this long passage, warm and replete in a narrow path of sunshine. He opens his eyes as we approach, and wags a friendly plumed tail at us but doesn't move. Tufts of grey hair around bright black eyes are the only things that give away his age.

'This gorgeous old gentleman is Shep,' Laura tells us, stooping to pat him.

'How original,' I hear Cassie mutter. 'Very *Blue Peter*.'

'Well, actually this is Old Shep.'

'Elvis, eat your heart out.'

'And that playful lad over there,' Laura points to where a younger version of Old Shep is currently chasing his own tail, round and round in never-ending circles, 'is his son, Young Shep.'

'It gets worse,' Cassie mutters, rolling her eyeballs.

'And this is my girl Meggie,' she refers to the animal still hugging her heels. 'Young Shep's mother.'

'Oh how lovely, a family of clichés,' Cas drawls from behind me.

'Old Shep doesn't actually live here. He thinks he does,' Laura strokes the dog's head affectionately, 'but he doesn't. He belongs to one of the men who work here, but he has a huge crush on my gorgeous girl, doesn't he, darling?' She transfers her affection to the silky head of the pretty collie sat quietly at her side. 'Which she fortunately reciprocates, hence the addition of Junior over there, who doesn't live here either, but is too stupid to realise it. They're lovely dogs to have because they're normally so intelligent, but unfortunately whilst Young Shep inherited his mother's looks, he inherited neither of his parents' brain capacity. He's a real sweetheart though. Very friendly.'

The young dog stops his tail-chasing. Finally realising that there are visitors, he charges toward us yelping frantically, tail wagging in a frenzy of excited greeting. He jumps straight up at Cas, his large front paws planted firmly in the centre of her stomach, making her gasp with surprise and indignation. To my own surprise, however, instead of the anger I expect she begins to chuckle, albeit dryly. Unfortunately, this moment of good humour is shortlived when she spots the set of muddy paw-prints Young Shep has left on her favourite pale-coloured sweatshirt.

'Bloody dog!' she hisses, shooing him away with the heel of one of her Kickers, as he bounds enthusiastically around her ankles.

'I think he likes you.' Laura smiles.

'Well, the feeling's not reciprocated,' my step-daughter growls. She sweeps a hand across her top to try to brush away the mud, but only succeeds in smearing it into a larger streak. Laura pulls an embroidered handkerchief from the pocket of her slacks and dabs ineffectually at the smear.

'Why don't we take you inside and pop that in the

washing machine? We'll soon get the mud out.'

We head back down the corridor toward the yard, Young Shep an over-excited escort at our heels. As we round the end of the wall, I hear the rattle of a car engine that's obviously seen better days, the unmistakable sound of a loose exhaust vibrating against the bottom of the car as it dips into a pot-hole, and then the air is violently rent by the squeal of a horn, which sounds a volley that could have come straight from *The Dukes of Hazzard*. An old S-registration Ford Capri is wheezing to a stop next to my blue BMW. Despite the cold, both windows are wide open, and Patsy Cline is blaring from the speakers.

Crazy.

As the driver opens the door with a protesting squeal of rusted hinges, the music gets even louder, and then thankfully stops as he removes his keys from the ignition, and pushes them along with their fake pistol key fob into the pocket of his low-slung faded denims.

A weathered old Cornishman, with a face like shrunken leather and eyes as bright and blue as the sky on a hot day, stands before us. At least I think he's Cornish. For all intents and purposes he could have just stepped into the yard straight from an episode of *Bonanza* – apart from the fact that none of the *Bonanza* boys drove an old rusted Ford Capri with cow horns affixed to the front of the bonnet. The seats of the car are covered with some sort of ponyskin-effect loose cover, which has left little black and white hairs all over the back of the red checked shirt this Cornish cowboy is wearing. The sleeves of his shirt are rolled back to his elbows to reveal stringy yet muscular arms, tanned to the colour of a new leather saddle. His jeans are held up by a wide leather belt with a buckle in the shape of a snake, and on his feet are worn dusty cowboy boots, with scuffed toes and scuffed heels, the leather tanned dark by days spent up to his ankles in farmyard. Our

visitor is thin and pigeon-chested, with legs so bowed
they're like a frame to the constantly changing picture
you can see between them.

Cas's sweatshirt forgotten, my mother beams broadly
at this new addition. 'Girls, this is Hank. He helps me out
on the farm a couple of days a week, so you'll be seeing
him about quite a lot.'

'How do.' Hank raises the Stetson to reveal a head of
thinning grey curls and the leather face cracks into a
wide white-toothed smile. His accent is a curious mix of
rich heavy Cornish, and sheer Dallas Texan, with a bit of
Irish thrown in for good measure.

Cassie's shoulders are shaking with the effort not to
laugh.

'Hello.' I hold out a hand which he takes in his own,
the rough callused skin chaffing my own softer hand as
he shakes with a vigour that belies the frailty of his
demeanour.

'Hank doesn't normally come in today, but we've got
a delivery to go out,' Laura explains, going over to the
battered grey Land Rover that she has had since we
moved to Falmouth. A death-trap contraption with
pockets of rust spreading over its Army grey body like a
bad case of the pox, it is almost the same age as me. God
knows how it gets through the MOT every year.

Laura pulls at the rusted rear door, opening it with
difficulty. 'You've made it just in time to give us a hand,'
she tells us, taking a huge black key from her trouser
pocket, and handing it to Hank. 'Can you go and get the
stuff from the cattle shed, there's a dear? It's all boxed up
and ready, and the girls and I will chuck it all in the back
of the Landy, ready for you to take up to Connor.'

Hank nods briefly and ambles off down the long
passage, his walk a curious rolling gait that makes him
look like he's strolling along the deck of a ship sailing on
stormy waters. Laura is busy clearing the debris-strewn
floor of the small jeep, moving bits of frayed rope, old

chewed dog leads, empty boxes, and binning several empty Cornish fudge boxes with a guilty smile and shrug.

'Bit of a weakness of mine, I'm afraid, hence the hips.'

It takes Hank ten minutes to reappear with the first of Laura's cargo. He is carrying two large sealed cardboard boxes with apparent ease.

I wince as I bend to pick one up, and fooled by his example lift a touch too casually. 'What have you got in here?' I complain. 'Bricks?'

Laura smiles, but then turns quickly back to help Cas. 'Careful!' She grabs the end of the box Cassie's just pushed into the back of the old Land Rover as, balanced precariously on the box below, it wobbles dangerously, threatening to fall to the floor.

'What's in these anyway?' Cas echoes me, her curiosity fighting with her churlishness.

Laura restacks the box she has just saved from falling and looks at Cas with an infuriating air of mystery.

'Didn't you know the Cornish are a breed of smugglers? You don't ask them questions, and they don't give you answers.' She smoothes down the end of a *Fragile* sticker that is peeling away from the edge of the box.

'Take no notice,' I smile at Cas. 'She's not Cornish, she's from Hove.'

Cas sighs, unimpressed by what she apparently sees as a display of childishness more suited to people younger than her, than those who are supposed to be adult.

'I wasn't that interested anyway,' she lies.

'Good.' Laura smiles enigmatically at her. 'Because if I told you, I'd have to shoot you. Anyway,' she winks at me, 'I may be from Hove, young lady, but seeing as I've lived in Cornwall for over sixteen years, I feel I have the right to claim a little bit of her for myself.'

Cas has stopped stacking, waiting for Hank's next batch of boxes and is watching Laura with a strange, almost fearful look on her face. I can see her taking

71

stock, measuring my mother as though she is an arithmetic calculation that Cas hasn't as yet been able to work out. She'll struggle to do it in one afternoon. I've known her all my life and I still haven't managed to solve the equation.

We form a kind of human chain. Hank disappears down the long passage, returning every ten minutes with two more boxes, I carry them one by one over to the Land Rover, and my mother and Cas stack them in. There are only twelve boxes, but it takes us the best part of an hour to load the jeep. The longest part is waiting for Hank to return from wherever it is that he's fetching the boxes from, but Laura doesn't suggest that someone goes with him to help, and assuming she has a reason for this, I don't offer.

I watch Laura chatting away to Cas as they wait and as they work. Cas is hard work to chat to as she rarely answers anything put to her. I think Laura is having a little more success than I normally do, for I see Cassie's mouth move in response every so often to something Laura says to her; in fact, by the time we've finished stacking, they seem to be having quite a conversation, Cas even smiling at intervals. Small, sad smiles, but smiles nonetheless.

Hank returns from the long passage with what are apparently the last two boxes, and puts these in the back of the Land Rover himself. Laura shuts the door on them, brushes her hands together, and turns to beam at us all.

'Well, I think we've all worked jolly hard today. Cassie darling, why don't you pop the kettle on and make us all a nice cup of tea? Hank likes his strong and sweet, don't you, pet? Just the way I like my men.' She pinches his cheek affectionately and the silent man blushes to the roots of his curling grey hair.

To my surprise, Cassie does as asked, with no questions, or black looks. We follow her into the kitchen a few minutes later to find the kettle on, and Cas taking tea bags from the tin by the kettle and an assortment of mugs from a mug tree on the window ledge.

'That one's mine,' says my mother, pointing to one that's emblazoned with the words *The Boss*. 'The one with the Star Spangled Banner is Hank's, believe it or not, the yellow one's Luke's, who you'll meet another time. Pick one and stick to it. We drink an ocean of tea throughout the day, but tend not to wash up every single time, slatterns that we are.'

I can see Cassie's mouth draw thin in disapproval, as she misses the humour in Laura's voice, and then watch as she inspects the cup she's just pulled from the mug tree next to the kitchen sink. That's something else that is unusual about Cas. Unlike most teenagers who seem to develop the urge to live in chaos from the age of thirteen onwards, she is incredibly tidy. Almost obsessively so.

Her bedroom at home would pass the strictest squaddies' mess inspection. I know she leaves a trail of chaos behind her through the rest of the house, but I also know this is against her nature, and is done purely to irk me. The cup obviously passes inspection, because it is added to the tray that already has mugs, milk in a little jug with a Friesian cow painted on it, and a huge teapot that I recognise as having once belonged to my maternal grandmother.

A plate of biscuits is already set out on the table. Hank makes a bow-legged bee-line for this, sitting himself firmly down next to the plate and helping himself to a handful. Cas and I wait for my mother to sit down before choosing seats ourselves, visitors subconsciously watching out for a usual seating plan that we have no wish to invade by taking the wrong chair.

My mother apparently has no preference. I note subsequently that she will simply sink into the nearest chair, and Hank will always sit next to the biscuits, no matter where they are put. If they are left on the side in the tin, he will stand up and lean against the sink. I think if we put them on top of the huge oak dresser that stands against the wall by the stairs, he would sit on that and keep eating until the tin was empty.

Whilst we drink, my mother talks and Hank doesn't. She talks about the farm, and feeding and fixing and fetching. He simply nods in response to the questions directed at him, or shakes his head, whichever is the more relevant, all the time drinking tea, and devouring biscuits at an amazing rate.

Cassie is seated at the end of the table, as far away from everybody as possible, nursing a mug of tea with two sugars that she hasn't touched, and staring in awe at Hank's extraordinary outfit. Her initial fit of giggles has given way to a horrified fascination, and she has barely been able to tear her eyes away from him all afternoon, no matter how hard she's tried.

I sympathise with her predicament. Personally, I can't stop looking at his extraordinary boots. I try, but every time I look over at him my eyes just keep sliding downwards. They may have looked like an ordinary – well, ordinary for Cornwall, anyway – pair of cowboy boots from the front, but from the back they are as ordinary as riding an elephant down Rotten Row. Inconspicuous cracked tan leather toes give way to the most outrageously flamboyant cocktail of rhinestones at the back of the shoe. A Phoenix is rising in an explosion of sparkling gems from the dust of each heel, all in shades of pink from pastel to fucshia, with the exception of what I think must be the phoenix's eye, which is bright yellow gold.

I smile to Cas in camaraderie, showing her that I too share the same amused reaction to Hank's strange mode of dress, but she blanks me, and I cover my face with my mug to hide my embarrassment, pretending that I wasn't smiling, simply opening my mouth to drink.

'That's much better,' Laura announces after her third cup. 'You may as well pop off now, Hank. I think that's it for today. Take the cargo up to Connor, and then go on home, although you could just take a quick look at the latch on the goose pen before you go, I think it's a bit loose.'

Hank touches his forehead in affirmation, nods to Cas and me, and rolls out of the kitchen door. Laura turns to us, pushing up the sleeves of her sweater as she does so, and smiles a touch too brightly.

'Thanks for your help. Sorry to throw you in at the deep end, especially as you've only just arrived, but believe me it was much appreciated. I think we must have loaded that delivery in record time. How about we get these bags upstairs,' she indicates our pile of luggage just inside the door, 'and then that's the fetching and carrying done for today at least. Why don't I show you where you're sleeping? Nattie darling, you're back in your old room, of course. I've put you in the attic, Cas. A flower in the attic. We'll take you up there first, shall we? I want to show Nattie what I've done with the room. She won't recognise it.'

I'd find it hard to remember what the attic looked like anyway. I spent most of my brief time here closeted away in my bedroom, listening to melancholy music and dreaming of a brighter future, somewhere far, far away from Cornwall.

There is a flight of stairs leading off the kitchen to the first-floor landing. We head up them and put my bags in my old bedroom, which overlooks the yard, and then go back out onto the landing. Laura opens what looks like a cupboard door to reveal a narrow staircase winding up yet another flight.

She leads the way; Cas comes next and I bring up the rear. The stairs are steep and each step creaks protestingly as we climb. We emerge into a long room that runs the length of the house, with Velux windows to the front overlooking the farmyard, and to the rear looking out over the wilderness that is the neglected back garden, and the meadows beyond.

Laura is still talking nineteen to the dozen. I don't ever remember her being this effusive, but then it suddenly occurs to me that she is as nervous about us being here as I was about us coming.

There are picture windows either end, one facing toward the road, and the other looking out over the fields between the house and the ocean.

'If you stand to the right you can just about see the sea,' Laura tells us as I automatically head for the rear window. 'You'll get a better view if you open the window and stick your head out, but be careful not to fall.'

I lift the latch and on my mother's instruction lean gingerly out of the open window, certain that if I did lose my balance and tumble earthward I would be making Cassie's day for her. From here I can see above the square horseshoe of buildings that make up the main body of Whitsunday, beyond the Long Barn and the hay barn, and over their dark slate roofs to the gently sloping fields beyond. These roll down to a tumbling edge of land that drops at about sixty degrees to meet the beach and then the water.

I can see a small herd of cattle huddled around a long metal feed trough in one of the fields, and in the distance the seagulls rise and fall like yoyos on a high wind. I remember this room as being a haven for the hoarder that Laura is, full of boxes containing what most people would call junk, but that she called memories. It's very different now. A proper room. A lovely room actually, spacious and light, with walls painted a soft raspberry colour, wooden floorboards, and a sloping ceiling. There is a wooden desk and chair under the far window, which looks out toward the track that leads back to the main road; two single beds with damson-coloured duvets are tucked either side of the room under the eaves, and between them are a full bookcase, two rugs in soft shades of raspberry and cream, and matching scatter cushions on the floor.

'This is where you'll be staying.' Laura smiles at Cas hopefully. 'I hope you like it.'

'She won't,' I can't help muttering under my breath.

My mother catches this and half smiles at me in sympathy.

Cassie is standing in the middle of the room. She turns about her slowly, taking in everything, then she smiles at Laura – a sweet smile that spreads slowly across her face.

'Thanks. It's great.'

I'm almost knocked sideways by surprise. She must have heard me. I bet she only said thank you because I said she wouldn't.

I study her face, trying to read the emotion behind the smile, but her eyes are blank and I can't mind-read. Maybe I'm being unfair, basing my assumption on my own experience of Cas. Her best friend's mother is always saying what a delightful child she is, after all. Perhaps it's only me she's so downright awful with – and Petra too, isn't she the lucky one?

And after all, the room *is* perfect. It's a teenager's dream bedroom. Maybe if this had been my room when I was here I might have been tempted to stay for a while longer. I surprise myself this time. I'm surprised by the pathos behind what started out as a semi-humorous thought. I shake my head and tell myself it's just weird being back here, and I'm too old and too much time has passed to worry about how bad I felt when I was sixteen and still living in this place.

'I'm going to start dinner, so why don't you girls unpack and freshen up and then come down.' Laura is still smiling.

I find myself wondering whether her smile, too, is

forced, and behind it lies the truth of how difficult she might be finding this reunion.

She turns to Cas. 'The bathroom's the last door on the left on the floor below. If you get lost, just yell.'

I shower quickly, change without unpacking, and then head back downstairs. There's no sign of Cas, but Laura is in the kitchen preparing dinner, slicing the long green fronded tails from a bunch of earth-covered orange carrots with a wooden-handled knife. She looks up from her chopping board, knife in hand, her smile hesitant, yet welcoming.

'All right? Found everything you need?'

I nod. 'Yeah, thanks.'

'Dinner won't be long. I hope you still like shepherd's pie?'

'What can I do to help?'

'Well, you see that bottle of wine on the table?'

'Yep.'

'There's an opener in the drawer to the right of the sink, just behind the cutlery tray.' She indicates behind her.

'Found it.'

'Great. Now open the bottle, pour us both a large glassful, then sit down and put your feet up. You must be absolutely shattered after driving all the way down here, and then helping me load those boxes.'

I can't sit down whilst Laura works, it doesn't feel right.

'I'm fine, honestly,' I reply, easing the cork from the bottle. 'I'll admit I'm a bit tired,' I add as my body betrays me by forcing a yawn, 'but I'd rather help out if I can. Are you sure there's nothing I can do?'

'Sit.' She smiles determinedly. 'Relax, read the paper or something.'

Today's *Daily Mail* is folded in half on the vast scrubbed wood kitchen table. I pour two glasses of wine, hand one to my mother and sitting down at the table, open it up to look at the headlines.

I haven't read a paper for three days. I don't know how I could have gone quite so long in a literary wilderness. It's a bit like a smoker quitting cigarettes. I'm an avid reader, and as well as books I normally devour most of the dailies. In my job, I have to keep abreast of the news. Although I'm on holiday, I can't afford to get too out of touch with what's going on in the world.

There's obviously not much going on in the world today, though; the *Mail* is leading with a C List showbiz story that would normally be about page three, certainly not front-page coverage. I read it half-heartedly, and with a strange sense of relief that I'm not missing anything important.

Cassie finally descends. She has changed into clean jeans and a thicker, mud-free sweatshirt, her pale pink hair still damp from the shower. Like me she asks if there is anything she can do to help out, which I must admit surprises me a little. She must be on her very best behaviour. I wonder how long this period of politeness will last.

Laura hands her some of the carrots she has just rinsed clean under the tap in the stainless steel sink. 'You can give those to Chance for me if you like.'

Cas shrugs. 'If you want.'

'Borrow my boots, save you going back upstairs for your shoes.' Laura looks down at Cas's feet. 'I'd say you were the same size as me. Four, right?'

Cas nods, and goes to pull on the pair of green Wellingtons that Laura is pointing to just inside the kitchen door, under a coat rack that is almost buckling under the weight of the jackets, coats, hats and scarves that are hung there.

Cas struggles to open the heavy back door, but once she has pulled it to, stops almost immediately in her tracks.

'Oh my God!' She takes a step backwards into the room, and stares fearfully out of the door, before closing it again firmly.

'What's the matter?' I look up from the newspaper, but ignoring me Cas turns to Laura.

'There's a monster in the yard,' she tells her, half laughing, half tearful.

'A monster?' Laura replies unconcerned. 'What are you on about, Cassie?'

'The biggest dog you have ever seen – in fact, I'm not so sure that it is a dog. It's quite possible that it's a huge mutated pig.'

'Oh, that'll be Mac.'

'Mac?' I query, surprised that Cassie's odd description can elicit such a confident confirmation of identity.

'He belongs to Connor.' Laura smiles happily as though we both know who Connor is. 'He often comes down for a visit.'

'Who?' I joke. 'Connor or Mac?'

'Well, you usually get them both at the same time, but I think Mac's got a bit of a thing for Meg – he'll sometimes sneak down here on his own.'

'Well, he'll have to fight Shep for her.' I smile, getting up from my chair.

'I think Shep might concede on this one,' Cas murmurs, looking out of the window. 'It'd be a bit like a featherweight taking on Mike Tyson.'

I join Cas at the window. She is staring out into the yard, still unsure whether it's safe to venture outside or not. The biggest bull mastiff I have ever seen is lifting a powerful rear leg to water one of Laura's tubs.

'Wow,' I murmur.

'Exactly,' Cas replies without looking at me.

'He's completely harmless, very friendly, in fact,' Laura is saying over my shoulder.

'Are you sure?' Cas mumbles.

In answer, Laura opens the door and calls out to the

huge animal, who is now working his way round the edge of the loose boxes, nose to the floor, like a road-marker painting yellow lines against a kerb. Mac stops mid-sniff and looks up. My mother calls him again and, pausing to take a final sniff at Chance who has just thrust a curious friendly face out of the open top door of his loose box, he then ambles over toward her, large pink tongue lolling out of the side of the most incredibly crinkled set of black lips and gums.

'I don't believe it,' I hear Cas murmur, her voice an octave higher with fear. 'She's actually calling it inside!'

The huge animal ambles into the kitchen. He sniffs at my mother in a friendly fashion, tries to sniff Cas, who backs away in alarm, then pads his huge frame over to me and sniffs again.

I sit back down in my chair and hold out a tentative hand, which he immediately licks.

'I think he likes you,' Laura says reassuringly.

'I probably taste of chocolate.'

'Well, he does love chocolate.'

'Do you think he'll eat her then?' Cas asks my mother a touch too hopefully.

Mac doesn't attempt to devour me, but giving my hand a curling lick, he rests his chin against my knee and looks up at me with huge black eyes, whose lower lids hang like slipped socks against the socket bone below. Cassie looks on in astonishment as I stroke his massive crew-cut head, obviously convinced that because the dog has a mouth large enough to eat a human being, this is exactly what he intends to do with it.

'I think you've found a friend,' my mother observes in amusement.

'You can never have too many of those,' I reply, scratching the creased skin of his forehead, 'except when it comes to buying birthday and Christmas presents, of course. He's absolutely gorgeous.'

'You should meet the owner,' Laura smiles, then pausing, gives me a knowing look. 'Hmm, yes, you should definitely meet the owner,' she mutters more to herself than to me.

I choose to ignore this and the obvious intention behind it. I know it's well meant, but things like this just make me angry. Like it's a slur to Rob.

'Talking about the owner, shouldn't you really take him back home?' asks Cas, still eyeing the giant dog in concern.

'Oh, he'll probably stay the night. He often does – he'll take himself home in the morning.'

'Won't his owner worry?'

'Worry? About Mac?'

'Uh, yeah.'

'Oh no, he's very independent.'

'You make him sound like a human.'

'He almost is, aren't you, darling?' Laura coos, coming over to scratch the animal's huge head affectionately. 'Just make sure you bag a seat at the dining table before he gets there.'

Dinner is a stilted affair. We eat in a fairly awkward silence that Laura keeps trying to break with questions that Cas doesn't really want to answer. It's hard to know what to talk to her about. School is obviously a taboo subject at the moment. Having tried and failed to get Cas to tell her about Cheal, Laura tries to talk to her about music.

My mother loves music.

One thing I always remember from when I was young, was her having music playing constantly in the background. It didn't matter what she was doing, either the radio or the record player would accompany her. Jazz was her favourite – Nina Simone, Sarah Vaughan, Helen Carr, Julie London, then Frank Sinatra, Big Bands, Swing, with the odd classical moment, and a little bit of rock and roll thrown in for good measure. I'm surprised she doesn't have something on now. It would be better than the silence we lapse back into after Cas has told a confused Laura that she likes Limp Bizkit, Dido, and Sum 41.

'Are they pop groups?' Laura whispers to me in consternation.

'Sort of,' I whisper back, unable to help a small smile escaping onto my face.

Cas as usual picks at her food, pushing it round and round her plate until it is cold and no longer edible. I am not hungry either, but aware that Laura is watching me like a hawk, I try to eat a little.

We both help clear up. It's the first time I've seen Cas do this without being told to. I'm finding it hard to stifle my yawns, and am pleased that I can genuinely say that the long drive down has tired me out, so I can use the excuse of wanting an early night and the need to unpack, as a means to escape up to my room.

Moments later, I hear Cas follow me up, the heavy latch on the stair door clicking loudly into place. Soon, Laura's footsteps follow. I hear the sound of her door being shut, and moments after, the familiar sound of Radio Two on low volume. I stand in the doorway of my room with my back pressed against the door and look about me, the breath escaping from my body in a long slow sigh.

It's so strange being back here, in the room I used to have as a sixteen-year-old girl. When I've been down to see Laura before, I've always found some excuse to stay at a rather nice B&B down in the village, well away from any memories I want to avoid. Now I'm back in my old room. The same room without the childhood clutter. Not that I ever had much clutter as a child. I followed Laura's example in that I too was the typical rolling stone, although unlike her, the hoarder, I gathered no moss. I think my theory then was that if I didn't have anything I valued then I wouldn't worry about leaving it all behind as soon as I seized my moment to escape.

It's a large room with a picture window overlooking the yard, and a deep-set sill wide enough to sit on. There's an open fireplace, and the same big old brass bed, and antique pine furniture I had when I lived here.

The only difference is the walls that were once pink have now been painted a far more appealing shade of soft ochre, a colour vaguely reminiscent of the old gold walls in the kitchen, so much so that I can only conclude Laura has mixed some left-over paint with white emulsion and used it to brighten up this room as well.

The curtains and bedlinen have been changed too. I had pink floral – tiny roses on a white background, which I hated with a vengeance for being so bloody girlie. Now it's tiny yellow daisies on a white background, a slightly fresher kitsch that I think I can live with for the four to five weeks we've elected to stay here.

My case is on the bed – something practical to tackle. I take my mind out of my melancholy and my clothes out of my suitcase and hang them in the wardrobe that I used as a teenager, pushing away this odd, almost inexplicable feeling of discomfort. It is only as I finally finish unpacking, and climb wearily into bed, that I notice it creeping back over my skin again like a cold hand running down my spine.

It is to be expected, I suppose. I should thank Laura; she's made sure that so far we haven't really had time to feel awkward. She just threw us in at the deep end as soon as we got here. The fact that we've all pulled together this afternoon has eased our way into Whitsunday far more than if we had simply turned up and tuned into the whole 'guest' thing. But I still feel that I shouldn't be here at all, and wish I was at home in my own bed, in mine and Rob's bed.

I start to wonder why I decided to come down at all. At the time I felt that it would be preferable to staying at home on my own with Cas. If I'm being totally honest, I couldn't face Christmas in that house without Rob. I managed to get out of Christmas last year, pretend it wasn't happening. This year I have to face it, for Cassie's sake if nothing else, but there is more to it than that.

Why *had* I accepted Laura's invitation to stay so quickly and so easily? Let's just say that to lose someone precious makes you reassess your own mortality, your values as well, and think about what's important to you.

A part of me thought it was time to find my mother again. Before it was too late, before I lost someone else I cared about.

I feel a strange tightness in my chest, like the pull of Victorian corsets being laced with a cruel vigour. I need comfort. I reach for my mobile. The signal keeps coming and going but finally, perched on the window seat with my head half out of the window, skin chilled by the cold clear night, I manage to get through. There's only one person I know who I can call at any time of the day or night.

'Petra? Hi, it's me.'

'Nattie!' She's pleased to hear from me. 'You got there okay? Why didn't you call me sooner? I've been worrying. How are you doing?'

'It's a bit weird, Pet. A bit strange.' I can hear music in the background, and then the sound of movement as Petra reaches to turn it down.

'Well, it's going to be strange, honey. How's your mother?'

'She seems okay.'

'And how are you?'

'You already asked me that.'

'Well, you didn't give me a proper answer.'

I'm tired, but I can't sleep. I'm with the only family I have but I feel as lonely as if I were on my own. I want to cry but I can't because my tear ducts don't seem to be working any more. I haven't cried once since the accident; my eyes are full of salt, but with no water to wash the irritation away. I've buried myself so deeply in my job for the past twenty months and now I'm scared to death because I don't have that occupation any more. I'm back in a house that I spent a year plotting an escape from because I couldn't stand it so badly.

I take a deep breath. 'I'm okay,' I lie.

'Honestly?'

'Honestly.' I unwittingly lace two fingers together to excuse the lie. 'I just wanted to let you know that we got here okay, and to see how you were. I'll give you a call in a couple of days, right?'

'Okay, as long as you're sure you're all right.'

I snap my phone shut and place it on the bedside table beside me, wondering why on earth I didn't just confess and tell Petra how I'm feeling. I think it's because I don't want to feel like this, and to acknowledge these feelings to someone makes them more real, more obstinate.

There's no point getting into bed. I'm so far from relaxed that I can't even close my eyes; they keep roaming round the room as though searching for something. It's at times like this that I usually work. I write to lull an uneasy mind.

There is a Cellophane-sealed folder of writing paper on the dressing-table – one of the pretty impractical kinds that people give as gifts but rarely buy to use themselves.

I fetch it and return to my seat on the window ledge, lured back by the clear black night, which is as refreshing as a cold glass of water on a hot day. I pull open the packet, take out the sheets of paper, and stare at the blank page in front of me, the plastic end of my Biro resting against the dry skin of my bottom lip. There is only one person I really want to talk to at the moment.

I begin to write.

*Dear Rob,*

*I can't believe how long it's been since I last saw you. It's so hard without you, so lonely. I feel lost – all alone in a world that no longer has a place for me. I've struggled so hard to keep going without you, buried myself in my work, made it more important than it is, trying to fill this huge gap that you've left in my life, this gaping hole in my heart. I still love you so much and I miss you so badly. I can't believe I'm never going to see you again. I miss how close we were, our friendship, the way you made me feel so happy, so loved, so cherished. Now I just feel numb, anaesthetised somehow, disconnected, disjointed. I don't understand what happened, Rob. Why it happened. The cruelty that took you away from me, and from Cassie.*

*Poor, poor Cassie.*

*She misses you so much too, and I know she feels as alone as I do. The anger I see inside her scares me. I know you hoped that we'd get closer eventually, but without you here she is simply drifting further away from me. I wish I could help her, give her the love you gave to me, but I am afraid she'll never turn to me, she'll never really want me in her life. I wish I could make her smile, make her as happy as you made me. I owe this to you. You gave me so much happiness in such a short space of time. But are the memories of this happiness enough to last me a lifetime without you?*

*I know you'd want me to live, Rob, not just go through the motions, but really live, feel, rejoice again, but I just can't seem to let go. I can't let go of you, I can't let go of myself. I feel I have to keep this tight control over my emotions just so that I can hold onto my sanity.*

*I didn't think that I'd survive without you, but I have. I thought I'd crumble, but I'm still here, still living, if you can call it that.*

*Would you believe that I am back at Whitsunday, and that Cassie is with me? You know, I always thought I'd bring you here some day. In my own time. But time is not my own. It took your death to make me realise that. I am governed by time, I do not govern it. If I did, you would be with me now.*

*How I wish that you were.*

*Always yours,*

*N x*

I fold the letter, place it in an envelope without rereading it, and write his name on the front. Then for want of somewhere more private to put it, I push it into the pocket of my coat which is thrown over the chair in the corner.

Despite being shattered, it takes me a long time to fall asleep. I lie in my bed, the bedside lamp casting a dim glow around the darkened room, and when I eventually drop off, I sleep fitfully. Strange noises, strange smells even, are enough to wake me from an uncomfortable slumber. There seems to be a constant scuffling in the darkness that I know must be restless animals out in the yard, but my irrational self tells me it is prowlers.

My sleep is usually full of ghosts anyway. Horrible nightmares about mangled cars, their shells crushed like fragile eggs . . . I wake with a start and cry out involuntarily, sitting bolt upright as though jolted by an electric shock. Belatedly I clamp a hand to my mouth, as my door creaks slowly open. I have obviously woken someone, and am filled with embarrassment, until I hear the click of long claws on the floorboards, and when a damp nose is pushed into my hand, I realise that my visitor is Mac.

Two huge front paws come up on the duvet beside me, and a concerned face is pressed directly into mine, so close that his wet nose leaves a trail across my cheek where he is sniffing me. The next minute, he heaves himself up next to me and with a heavy sigh, lies down beside me.

For a moment I lie still, stiff with surprise, unsure whether this uninvited visitor should be allowed to stay in my bed, or be evicted back to the warmth of the rug in the kitchen and the glowing embers of a dying fire. But then I begin to relax, lulled perhaps by the methodical breathing of the large animal, and with this solid warmth nestled comfortingly against me, I finally fall into a deep sleep.

# Chapter Three

It's light when I eventually wake up. *Too* light. I look across at the clock on the bedside table and am horrified to see that it's eleven-thirty. I haven't slept this late for a long, long time.

Mac has gone.

Feeling strangely awkward about using the shower without asking, I stumble downstairs in my nightgown and follow the noise of the radio into the kitchen, where I find Laura washing up used breakfast dishes at the kitchen sink.

'Morning,' I growl, rubbing sleep from my eyes.

Laura looks up from her suds and smiles. 'Good afternoon,' she replies lightly.

'Why didn't you wake me?'

'I decided you needed the rest.' She pulls her hands from the sink, shaking the suds from them, then drying them carefully on a towel slung over the handle of the long black Aga. She then pours me a cup of tea without asking, and pops two slices of bread into the toaster.

'Did you sleep okay?'

'Of a sort, yeah, thanks.'

Laura pours herself a cup of tea, and joins me at the long wooden table, which dominates the back of the kitchen.

'I understand you had a strange gentleman in your bed last night.'

I look at her in puzzlement for a moment before I

realise she's talking about Mac.

'Oh yes.' I laugh lightly, breathing in the steam from my tea. 'An uninvited guest.'

The toaster snaps two pieces of lightly browned bread from its mouth with a heavy metallic thud. Laura immediately rises again, fetches the toast and butter and places them in front of me, her face falling in disappointment as I ignore them and simply continue to sip at my tea.

'Where's Cas?' I ask.

'I sent her outside,' she replies with a slight rise of her eyebrows. From Laura's expression and tone of voice it would appear that Cassie's period of good behaviour was incredibly shortlived.

'What – to stand in a corner with a pointed hat with a D on the front?' I enquire lightly.

Laura smiles but the smile has a slightly hard edge to it. 'Oh, she's far from stupid. In fact, her put-downs are practically verging on genius for someone that age.'

'Oh dear. She's hard work, isn't she?'

Laura nods.

'I'm sorry if she's been obnoxious.'

'Would you have expected any different?'

'Well yes, actually, she's normally polite to everyone else except me.'

'Perhaps I should feel privileged that I'm an exception. Actually she hasn't been too bad.'

'Really?'

'Well no, she's not directly impolite to me. She just has an opinion on most things.'

'That's true.'

'And her opinions don't seem to be very flattering at the moment.'

'I'm sorry,' I say again.

'Don't be. I've got my own back.'

I raise my eyebrows at Laura in question.

'I sent her out to feed the geese.'

'I hardly call that a punishment,' I begin, then notice that the smile Laura is wearing as she speaks has a slight sadistic edge to it.

I'm just about to enquire further when, as if on cue, the air is rent by a small shrill scream. This is followed immediately by a loud crash as a metal feed pan hits the ground, the outraged squabbling of a large and angry bird, and an intensely loud rustling of feathers as though a flock of vultures have just made a group landing in the stableyard.

We both rush to the door, to see Cas being pursued across the yard by the biggest goose this side of a Christmas pantomime. Its wings are back, beating her forward, raised so high that as it runs, it almost glides across the ground like an ice-skater hitting the rink at great speed. Its neck is coiled back like a snake about to strike, and it's hissing loudly like a spiked tyre.

'That's Gertrude,' my mother tells me, her eyes full of amusement, and I'm surprised to see no concern in them whatsoever. 'As you can probably tell, she's not exactly the friendliest of creatures.'

I've never seen anyone move so fast.

Cassie hurls herself into the Land Rover, which is parked just outside the kitchen window, slamming the door just as the goose's beak is making a final lunge for her trailing foot. Laura watches without undue concern as the two slightly smaller birds that make up the rest of the flock beat a hasty escape through the open gate, simply sighing gently, but still smiling, as they are closely followed by the chickens and then the slower ducks.

'My dear Cassie,' she calls across to her, 'I thought I told you to make sure you shut the pen gates behind you.'

Cassie's face peers out of the window at us, as black as thunder.

Laughing softly, Laura picks up a walking stick from the umbrella stand by the door and steps outside.

Halfway across the yard, she turns and raises her eyebrows at me. 'Come on, then. Aren't you going to help me round up the girls? They won't bite,' she urges again as I hesitate.

She marches toward one of the geese, which is pecking hopefully around the bottom of Chance's stable door, picking up crumbs dropped from his last feed with a frighteningly long and strong-looking beak.

'Are you sure?' I call hesitantly after her.

'They can't bite – they don't have any teeth,' she calls back as I don't move. 'They can give you one hell of a nasty peck though,' she adds in an amused undertone.

'Don't expect *me* to come out and help you!' Cassie calls to us through the open top inch of the car window. 'I'm not moving until that . . . that . . . Rottweiler masquerading as a fowl is back behind bars.'

Reluctantly I pull on a spare pair of Wellingtons, the rough insole feeling cool, slightly damp, and uncomfortable against my bare feet, throw Laura's stiff old Barbour on over my short night-shirt, and then rummage in the umbrella stand for the sturdiest-looking walking stick I can find. I select a thick, twisted, beautifully polished walnut branch, with a carved owl's head for a handle, and follow my mother outside.

Laura has put goose number one back in the pen, and has turned her attention temporarily to getting Cas out of the Land Rover to help.

'Come out of there, you wimp.' Laura attempts to wrench open the car door, its rusted hinges groaning in protest at her rough handling, but Cas has pushed down the lock. 'You have to show them you're not scared of them,' she says impatiently. 'It's the only way to handle them.'

'Who on earth said that I *want* to handle them?' Cas mutters sulkily through the glass, refusing to budge. 'I certainly didn't. In fact, I'm never going near the awful things again.'

No amount of cajoling or encouragement will get Cas out of the Land Rover, so it is left to Laura and me to attempt to round up the rest of the escaping flock. I decide to take the bull by the horns, or should I say the bird by the beak, and as my mother expertly herds her second goose back into the pen, I go for the ringleader. Copying my mother's stance, I head for Gertrude, gaze steady, arms outstretched, the walking stick held outwards in my left hand in an attempt to herd her to the right. Instead of being gently guided back to her home, however, Gertrude decides to go on the offensive, jerking her neck backwards and forwards in a threatening manner. The wings come back, she begins to hiss.

The next thing I know, it's me being herded across the yard, as Gertrude launches an attack, hurtling after me far faster than I thought a goose could ever go. This isn't right – it's supposed to be *me* herding Gertrude, not the other way round. It doesn't help that Laura is now literally howling with laughter at me. Neither she nor Cas attempt to help me.

It's hard to run quickly in Wellingtons that are too big for you. My harsh cry rents the clear cold air as an even harsher beak sinks with relish into the soft flesh of my backside.

Laura finally comes to my rescue with the aid of Meg, who has appeared from the long passage running between the end of the stable block and the Long Barn that sits at right angles to it. Between them they guide a hissing Gertrude back into her pen, and soon have the family of ducks back where they belong too. The chickens are tempted into their abode with a pan of corn, and then Laura, still laughing, turns her attention to me. Cas remains cowering in the Land Rover with the doors firmly locked. Me and my abused backside are cowering behind it.

'It's not funny,' I complain at the sight of Laura's grinning face. 'I think I'm bleeding?' I attempt to twist my head round to inspect my injuries, pushing futilely at the heavy material of the borrowed coat.

My mother marches up to me still smiling broadly despite my protestations that my plight is far from amusing. I've managed to push the heavy coat to one side, and am gratified to see a spot of blood seeping through onto the pale grey of my short night-shirt.

'See? I told you! It's not funny, I was right! I'm bleeding.'

'Bleedin' useless,' chuckles Laura. 'Here, let me have a look at you.' And she unceremoniously pulls up my night-shirt and peers at my bum.

'Oh my goodness, I don't know what's more humiliating, being beaten up by a goose, or this,' I sigh, as she gets her glasses out of her pocket and pushes them on for a better look. Even Cas winds down the window of the Land Rover and peers round, her scowling face now replaced by a slight fit of the giggles.

'Tch.' Laura tuts at me. 'Don't be such a baby, it's only a scratch.'

'A scratch? It really hurts! If I had a bone down there I'd swear I'd broken it!'

'Stop complaining or I'll get Gertrude back to kiss it better for you.'

'The only way that bird is getting near me again is on the end of a fork. Vicious bloody thing.'

'Do you realise I haven't been this close to your backside since you were a toddler,' Laura chuckles.

'Well, what are you still doing down there?' I mutter crossly. 'Waiting to powder it for me?' I look down at Laura, she peers up at me, the hem of my night-shirt still lifted high in her hand. For a moment we stare at each other tight-lipped, and then simultaneously, we burst out laughing.

A shared laughter that is broken a few moments later by a slight cough. A cough that is then turned into a slightly louder one. I turn around in horror as I realise that Laura and Cas aren't the only ones getting an eyeful of my goose-bumped backside. The severe burning of my face takes over from the burning sensation in my butt cheek, as a full body blush descends upon me.

'Good morning,' lilts a laughing Irish voice.

A man is standing at the yard gate, blue eyes bright with amusement.

'The moon's made an early appearance today, I see. Still, that's often how it is in winter.'

My mother, who had been as frozen as me, bursts out laughing again and drops my night-shirt down to cover my modesty.

'I'm going to die,' I mutter without moving my lips.

'Don't be silly, it's only a little thing,' Laura replies, deliberately misinterpreting me.

'Technically speaking that's not true, but I suppose it depends on whether you're talking about the bite or the arse,' Cassie calls loudly from the safety of the Land Rover, eyeing me with evil amusement.

'I was looking for my dog,' the newcomer tells us.

I shoot Cassie a warning look before she can make any comment about growlers, or whatever other acid witticism is waiting on the end of that sharp tongue. I'm torn between flight and a pretence at dignity. The kitchen door is still wide open, only a few short steps away. Fighting the urge to leg it inside, instead I hold out a shaking hand as calmly as I can to the man standing in front of me, as though it's the most natural thing in the world to be standing in the middle of the yard on a winter's day in my night-shirt and a pair of Wellingtons.

'You must be Connor, Mac's owner.'

'And you must be feeling the breeze a bit this morning,' he replies with amusement.

Cassie giggles.

He looks down at my short night-shirt, the lengthy gap between the top of the old Wellingtons and its hem feeling suddenly as wide as the Grand Canyon. I blush again, conscious that he is fully aware of the fact that I don't have any knickers on. I am *so* embarrassed, but he simply turns to Laura to ask: 'I'm looking for Mac. Guessed he'd probably be here, gate-crashing as usual.'

'Snoring by the Aga,' Laura nods.

'Lazy great lump.' He laughs with obvious affection. 'Not the best time for him to go walkabout. I'm off up to Plymouth today, so thought I'd better find him before I go, or he'll get home to a locked and empty house.'

'You may as well leave him with us then.'

'I was hoping you'd say that. Dog hotel now, eh?' He indicates Shep who is just sliding in through the front gate no doubt on a visit to Meg. 'I'll be back later tonight. Is it all right if I pick him up then?'

'Whenever you like. If we're not here, we'll be at the Ship.'

As Connor turns to leave, Cas finally deigns to get out of the Land Rover. He stops and smiles at her in pretend surprise, as though he hasn't noticed her hanging avidly out of the jeep.

'And where did you come from all of a sudden?' he asks pleasantly.

'She was being a wimp and hiding from Gertrude in the Landy,' Laura explains.

'And who might you be then?' he tries again.

'Cassie,' she replies cautiously.

'Ah yes, Laura told me about you, so she did. Cassie, now what would that be short for . . .?'

'Cassandra.'

'That's a fine name, so it is.'

'My mother chose it,' Cas replies loyally. I know full well she hates the name. If anybody ever tries to call her by the full version she goes mad at them.

'Greek legend says that Cassandra was a Trojan Princess.'

'Yeah,' Cas nods. 'She was captured by Agamemnon and brought back to Greece as a concubine, only to be

98

murdered by his jealous wife Clytemnestra.' Am I imagining it, or does Cas look over at me as she says this?

'Ah, so you know your history then, very impressive. Nice to meet you, Cassie.' He holds out a hand which she takes for a brief moment. 'And very nice to *see* you too.' He turns and winks at me. 'Cheers, Laura, I'll be catching you later on.'

Laura waves as he strolls back to his car, which is parked beyond the closed gate. Heaven knows how long he'd been standing there. I certainly didn't hear his car pull up. It must have been during the commotion Gertrude was making as Laura finally got her back in the pen.

'Oh my God,' I hiss, as he drives away. 'I don't believe that just happened.'

'Tea!' cries Laura brightly, swiftly changing the subject and beckoning us inside. 'I don't know about you two, but I need a nice cup of tea.' She heads into the kitchen and begins to fill the kettle at the sink.

Mac looks up from the rug as we follow her inside, but doesn't bother to move, apart from a brief wag of his short stumpy tail.

My mother busies herself with the kettle, throwing tea bags into the huge old teapot, and pulling mugs from the hooks that line the dresser shelves. Taking a tin from one of the cupboards, she removes a large square fruitcake and begins to cut it into slices.

'Well, that was certainly an energetic start to the day,' she chuckles, putting a piece on a plate and handing it to Cas who has kicked off her boots and is sitting on the rug next to Mac, scratching his ears absentmindedly, no longer fearful of the large dog. 'You know, I never thought you'd be someone who wouldn't say boo to a goose, Cassie dear,' Laura teases her gently. 'I don't see that you'd normally be afraid of confrontation.'

'I'm not afraid of anything,' Cas states, tilting her chin defiantly. 'I'm not,' she adds, trying to convince us.

'That . . . that,' she searches for the right word to describe Gertrude, '*thing* was bloody vicious. It would have been stupid to go near it.'

For once I agree entirely with what she's saying.

'Only an idiot would have tried to get that thing back in its pen on their own,' Cas declares, picking a cherry from her cake and pushing it into her mouth, looking over at me so that I'm fully aware I am the idiot she's referring to.

'Thanks,' I tell her dryly.

Laura, who so far has been teasing, senses a sudden dangerous swing in mood, and somewhat perversely starts to laugh.

'I don't know what you're finding so funny,' I tell her haughtily. 'I could sue you for not keeping a dangerous animal under proper control.'

'Oh come on, darling, you've got to see the funny side of things.'

'The funny side that everybody saw being the back-side of Natalie,' Cas murmurs, an evil grin sliding onto her face.

My mother throws Cas a look. 'If it's any consolation, she's on a short-term contract,' she tells me soothingly, carrying the tea tray over to the table.

'What do you mean?'

'Well, Christmas is coming and the goose is getting fat . . .' Laura puts down the tray and makes a melodramatic cross of her throat with a finger.

'You mean she's on the Green Poo mile,' I reply, feeling the corners of my mouth begin to twitch. 'Oh dear, that makes my comments about Gertrude and a fork a bit crass, doesn't it?'

'Well, to be honest she deserves it,' my mother finally admitted. 'If she was a dog she probably *would* have been put down under the Dangerous Animals Act by now. I don't think I've ever met such a cantankerous creature before in my life.'

'Now you tell me,' I complain, accepting a hot mug of tea from her. 'An advance warning would have been a good idea before I decided to tackle her on my own.'

'I did say that she's not particularly friendly.'

'That's the understatement of the decade,' Cas snorts crossly, feeding a large piece of her cake to Mac.

Laura is struggling not to laugh again.

'It's not funny,' I moan at her.

'Not funny?' she chokes. 'You should've seen your face!'

I'm trying to keep my hurt expression intact, but I can't help a snicker of laughter escaping through my nose.

'Well actually,' I tell her, the grin getting wider, 'I'm more concerned about who saw my arse!'

Cas hesitates for a moment, her face poised on the edge of a frown and then to my surprise she too starts to grin.

Dinner this evening is slightly more relaxed. I peel and cut, my mother cooks, and Cas lays the table. A real joint effort.

I can't escape to an early bed again, however, as Laura announces over the washing-up that we've been invited down to the local pub for a night out.

'Hank's wife Orlaithe is the landlady, and she very kindly offered us drinks on the house at eight o'clock,' she tells us, handing me a plate to dry.

'Ooh, Happy Hour at the local spit and sawdust,' pipes up a sarcastic voice from the corner, where Cas is curled in a chair keeping out of the way in case we rope her into more chores. 'How can I possibly calm my excitement.'

I'd reprimand her, but I'm about as keen on the idea as Cas is. Despite having a long lie-in this morning, I'm completely shattered. All I want to do is curl up somewhere warm with a good book.

101

My mother is having none of this though. By seven forty-five, we have been cajoled into the Land Rover, and are heading down into the village, Cas and I pressed closer on the front bench seat than we have ever sat before, the only other option being to perch upon an upturned bucket in the back, and be thrown from side to side every time we take a bend or corner, like an empty drinks can rolling loose across the floor. I can feel her flinching away from me every time we are flung together by my mother's Grand Prix-style driving.

The pub is only about three miles from Whitsunday, but it feels like a lifetime of bruises away. We finally pull over the crest of a hill and descend upon a cliffside road into a car park, where Laura handbrake turns the rusted jeep into an empty space. Pocketing the small screwdriver she uses to start the thing instead of a key, she smiles happily at Cas and me who, white-knuckled and petrified, begin to breathe again.

The car park is cut into the edge of the cliff, bordered on one side by a steep face of rock, and on the other by a vertical fall down to the ocean. As I step down out of the jeep, I can hear the roar of the waves as they crash against the black volcanic rock below our feet, and taste the salt in the spray that hits our faces as we follow my mother down the sloping length of the car park to a narrow path, which winds around a hill into a dark oblivion.

She marches ahead of us, cheerfully whistling a Frank Sinatra song, occasionally throwing a glance over her shoulder to make sure that we're still following and haven't slipped over the edge and plummeted fifty feet into the boiling ocean below. I am relieved to see a well-lit building come into view, the lights of Trenrethen village a twinkling backdrop behind it about half a mile away as the crow flies.

The Ship Inn is an old harbourmaster's house of whitewashed stone, with a roof of grey slate, and green shutters flanking the sixteen windows it boasts. Nestled into the side of a cliff overlooking a small natural harbour in the Atlantic Ocean, it has, on occasion, lost the odd drunken customer to the waves below, despite the prominent signs just beyond the tables on the terrace which advise all customers to *Beware of the Edge.*

Before we go in, I pause and look across the darkness. About half a mile offshore sits a large barren island of volcanic rock, almost menacing in the gloom.

'Breathtaking, isn't it?' Laura's voice is close behind me. 'The guide books say this place has one of the best views in the whole of Cornwall. They take guests and the rooms are always booked out.'

Hank and Orlaithe, my mother informs me, live in a low-eaved flat on the second floor nestled under the roof. We step from the cold of the night into the warmth of the pub, with its real fire, bright red patterned carpet, dark wood, and clutter of all things 'Mariner'. Old sextants adorn the walls, as do ships' wheels, anchors, stuffed fish in glass cases; the beamed ceiling is even hung in places with net, a few plastic fish and the odd shell and starfish captured within.

I don't know what I was expecting Hank's wife to be like. Despite the flamboyant mode of dress, Hank as a person is unbelievably quiet and unpretentious. He barely speaks. When he does, it's through sheer necessity, and normally words of two syllables or less.

If Hank is a silent movie star, Orlaithe is Mae West. Spilling out of a bright red dress that's cut just about high enough to cover the nipples of her ample bosom, I soon learn that Orlaithe Doyle is as vocal as Hank is silent. A vivacious red-headed girl from County Cork, she looks about forty but must be older; her skin is the colour and texture of double cream, and she has huge amber eyes and a smattering of freckles over a small tip-tilted nose. And her smile is as welcoming as a warm fire on a cold night.

Swooping down upon us the moment we step through the front door, she folds us into her ample bosom as though we are long-lost friends instead of new acquaintances.

'Oh my goodness, 'tis wonderful to be meeting you at long last. I've heard so much about you from your mother, Nat, that I feel as if we know each other already. And this must be Cassie. You poor wee girls. Such heartache! You come and sit with me, why don't you, and have a drop of the good stuff to warm you.'

Freeing us from the Anaïs-scented voluptuous warmth of her embrace, she herds us ahead of her to some stools by the busy long bar, and then heads back to the optics to pour four large shots of Bushmills, which she proceeds to hand round to myself, Laura and Cas.

Cassie is holding her glass of whiskey in bemused delight, like she can't believe her good fortune. Realising her mistake, Orlaithe hurriedly takes Cassie's glass of whiskey back, tips it into her own, and cracks the top off a bottle of Diet Coke instead, replacing it in Cas's hand before her fingers have even had a chance to close. Then, spotting my step-daughter's disappointment, Orlaithe grabs two bags of Maltesers from the shelf below the optics, and thrusts those in her other hand. Coming round from the pump side of the bar, she then sits her plump backside down on a barstool and patting the two either side, urges Cas and me to join her.

'You've had such a God-awful time haven't you,' she tells Cassie and me, 'but don't worry you're here now. We can look after you properly, so we can, can we not, Laura darling?'

My mother nods her agreement. 'We can try to, but I'll warn you, these two are fiercely independent.'

'Nonsense, everybody needs a little pampering now and then, so they do.' She clasps a hold on Cassie's arm. 'Laura tells me you're a dancer – a ballerina, by all accounts. I used to dance when I was your age, but only the Irish jig!' She bursts into a great belly laugh, her rolls of flesh doing a jig of their own in response. 'Do you sing?' is her next question.

Laura leans over to Cas, whispering to her that Orlaithe sings.

'Oh, just a little now.' Orlaithe flutters a pink finger-nailed be-ringed hand to her ample bosom and tries to look coy.

'A little?' My mother raises her eyebrows.

'Well, rather a lot actually.' The belly laugh rolls out again. 'Any time I can get me hands on the microphone.'

This point is proven an hour later, when after several more glasses of Bushmills, and hardly having stopped speaking to draw breath, Orlaithe shouts across the room at a new arrival, 'Denzel, about time! How about a little tune on the old piano for us?'

A small bald man in a suit that looks like it came straight out of the window of a Red Cross shop, and was made for a man two sizes larger, nods his approval, and promptly throws himself down onto the stool of the old black piano he is leaning against, cracking his knuckles so audibly it makes me wince. To my utter surprise, instead of a rousing chorus of 'Roll Out the Barrel' or something of that ilk, he begins to crank out a mellow rendition of 'A Rainy Night in Georgia', joining in with a voice marinated in sixty years' worth of stout.

Imagine Val Doonican singing the blues.

Deep South Blues.

Before Denzel's even finished, Orlaithe is being per-suaded onto the microphone. 'Oh, I couldn't possibly. Oh no, I couldn't . . . Oh, go on then.' She takes the stand to tumultuous applause, and begins to belt out something country. A Dolly Parton song I think, about someone stealing someone else's man. She's really rather good.

Even Cas joins in the hand-clapping that is the pub clientèle's encouragement for her to sing a second song when she's finished the first. Thus encouraged, Orlaithe regales us with at least three more songs.

During the fourth, the main door is pushed open and a man walks through into the room, a blast of cold wind following him, enough to make the flames of the fire flicker in protest, before the door swings shut again. I see my mother smile in recognition and immediately recognise Connor. To my dismay he acknowledges Laura's greeting and heads over toward us. On the pretext of going to the loo, I quickly excuse myself, pushing my way through the singing throng.

In contrast to the nautical theme of the main bar, the ladies' loos are small and very pink. Pink carpet, pink walls, and plastic pink flowers in little pink vases. Even the air fresheners are little pink plastic pots of something girly and floral. Indicative, I would imagine from what I've seen so far, of Orlaithe's overtly feminine taste.

I have a pee and then spend a while brushing my hair in the hope that Laura will have done her hello's and I'll be able to slide back to my bar stool without having to speak to the man to whom I was introduced in such an unfortunate manner this morning.

As it turns out, I couldn't have picked a worse moment to emerge into the crowded bar. The pianist has found a new friend. Denzel is still rattling away at the ivories but Orlaithe is back behind the bar, and he is now being accompanied by a new vocalist, whose singing skills are somewhat marred by the fact that he is obviously staggeringly drunk. He is also working the room like a Vegas regular, descending from the stage to chat up the diners. I walk straight into the path of an amateur Karaoke star carolling his way round the pub, on the prowl for his next victim.

To my dismay, the next victim turns out to be *me*.

Instead of slipping inconspicuously back to my seat, and therefore avoiding Connor, I am accosted by the singer, who grabs my hand as I attempt to sidle past him,

106

and then stands swaying in front of me, serenading me loudly in his beer-drenched breath. I stand asphyxiated and paralysed with embarrassment before him, a forced smile clamped to my face like the wooden grin of a ventriloquist's dummy. When the song has finally dragged to a tortuous end, he raises my hand to his purple lips and plants a horrible sticky wet kiss on the back of it.

Cas is smirking, acutely aware of my discomfort. My misery is complete when I realise that Connor is also a witness, his eyes bright with mirth, his own mouth curled at the corners with suppressed laughter. He catches me watching him and at least has the heart to roll his eyeballs in sympathy.

It feels like everybody is watching me, the whole pub – the little scene of the drunk and the red-faced woman is the highlight of their evening, the cabaret. There's nothing else I can do, apart from turn round and go straight back into the toilets and emerge later when hopefully everyone will be too drunk to remember my moment in the spotlight. Holding my head high, I march back to my bar stool, a serene smile on my face, hoping the red flush doesn't give my shame away too much. A surprisingly good voice sings quietly in my ear, a repeat of the song with which the pub singer so drunkenly serenaded me. I turn to find Connor standing beside me.

'You walked right into that one, didn't you?' he beams.

'It's not been my day,' I reply, smiling a little stiffly.

'If it's any consolation, you've made my day . . . now how can I put it? . . . far more interesting.'

My eyes narrow in distaste at his apparent vulgarity, and he bursts out laughing. 'I'm sorry, I couldn't resist it. I feel I should introduce myself again. It was hardly a *proper* introduction this morning, was it?'

'Don't,' I mumble. 'You would not believe how embarrassed I was.'

'Would it help if I told you I didn't see anything?'

'Would you be lying?'

He nods. 'But if it makes you feel better, I never saw your backside at all, especially not the small dimple you have on your left cheek.'

He's teasing me again, but the smile is friendly and easy, and I lose the feeling of discomfort. I can't help smiling back.

'That's better.' He holds out a hand. 'Connor, Connor Blythe.'

I take it. 'Natalie Forester.'

'Pleased to meet you, Natalie Forester. Although of course I've heard all about you already from your mother.' He pauses and looks over my shoulder, then ducks his head and whispers confidentially, 'I had better warn you that your new friend is heading back in this direction.'

I turn around to see the drunken singer staggering over toward me. 'This is my cue to go home.'

I use the fact that Cas is wilting on her bar stool, eyes closing like a Tiny Tears doll being lain on its back then popping open as she forces herself to stay awake, to persuade Laura to call it a night. The only problem is, when I ask my mother if she's ready to go yet, she announces that she's had far too much drink to drive.

'Blame Orlaithe and her never-ending bottle of Bushmills,' she smiles apologetically at me. 'It took me half an hour to work out why my glass wasn't going down. By the time I noticed, I'd already had the equivalent of three measures so there was no point in stopping there. Why don't we walk home and let Hank bring the Land Rover back in the morning?'

'Do I hear that you need a lift?' It's Karaoke Man, pushing his way into the conversation by stumbling so hard into Laura that she has to grab the brass rail that runs along the bar to stop herself from falling.

'I wouldn't dream of letting three gorgeous young

things walk all the way home on their own.' He's trying to take my hand again. I quickly stuff them both in my jacket pockets.

Orlaithe hurries over and steadies a still swaying Laura. 'He's knocked back so much Jim Beam, he'd probably reverse straight out of the car park and over the edge of the cliff,' she warns her.

I look at him in horror. How could he even think about driving?

We are rescued by Connor. 'It's all right, Davey, I have a prior claim. I already agreed I'd give Laura and the girls a lift home so I did.'

Laura quickly nods her agreement, her relief evident. Orlaithe sees the look of disgust on my face, and smiling reassuringly, whispers that Davey has left his keys behind the bar, and won't be given them back until the next day.

'You'll not be driving anywhere tonight, Daveth Brann,' she tells him sharply.

'I won't?' He rolls around to face Orlaithe. 'In that case I'd best be having another drop of the good stuff then, hadn't I?' He props himself up against the bar and orders another pint of bitter with a whiskey chaser, then turns and doffs a non-existent hat to us. 'Ladies, I'll bid you goodnight.' Leaning forward, nearly falling off his stool, Davey takes hold of Cas's hand and pulling it to his mouth, plants a wet kiss on her white knuckles.

My smile finds its way back to my face as Cas, bottom lip drawn back in horror, surreptitiously begins to wipe her hand down the side of her jeans.

Connor has a Land Rover too but it's nothing like my mother's. It's almost brand new – a big black shiny vehicle with central locking and a sound system better than the one I have in my house. It also, thankfully, has more seats – dark grey leather ones that don't smell of damp, and aren't covered in dog hair. He is also a far better driver, negotiating the narrow winding roads with skill and care.

Mac comes out of the house as soon as Laura opens the kitchen door, and without bidding jumps into the still-open door of Connor's car, settling down in the front seat. We chorus our thanks as he drives away.

'He's such a nice man,' Laura hiccups gently as she waves him goodbye.

'A very, very, very nice man,' Cas quips, taking her arm. 'Cheaper than a taxi anyway.'

We go inside and help a swaying Laura up the narrow stairs to her room. Her bedroom is very 1980s Laura Ashley. It could almost be a still from one of their old catalogues. Lilac-painted walls, the linen pretty florals in pastel colours, pinks and lilacs, several matching rugs thrown carefully yet casually across the stained wood floor. The old-fashioned wrought-iron bed is smothered with a huge cream quilt covered in tiny lilac flowers. The window ledges and dressing-table are adorned with elegant pottery bursting with dried flowers. There is a wooden chair in the corner with a sun hat covered in daisies thrown over one corner. The pretty lamps on the twin bedside tables are edged with butterflies – copies of Tiffany ones, I think.

There are no wardrobes in here. Laura has a separate room for her clothes. If she put them in her bedroom there would be no room for a bed, and then where would she sleep? The smaller of the bedrooms opposite my room has become a walk-in wardrobe, filled to the brim with suits and skirts, elegant blouses, well-cut trousers, soft jumpers, evening dresses, all in warm pastels or autumnal shades to suit her peaches-and-cream colouring.

She doesn't have a lot of money to spend, but she simply never throws anything away. Everything is tended with a loving care. This collection is an accumulation of over thirty years of clothes buying.

The most prominent thing in the room, however, is the three-tiered rack that stretches the entire length of one wall, covered in neat racks of size four shoes.

'Imelda Marcos eat your heart out,' was Cassie's first comment when shown into this haven of fashion.

Laura falls back onto the bed, which creaks gently in protest and bleats wearily for a cup of coffee. By the time I've gone downstairs, made the coffee and returned to her room, she is fast asleep, snoring gently. Cas has gone to bed too, but I note that she has first removed Laura's shoes, and covered her carefully with a spare blanket.

It is raining. Torrential rain, thundering against the roof as if God is throwing stones from the clouds, using the dark-grey slate as target practice. It has been raining for three days, so heavily that Laura has begun to joke about building an ark and loading the animals onto it as soon as possible. I can see her in the yard now, covered from head to foot in a huge black mackintosh, feeding the wet sorry-looking troupe of chickens that peck half-heartedly at her feet, torn between eating and running back into the small stable that acts as their coop.

Cas is curled up in a chair by the fire, an abandoned book, spine bent open, at her feet. She has been in practically the same position for the same time as the rain has been dogging us, her expression getting sourer by the day. Although I wouldn't have thought it possible, she is looking more miserable than usual at the moment. So much so that I decide to take the easy option and after a brief, 'Good morning,' which she doesn't return, pull on a waterproof and go out to the yard to help my mother feed the geese.

'Lovely day, isn't it,' Laura grimaces, looking up at the black clouds banked in the sky above us as I join her at the gate of the pens. 'Even the ducks are beginning to get fed up with so much water.' She points to where the small band, looking decidedly bedraggled, are huddled together against the wall of the Long Barn, seeking shelter from the driving rain under the overhang of the roof. My mother opens the door to their own stable, which has blown shut in the wind, and the five ducks waddle quickly inside.

'Only Chance left to do. Do you think you could refill his hay net for me? I'll do his water bucket seeing as I'm already soaked through. I could just wring my clothes into it, couldn't I, instead of taking it to the tap.'

I take Chance's empty net and sprint down the long passage into the left-hand barn, where the hay is kept. Meg is inside, sheltering from the rain whilst rat-watching, her favourite occupation. She has found a hole in the back wall that looks promising and has been stationed outside of it for most of the last three days, determined that should anything dare to emerge, and she's certain she can smell something in there, it will be here. I only wish Cas could be occupied so easily.

The morning stretches into one of those endlessly boring days where there is absolutely nothing to do. The fact that it's the third one in a row seems to have stretched my step-daughter's limited patience to the end of its endurance. She's like a captive animal, prowling backwards and forwards in a cage that's too small, ready to bite the first person who sticks a friendly hand through the bars in an attempt to cheer or comfort.

Laura has been trying to think of things for her to do, but whatever she suggests Cas abruptly vetos. She doesn't want to watch an old black and white film on television; she must have seen it at least 'twenty times before' and it was bloody boring the first time. She has apparently read every single thing worth reading in the entire house, despite the fact that Laura has a small study, just off the sitting room, that has a fairly decent collection of books. She has complained quite bitterly about the fact that Laura doesn't have satellite tele-vision, and her derision when she discovered that the portable in the kitchen was the only television in the house, and Laura doesn't even have a video recorder, was scorching.

She's turned down my offer of shopping and the cinema, Laura's of taking her to the local swimming baths (who wants yet *more* water?) and has refused Orlaithe's offer to go down and help out in the pub for a little pocket money.

I think she wants to be a martyr. She wants me to see how much she's not enjoying herself here and feel guilty. The thing is, I do feel guilty, dreadfully so, only not over Cas. I feel bad for Laura.

My mother has been positively saintly in her handling of Cas's bad moods, always cheerful, refusing to let her smile slip to the level of Cassie's sneering, while constantly trying to bolster my flagging spirits.

Cas looks up at me when I go back into the kitchen half an hour later, her eyes glaring her discontent. I look away. Maybe if I ignore her, she will do the same. She continues to stare at me, however, her eyes burning into the back of my head as I make Laura a pot of her favourite Earl Grey tea.

'I hate it here. It's the pits. It stinks. It's awful. It's worse than being at school.' She spits out the words like broken teeth from her mouth.

I stop in my tracks and simply stare at her, surprised not so much by the verbal assault as the level of venom she carries in her voice, as though we are all to blame for every misfortune she has ever suffered.

This is the first time Cas has actually initiated a conversation with me.

'It must be awfully liberating not to worry what other people think of you,' I eventually reply, as calmly as I can.

'Take me or leave me, I don't care either way,' she challenges, tilting her chin haughtily.

'You're a guest in my mother's house, and you were

brought up to have better manners.'

'Oh, you know that, do you? You know *sooo* much about me, don't you? Well, you're kidding yourself – you don't know me at all.'

She's expecting an argument, she positively *wants* an argument. She wants me to raise my voice and yell.

I fight to keep calm. 'Why won't you just give me a chance, Cas? How can you dislike me so much when you've never even tried to get to know *me*?'

'Oh I know you – I know all about *you*.'

'Really? Even though you say that I know nothing about you at all, you know all about me, do you?' I throw her own words back at her. 'Well, what am I thinking then? What exactly am I thinking now?'

She looks at me as if I've gone mad. 'How the hell should I know?'

'Exactly. You can't read my mind, so how can you assume you know exactly what's going on inside my head?'

Cas looks away sharply, her gaze turning from me toward the door, and I realise that Laura has come back in and is standing in the doorway silently watching us. I, too, fall silent.

Laura looks at me, then turns her gaze to Cas. 'I'm driving down to the village – there are a few things we need from the store. Why don't you come with me?' Without giving her a chance to answer, my mother takes Cas's jacket from the stand by the door, and picking up her shoes walks over to her, holding them out for her to take.

To my surprise, Cas complies without a murmur, putting on her shoes and jacket and following Laura out into the yard, leaving me standing there on my own, our altercation still echoing in my ears.

Although I listen for voices, Laura and Cas are ominously silent as they get into the Land Rover, the only sound being the grating of rusted metal as they each wrench open the old jeep doors. I hear the motor crank reluctantly into life, and then sink down on the chair Cas has just abandoned, my breath exhaling in a long trembling sigh. The unexpectedness of her attack has thrown me. Upset me far more than I would have dared to show to Cas.

*Why does she hate me so much?*

Have I let her down?

I promised I would always be there for her, but have I been?

Haven't I just hidden myself away from her as I have done the rest of the world?

Haven't I simply let her walk away from me because it was easier, when I should have been fighting to build a relationship with her?

Haven't I locked myself away in my own misery like my mother did when my own father died?

I look about me, at the cosy yet quiet room, the only sound the loud ticking of a clock in the sitting room, and the faint lowing of cattle from the fields beyond. Maybe Cas is right; maybe we shouldn't have come here. At least at home she had all of her things – her stereo, her books, satellite TV, her computer, things to pull you out of your own miserable mind.

*At home.*

I suddenly feel terribly homesick. But I know it's not the house in Hampstead that I'm missing so badly. It's Rob. There's nothing I want more in the world than to feel his arms around me, to hear him tell me that everything is going to be all right.

I feel the need to get out of here as much as Cassie obviously did. Grabbing my coat and bag, and the keys to my car, I head outside into the pouring rain. Starting up the car, I drive out of the yard and down the long track to the main road then, not quite sure where I'm going, I turn right at the end of the track and keep on, following the road, not really looking where I am or

SARAH HARVEY

where I'm going, driving on auto-pilot, lost inside my own head.

Through Trenrethen, through Sennen, following the narrow winding road until I see the signs for Land's End itself and suddenly wonder where the hell it is I think I'm going. I slow down, look about me, and then finally pull into the car park for want of a better idea. I turn off the engine and sit in my car, suddenly filled with a silence so empty I can almost hear my own heart beating, and yet I cannot hear the usual soft sigh of my own breath. This is silent, almost as though I have stopped inhaling, my lungs fed by anxiety instead of oxygen.

I must be sitting there for about fifteen minutes before I finally return to the tangible world. I look about me. The large car park is practically empty. There must be about twenty cars in all, when there is room for at least five times that number. I don't quite know what I'm doing here, and still not quite sure why I'm doing it, I get out of the car, pull on my coat and pay the parking fee, then walk across the gravel to the entrance.

This isn't the Lands End that I recall from my childhood.

I vaguely remember reading an article about it having been bought by Americans and turned into a tourist attraction, with rides and games and shops selling Land's End T-Shirts and Land's End Jam and Land's End Fudge. The place is very quiet – there aren't many people here, but most of those seem to be inside the shops or the attractions, sheltering from the rain. A few more hardy visitors are struggling with the zips on their cagoules, catching their hats to stop them flying off like kites on the wind.

I walk through the buildings toward the cliff edge. A couple of soggy Japanese tourists are taking each other's photograph at the sign that states that *New York is 3147 miles*, *John O'Groats 874*, and *London 323*. I look towards the inn. There are people inside the restaurant, families

116

with small children, couples sheltering from the rain, eating, drinking, laughing, talking, arguing even. One couple are having a furious hushed row. I can't hear them, of course, but I can see their strained faces, lips moving in harsh whispers, until she looks angrily one way, and he the other, toe tapping furiously against the floor as he tries to still his anger, her pretending to reapply her lipstick, but actually using her mirror to check to see if he's looked back at her again.

I want to go and shake them. Demand that they don't take each other for granted. Make them realise that sometimes time is more precious than principle. Ignoring the *Danger* signs I turn away and walk out across the rocks and grass toward the cliff edge, look out towards the sea, then down to the rocks below me. Not really thinking, just looking, feeling the world bluster around me as though I am somehow separate from everything.

I think we are all looking for somebody who understands us completely. Someone we don't have to explain things to, someone who doesn't take something we say or do the wrong way, and then wonder why we get upset. Not someone who thinks they know you better than you know yourself, whilst totally misunderstanding what you are thinking, totally misreading your words, your facial expressions, your actions.

That was the one thing about Rob I don't think I could ever replace.

He knew me.

He really knew me, and I him. We could communicate volumes with just a single look. I miss this intimacy more than any other.

I know it sounds a cliché to say a part of me is missing, but when you are so close to someone, then that is exactly what they become. The most unknown part of a person medically is their mind: we cannot see it, feel it, touch it, we cannot even explain it, but it must be by far the most important organ of our body. Rob knew my mind as well as *I* knew my mind – so much so, that he became a part of it, a part of me, and now that part is gone.

I miss him so much.

*Cas misses him, too.* I see it in her anger, an anger born of a pain that she thinks no one else can comprehend. If only she knew, if only she could see those feelings echoed in my own eyes.

Instead of heading back to the car park, I begin to walk along the coastal path, striding furiously, almost running, as though if I go fast enough I'll leave it all behind me. My hair is blown around my face like frayed rope blinkers. The only thing I can see is the rock beneath me where my feet stumble as I struggle on, the intermittent blasts of wind so strong they are like an explosion around my ears.

It is only when my legs begin to tire that my mind, as if in conjunction, ceases to race quite so much, and I stop and look around me. I don't know quite how far I've walked. I only know that it has been a long way. I guessed that very soon, if I kept walking, I'd pass Sennen Cove, and the Ship, and end up back at Whitsunday.

Perhaps that would be the best thing to do. Leave my car in the car park, and ask my mother to take me back to fetch it tomorrow. I suddenly feel interminably weary. The rain has slowed to a drizzle. There are no houses nearby and I cannot see the road. I think I'll just sit down for five minutes, rest my aching legs, and then make my way back. To go home without my car would elicit questions I have no desire to answer. As it is, I can stop at the village shop on my way home, and swear that I had a sudden uncontrollable craving for some kind of food that we don't have in the house.

I look up, try to get my bearings. There is a small grey building just ahead of me. A sign says that it's a National Trust property, but doesn't tell you what it is. Its black shutters are firmly padlocked, protected against the

118

invasive wind that charges in from the sea, rides the waves like a warrior on white horseback from the west.

I would imagine it's a Huer's hut. A solitary but necessary job at one time. The hut gave shelter to the Huer, on the look-out for the shoals of sardine that were prized by fishermen then. It offers no shelter to me now, nowhere to rest before the journey back. Instead I walk beyond it, down a slope toward the cliff edge, where a natural outcrop of grey stone stands, like a tumbledown building. Stepping toward the largest of the stones, I feel the wind drop significantly. There is a small path weaving down between the rocks ahead of me. I walk beyond the largest stone, following the path through a partially hidden opening and find myself in a hollow, completely surrounded by the cliff and rock, protected from the elements. Directly ahead of me, about a metre away, the ground disappears to nothing. I step forward, my toes almost touching the edge.

From the smooth rock below my feet, I can look straight down about fifty feet to the sea below, the waves crashing violently against the pitted rock as though trying to reach up to me.

One thing about having nothing left to live for is that I no longer fear my own death. I step a little toward the edge, aware that the rock beneath my feet is slippery with sea spray and sodden lichen. One gust of wind could send me reeling forwards, tumbling down into the vast empty blackness of storm-stirred ocean.

I fling my arms wide, throw back my head. And then I scream. Scream into the wind until my lungs are empty. But the sound is carried away from me, enveloped and swallowed in the wail of wind and sea, so that my pain is silent to anything or anyone other than myself. And yet to me that scream is louder than a thousand decibels echoing. And then I sink back, sink back into the hollow until I feel the granite hard against my back, and I am covered from the rain by the overhang, and I cradle my head in my arms, drawing my knees to my chest.

Rob used to love the sea. We'd get away to the coast for a weekend as often as we could, sit silently together for hours on a beach somewhere, side by side, shoulders and thighs pressed together, occasionally my head upon his shoulder, sometimes laying his head in my lap, and listen and watch. Hypnotised. Mesmerised. Calm.

There's something about the ocean. Something that just draws your eyes and your thoughts. Something magical and mysterious. I never managed to bring Rob here. In a way I'm glad we didn't come here together. It somehow makes it easier for me now. I don't look around me and see memories instead of views.

In this place I am protected from the wind and the rain by the rock surrounding me. So still, so quiet, almost ethereal. I can see him and feel him so clearly, he could almost be with me. If I closed my eyes, I swear I would feel his reassuring touch upon the cold pale flesh of my cheek. But logic tells me I'll only be disappointed, so I keep them resolutely open, focused on the restless beauty of the tumbling water in front of me.

Solitude is only beautiful when you are surrounded by things that are beautiful, and your head is empty of sad thoughts.

I get to my feet, and turn back.

It is dark when I finally get back to my car, and I am shocked to find that it has gone five. Although a trip to the shops wouldn't have taken me the four hours that I have been absent from the farm, I attempt to cover my tracks by stopping at the small shop in Land's End to buy chocolate. Then as an afterthought, I pick up a couple of bottles of wine, then stop at the takeaway further down the road for fish and chips.

The kitchen is a haven of warmth, the old gold walls licked with the glow of the flames from the huge fireplace. Cassie is seated at the long table, her feet curled underneath her, several papers spread in a radius in front of her. She glances up as I come in, but seeing that it is me, her eyes dart away again without acknowledgement.

My mother is standing at the kitchen sink peeling potatoes. She turns and smiles as I come in, gesturing to the ever-present teapot on the table, to indicate that there is fresh tea if I want it. To my relief she doesn't ask where I've been, simply gives me a look that is tinged with obvious relief that I have returned in one piece.

'I bought dinner,' I tell her, waving my brown paper bags.

'Ooh you're an angel,' she smiles, putting down the potato and stabbing the small knife into it almost symbolically. 'I really wasn't in the mood for cooking tonight, as you can tell by the fact that I've peeled exactly two potatoes so far as my contribution towards tonight's meal.'

She washes the starch from her hands, gathers condiments from the cupboard. Salt and vinegar, sauce, a freshly baked loaf, butter, huge home-made pickled onions in an old coffee jar.

It reminds me of the Friday-night suppers we used to have when I was young. Dad would always come home with fish and chips on a Friday: a happy childhood memory that I had somehow managed to forget. You think I'd remember them all, having convinced myself that happy childhood memories were so few and far between.

Cas is quiet; no mention is made of our earlier row. She eats more than I've seen her eat for a while. I open one of the bottles of wine and she accepts a half-glass with a small 'thank you', her eyes looking at me then darting away again.

When we have finished eating, Laura begins to clear the table, and Cas helps without being asked. Then whilst Laura begins the washing-up, she settles back down at the table with a new magazine she must have picked up in the village whilst out with my mother.

The radio is playing.

Refusing my offer of help, Laura is standing at the sink, swaying from foot to foot in the way that she does to music when her movement is restricted by a task in hand, her shoulders bobbing slightly, but rhythmically. She starts off singing quietly in accompaniment to a Jill Ireland song, then her voice rises in a soaring contralto, and suddenly she backs away from the sink with hands dripping suds on the floor and begins to sway solo around the kitchen like an egotistical *Come Dancing* contestant who can't bear to share the limelight with a partner and therefore Tangos, Foxtrots and Cha Cha Chas alone in the glorious warmth of the spotlight.

Cas looks up, a smile fluttering across her lips, then dying as she looks away as if embarrassed by Laura's behaviour. Then the music changes pace. She begins to jive, so well in fact that Cas stops pretending to be embarrassed and watches her in fascination. She doesn't dance alone for long. Looking up, she sees me watching her, and smiling, holds out her hands to me.

I ignore them. She beckons for me to come forward, still swaying before me like a snake in front of a charmer, a smile of pure indulgence on her face. I shake my head, and my mother turns to where Cassie is seated at the table, pretending to read the magazine once more, but in reality watching out of the corner of her eye.

Swooping down on her, Laura grabs her hands and pulls her to her feet. The surprise and the momentum of the movement give my step-daughter no opportunity to back out, and the next minute my mother and Cassie are dancing together round the kitchen. At first she is annoyed and embarrassed, her body stiff, her feet dragging and reluctant, but Laura's enjoyment is infectious, and Cassie is soon drawn to display a skill that rivals my mother's when it comes to jiving. And then the music changes and Laura pulls the young girl into a gloriously over-the-top tango, flinging her unceremoniously about the kitchen in a series of dips and twirls. Then Cassie begins to smile, and to my total amazement, the smile is soon followed by breathless laughter.

Catching the mood, the dogs begin to jump around them in excitement, poised on hind legs, paws scrabbling in the air, as if they are trying to dance themselves, like marionettes jerked by invisible strings.

And then the record ends, and the spell is broken. A moment's awkward silence, everyone standing still, even the dogs crouched and waiting – for what I'm not sure – maybe an explosion of some kind and an expression of annoyance from the volatile Cassandra, but then laughing, Laura sweeps Cassie, whose hands she is still holding, into her arms and hugs what little breath she has left out of her.

I watch as Cassie's body goes resistant at the uninvited embrace, and then as if her whole body has given a massive sigh, she relaxes, her own arms wrapping around my mother's waist and her head falling against her shoulder. Momentarily I see her arms tighten as she squeezes my mother in return, and then they both draw back, and I see that Cassie is smiling up at my mother, her face flushed with the first colour I have ever seen on her alabaster-pale features. My mother reaches out and, as if it is the most natural thing in the world, tucks a lock of Cassie's pale-gold hair that had fallen across her face, behind her ear, and Cassie continues to smile up at her.

My mother the miracle-worker.

The smooth commentary from the DJ glides over the intro of another track, and Laura returns to the sink, and her washing-up. Without a word Cassie picks up a tea towel and joins her.

Although it is they who have been dancing about the room like mad things, I suddenly feel very hot. I had backed up against the door to get out of the way of them dancing, and feeling the handle behind me, I turn it and quietly slip out into the yard. It's a cold clear night; the black sky is littered with a million bright stars, and the moon is as pale, and as distantly enigmatic as Cassie's face.

My breath is a cold vaporous pool in front of me as I sigh heavily. The rain has ceased and the fields stretching out beyond the Long Barn are sugar-frosted. I can hear a dog howling in the distance, and the grumble of an engine as an old car heaves its way up the Sennen Cove road.

Hearing my footsteps, Chance emerges from the dark shadows of his loose box, blowing down his whiskered nose at me in friendly greeting. I go over to him and he breathes in my face and my hair, his lips mumbling against my jacket as he searches for the treats he feels sure that I've brought him. Finding nothing, he *harrumphs* heavily into my right ear in disappointment, but instead of walking away, back to the straw-deep warmth of the far corner, he merely stretches his long neck further out of the half door, and rests his warm whiskered chin against my shoulder, his cheekbone pressed to mine, his breath warming the back of my neck.

I close my eyes and lean gratefully against him, consumed with a loneliness that is so intense I feel as if I am falling into blackness.

I'm not sure how long I stand there, with Chance blowing warm, sweet, hay-scented breath across my face, but when I finally open my eyes, I find myself looking straight into his, and see an intelligence, sympathy and understanding that is surely beyond an animal.

# Chapter Four

I should thank Laura.

There is a new warmth in the household, one that doesn't really include me, but one for which I am nonetheless grateful, because it does make life a little easier to see Cassie looking happier.

I don't quite know what Laura has done to achieve this new *entente cordiale*. I do know they 'had a chat' while I was traipsing around Land's End in a thunderstorm, because my mother told me, but that is all she told me. Whatever it was that she said or did, it seems to have broken the hard layer of permafrost in which Cas had encased herself, and they are now friends.

I can't help feeling the odd pang of jealousy. My mother has developed a better relationship with Cas in the past week than I have managed to achieve in the three years that I have known her.

I'm also finding it a little difficult to see Cas getting the affection from my mother that I so desperately craved at her age, but never received. I try to tell myself that it is all in the past, and I should be over it by now, but it's all very well trying to act like an adult, when you feel like a child who just wants to be held and told that everything will work out in the end.

I sleep late again on the Monday morning, and come downstairs to find that the other two have carried out all the chores between them, such as feeding and watering the menagerie, and collecting the post from the American-style box at the end of the track. They are now cooking breakfast.

Laura, who was frying bacon, puts down her spatula, and pours me a cup of tea.

'You should have woken me, I'd have helped,' I say a little grumpily, accepting the hot mug from her.

'Don't worry, we started early. Cas and I are going shopping in Truro. There are a few bits that she needs to get.'

I refuse breakfast, preferring to nurse my mug of tea until it is cold.

Laura and Cas sit down to full English. They chat as they eat, a new camaraderie between them. It would be nice if their conversation included me, and I feel slightly disappointed that I'm not invited on this jaunt of theirs, especially as I watch them leave with hardly a backward glance in my direction.

Once more I have to remind myself that I'm a grown woman, not some silly schoolgirl in a sulk because she feels left out of the fun.

The weather has broken as well, perhaps in response to Cassie's new sunnier nature. There is no sign of the rain that has been dogging us for days; in fact, the sun is shining in a pale blue cloudless sky, and if it weren't for the chill so noticeable in the air, it could be a summer's day, August instead of December.

I feel cooped up and restless in the house on my own. I try to work but can't seem to settle to it. After staring at the blank screen of my laptop for half an hour, I give in and decide to walk the two miles or so down to the village, and do a little shopping of my own.

Trenrethen is a typical picturesque Cornish hamlet of quaint cottages and assorted tourist appeal shops selling fudge and jams and tiny gold-plated Cornish Piskies perched cross-legged on a piece of Cornish rock. It nestles in a cleft of land that dips down like a crease to the sea, the houses clinging to the gentle hills either side of the long main street.

I cut across the fields, joining the road only as I reach the outskirts, walking its steep length down into the heart of the village. I can see the roof of the Ship in the distance to the west, and to the east a church sits just above the highest house on the opposite hill. Walk east for salvation, west for ruination.

I wander around the shops. It doesn't take long as there are only four: a post office, a bakers, and two gift shops, one traditional, one more ethnic, selling crystals and silver charms, scented candles and aromatherapy oils. I buy some rum and raisin fudge for Laura from the first gift shop, and an oil that's supposed to relieve stress from the second for me, then a paper and a couple of postcards from the post office, before heading across the road and down a little to the small café that overlooks the spectacular natural harbour we first saw from the Ship. The café is empty apart from the jolly Rubenesque lady who runs it. Judging from her rotund appearance I guess that the food here is pretty good, and order a cafetière of real coffee and a large slice of home-made coffee cake, and take them outside to sit at one of the small terrace tables in the sunshine.

I eat quickly. I'm not surprised that I'm hungry. I've got used to Laura's huge breakfasts, one of which I refused this morning in what I now recognise as a fit of pique at being left out of the shopping trip. To distract myself from going straight back inside the café and ordering another piece of cake, I open the oil and take a big sniff. It smells gorgeous, but it doesn't stop me feeling hungry, and unfortunately it doesn't make me feel any less uptight either. Not instantly anyway; maybe it takes a while to work. I rub some on my pulse points, determined to sniff each time Cas pops into my mind.

Blinking slowly in the rare sunshine, I pour a second cup of coffee and take out the post cards that I bought

127

from the post office. The first one is of a large dumb sheep, with an enormous backside standing on the edge of a cliff at Land's End, that I bought to send to Petra. I was going to caption it with something stupid to make her laugh.

*Natalie contemplated throwing herself off, but knew if she landed arse first she'd just bounce straight back up again.*

Smiling to myself I pull a pen from my handbag, and start to write. *Dear* ... But instead of Petra's name, another name begins to flow from my pen.

> *Dear, Dear Rob,*
> *Wish you were here. That's the usual way to start a postcard, isn't it, but I don't think it could ever have been so heartfelt before. I feel so lonely without you.*
> *Love always,*
> *N x*

I sit back and look at the card on the table in front of me, surprised by my own actions. And then I hear a friendly voice calling my name. 'Natalie!'

It's Orlaithe. She's coming out of the quaint village post office, opposite the café, the bell on the door ringing as she first opens it and then shuts it behind her. I hastily push the card into my jacket pocket, feeling rather foolish, but a little better somehow.

Orlaithe is crossing the road toward me. 'I thought it was you, so I did,' she calls brightly. 'What are you doing out here all on your own? Where's Laura and Cas now?'

I smile a greeting. 'They've gone shopping in Truro.'

'And left you all alone?' She raises her eyebrows in sympathy.

'It's nice to get some peace,' I lie unconvincingly, 'and a decent cup of coffee,' I add, trying to sound more cheerful. 'Laura doesn't believe in coffee.'

'Well, why don't I join you for another cup? You're not rushing off, are you?'

'No, I'm in no hurry. That would be nice, thank you.' I go to get up, but Orlaithe gestures for me to stay where I am.

'No, no, I'll get it. You stay where you are – I'll be back in a minute.'

Orlaithe disappears inside, returning minutes later with a fresh pot of coffee and to my chagrin two more desserts. She puts a plate of chocolate cake in front of me, silencing my untrue protests that I couldn't possibly eat another one.

'Nonsense – you look like you need something inside of you, skinny little thing that you are.' She pats my hand. 'It's such a beautiful day we're having, isn't it?' she smiles, sitting down opposite me, and breathing in the fresh clear air with obvious relish. 'Far better than all that horrible rain.'

'Lovely.' I nod.

'I never thought it was going to stop – rain, rain, rain, nothing but rain for three whole days.' She picks up her fork, and starts to ease the fudge icing from the top of the sponge cake with the edge of it. 'So how are things then, Nattie? How are you getting on staying with your mother?'

'It's good,' I reply politely.

'Sure 'tis a beautiful place Whitsunday, such a lovely position so close to the sea.'

'Yeah, it's great. I'd forgotten how beautiful it is here.'

'You'll soon settle into life at Whitsunday. You'll be getting to the point where you won't ever want to go back to that dirty great city; you'll want to stay here for ever. And your mother, she'll be looking after you so well, you'll never want to be leaving.'

'How long have you known her?'

'Your mother? Ooh,' Orlaithe purses her lips as she ponders. 'It must be a good ten years now, since Francis and I first took over the Ship.'

'Francis?' I query.

'Frank – Hank. The original Texan wannabe, but he's Irish through and through, and a good Catholic boy is my Francis.'

'I didn't know. I mean, I could see he wasn't American . . .'

'Oh no!' Orlaithe throws up her hands in mock horror. 'Don't tell him you can see through his careful disguise, he'll be absolutely devastated.'

'. . . but I thought he was actually from Cornwall.'

'Well, I'm from County Cork originally, and Francis, I mean Hank, is from Dublin, but he's been living over here since he was a small boy, whereas I only came over – ooh, let me see now, in seventy-nine, no, no, I think it was seventy-eight. Yes, I came over in seventy-eight. Twenty-three years ago, would you believe that now, and a handsome young woman I was then. It was a catch that Francis Doyle got himself, so it was,' she smiles, her eyes sparkling brightly with humour.

'He's a fair bit older than you, isn't he?'

Orlaithe nods. 'Twenty years.'

'Twenty years? You're kidding, aren't you?'

'Twenty years, three months and two days to be precise,' she affirms.

'Then that makes him . . .'

'Seventy-two. Doesn't look it, does he? As fit as a man half his age, is my Francis.'

We are both silent for a moment sipping at our hot coffee.

'So your mother and Cas have gone shopping, have they?'

I nod.

'She's a pretty wee thing isn't she, your Cas?' 'My' Cas. She's never been called 'my' Cas before. It's strange to realise that this is how other people must view her. And, to my surprise, I quite like it. I nod again.

130

'Although I should imagine she's not as delicate as she looks. I daresay she can be a bit headstrong sometimes.'

'You see that, do you?' I laugh dryly.

'Sure, but still it's good that she's getting on with Laura so well.'

'Yeah.' I sigh.

'And of course she thinks the world of you, you know,' Orlaithe adds, looking at me keenly.

I merely look back at her, unable to agree with her on this one.

'So, are you finding it strange, being back here then?' Orlaithe asks quietly as I remain silent. 'And this time with Cassie?'

I open my mouth to say that it's great again, but instead, under the steady gaze of those warm and friendly amber-coloured eyes, I find myself telling Orlaithe that yes, that is exactly how I feel. Strange. I tell her how odd it feels to be back here once again, to be staying at Whitsunday in my old room, how I thought that the next time I came to Whitsunday I would be bringing Rob with me, how I cannot associate the sad withdrawn woman I remember as my mother with the endlessly cheerful and supportive Laura who has greeted Cas and me so warmly, and my guilt at staying away for so long. I say to her all the things I wanted to say to Petra the other night but couldn't bring myself to speak aloud.

Orlaithe listens without comment, then reaches across the table to take my own cold hand in a warm, reassuring grip.

'Of course it will be strange for you, darling; your whole life's been turned upside down, so it has. But she's a wonderful woman, your mother; she'll soon have you feeling a hundred per cent better. And as for Cas, she's a good girl deep down, so she is. You'll find the way, don't doubt it.'

Orlaithe sits back in her seat, her copper curls fanning

behind her in a sudden breeze that rushes up the main street from the sea. The sun has disappeared behind a long low cloud, and the temperature has suddenly dropped at least ten degrees.

She shivers. 'Sure and 'tis getting cold now. Where's your car?'

'I walked down.'

'Then I'll run you back up there when you're finished your coffee. We'll see if the other two are back from their shopping trip yet, shall we?'

'No, I couldn't possibly make you do that. I mean, it's really kind of you, but it's in totally the wrong direction for you. Besides, I'll enjoy the walk.'

''Tis no trouble.'

'Thanks, but no, it's okay, I'll walk back. I'd like to.'

'If you're sure?'

'Certain. Thanks though for the offer, and for the coffee and the company.'

'Anytime, darlin'. We'll be seeing you down at the Ship soon, no doubt?'

'Absolutely, yes.'

She stands up to leave, gathering her numerous shopping bags into strong bejewelled fingers.

I stand up as well. 'Orlaithe, thanks. You're a good listener.'

'Well, you can't stand behind a bar for thirty years without being that, my love, but it was a pleasure, Nattie, truly. You take care now.' She takes my shoulders and plants a vibrant pink kiss on both of my cheeks.

I arrive back at Whitsunday to find that the others have indeed returned. Bags of shopping are abandoned on the floor – Boots and Superdrug have been raided with a vengeance. Cas is setting the table for dinner, which is nearly ready.

'We were too hungry to unpack,' Laura explains from the Aga. 'Thought we'd have dinner first.'

It's Laura's favourite meal – liver and bacon, with mashed potato and onion gravy. The first time it was served, Cas almost fainted with horror, and immediately insisted that she was vegetarian, despite the fact that she'd consumed a vast bacon sandwich for breakfast that day. However, Laura still managed to persuade her to try some.

Laura has a way of dealing with Cas that I have never mastered, and yet dearly wish I could emulate. She is calm yet firm, unyielding yet always fair, and Cas responds to her. When they are together I see a different person from the wilful, rude uncooperative girl that is the Cassie I know.

After dinner I find that Laura has somehow persuaded Cas to try other things she's adamant she doesn't like, and not just food. The shopping trip to Truro apparently wasn't just to stock up on shampoo, socks and new eyeliner. Among Cassie's many purchases is a large cardboard box. The box contains a pair of riding boots.

From loathing all of the animals in the yard, in particular the fowl, Cas has now taken up their care as one of her regular chores, ensuring that she feeds and waters them twice a day without fail.

Laura now tells me quietly that Cas has also agreed to start riding Chance. Although still claiming she has no interest in horses, she has agreed to exercise him, 'purely to help out Laura', she insists, not because she wants to. She hasn't ridden for at least three years, it being a somewhat 'childish' pursuit apparently that interfered with her dance training. Her school is over-run with young girls with a sad unhealthy fascination for all things 'horse', she tells us, wittering on about ponies, and pony clubs, and rosettes, clutching their Christine Pullein-Thompsons, and dreaming of Olympia at Christmas.

For someone who's trying to be the epitome of cool it was hardly a scene worth getting involved with, and yet

Laura has once again persuaded Cas to change her view. In fact, the very next day I get up to find them both down in Mile Meadow, Cas gently cantering Chance in a wide circle, whilst Laura shouts at her to sit up straight and get her heels down.

The sun that graced us fleetingly with its presence yesterday has returned, if a little pale and wan, to hang limply in a washed-out pale blue sky. The ground is still sodden, Chance's heels kicking up a spray of dirty water as he canters good-naturedly round and round the pivot that is Laura. Cas actually rides very well – she has what horsy people would call a 'good seat'. I also notice she has an audience.

Hank is standing at the bottom of the ladder, at the end of the Long Barn which faces into the field, one weathered hand shielding his eyes against the sun, as he watches her, nodding his approval at the way she easily handles the big horse. She is also being watched by a young man with tousled sea-bleached hair who, despite the fact that it's far from warm, is balanced on the roof of the Long Barn in just ripped jeans and a faded blue Fat Face T-shirt that almost matches the faded blue of the clear sky above us.

'Who's that?' I ask Laura, as she unclips the lunge rope from Chance's bridle and instructs Cas to take him across the field on her own.

'Luke.'

'Luke?'

'Local lad – comes to help Hank out sometimes when a job's a bit too much for him, not that he'd ever admit that anything's too much for him, mind. Some slates have come loose, so Luke's supposed to be up there fixing them for me. To be honest, I think he finds things down here far more interesting at the moment. If he leans any further over next time Cas rises to the trot, he'll fall off!'

'She's too young to have an admirer.' I frown up at

the blond boy, silently urging him to get back to the job in hand and stop ogling my step-daughter.

'It's her sixteenth birthday next Sunday.' Laura watches me in amusement.

'I know. But she's still too young.'

'Whilst we're on the subject, what are we going to do about it?'

'Her birthday?'

'Exactly.'

'I don't really know. I've been trying to think of something, but I wasn't sure she'd want a big fuss.'

'Well, I think it's a good idea to make a fuss of her. We could have a party.'

'I suppose, but it'll be rather strange for her though without any of her friends here.'

'We could invite Luke,' Laura says teasingly as I throw the boy yet another wary glance. 'And she has us.'

'Some consolation,' I mutter.

Laura's enthusiasm is not to be dampened. 'I'll ask Orlaithe to make us a birthday cake. She makes the most fantastic cakes and biscuits. I'd do one myself but I'm not exactly good at baking, unless you think you could give it a shot?'

I shake my head.

'Orlaithe, then. Right – what about presents? What do you think she'd like?'

I shrug. 'Don't ask me, I haven't a clue what to get her.'

'Well, *think*. What does she need most?'

'I was thinking along the lines of clothes or something.'

'Okay, she may like that, but what does she really *need*?' She repeats cryptically.

I glance over at Cassie who is concentrating too hard on her riding to have noticed that we are talking about her. Why is my mother being so obscure? I still don't know what she's getting at.

'Not material things,' Laura prompts me. 'Forget

135

clothes, and CD players – what does that girl need the most?'

'Manners,' I scowl.

Laura pulls a face at me, as she too glances across at Cas to make sure she can't hear us. 'Try again,' she perseveres. 'What do you miss the most, now Rob is gone?'

I pause for a moment as a thousand things flood my mind, but my heart speaks the loudest. 'Love,' I state quietly.

'Well, there you have it then.'

'Then I have what?'

'Your answer. She needs love.'

'You can't buy love.'

'No, but you *can* buy her a dog.'

'What! You're kidding, aren't you?'

'Not at all. It would be good for her.'

'But a dog? It's not practical. We go back to London in a few weeks' time, then Cassie will go back to school.'

'You can take care of it then – it will give you something to go home to.'

'I don't need something to go home to. I've got work.'

'You can't work twenty-four hours a day, no matter how hard you try.'

'And I've got Petra . . .' I trail off as my mother looks at me.

'Who has a very busy life of her own.'

'And I've got Meryl,' I add feebly.

'Meryl? Who's she?'

'My goldfish,' I reply with a grin. 'Petra's popping round to feed her whilst I'm away. Okay, I give in, I need something to come home to, but I don't think that something should be a dog.'

'It would be good for you, and for Cas of course. It would give her something to look after, something to think about other than herself. Take her mind off her problems. You never know, it might actually help her look forward to spending some time with you in the school holidays instead of going to whichever friend will have her.'

I nod thoughtfully. What Laura is saying actually does make sense.

'They take a lot of looking after,' I demur. 'And it wouldn't be fair to leave it at home on its own all day.'

'You could always pretend it's a guide dog and take it into work,' Laura jokes.

'What – and tell them it's for people who are blind drunk?' I laugh.

'At least think about it. It really would be good for Cas.'

'You're probably right, but it's not very practical,' I repeat.

'At least promise me you'll think about it.'

I look at her hopeful face, and sigh. 'Okay, okay, I'll think about it.'

Laura beams broadly. 'Lovely. A friend of mine down in Helston has a gorgeous Labrador bitch who gave birth to puppies about ten weeks ago. I'll give her a ring if you like, see if she's ready to let them go yet. I'll tell her you're going to come down and have a look.'

She turns away as Cas trots Chance up to a halt beside us, enthusiastically patting the sweating muscle of his long chestnut neck, her half-smile expanding quickly into a broad beam.

'Well done, darling, that was excellent.'

And that was that.

Two days later I find myself driving down a row of large detached houses in Helston, looking for number thirty-three, and Mary Ray.

Number thirty-three Orchard Drive, it turns out, is a 1930s bungalow, the type with an arched porch edged with red brick, and large bay windows to either side. Each bay is again made of red brick, and the rest of the walls are pebble dash, painted a soft pink, which clashes wonderfully with the dark green front door. Two perfectly shaped bay trees flank the archway, and a small concrete ramp turns the step of the porch into a slope. I notice that to the right of the door just next to the thick brass doorbell, there is a metal hand-rail, painted white, yet worn to pale grey in areas, with use.

The woman who answers the door stands barely over five foot in her floral slippers; her back is bent and she is leaning heavily on the strong wooden cane she holds in her left hand.

I smile nervously, pushing the hair that the cold northerly wind has blown into my eyes away from my face. 'Mrs Ray? I'm—'

But before I can finish she holds out a friendly hand in greeting. 'You must be Natalie.'

'That's right, I am.'

'Well, there's no doubt about that. You've got your mother's looks.'

'I have?' I ask in genuine surprise.

'Very much so. Not her colouring, of course, you're much darker, must take after your father there, but there's no mistaking the fact that you're Laura Dunne's daughter.'

Nobody has ever told me I look like my mother before. Then again, I've hardly seen her enough to be compared with her; we don't have mutual friends, unless you count Petra who, although she hasn't met my mother often, has always got on well with her whenever they have come together.

'Come in, come in,' she opens the door wider for me, 'your mother phoned to say you were on your way. The dogs are through the back in the conservatory; it's slightly warmer in there than the rest of the house at the moment. We've been having some dreadful weather, haven't we? Still, at least the rain has stopped now . . .'

Mrs Ray takes me through an immaculate lounge

138

with dusk-pink carpets and dark oak furniture that has the kind of sheen only achieved by many years of loving attention with a cloth and layer upon layer of polish, to a conservatory that runs the entire length of the back of the house. This overlooks a garden laid to lawn, which despite the weather is well kept, cut in neat vertical stripes like a well-tended bowling green.

At the far end of the glass room, against the wall, and beneath a radiator that is currently on at full blast, is a large, dull red plastic dog-basket. In the basket, stretched out on a blanket set upon a faded floral cushion is a large black Labrador. She lifts her head as we enter the room, and feebly thumps her tail in greeting, but makes no move to approach us.

'Poor darling's shattered.' Mary Ray smiles adoringly at the animal. 'I think in dog years her offspring must be at the same stage as human children when they hit the terrible twos. This will probably be the last litter she has, she's getting a little too old now for another.'

There are five puppies.

Two are in the basket with their mother, asleep half on her and half on each other. Two others are playing a vigorous game of tug o' war with an old torn silk scarf. There are three black, one yellow and a small tawny-coloured animal.

'Do you want a dog or a bitch?' Mary Ray asks, walking slowly over to them.

'You know I hadn't really thought . . . What would you suggest?'

'If you don't mind what sex it is, then why don't you just see which one you like the best? This is the pick.' Struggling to bend, she lifts up a fat wriggling animal, one of the two that was play-fighting, and holds him out to me, but he isn't interested in being petted. He struggles to be released from my unwanted attentions, keen to be back on the floor with his brother, who has now claimed ownership of the scarf that was the bone of contention.

I put him down and he rushes off to restart the fight.

I look at the two asleep in the basket. They're so cute, but seem so comfortable nestled up to their mother's belly. It would be difficult to even lift them away from her now, let alone take them away from her for good.

The fifth puppy, the tawny one, is sitting a little to the side, not joining in the games. He is slightly smaller than the rest. I look at him, he looks back at me with huge brown eyes and cocks his tiny head to one side and to my utter surprise I am suddenly drenched by a warm shower of maternal feeling.

'What about this one?' I ask, bending down and holding out my hand to him.

'Are you sure?' Mary asks me in surprise. 'He's filled out a little now, but he was the runt of the litter.'

'I like him,' I reply, as encouraged by my waggling fingers, he wanders over to sniff at them, then lick them with a small pink, very rough tongue.

'He's not the most handsome, but I must admit he does have a lovely nature.'

'This is the one I want. If that's okay with you?'

Mary Ray smiles broadly. 'If you're sure then yes, that's good.'

'Can I take him with me?'

'Well, they are ready to go if you want him now. Your mother did warn me that you might . . .' Her voice breaks a little.

'Are you okay?' I ask in concern.

She sighs a little and shrugs her shoulders as though shaking off a feeling. 'Do you know, no matter how many times I do this, it's always hard to say goodbye to the little loves when the time comes for them to go to their new homes, but I'm sure you'll take wonderful care of him. Let me go and find you a box and a blanket and we can make him comfortable for the journey home.'

'How much do I owe you?'

'Oh no, I don't want any money for him. I'm just pleased that he'll be going to a good home.'

'But he's a pedigree!' I insist, knowing full well that I'd be expected to pay several hundred pounds for the dog in London.

'You're doing me a favour taking that one.'

'Now that I *don't* believe.'

'In that case, let's just say I'm paying a debt of gratitude to your mother,' she tells me. 'The Lord knows how many times she's helped me out over the years. In fact, I have something I'd like you to pass on to her if you don't mind.'

'Do you know Laura well?'

Mary Ray looks at me thoughtfully for a moment, and then smiles. 'Would you like a cup of tea?' she asks.

I leave number thirty-three Orchard Drive an hour later with a new puppy, and a slightly new perspective. It's an eye-opener to see my mother from someone else's point of view. To me, Laura Dunne my mother was a cold, withdrawn woman who never seemed to want me in her life. To Mary Ray, she is a kind, thoughtful friend who has always been on hand to help whenever needed.

I realise that I don't really know her at all. I have seen this over the past week or so. She's not how I remember her – but then how balanced could the perspective of an unhappy sixteen year old be? I only have to look at how Cas views me to realise that sixteen-year-old Natalie never really knew her mother at all.

There are four handsome fat male pheasants in the yard when I get back. They remind me of slightly startled country vicars, with their pristine white dog collars, and fussy gait, walking as though their hands, if they had any, would be firmly clasped behind their plump rust-coloured backs. Laura tells me that they come here from the Treloar estate nearby to escape the huntsmen, and to

141

steal corn from the chicken coop. They scatter quickly as
the kitchen door is flung open and Laura hurries out to
meet me.

'Did you get it? Did you get it?' She is almost climbing
in the car as I drive through the gate in her eagerness to
get a look at what's in the box on the seat beside me.

I pull my car to a halt in the space at the end of the
stables, and she wrenches the door open, diving straight
into the open box with a smile of anticipation on her
face.

'Oh my goodness, it's adorable, she'll love it.'

'Do you really think so?'

'Don't look so worried – how could she not?'

'Quite easily. It's from me.'

'He or she?'

'He.'

'Don't worry, she can't fail to love him. Everybody
loves dogs.'

She lifts the box from the seat, and carries it towards
the house, the puppy clearly trying to escape as they go,
his silken head bobbing above the edge of the cardboard,
his tongue trying furiously to lick at Laura's fingers as
she carries him.

I get out of the car and follow her into the kitchen.
She has scooped the puppy out of his box and is cradling
him to her, laughing with delight.

'Cas'll love him. He's absolutely gorgeous, aren't you?'
She holds the wriggling animal up to her face, and
giggles as he covers it in wet tongue kisses. 'You're
gorgeous, aren't you, little fella? Yes, you are.'

'Where is she?'

'Out riding.'

'I'll have to give him to her when she gets back then.'

'Nonsense! We can keep him a secret between us until
her actual birthday.'

'Where on earth can we hide him until Sunday?'

'He can go home with Hank tonight, then Hank and

142

Orlaithe can bring him with them to the party.'

'He won't mind?'

'Not in the slightest. In fact you'll be lucky if he brings him back. Hank's never had children, so he gets a bit broody over puppies.'

I can't imagine Hank getting broody over anything except his car. He loves his car, great monstrosity that it is.

'Oh, Mary Ray said to say "hi", by the way. She sent you this.' I hand my mother the package that Mary entrusted to me. It feels weighty. Like a bottle.

Laura puts it down on the table and calls Hank in from the hay barn, where he is happily tinkering with the engine of the old red tractor. Ten minutes later, tractor totally forgotten, a gooey-eyed Hank is despatched with the puppy, and strict instructions to bring him back on Sunday morning – an order, I am a little concerned from the lovesick expression on his lined face, he might have some trouble following.

Hank and the puppy gone, Laura turns her attention to the package that Mary Ray has sent her.

'Ooh lovely!' she exclaims. 'I was hoping it would be this.' And she pulls out a bottle full of dark damson-coloured liquid.

'What is it? Wine?'

Laura shakes her head. 'Sloe gin. Mary makes the best ever. Here – try some.'

'But it's two in the afternoon,' I protest, as she starts to unscrew the cap on the bottle.

'Just time for last orders then.' Laura fills a small glass and holds it out to me. 'Go on. One small glass won't hurt.'

I sniff at the dark purple liquid. It's so strong, just the smell of it makes me cough.

'Put hairs on your chest, that will,' Laura jokes, already halfway through her own glass, and licking her lips appreciatively.

'I have enough trouble depilating my moustache as it is,' I joke, taking a tentative sip.

'So what do you think?' she asks.

I feel the sweet liquid run over my tongue, and course a warming path down my throat into my stomach.

'Wow. That's really good.'

'I told you, she makes the best.'

'Umm.' I nod my agreement, bringing the glass back to my lips again.

Laura watches as I finish the small glassful, then holds the bottle out to me. 'Another?'

I smile at her, lips sticky sweet and slightly tingling. 'I don't think I should.'

'Oh come on,' my mother urges, refilling her own glass. 'How about a toast?' She raises her glass and refills my own. 'To having my daughter home again.'

Despite the fact that I'm late up again the next morning, I'm still up before Laura, which is a first.

I'm not sure how I manage to get up at all. I don't know what Mary Ray makes her sloe gin out of but I haven't had a hangover this bad since Rob and I went on a tequila binge on our honeymoon in Mexico. It didn't help that Laura and I sat down last night and drank nearly the entire bottle between us, watched by a frowning Cas, whose lips were tight with disapproval.

Even the stinging needles of a cold shower can do little to shake the fug of my hangover from my throbbing head, and I stumble downstairs feeling decidedly sorry for myself.

Cas has done the chores on her own and is now in the kitchen making breakfast, a martyred look on her face. I slink into the room like a severely chastised dog, and slump down at the table, head in hands, deciding that I'll make a cup of tea as soon as my legs have stopped shaking from the effort of coming down the steep narrow stairs.

'How's your head?' she asks without looking at me. It's not a concerned query, it's a biting rebuke.

'Still there,' I reply, feeling it gingerly with my fingers. 'I think.'

Cas throws the hot frying pan in the soapy-water-filled sink, where it sinks spitting to the bottom, then pulling on an oven glove reaches into the dark belly of the Aga. I close my eyes, then open them abruptly as she dumps a hot plate in front of me.

'You're just trying to finish me off, aren't you?' I groan, looking at the plate heaving with bacon, mushrooms and more noticeably, two eggs sunny side up, sitting slimily side by side like staring yellow eyes, boring into my throbbing head.

'Would it were that easy,' Cas bites back at me, fetching a mug of tea and banging this down so hard next to my breakfast that the brown liquid slops onto the table.

She leans against the sink, arms crossed, and watches me as I warily prod a sausage with my fork, trying to decide whether I'm too nauseous to try and eat, or too nauseous not to eat.

I take the lesser of the two evils and grasp my mug in shaking hands. Cas is still watching me, lips pursed.

'What?' I find myself snapping at her.

'You drink too much,' comes the quiet reply.

'So?'

'It's not good for you.'

'So?'

'All right then, drink yourself to death – see if I care.' She throws the tea towel she is holding onto the drainer, and stalks across the room and up the stairs. I hear the latch rattling as she attempts to slam a door that is too flimsy to make much of an impact.

After half an hour there's still no sign of Cas re-emerging from her room, and Laura is still snoring away under her quilt. I still feel as if I'm coming down with something, although I know it's only a hangover, and decide that as everybody else seems to be spending the day in their rooms I may as well head back to mine. I was supposed to be going back out today to try and find Cas something else for her birthday, but can't face fighting my way through the ravaging hordes of Christmas shoppers.

I feel decidedly green, and I'm not sure that my legs are working sufficiently to carry me round Truro. What I need is a personal shopper to go and do it for me. I dig in my bag for my mobile and curl up as far into the window as I can to get a signal.

'Hello, Petra.'

'Nat! How are you?'

'I'm okay, what about you?'

'Oh, don't ask!' she wails.

'Why, what's the matter?' I reply in concern.

'Christmas,' she states brusquely.

'Oh, don't tell me Peter's cancelled on you.'

'Oh no, no, not at all, he hasn't done that, although in a way I wish he would. No, I don't mean that, I shouldn't say that.'

'Then what's the problem?'

'Well, *I'm* cooking Christmas Dinner.'

'Oh dear.' Petra can't cook. She can't even boil an egg.

'I need some advice, Nat. If I tell you what I've done so far, will you tell me if I'm getting it right or not?'

'I'll try.'

'I wasn't sure what size turkey to get so I've ordered a twenty pounder. Do you think that'll be big enough?'

'For two people?'

'Yeah. Oh, it's not big enough is it, Nat? I knew I should have got a bigger one!'

'Trust me, Petra, it's plenty big enough. In fact you probably won't need to buy another one for Easter, it'll last you that long.'

My friend sighs. 'I didn't know, did I? In fact, I'm a Christmas Dinner virgin!'

'Couldn't you just order in or something?'

'No!' she wails. 'I've got to do it myself, I want it to be just right. More than right, I want it to be absolutely perfect.'

'In that case, you'd definitely better get someone else to cook it for you.'

'I should be insulted, darling, but seeing as you're right . . . It's insane, isn't it? I mean, look at me – I'm independent, successful, and I can't even butter toast.'

'Maybe it's about time you learnt. Have you got any recipe books?'

'I don't think so, but I'm pretty good at stirring.' She jokes, 'How about if you just tell me what I've got to do with the blasted turkey, then I think I can handle the rest.'

'Okay. First of all, you'll need to stuff it.'

Petra interrupts me with a gasp of horror. 'You mean I actually have to stick my hand *inside* a dead animal?'

'I think that's where the term stuffing comes from, yes.'

'Oh my goodness. I'm not sure I can do that, Nattie.'

'You've got to.'

'So to get a good meal, I have to stick my hand up a deceased turkey's butt?'

I burst out laughing. Petra joins in.

'Tell you what, why don't I just go down to Harrods, and see if they've got any personal shoppers in the Food Hall.'

'That sounds like a much better idea. Apart from learning to cook, are you busy at the moment?'

'I know that tone of voice. You want something, don't you?'

'Me? I was just phoning to say hello to my oldest and dearest friend, that's all.'

'Gee, that's nice, honey. Now tell me the truth.'

147

'Okay, so I need a favour.'

'Anything, darling, what is it?'

'It's Cas's birthday on Sunday. I've got her a few bits – in fact, I've got her quite a few bits – but I wanted to get her something nice to wear. I've looked here and there are some quite nice shops but I can't find what I want.'

'What do you want?'

'I don't know, I think that's half the problem.'

'Are we still talking clothes for Cas here,' Petra jokes, 'or life in general?'

'Probably both,' I reply, laughing lightly. 'Just get her something special, okay? It's her first birthday with me since Rob's accident, and I want to make sure it's as good as it can be.'

'There are a lot of firsts to go through after something like that, Nat. For you as well as Cas.'

'I know,' I sigh, 'but can you do it for me? You'd be helping me out big time. I'd owe you a huge favour.'

'You give me an excuse to go shopping and you say it's *me* doing *you* the favour? Of course I'll do it for you. When do you need something by?'

'You're going to have to post it to get it here by Saturday.'

'Of course. Consider it done. Knightsbridge, here I come.'

The very next day I am greeted by the rare sight of the postman's red van winding its way up the track to the house. There is a large box to sign for, sent Special Delivery and postmarked *London*. Petra has carried out my request in record time. There is also an envelope postmarked *Greenwich* that I know must be from Louisa-May. I hide this in the dresser drawer, and then hurry up to my room before anyone spots the delivery and asks me what it is.

Closing the door firmly behind me, I sit on my bed and start to pull the brown paper from the parcel, unearthing two flat Nicole Farhi boxes. The first

148

contains a beautiful terracotta-colour jumper, of the softest lambs' wool. The second a gorgeous pair of cream velvet trousers. There is a note from Petra inside the second box: *The trousers are from me. Tell her they're from her Auntie Petra and hopefully she'll be so shocked, she'll lose the power of speech for at least one day, giving you a memorable birthday present too!*

Laughing, I unearth the wrapping paper and the card that I bought in Penzance on my way to get the puppy, wrap the two boxes individually and then, going to my case, I pull out an old jewellery box from the inside zip lock, and wrap this as well, putting the two boxes with the rest of Cas's presents under my bed, but placing the jewellery case in the top drawer of my bedside table.

Sunday morning dawns, bright, clear and cold. The house is strangely quiet. I can normally hear some activity – Cas in the bathroom, Laura in the kitchen – but today there is nothing, just a silence that hangs in the air like a presence.

Cas hasn't mentioned her birthday at all. I think she expects it to be a bit of a non-event this year, despite the fact that it is her sixteenth. Because it was so near Christmas, Rob always tried to do something extra-special to make her birthday stand out from the frenzied blur of Christmas festivity.

I'm a bit limited geographically, but in an attempt to emulate her father in some small way, I've really gone to town on her presents, totally over the top in price and quantity. I know I'm an idiot, I know that in some way I'm trying to buy her affection, even though I'd deny it vehemently to anyone who dared suggest the idea. Despite the recognition of my foolish generosity, even now as a last gesture I slip a cheque for one hundred pounds inside her birthday card, and seal it quickly before I can change my mind.

It's funny. I celebrated my sixteenth birthday here too.

But instead of clothes, make-up, magazines or music, the usual teenage wants, I used the money I was given for my birthday to buy my train ticket to London. My ticket to freedom, or so I thought back then.

Cas seems so young. And yet it was at that same age that I left to forge a life on my own. They say that children and teenagers grow up more quickly in this day and age. I don't agree with that. I think they just take more liberties and have a louder opinion, which they're happy to voice at all times, giving them an air of adulthood that they don't actually possess.

I can't imagine Cas being able to look after herself. Or maybe it's because I'm older myself now that she seems so young, and so incapable of being on her own.

The door between the bottom of the stairs and the kitchen is shut. I push it open to be promptly pounced upon by Laura, who is wearing a pointed striped party hat. A party blower blares out from her mouth.

'Surprise!!!' she yells, showering me with a handful of confetti, and then drops the party blower as she realises it is me and not Cas. 'Oh good, it's you. I thought you were going to miss the fun.' She kicks the door shut with her foot and reaches behind her into a box on the dresser. 'Here, put this on and get ready. She must have finished in the bathroom at least an hour ago, so she should be down any minute. Heaven knows what she's been doing up there for so long, and so quiet as well.' Laura hands me a party hat, and a plastic horn.

She has decorated the kitchen with balloons and streamers, and a banner that says *Happy Birthday* is stretched across the wooden lintel above the fireplace. The table is piled high with the presents we have been hiding for the past week, and a bottle of champagne with a bow tied around its green neck, along with five glasses, sits next to a jug of orange juice.

I can smell fresh croissants warming in the oven, and to my surprise and delight, instead of the usual teapot, an old percolator has been unearthed and is currently spitting small drops of water into a filter jug full of real coffee. Even Meg is sitting expectantly on the rug by the fire, her fur brushed neatly, a matching bow around her neck.

'Wow, you have worked hard, haven't you? You should have woken me, I'd have helped.'

'Well, I must admit the balloons took a while, but you were sleeping so peacefully when I looked in this morning that I didn't want to wake you. I'm surprised Cas isn't down yet though. I heard her having her shower simply ages ago. It must be an hour at least.'

I picture Cas sitting alone in her room on her sixteenth birthday, and suddenly feel desperately sorry for her. I remember how lonely I used to feel in this house, and at least I had my own mother here, no matter how distant she was. I must make more of an effort with Cassie. I smile at Laura, put on my party hat and pick up the box of confetti that she has left on the side.

There are soft footfalls on the stairs.

'Quick, quick,' Laura hisses, elbowing me with excitement. 'Here she comes now.' We both shuffle to where Laura was originally hiding behind the door before I came in.

The door creaks open.

'Surprise!!!'

We spring out from our hiding place, throwing more confetti, Laura's blower squealing, me honking my horn.

For a moment Cas looks as startled and about as pleased as a rabbit about to be hit by a speeding car, and then her pale face breaks into a huge smile as we both yell, 'Happy Birthday!' and rush to hug her.

Cas hugs Laura hard, me briefly, and then wriggles out of my embrace like an eel, happy to be taken by the arm by an over-excited Laura and led to the table which is groaning under the weight of her presents.

'Me first, me first!' Laura cries, picking up the closest

parcel and handing it to her. Laura has bought her a book on horse care, a pair of jodhpurs, to replace the tatty old jeans she's been wearing to ride out in, a pair of riding gloves and her own hard hat. She's been borrowing an ancient one of Laura's that is a touch too big for her, and has a tendency to slip over her eyes at crucial moments.

Cas puts on the riding hat, making Laura laugh, and opens the envelope from her grandmother. There is a brief message inside the card, wishing Cas a very happy birthday and saying how much Louisa wishes she were with us. This Cas reads aloud to us; a longer letter that accompanies the card, she puts aside to read when on her own. Louisa has also sent her a cheque for a hundred pounds, which Cas waves delightedly at Laura before folding and slipping it into her back pocket. When it comes to my heap of presents, Cas's eyes open wide with a sort of wary incredulity.

I have bought her the jumper, a pair of expensive leather fashion boots Laura told me she admired when they were out shopping, a new pair of Levi's, a personal CD player, some CDs to go with it, and some small diamond earrings.

'Are they real?' Cas asks in disbelief, holding them up to her ears in the large mirror above the fireplace.

'Uhuh.' I nod. 'Do you like them?'

'They're really pretty. You must have spent a fortune.'

The way she says this makes it feel like a chastisement. She has an air of nonchalance about my gifts that is both infuriating and belittling, opening each with a strange knowing look, as though she were Hercule Poirot unearthing evidence in a murder case that backs up his already thought out theory on 'whodunnit'.

*I know you're trying to buy me and it's not going to work.*

I hand her the last box. 'This is from Petra.'

She looks at me in disbelief. I almost expect her to say, 'Are you sure?' but she simply takes the box and begins to open it, throwing me wary glances every so often as though I'm playing a trick on her, and she's expecting the box to blow up as soon as it's opened or something.

Of course it doesn't, and as she pulls the velvet jeans from their layers of tissue paper, the surprised concerned look gives way to a surprised pleased one.

'They're really nice,' she says in disbelief.

'They go with your jumper.'

'Thanks.'

'Don't thank me, thank Petra, next time we speak, yeah?'

'Okay.' Cas nods unconvincingly.

The tuneless horn of Betsy echoing around the yard, tells us that Orlaithe and Hank have arrived, bringing with them the puppy. I cheer up a little. She can't help but love the puppy, he's totally adorable. I even had Orlaithe on the telephone the night Hank took him home to ask where I got him from, because she and Hank were considering adopting one of his brothers or sisters.

Laura opens the door for them, as they stagger through under the weight of their packages.

Whenever Orlaithe walks into a room it's as though someone has just flooded the place with laughing gas, with her bright copper hair, ever-present smile, and infectious cheer. She is currently grinning like a banshee and singing a rousing chorus of 'Happy Birthday', Hank humming along in the background. Hank is carrying a large box, and so is Orlaithe, who also has a gift-wrapped parcel on top of this and another under her left arm.

'Apparently the cake's in one, and the puppy's in the other,' Laura whispers with a grin. 'I just hope we don't get them confused and take the cake for a walk and try and stick candles in the dog!'

It's a pathetic joke to try and make me smile, but I am more than grateful for it. Cassie's somewhat blasé acceptance of my gifts did not go unnoticed.

'Happy Birthday, sweetheart.' Orlaithe puts her parcels down on the table, and sweeps Cas into her arms for
a hug and two kisses, one to either cheek.

Hank is still standing uncertainly in the doorway
looking smart if a little stiff in his best starched shirt and
navy jeans. Laura draws him inside and closes the door
behind him, then gestures excitedly for me to come and
take the box he is carrying.

Orlaithe has really gone to town. The open box has
been gift-wrapped, and as I peer inside I can see that the
puppy is now wearing a huge blue ribbon around his
neck.

'Cas.'

Cassie looks over Orlaithe's shoulder.

'This is from me. And Laura,' I add, wanting my
mother to take some credit, as it was she who persuaded
me to buy him.

Laura looks pleased and mouths, 'Thank you,' at me.

Cas walks hesitantly over, a little overwhelmed I think
by the attention and the number of gifts. She runs a
hand through her short faded pink hair and then
reaches out to take the box, jumping back as the puppy
chooses this moment to try and escape, scrabbling
upwards and onwards like a wayward jack-in-a-box.

I gently catch him round the middle to stop him
falling to the floor, and hold him out to Cas with a stupid
grin on my face, but she simply stands and stares at me
as though I'm trying to get her to clear out Chance's
loose-box with her bare hands.

'Another dog!' she drawls insolently. 'There are
already far too many of the stupid things around the
place already.'

Laura and I exchange unhappy glances.

I stand there awkwardly, still clutching onto the
puppy who, oblivious to his less than warm reception
from his new mistress, is attempting to lick away all of
my make-up.

Orlaithe wades in to save the moment. 'Here, why don't you open this one.' She puts an arm around Cas's shoulders and steers her away from me and the puppy and back to the table. 'It's from me and Hank, so it is.'

Laura comes and takes the puppy from me as I stare open-mouthed after Cas. Rolling her eyes to heaven, and shaking her head in sympathy, she puts him down on the rug next to Meg, who casually bends to sniff at the newcomer with a curious disinterest. I feel a warm and reassuring hand on my shoulder, and turn in surprise at the sound of an unfamiliar voice.

'She'll come around soon enough. You'll see.'

I think those are the first words Hank has ever spoken in my presence. I can't decide whether to cheer, faint with surprise, or slink into a corner to lick my wounds, whilst Cas goes into raptures over Hank and Orlaithe's gifts, and studiously ignores the tiny Labrador, who is wobbling slightly on the rug, his big eyes full of bewilderment.

Cas is currently examining a scrap of silver material that Orlaithe informs us is actually a dress, with great and obvious delight. The next present turns out to be a pair of high-heeled strappy silver sandals to go with it, which Cas promptly puts on over her pink stripy socks, tottering around the room in heels and her hard hat, making everyone else roar with laughter.

Laura opens the champagne bottle with gusto, shooting the cork so hard from the neck that it makes a dent in the ceiling, the liquid frothing and foaming onto the floor until Orlaithe rushes to capture it with a glass.

They both hand round glasses, Orlaithe and my mother, and aim more sympathetic smiles in my direction, and then Orlaithe turns her attention to the second box.

'And now for the *pièce de résistance*, even if I do say so myself. Drum roll, please, Francis.'

Hank uses two strong brown fingers to tap out a drum

roll on the kitchen table as Orlaithe opens up the other box and pulls out a huge lurid pink cake. It's an extraordinary thing, and it takes me a little while to work out exactly what it's meant to be. And then I realise it is an exact, life-size, although in 2D instead of 3D, copy of the puppy. A bright pink Andrex puppy, with a black fondant icing tongue.

'Ta da!' she flourishes it before us, her face lit up with pride.

This version of the puppy gets a much better reception than the original.

'A cake!' Cas exclaims. 'I'm far too old for a cake!' But she's smiling as she says it, and doesn't take much persuading to blow out the sixteen candles, to a huge round of applause.

'Happy Birthday to you, Happy Birthday to you,' Orlaithe begins to sing again.

Laura hands Cas a long knife, and as she sinks it into the icing, Laura flicks the switch on her tape recorder and Stevie Wonder starts to sing his own rousing version of the birthday song.

'Happy Birthday to you, Happy Birthday . . .'

Party poppers bang, streamers flying over the birthday girl to tangle in her hair and wind around her shoulders in multicoloured layers. There's the flash of a camera bulb as my mother takes a photograph, the sound of crystal against crystal as a toast is proposed, loud laughter, excited exclamations, and yet all I can hear is the hollow echo of the emptiness I feel, knowing that Cas, the only living part of Rob I have left, can feel nothing of the love he felt for me, only a sad, destructive hate.

It is early evening. Hank and Orlaithe have gone home, Orlaithe more than a little merry on champagne, Hank replete from at least five slices of birthday cake. Laura is seated by the fire, the puppy fast asleep on her lap, her own eyes threatening to close; she is tired from the day, the warmth, and the effects of the champagne. Cas is curled up at her feet, the earphones of her new CD player firmly over her ears, the tinny sound of the volume turned to high the only noise in the kitchen apart from the odd crackle of burning logs in the grate.

There is one remaining gift that I haven't given to Cas. It's in my pocket. It's been there all day, the solid weight awkward and obvious against the flesh of my thigh, a constant thorn pricking the so-far still-inflated bubble of my indecision.

I didn't know whether I should give this final gift to Cas. My intentions are good, but that doesn't mean she'll take the gesture the right way at all. Knowing Cas, she'll find the wrong in it, rather than the right, rather than the pleasure I'm hoping to give her.

'Cas.' I speak before I can change my mind.

Laura's eyes blink open, but Cas doesn't hear me.

'*Cas*,' I call a little louder.

Cas looks up and takes off her headphones.

'There's one more thing I wanted to give you.' I walk over to her holding the gift out for her to take.

'You've already given me enough,' she states flatly.

'Please, take it.'

Laura raises her eyebrows in question, but I am watching Cas's face as she unwraps the paper, and opens the small velvet box. Inside is a watch. A man's watch, an old Cartier with a brown leather strap, a handsome watch, but not so masculine that a girl could not wear it.

'It was your father's.'

'I know,' Cas murmurs, running a thumb over the glass of the watch face.

'I had it restored. I thought you might like to have it.'

Her eyes have filled with tears.

'I hope . . . I mean, I . . . I wanted you to have something of his . . .'

157

Cas pushes past me and runs to the kitchen door, tugging it open with a blind and clumsy urgency, before fleeing into the darkness of the yard. I go to follow her, but Laura's hand on my arm restrains me.

'Let her be.'

'But . . .'

'She needs some time to be alone with her thoughts. You understand, don't you? Today's been hard for her.'

'It's been hard for me too. Don't you think I know the one thing she wants for her birthday is the one thing that I can't give her? That I can *never* give her! How do you think that makes me feel?' Laura pulls me into an embrace and although I fight against the comfort she is trying to give me, I finally rest my head against her shoulder for a brief moment before she allows me to pull away again.

Half an hour later Cas comes back in.

Very quietly she opens the door, walks across the room and hugs Laura, hard, announcing that she is really tired and if we don't mind she's going to go up to bed. She says thank you for the day, and for her gifts, as Laura plants a gentle kiss on her forehead, and then turns to me and puts out a tentative hand. Blinking with surprise, I reach out and take it with my own, squeezing her hand gently. Then to my bewilderment, she steps quickly forward and hugs me briefly.

I notice as she heads up the Stairs that Rob's watch is clasped firmly about her left wrist.

I cannot sleep again that night.

At two in the morning I am still huddled in the window seat staring out into the night, my body so weary, but my mind racing with what feels like a thousand disturbing thoughts. And yet I know they are only the same things running over and over again in my head like a scratched record.

158

Once more I find myself reaching for pen and paper.

*Dear Rob,*
*It was Cassie's birthday today. I tried to make it right for*
*her, but I think I blew it. I wish I knew how to make her*
*happy, how to turn things around so that we can be*
*friends.*

*Beneath her icy exterior I know there is just a fright-*
*ened little girl, who's lost almost everything in the world*
*that she cares about. I remember, too, how it felt to lose my*
*father when I was six years old. It was hard for me so for*
*a hormonal, emotional, unhappy fourteen-year-old it*
*must have been doubly difficult.*

*But I don't know what she wants from me.*

*She doesn't attempt to be friends, choosing to ignore me*
*wherever possible. I don't know which is worse, when she*
*blanks me, or when she deigns to speak, in order to*
*ridicule me.*

*No, Cas does nothing to encourage me to love, or even*
*like her, and yet I so want to. Worse still, I want her to like*
*me. Not just for your sake, but for hers, and my own. I*
*know I resented my mother when I was her age, but I'm*
*not her mother. I don't really know what I am to her. An*
*annoyance – I know that much! In her eyes, I have no*
*right to tell her what to do, how to behave. In her head,*
*I'm not attempting to guide her for her own good, I'm*
*interfering for my own perverse pleasure. If only she knew*
*how much I hate having to do so. I'd stand back and let*
*her get on with her life as she sees fit, if only I didn't feel*
*this need, deep inside me, to steer her in the right*
*direction.*

*I feel like a small boat struggling to sail against the*
*wind. I keep thinking I've moved forward, and then I find*
*I have gained no ground at all. I wish you were here, Rob,*
*you'd know what I should do.*

*Love always,*
*N x*

★ ★ ★

This letter is folded and sealed and placed with the first and I climb into bed feeling a little better, ready to try again with Cas, and to keep trying, no matter how badly I seem to be doing.

# Chapter Five

Two days after her birthday, Cassie stumbles downstairs, rubbing sleep from her eyes, her blonde hair sticking up in spikes, jeans pulled on over her pyjamas. She pours herself a glass of milk, and steals a slice of toast from Laura's plate, attempting to drink and eat whilst shrugging on her jacket.

'I've done the chores,' Laura tells her.

'Oh right, thanks.'

'And I've fed and watered Chance,' she adds quickly, as Cas automatically begins to pull on her riding boots.

Cassie stops and looks at Laura in question. 'But why?'

'We're going out for the day. Thought we'd have a little belated party for your birthday.'

'But we had a party *on* my birthday,' Cas frowns.

'Okay, so it's just an excuse for a booze-up,' Laura admits cheerfully. 'Well, a picnic actually.'

'A picnic? It's the middle of winter – we can't go on a picnic.'

'Nonsense, it's a beautiful day. It's perfect.' My mother pulls Cas to the window, and breathes in deeply as though trying to fill her lungs with fresh air, despite the fact that the window is shut. 'Just look at that sunshine.'

She lets go of the girl's hand. 'Now go and have a shower and put something warm on, there's a good girl, while Nattie and I get everything ready.'

Cas pulls a face, but heads up the stairs nonetheless.

Laura turns to me. I'm still sitting at the kitchen table.

'Come on then, what are you waiting for?'

'I'm inclined to agree with Cas. It's the middle of winter, hardly picnic weather.'

My mother tilts her head to one side and gives me one of her old-fashioned looks, the kind she uses on Luke to get him out of the kitchen when tea break is well and truly over, but I'm determined it won't work on me. The last thing I feel like doing today is shivering on a blanket in the middle of a field whilst my mother sits there in a T-shirt, feeds us cucumber sandwiches and tells us that the chill we're feeling is purely psychological.

'Don't be such a wet blanket, Nattie. It'll be fun. If you look in the cupboard under the sink you'll find a cool box.'

'Ooh good, I can sit in that to keep warm,' I reply sarcastically.

Ignoring me, Laura turns and opening the fridge door begins to rummage inside. 'It might be a bit dusty – it'll probably need a wash-down. I haven't used it since Harvest Festival.'

'Oh great, it'll probably be full of rotting vegetables.'

'No, but there might be a few bottles of Stella rolling round in the bottom.'

'Beer in church?'

'Of course. You get red wine, don't you? Why not beer for those that don't drink plonk? In fact he's a very progressive Vicar, Reverend Stanley. I think he even mentioned putting optics up along the altar for those who fancied something a bit stronger at Holy Communion. You know, drag the drinkers in for Sunday service, better than them propping up a bar somewhere.'

I drop the shocked expression as it dawns on me with this last bit of pastoral information that she's only joking. She turns back to me, hands full, and pushes the fridge door shut with her backside. 'No, seriously, the bottles were for the harvest supper at the Church Hall. The

Reverend is quite a forward thinker but I don't think turning the church into a fun pub would be quite his style. He's a lovely man though. You'll have to meet him sometime – I think you'd like him. As a friend,' she adds as she sees my eyes narrow at this comment. 'I only meant as a friend. He's married with about nineteen children.'

Taking the cool box from me, she removes the lid, and peers inside, sighing in disappointment. 'No beer. That means we'll have to stop off on the way.' She wipes out the inside before placing the large greaseproof-paper-wrapped packages she took from the fridge inside it. 'Nat, there's an old picnic hamper on top of the wardrobe in your bedroom – would you get it down for me?'

I go upstairs. The door to the attic stairs swings open as I reach my room. Glancing back I see Cas step through and head down the second flight of stairs to the kitchen, hair still slightly damp from her shower, warm in burgundy boot-cut cords, and I'm amazed yet pleased to see the sweater I bought her for her birthday. I got the distinct impression she didn't like it, so to see her actually wearing it cheers me greatly.

In my room, I can see the picnic hamper perched on top of the old wooden wardrobe. It's an old-fashioned wicker basket, with a handle made of plaited rope. Funny, but I hadn't noticed it there before. I can't quite reach it, so pull the chair from the corner of the room, and stand on it.

There is something else on top of the wardrobe as well as the picnic basket. A green shoe box, very old, but still with the drawing of the shoes it once contained stuck to the side. Size four leather courts with the stylish name of Olivia. Easily recognisable from the distinctly 1950s-style of shoe as a pair that once belonged to my mother. The box is tied with a pale green ribbon, and a note scrawled on top in thick black marker pen in my mother's handwriting states *Important, Do Not Throw* with three exclamation marks to follow.

My curiosity is instant, but not insatiable. Probably more photographs. Definitely not shoes any more. To leave shoes unworn in a box would be pure sacrilege to my mother. They should be worn, displayed to the world and appreciated as works of art.

I pull the hamper from the dusty surface, and with only a moment's hesitation over looking inside the shoe box, head back downstairs. The open kitchen door tells me that Cas is now outside. My mother is just putting down the telephone receiver.

'Thought we'd make a party of it,' she tells me, but doesn't say who she was calling.

While Laura checks the hamper, refilling the tiny glass salt cellar and pepper pot with fresh, and rinsing the six plates, glasses and cutlery sets that it contains, I take the thickest jacket I possess from the hat stand, and go out into the yard to load the now full cool box into the back of the Land Rover.

Cas is placing fresh hay in Chance's hay net, despite the fact that Laura has already filled it almost to bursting, chatting to him while she works, as he blows eagerly at her hands, determined that as well as hay, there is also room for his muzzle in the blue netting. Finished, she reaches around the open top half of the stable door, and hangs the net back on the small hook set there for this purpose, then leaning in towards Chance who is beginning to pull at the hay with yellow teeth, uses the sleeve of her one hundred pound sweater to wipe a large blob of green sleep from the corner of one of his black eyes.

My pleasure at the fact she's actually wearing my gift takes a dip. Why didn't I just buy her one of those throwaway things, from a cheap high street shop, the sort of garment that most of her contemporaries would be wearing? I can feel my anger build. I know it's only a little thing that shouldn't really matter, but it's indicative of the contempt with which she treats me. I almost call out to her, but then I see Cas check herself, and look down at her sleeve in horror as she realises what has happened. She pulls a handkerchief from her trouser pocket and begins to rub furiously at her sleeve, muttering to Chance about what a mess he's made of her gorgeous new jumper.

And suddenly I am angry with myself instead of her. We really need to talk. I can't let my frustration build inside me like hot lava in a volcano, just waiting to erupt and cause major devastation. The problem is, Cas and I don't talk. It's just something we don't do.

Laura comes out of the house, pulls the kitchen door to behind her and locks it with the great brass key, which she then places in the tin bucket full of winter flowers that hangs by the side of the door. She turns to me, the hamper clutched in one hand, heavy, making her stoop a little to the left.

'Everybody ready then?' she beams.

I pick up the cool box from where I had placed it on the cobbles whilst watching Cas, and open the rear doors of the small jeep.

'Now where are those bloody dogs?' Laura looks around for Meg, and Young Shep, who seems to be with us on an extended visit at the moment.

Cas has rechristened Young Shep. She announced that it was bad enough having an old Shep, and it was no wonder that Young Shep behaved like a slightly dense adolescent when he didn't even have a name he could be proud of. The fact that she now calls him Jasper, or Jas to be precise, because he reminds her of her best friend's 'arse of a younger brother' probably hasn't done the poor animal's self-esteem any favours though.

Laura thought he might get confused if we changed his name, to which logic Cas replied that he was already permanently confused so a little more confusion wouldn't hurt him. As the dog refuses to respond to whatever you call him, I feel it won't hurt, and after all I must admit 'Jas!' is easier and far less embarrassing to yell than 'Young Shep!'

As I put the box inside the dusty junk-filled rear of the motor, Meg and Jasper appear as if from nowhere and pushing past me, jump into the back to sit side by side next to it. They are smiling in that beaming way dogs do, panting and eager, aware by some clairvoyant canine instinct that today we are going on a trip – probably aided in this opinion by the appearance of the cool box, which Jasper promptly puts a wet nose to, to see if he can smell what's inside through the thick dimpled blue plastic.

Laura is already in the driving seat, reaching inside the open-fronted glove compartment for the red screwdriver. I climb in next to her, as she thrusts the screwdriver into the broken ignition.

'One day you're going to push that in too far and electrocute yourself,' I mutter in concern.

'When I win the lottery I shall buy myself a nice new one.'

'Range Rover?'

'No – screwdriver.'

'You need a new car,' Cas agrees as she squeezes in beside me, clutching a wriggling excited puppy to her chest. Her jumper is now thankfully protected by an old jacket.

'Well, why don't I just pop down to the showrooms and pick myself up a brand new Ferrari?'

'I'll lend you the money. I've got plenty.'

My mother and I both look quickly across at Cas, eyes narrowed, but she is staring resolutely ahead through the muddy windscreen. It's the first time Cas has ever made any reference to her inheritance, which is substantial, but the majority of which is in trust until she is twenty-five. She gets a very generous monthly allowance, her school fees are paid, and I receive an amount to cover the cost of keeping her for the time that she is with me – clothes, food, bills etc. – most of which I've stuck in an account in her name, as I hardly ever see her. Of course there are clauses that mean she can break that Trust with the agreement of her executor – *ie* me – if she ever wanted a lump sum for something, say a small car when she passes her test, or a holiday, or maybe an expensive school trip that would otherwise be too much, but so far she has never asked me for anything, nor even mentioned the fact that the money exists.

Laura raises her eyebrows at me, and then smiles at Cas. 'Thank you, Cas. That's very sweet of you. But this old bus and I have been together for a long time, haven't we, darling?' Laura pats the dusty dashboard affectionately. 'Through thick and thin, mud and flood. I think I'll stick with her for another few years at least.'

We stop at the village shop for beer. I go in with Laura, and whilst she prevaricates over the different brews, pick up a couple of bottles of wine, a cheap corkscrew and some plastic cups, then when I get to the counter, ask the assistant to hand me a large box of chocolates from the cigarette-laden shelf behind her.

What the hell – if I'm going to freeze my butt off in the great outdoors, I'm going to do it in style. Cheap white Rioja or a rough Chianti out of those white plastic cups that split when you grip them too hard after a couple of glasses have warmed your toes and made you desperate for a pee behind a bush somewhere, and a box of Black Magic: what more could a girl want?

Laura drives down toward Land's End, turning off at Sennen onto the narrow coastal road that leads down into the Cove.

'This is where the dolphins often swim,' she announces, stepping heavily on her non-existent brakes as she takes a sharp right turn into a long sloping car park.

'Seriously?' Cas questions, immediately looking out to sea.

'Absolutely. I've seen them here quite a few times.'

Pulling to a halt by a low wall of crumbling grey stone, she wrenches on the unreliable handbrake, then stepping out of the car, puts a brick that lives under the seat, in front of the rear wheel. Coming back to the still open door, she reaches into a side pocket and pulls out a leather case.

'Binoculars,' she explains, handing them across me to Cas, 'just in case we're lucky.'

Getting out of the car I see that Hank's Betsy is parked a couple of spaces away, and looking down on the beach, spot Orlaithe perched on a bright pink blanket, her flame-red hair streaming behind her in the breeze that's skipping like a stone across the small white peaks of a calm ocean. She turns and spotting the Land Rover, waves to us enthusiastically.

Laura opens the back doors and the dogs spill out, barking excitedly. Racing away from us, they jump the low wall to join the path below, which slopes down to the beach. They speed down the path and onto the beach, kicking up sand in their wake as they run eagerly into the sea, soaking the long hair of their black and white bodies before racing all the way back up to us to shake and soak and sniff around the picnic basket once more.

Still clutching my carrier bag with the wine and chocolate, I take the cool box from the rear of the Land Rover then walk back around the front to wait for Laura and Cas who are getting the rest of the things from the car.

I think Sennen Cove must be one of the prettiest places in England. To my left is the long promenade, an endless front of small grey or white cottages with huge windows like pretty little does with large blinking eyes, at the end of which sits the Lifeboat Centre sheltered by the greeny-brown curve of the stone harbour wall. To my right is the beach: Whitesands. A pretty arc of palest sand that runs for almost a mile along the coast, so beautiful even the great churning waves of the Atlantic are tamed here to a caressing gentleness.

There are no sheer cliff faces here; instead the land drops steeply from above in a tumble of brown earth and the rich green and white of the sea grass which clings to it in great fronds. I breathe in deeply, filling my lungs with the cold fresh salty air. Perhaps Laura's idea wasn't as insane as it first seemed. Yes, it's cold, but somehow here it doesn't seem to be as biting; the sun is peering around the edge of a smattering of white mashed-potato cloud, and it's breathtakingly beautiful, the kind of place where you just want to sit and stare at the stunning nature around you, soak it into your skin as though it will soften the harshness of life.

Cas comes and stands beside me. She has the picnic basket in one hand, and a red tartan rug under the other arm.

'What a gorgeous place,' she murmurs.

For a moment I think she is speaking to me, but when I turn sideways to look at her, she is staring ahead, thoughts lost in the deep aquamarine of the ocean, and it is obvious she is simply saying aloud what I am thinking to myself.

Laura is finally ready. She emerges from the back of the Landy, carrier bag full of beer bottles in her left hand, a huge white box balanced a little precariously on the palm of the other. Not wanting to walk the length of the car park to get onto the path below, she places both items on the wall, and swings herself over, dropping carefully the four feet or so downwards, before retrieving them.

'Come on then.' She grins up at us, as Cas and I both hesitate. 'What are you waiting for?'

Cas smiles at Laura and with the poise of the ballerina

that she is, jumps lightly over the wall. As usual the athletic strength of such a willowy slender body surprises me as she simply carries the basket and the blanket over with her. Jasper follows. Within seconds he has sprinted the two hundred or so yards back into the sea and is chasing foam horses again. The only one who waits for me is Meg, looking up at me from the path with her solemn black eyes, urging me to follow her.

Lowering the cool box over the edge I then proceed to climb over the wall myself, using the blue box as a step to shorten the height I have to drop. I'm not worried for me. Heights don't bother me normally, but I'm carrying a precious cargo. The wine bottles clank together reassuringly as I follow the footprints of the others down the beach to join them.

Orlaithe beams at me broadly as I come close enough to make out her features. She is perched squarely on a huge soft pink blanket, resplendent in a fake fur coat, that is wound so tightly about her body, and so firmly rooted beneath her legs and backside that I'm sure she'd have trouble moving if she tried. Perched on her head, doing nothing to stem the attempted escape of those tight titian curls, which are sailing on the breeze like an unfurled banner, is a hat of the same material. She looks like a large fluffy bear with a pink face and red lipstick.

'Nattie, darlin'! How the devil are ye? What blessed idiots we are to be out in this weather, but what fun we'll have, eh? Laura's picnics are absolutely legendary, although 'tis only a small gathering today. Do you know, I'm sure your mother invented the overnight rave party, so she did. The last time we did this there must have been at least a hundred of us, and the music and the drinking went on until the sun went to bed and then came back up again to join us once more the next mornin'.'

'She's exaggerating as usual.' Laura grins as she lays down the tartan rug alongside the fuchsia one. 'There certainly weren't a hundred people.'

'All right – about fifty of us then,' Orlaithe counters. 'Although I'm sure we drank enough for a hundred!' She pats the place on the blanket next to her. 'Come and sit beside me, Nattie. Let me great backside be a wind-break for you – you've no fat of your own to keep out the chill, that's for sure. Look at you, I couldn't get one of me arms inside that jumper, and as for those jeans, there's about enough room for a third of my backside.'

She scrutinises my jeans-clad rear as I bend to place my box and my bag on the floor. 'No, make that a third of a third of me backside.'

I sit down beside her and begin to rummage in my plastic bag. 'I can't believe how warm it is here. It's as if we're in a different country.'

'It's sheltered here, by the rocks on either side.' Orlaithe points to the west and to the east. 'That's why the dolphins come. The waters are warmer here than anywhere else along this part of the coast.'

'Have you seen them too?' Cas asks her, suddenly remembering the binoculars she has thrown over one shoulder and uncasing them.

'Many times,' nods Orlaithe, 'and seals too – although they're usually further up the coast off Hells Mouth.'

Cas sits down in front of us and puts the glasses to her eyes. 'Oh my goodness!' she exclaims.

We all look up and strain to see where her glasses are pointed.

'What is it?' Laura asks her. 'Have you seen something?'

'Over there!' Cas points and we follow the direction of her finger to make out a black head bobbing through the water.

'That's a dolphin?' I ask in disbelief.

'No, it's that stupid dog!' Cas puts down the glasses and I can see that she is smiling. 'Jasper. He must be at least half a mile out by now.'

'He's probably chasing a buoy,' my mother replies,

unconcerned. 'He thinks they're balls, you see.'

'Will he be all right?' Orlaithe asks in concern. 'He's one heck of a long way out.'

'He'll be fine,' Laura replies. 'Beer, any one?'

I'm watching Cas. I don't see her smile often enough. I know it's a cliché to say it, but it completely transforms her face. I wish I could make her smile. I only seem to have the opposite effect though. Even now, as she catches me watching her, the smile slips into oblivion. Embarrassed, I return my attention to the wine. The white is too warm and the red is too cold, so I refuse my mother's offer of a bottle of Stella, throw caution to the wind and open both.

'Where's Hank?'

'The lads are off over the rocks collecting driftwood,' Orlaithe explains. 'They've been gone a while though. A girl could've caught her death waiting for them to come back.' She refuses a beer and accepts a glass of warm white wine. 'Hank's going to be an In'jun instead of a cowboy for once and start a fire for us.'

'Lads?' I query the plural.

'Connor's with him.'

'Oh good, he decided to come then,' Laura chirps happily.

'You didn't tell me *he* was coming,' I find myself snapping.

My mother looks at me curiously for a moment and then laughs. 'Don't tell me you're still embarrassed about the first time you met him. I'm sure he's forgotten all about that.'

'Forgotten about what?' Orlaithe asks, her eyes bright with interest. 'What happened the first time you met him?'

'It's a long story.' I try to fob her off. 'And very boring.'

Orlaithe looks over at Laura who is trying to suppress her laughter. 'I like long stories, and from the look on

172

your mother's face it's far from boring.'

Whilst I cringe into my plastic cup, Laura tells Orlaithe about the first time I ever met Connor Blythe.

'He saw your *arse*?' Orlaithe shouts far too loudly when Laura gets to the most embarrassing part of the tale.

I nod, certain that my cheeks are now as bright red as Orlaithe's hair.

Orlaithe tuts and shakes her head. 'No wonder you don't want to be seeing him again. Perhaps he should show you *his* to redress the balance,' she jokes.

'Er, I don't think so.' I laugh uncomfortably.

'Well, *I'd* certainly like to see his arse.' Orlaithe winks heavily at me. 'Those sweet young firm cheeks encased in denim.' She takes a long draught from her wine. 'Ooh, if only I were ten years younger, and didn't have a man I couldn't possibly cheat on because I love his kind, sweet-natured, bow-legged little body to death . . .'

Not at all amused by the turn of the conversation, Cas has got up from the rug and is introducing a bemused yet excited puppy to the sea. He's never seen it this close to before, and isn't quite sure what to do with it or about it, especially when he bends to sniff and gets salt water on his delicate little black nose, which he automatically licks with a small pink tongue. Deciding that salt water doesn't actually taste too awful, he returns to the water's edge for a deeper drink, only to be chased back up the beach by a wave, with a look of total astonishment on his face.

Cas follows him back up, scooping him into her arms, his paws leaving sand prints on the black padded jacket she has pulled on over her sweater.

'It's only water, Stupid,' she tells him. 'Look at Jas – that's what you're supposed to do with it, although,' she adds, as Jas appears to swim even further away from us, 'maybe he's not the best example for you to follow.'

Laura looks up at this and spotting how far out Jasper

actually is now, whistles sharply. We all stand. Even Orlaithe the bear struggles to her booted feet and hollers.

Two figures appear from the rocks to my right. At the sound of our panicked voices they break into a trot and then a run. As they come closer I see that the person lagging behind is Hank, resplendent in the black Stetson he wears on days off.

The other figure, making better headway on the soft sand, is Connor. He skids to a halt beside us, breathless, worried. 'What's going on? What's all the yelling about?'

Cas points out to where Jasper is steadfastly beginning the first solo dog journey across the Atlantic.

'Is that all? The dog's having a swim? You scared us. I thought we were going to have to call out the lifeboat.'

'We still might.' Laura's face is pinched with concern.

Connor shakes his head and putting his little fingers to either side of his mouth, whistles so shrilly that Orlaithe, Cas and I cover our ears at the sound. As if by magic, Jasper pauses, and then executes a perfect U-turn, beginning to slowly doggy-paddle his way back in the right direction toward the beach.

'Stupid dog,' my mother sighs, but she's laughing again.

'Do you know something? I don't think he's as stupid as we make out.' Cas looks at Laura in question. 'I think he might just be a little deaf. You know when you tell him to sit or something, and he just looks at you with his head to one side, and this daft grin on his face. But if you do the Barbara Woodhouse thing – with your hand as well,' Cas demonstrates with her right hand, 'he always sits then.'

'The girl might have a good point there.' Connor nods.

Cassie heads down to the water's edge to test out her theory by encouraging Jasper to swim to shore with enthusiastic hand claps.

Minor incident over, Orlaithe turns to admonish

Hank. 'Where on earth have you been?'

As usual Hank responds with little more than a raising of his bushy eyebrows, so Connor replies for him. 'There's plenty of wood on the shore, but not most of it dry. We had to go beyond Farmer's Point, almost back to the Loft.'

'Connor lives in an old farm cottage, just beyond the furthest point,' Laura tells me, pointing into the distance. 'You can't see it from here, but if you go round the next bay, just beyond the last one you can see . . .'

Connor is smiling at me. 'Hello, Natalie Forester. How are you?' He kneels down in front of me, placing the bundle of wood carefully next to our blanket.

'She's cold, aren't you, darlin'?' interjects Orlaithe. 'Like the rest of us. Oh well. At least the wine's warm.' She winks a green-painted eye at me, raises her plastic cup to her lips again, and drains it, then hands it to me for a refill.

Connor smiles indulgently at Orlaithe, and begins to lay out a circle of stones, a little way from the blankets. He takes a little sand from within their circumference, making sure that he doesn't go down deep enough to encounter wet sand, and fills it with the wood that he and Hank have collected. First the smaller branches, the twigs, along with some screwed-up balls of newspaper, then the larger branches on top. Pulling a box of firelighters from the pocket of his abandoned jacket, he strikes up a light and, hand shielding the small flame from the sea breeze, leans in toward the kindling he's placed at the bottom.

It takes four attempts for the fire to catch, prompting Orlaithe on the third to point out helpfully that Hank should breathe on it as 'he's drunk that much whiskey in his life he should have a flammable warning stamped on his forehead.'

When the fire is blazing strongly, Laura begins to cook. The greaseproof paper parcels she brought along turn out to contain huge links of fat sausages, which we place on wooden toasting forks made from sticks quickly whittled by Connor with his penknife.

The dogs return to us, drawn by the warmth of the fire and the tempting smell of cooking meat. Mac, who ambled back over the rocks in his own sweet time, about half an hour after his master, comes and sits beside me, leaning his heavy frame against mine, accepting pieces of hot sausage with a delicacy that should belie such a large dog. He cannot, it seems, discriminate between my mouth and his own, practically following each piece of sausage that goes to my lips with his head until we are almost kissing every time I eat.

'I think he likes you,' Connor is prompted to say, as I find myself once more staring eyeball to eyeball with Mac.

'Cupboard love,' I reply.

'Sausages.' Cas giggles doing an impression of the dog from the TV adverts.

'How many glasses of wine has she had?' I whisper to Laura.

'I'm not sure, I lost count from *my* fifth.' She grins.

'You're supposed to be driving,' I snap at her.

'We normally just sleep it off.'

'On the beach?'

'Yes, on the beach.'

'All night?'

She nods. 'It normally takes that long to sober up. Don't worry, we've got more blankets in the car.'

'What if it rains?'

'She's having a joke with you, darlin'.' Orlaithe is beginning to slur a little. 'Old Davey's coming down for us with his minibus.'

'And who's to say he'll be any more sober than us?' I reply in concern, remembering that the few times I've met Davey, he's been singing up a drunken storm in the Ship.

'Don't worry, he drives better when he's had a few,' Laura quips.

'How the hell can you say that. It's not something to joke about . . .'

Laura's face, pink from the fire, turns puce, and she puts her hand to her mouth in horror. 'Oh Nattie, I'm so sorry. I didn't think.'

'It's okay,' I sigh, suddenly embarrassed by my outburst, and the fact that Cas has thrown me a look I can't read, and then abruptly left the fireside to march down to the water's edge.

'No, it's not okay,' Laura rasps tearfully.

'Forget it, please,' I stress, but my mother, looking mortified, has slipped into a glum silence, turning to look out over the sea so that I cannot see her face.

Orlaithe struggles to her feet and turns to Hank, who is polishing off a charred sausage with obvious relish. 'I think we need to collect some more firewood.'

Hank looks in puzzlement at the more than sufficient pile of branches that he and Connor have already collected, but a meaningful look from Orlaithe gets him on his feet and he follows her down the beach nonetheless. I can hear her explaining to him as they walk: 'It was a drunk driver who forced the poor wee girl's husband off the road so it was.'

Connor looks from Laura to me, smiles sympathetically, and then getting to his feet, heads down to the sea and to Cassie, calling the dogs to him, distracting her with their antics.

Laura is shaking her head in disbelief.

'I'm sorry,' I tell her. 'I shouldn't have reacted like that.'

'No,' she says, 'it's me that should be sorry. That was so thoughtless of me.' She upends her beer bottle, stabbing the neck quite viciously into the sand, so that the contents drain away, her eyes still unable to meet mine, her cheeks still white, drained of colour.

I catch her arm. 'You have been wonderful,' I state slowly. 'I have no right to make you feel bad about something that wasn't your fault.'

Laura bites her bottom lip.

Reaching behind me I take hold of the heavy wine bottle, and pour Laura a cupful, holding it out to her. 'Please . . .'

She hesitates, so I refill my own plastic cup, and raise it to her as though making a toast. She half smiles and takes the one I am holding out to her.

'Thank you,' I tell her, and raise the wine to my lips. 'Thank you for putting up with us both.'

Connor and Cas, who has definitely now decided that Jas is not stupid, but merely slightly deaf, are attempting to teach him to sit, stay and fetch with hand signals, using the leftover sausages as encouragement. This is probably not the best method as he is far too distracted by the knowledge Cas has a sausage in each pocket to take any notice of what she is signalling to him.

After half an hour, Connor gives up. He flops down on the blanket next to Laura, sighing and pretending to wipe non-existent sweat from his forehead.

'I think *you're* right: he's not deaf, just a few potatoes short of a chip butty, that's all.'

'You look like you need a drink.' I pass him a cup of wine at the same time as Laura passes him a bottle of Stella. He looks from one to the other, then smiles and takes both.

'Cheers.' He bangs his plastic cup against mine, spilling some into the fire to make it hiss and spit in protest, then salutes my mother in the same way with the bottle.

The box my mother was carrying turns out to contain a huge chocolate cake. Orlaithe and Hank have also made their way back to us across the beach, Hank's arms full of damp driftwood.

Orlaithe has brought a bottle of Babadillo brandy,

exceptionally delicious paint-stripper purchased on their last Spanish holiday. She has also brought a bottle of champagne and insists on mixing the two together, the bubbles from the champagne force-feeding the alcohol from the brandy into my bloodstream far too quickly. We eat cake and drink too much, and lie replete and half-cut on the blankets, gazing up at the ice-blue sky above us, the dogs dozing in the warmth of the fire, so close you can smell the damp hair of their coats begin to warm and then gently singe.

Hank, Laura and Orlaithe are all asleep, mouths open, Hank snoring the constant drone of a large sleepy bumblebee. Cas is lying on her stomach, next to Laura, chin in her hands as she gazes out to sea.

Connor, who is lying to my left, touches my arm, puts a finger to his lips and points up into the sky to his right. Twenty feet away, a small bird of prey is hovering on the wind, dipping and swerving like a kite on a string.

'What is it?' I whisper.

'It's a kestrel. They're quite rare – we're lucky to have spotted it.'

'Laura says that you can sometimes see dolphins swimming here as well.'

He nods, and indicates to Cas. 'That's why Cas has had her eyes glued to the sea for the past hour, but it's Murphy's Law you never get to see them when you're watching out for them.'

'Have you seen them?'

'Quite a few times, but then I spend a lot of time down on the beach.'

'Yeah? What do you do, Connor?'

'I'm an artist,' he replies.

'Piss artist? Con Artist?' I tease gently.

'Trapeze artist,' he laughs, joining in.

'What sort of art?'

'Paintings mainly.'

'Really? You make a living out of it?'

'I scrape by,' he murmurs, staring beyond me out to sea. 'What shoes was your mother wearing today?'

'I'm sorry?' I ask, confused by the sudden change in conversation. I follow his gaze. Jasper is bounding around in the surf, something fairly large lodged in his mouth.

I look over to the slightly dozing body of Laura. She has taken off her thick scarf and rolled it up to form a makeshift pillow; her feet are swathed in thick red socks, her heavy walking boots kicked off for comfort whilst she sleeps. Only one of the boots still stands at the side of her blanket.

'Jasper!' Connor and I both yell in unison, struggling to our feet.

He is quicker than me, running down to the water's edge, calling for the dog to come to heel – a command that Jas as usual refuses to acknowledge, simply splashing through the water a few yards away from me, the laces of Laura's boots hanging from his mouth like ribbons of spaghetti he's forgotten to swallow. We dance around like idiots at the water's edge, shouting his name until we're hoarse, and yet still he ignores us, until Connor whistles piercingly and Jasper finally turns to us.

'Come here, you idiot,' I shout, and then remembering Cassie's theory, bend to pat my knees in encouragement. He hesitates for just a second, and then to my relief comes bounding back toward me.

'That's a good boy,' I croon enthusiastically. 'Now give me the shoe.' I reach out and try to pull it from his mouth, but thinking that I'm playing, Jas refuses to give up his prize. A tug of war ensues that pulls me into the shallow water alongside the dog.

Connor is running toward us, his mouth twisted with amusement. I hear Cassie and my mother call out to me, and turn my head to look at them. And then Jasper lets go.

I am pulling against a force that is no longer there.

There is only one way for me to go.

Backwards.

I fall into the cold churning water shrieking loudly, sinking just deep enough to cover my ears but not my whole face, but I'm still spluttering as if I would drown, as I surface and drag my body, heavy with the weight of the water saturating my clothes, into a sitting position.

Connor is beside me in a moment, running straight into the sea, his own shoes soaked within seconds, the light blue denim of his jeans going dark with salt water. He can't stop laughing as he offers me his hand to pull me upright.

'It's not funny!' I exclaim.

'Oh, but it is.' He grins insolently down at me. 'You haven't seen the state of yourself yet, have you?'

Laura's boot is floating unrescued in the sea about a foot away from me. As Connor reaches out to me, he bends a little to pick it up with his other hand. But Jasper is too quick for him.

He splashes through the surf and snatches at the boot just as Connor's fingers go to close around it, whisking it away from his reach so that he is grasping at thin air. Caught half-turned, unbalanced, Connor tumbles heavily into the water.

I'm howling with laughter as he drags himself up beside me, hair wringing wet, salt water streaming down his face, and for a moment our eyes catch. And for that moment I feel a charge, a connection between us.

I am unable to move, to unscramble the torrent of emotions that are washing through my head like the waves that are washing over my body.

I think of Rob.

And then, boot finally abandoned on the beach at Laura's stockinged feet, Jasper bounds between us, splashing our faces with water, barking, jumping, pulling at my clothes with sharp teeth, tail wagging furiously at the fun of such a riotous game. And Connor is standing and offering me his hand to pull me from the water again, and we are both suddenly a little awkward, and welcome the chance to pull away from each other when on returning to the sand, we are met by the laughter of the others.

*Dear Rob,*

*I have always believed that one day you and I will meet again. I cannot accept that you are gone completely. How can someone who was so alive, so full of passion and promise be confined only to the realm of memory? I would swear that somewhere, some part of you lives on.*

*I have to keep hold of the belief that you will be waiting for me wherever you have gone.*

*But now I have a new agony to torment me, one that has been awakened by the look I saw today in Connor's eyes, and the disturbing feelings this awoke within me: if you will be waiting for me, was Eve waiting for you?*

*The perfect Eve. The first woman.*

*I've got to believe that there is something after this life, but if there is, then she will be there too. Are you together again? Or is it truly, only till death do us part? If this is so, then you are no longer my husband, and yet to me it feels that you will always be so.*

*For the sake of my sanity I cannot torture myself with this madness. How can I be jealous of a ghost?*

*If you could see me now, see inside my head and my heart, would you be jealous too? Jealous that I have seen a glimpse of you in another man's eyes?*

*N x*

# Chapter Six

The rain has returned.

'It's a good job we had our picnic yesterday,' Laura mutters, staring out of the window at the heavy grey sky with its loaded clouds ready to burst upon us at any moment.

In the yard, Cas is quickly grooming Chance with a red plastic Dandy brush, looking up at the sky every few seconds as though willing the clouds to hold on until she has finished.

'Oh well, it's time I got back to work anyway.' Laura hauls herself from the chair and puts her empty teacup in the sink.

'What do you mean, get back to work?' I ask. 'You've been hard at it all the time since we arrived.'

'On the farm you mean? Oh, that's not work.' She goes to the door and bends to pull on her Wellingtons.

'It isn't?'

'Not paying work anyway, unfortunately – apart from the eggs. No, I simply discovered a new vent for my artistic nature,' she mocks herself, winding a long woollen scarf around her neck. 'Don't wait up, I'll probably be some time,' she quips, as though trekking out into the Antarctic.

I watch in bewilderment as she heads outside, but at the door she hesitates and turns back to me. 'Do you want to come and see?'

'Yeah,' I nod eagerly. 'I do.'

Intrigued, I pull on a jacket and follow Laura out of the kitchen and across the yard. We tread hurriedly down the long passage by the stables, fighting our way against a nasty easterly breeze that is blowing up from the sea. We go through the gate into Mile Meadow and turn left through a gate in the top hedge that I haven't seen before, and we are back on ourselves – if I calculate correctly, somewhere behind the stables. Laura leads me across the top of this field to a cattleshed that is nestled beyond the far hedge of Mile Meadow in the field before the one where the small herd of Jerseys are huddled around their feed trough.

I've never really taken much notice of it before, but now as we approach I see that the black wooden door of the squat, whitewashed building is padlocked with a heavy metal clasp. Laura reaches inside her pullover, and pulling a chain from around her neck, removes the small brass key that hangs upon it, and opens the lock.

The door swings back against the wall and my mother gestures me inside out of the icy wind. She pushes the door to behind us, unwinding her scarf from her face and pulling off her gloves, puffing with exertion and cold.

It's warm in the shed. Warm and cosy, with a low ceiling, and a concrete floor covered in rush matting. An old waist-height cupboard sits in the corner opposite the door, and upon its wooden top is a metal kettle, a couple of cracked mugs, an old brown teapot and a tin containing tea bags. On the window ledge is a worn red plastic radio cassette that I recognise as one that I had in my early teens. Laura heads straight for them, flicking the switch on the kettle, and pressing the cassette to 'on'. Jerri Winters starts singing about the fact that somebody loves her.

Laura shrugs almost apologetically as I look around me in amazement. 'Welcome to the World of Laura Dunne originals.'

In the centre of the room sits a potter's wheel; in the corner opposite the door, a huge kiln, which explains the heat in here, and circling the entire room are shelves, rising in three neat ranks to the ceiling, completely laden with little clay sculptures.

'This is what you helped me load the day that you arrived,' Laura tells me.

'Oh my God!' I exclaim in disbelief. I gaze in front of me at what can only be described as a shelf full of pottery penises. 'You've never told me about this,' I say almost accusingly, circling the small room, eyeing the contents of the shelves with my mouth wide open.

'It's not exactly the sort of thing I advertise very broadly.'

'They're um . . . very unusual.'

Laura grins as I reach out and take one of the items from the lowest shelf. 'I call them ethnic.'

'Change that to phallic and I think you'd be closer. Ethnic? South Africa maybe, but Ethnic Cornwall?'

'You may mock, young lady, but I'm a big hit in Covent Garden.'

'Yeah, I bet you are.' I pick up a pottery willy and brandish it at her. 'Just add batteries, eh? Who sells them for you?'

'Connor introduced me to a delightful young man who has a small gallery just off Neal Street. He has my ashtrays on back order.'

She waves a familiar-shaped piece of pottery at me. I take it from her and examine it.

'It's a . . . it's a . . .' I mouth.

'Exactly. If you can't quit, use a clit,' she jokes.

'And you sell a lot of these?'

'As many as I can make. Apparently they're a great talking point at dinner parties.'

'But they're so . . . so . . .'

'Much fun?'

'Politically incorrect.'

'Aren't all of the best jokes?'

I pick up another statue of lovers entwined, the woman reclined across the knee of the man, arms about each other, a clear piece of plagiarism of Rodin's *Kiss*, but it is impressive nonetheless.

'This is good.'

Laura glances up from the row of electricity switches; one is marked up with a little sticker that says *wheel*, and another predictably marked *kettle*.

'That? Oh, that's not to sell, that's a gift. I took a little more time with that one. Would you like a cup of tea? I've only got peppermint or camomile here, I'm afraid, but it means I don't have to worry about whether I've remembered to bring milk or not.'

'You don't need to – you could just nip out with your teacup,' I joke, indicating a large black and white Friesian clearly visible just beyond the hedge, 'and get it fresh.' I turn to another shelf and pick up something that resembles a double eggcup, but is really a pair of breasts, and gaze at it in wonder.

'It means that we just about scrape by at the moment.' Laura is standing behind me, looking nervously over my shoulder. 'You're not totally shocked with me, are you? It's not as though it's pornography. Heavens, if it *was* the money would be far better. It's just things are a bit tight at the moment.'

I turn, a broad grin on my face, and wave a clitoris ashtray at her. 'I suppose selling these helps you out of a bit of a hole?'

I leave Laura to work, and head back to the farmhouse. Apparently, my mother's pottery sideline has been providing her with a much-needed source of income for several years. Her confession that money is tight didn't come as a shock to me. Not as much of a shock anyway as the methods she is using to raise cash! Surprised as I am by her recently revealed occupation, it explains to me how she has managed to struggle on for so long with mounting debts.

There is a post box at the end of the track that leads down to Whitsunday. The track is about a mile and a half long, and I have taken to walking down there in the morning to collect the mail, if there is any. Meg and the puppy, whom Cassie has inadvertently christened Stu, short for Stupid, and occasionally Jasper, often walk with me, covering at least twice the distance that I do as they run backwards and forwards investigating interesting smells, and strange and tempting movements in the hedge that borders the rough road, in the hope that it may be rabbits for them to chase.

Stu is still tiny for his age, and sometimes struggles to keep up, but he has a fierce spirit that will not allow him to lag behind for too long. I think I should take a leaf from his book with regard to determination. He has slowly been winning his way into Cas's heart over the past few days. No matter how much she spurns him, he still follows her with a determined and unshakable devotion. Poor little thing. Handicapped from the outset by the fact that it was *I* who gave him to her, he is managing to creep into her affections as steadily and unrelentingly as the ivy grows on the north wall of the farmhouse, despite the bitter winds and harsh frosts that try to thwart its progress. His loyalty is unstintingly *dogged*, and on Cas's part there's a reciprocity of affection that she's quick to deny if I'm ever around.

Perhaps if I was as undeterred as he by the barriers she puts up, I could tread a careful path into Cassie's good books, too.

As well as the two sheep dogs and the puppy, quite often I have turned around to find that Mac has joined the daily walk as well. It's surprising how such a large dog can move so stealthily. I am rather pleased by the amount of time he chooses to spend with me, often appearing when I'm out walking, or waiting for me by the fire in the hope that I will feed him more sausages.

Meg will join us straight from a night spent ratting. She never sleeps in the house overnight, preferring instead to disappear into the darkness. In fact, I very rarely see her sleep except sometimes in the evening, when my mother is sitting by the fire, and then she will lie at her feet, and slumber deeply, legs twitching as she dreams of chasing hares.

The dogs in this community appear to be communal. I think this is a reflection of the attitudes people have in the village. Everywhere you go, you always get a friendly greeting, the offer of a cup of tea. People aren't afraid to look you in the eye, nor are they afraid to talk to strangers. When Cas and I first came here, I found this a little intrusive. Everyone seemed to know who I was without introduction, to know what had happened in my life.

Now I like the sense of security it gives me.

I wouldn't walk alone in London in the middle of the night. I certainly would never walk into a public house on my own, but I know here, if I ever felt the urge to do either, I would be safe or I would receive a warm welcome and soon have not one but several drinking companions.

I have even struck up a friendship with the young girl who drives the post van, Morwenna, who I sometimes bump into delivering the post. What post we get, that is. Laura never seems to get much mail, but I have noticed a good deal of the letters that she does receive are from the bank, and most of the bills are marked *urgent*, or are ominously red through the thin white envelopes.

It hasn't taken me long to work out that Laura and Whitsunday are in trouble. I just haven't quite got an idea of the level of debt she is facing. I really want to help out. I struggled for money when I was younger, when I first moved to London. Consequently I have always been quite careful, but I have been earning a good living for some time now, have my own flat, which I've been renting out on a short-term lease, and some savings of my own. When Rob died I was left more than comfortably off although this is something that I've consciously not thought about at all.

I'm learning, however, that my mother is vastly independent. I'm also learning that, although by no means destitute, things have been far from easy for her over the years. The insurance money invested after my father's death gives her a small monthly income, but as much as I made fun of her somewhat insalubrious pottery it has obviously been a lifesaver for her.

The farm, which is her main occupation, in so far as it takes up more of her time than anything else, earns her next to nothing. She views each motley member of her livestock as a pet, and has taken nothing to market for over three years, making practically no money from her menagerie. She has an ongoing egg order with the local corner shop, and some of the B&Bs along the coast, and she will occasionally send one of the foul fowl down to the local butcher to be popped, plucked and stuffed and returned looking like Sunday lunch, but apart from this, the smallholding seems to be a major drain on her resources rather than a boost to them. She insists that her reward is pure pleasure, but I can't really see what pleasure she gets from having to rise every morning before the sun to feed and muck out a bunch of not altogether grateful animals.

Then there are the 'men'. Hank works afternoons only, Tuesdays and Thursdays, doing the 'heavy' stuff – drystone walling, fixing fences. Luke comes in only occasionally, normally in case of fire, flood or emergency, but he still has to be paid for his time.

Despite it all – the early starts, whatever the day, whatever the weather, and the money worries – I get the feeling she wouldn't have it any other way.

She won't accept any money for our keep, so I have

taken to going into Truro once a week to stock up at Sainsbury's, but I wish that she would let me do more. If *only* there was some way I could persuade her to let me help.

The post that I collected from the box this morning is still on the table, ignored and unopened as usual. Feeling a touch guilty, I pick it up and take it to my room.

Two days later, Cas is at the kitchen table eating boiled eggs, dipping toast soldiers into their ochre-yellow centres. She is wearing blue jeans, a thick red polo-neck sweater, and thick pink and green stripy socks. She is reading an article in a magazine, so engrossed that she doesn't notice me come downstairs and enter the room, my feet soundless in the thick socks I too am wearing. Laura is at the end of the table, facing the stairs, poring over the blue ledgers that I recognise as her account books.

She looks up and smiles, a little stiffly so it seems, unless I'm imagining things. 'Morning.'

Cas also looks up but doesn't speak, simply raises her eyebrows in silent greeting.

'So, what are you up to today?' I ask, taking the maintained eye-contact as an opportunity to talk to her.

'I'm going riding,' she replies, shutting the magazine, and getting up from the table. The leather knee-high boots she bought in Truro are standing by the door, freshly polished. She tucks her jeans into the woollen socks, and pulls the boots on over the top, then struggles into a thick blue padded jacket that makes her look a little like a navy-painted Michelin Man.

'I know it's not exactly high fashion,' she says to Laura, who is laughing at the sight of her, 'but it's the warmest one I've got and it's bloody cold out there. In fact,' she reaches towards the hat stand, takes a knitted bobble hat from one of the laden prongs, and pulls it defiantly over her pale blonde curls.

As Laura begins to sing 'Frosty the Snowman' at her, she sticks out an insolent tongue.

'What the hell! If you're going to take the piss, I may as well go the whole hog,' and reaching for the matching scarf, Cas winds it tightly around her neck, securing it with a thick knot under her chin.

'Now if you'd have asked her to wrap up warm she'd have gone out in her underwear,' I tell my mother in admiration as Cas kicks the kitchen door shut behind her.

'Kids don't like being told what to do. Find their weaknesses, Nattie,' she jokes. 'Use them against them. Gain ascendancy!' Then she closes the ledgers with a heavy sigh. 'I'm not getting very far with these.'

'Problems?' I query casually.

'Well, they don't add up – let's put it that way.'

She gives me a strange look, and then placing one on top of the other, she takes them from the room, back into the small study where they live on her untidy desk. A couple of minutes later her head pops back round the door.

'Nat, you're not going anywhere, are you?'

I shake my head, puzzled. 'No, no plans, why?'

'I need a word. I just have to make a phone call, to check something, then I'll be back.'

I make myself a cup of tea and sit down at the table in Cas's recently vacated seat. It's still warm; the magazine she was reading has been pushed away across the table. I reach out for it. It looks familiar. It must be one I've already read. It takes me a moment to realise that Cas was flicking through an old copy of *Naked*. Not just any old copy, however, but *the* issue. The story that started it all. Laura must have kept it.

With trembling hands, I turn to the page number I know by heart, my eyes alighting on the familiar photograph of Rob that heads the piece. I always thought it was a gorgeous photograph of him. He used to hate having his picture taken, and he does look slightly uncomfortable, but he also looks strong, and handsome and very much alive, as though the past twenty months have never happened.

I trace the contours of his face with my finger, the page feeling cool and smooth beneath my touch. I must sit silently for at least a quarter of an hour, simply gazing at the photograph of Rob, looking, not thinking, just looking at the face of the man I love. A face I will never touch or kiss again in my lifetime. And I find myself wishing that my lifetime could be as short as his, that it could end, now, at this very moment, so that I could be with him again.

The door slams behind me, making me almost jump out of my skin.

'You paid Camleys?' Laura's voice is almost accusing.

'Sorry?'

'You paid the feed bill.'

'Ah.' I close the magazine slowly, and turn to face her. 'I forgot to tell you. He came round while you were out, and so I paid him.'

'I'm not destitute, you know,' she snaps.

'I didn't say you were. You won't let us pay any board, so I reckoned I needed to repay you in some other way. I was going to tell you – it just slipped my mind.'

'Oh it did, did it?' she asks in disbelief.

'Yes. Please don't be angry. I just wanted to pay my way.'

'By settling a bill for nearly one thousand pounds?'

'I just wanted to help, that's all.'

'And you think I needed that sort of help? I've managed to pay my way for the sixteen years you've not been around.'

I am surprised by the tone of her voice, which is almost accusing. 'This isn't just about the money, is it?' I say softly.

Laura sighs and pushes her hair out of her face. 'I

thought it was, but no, maybe it isn't.'

'Then what is it? What's the matter?'

'That's just it, Nat. I've survived on my own for sixteen years. *Sixteen years.* Half of your lifetime, and a great big chunk out of mine.' Her voice drops to a whisper. 'Did it never occur to you that I might miss you?'

I reach out and squeeze her arm in an attempt at reassurance, but I don't reply. I know we need to talk, but I can't face it right now, not after seeing that article. There are too many other things that I'm struggling to come to terms with, without an emotional afternoon going through the reasons why Laura and I had drifted apart so badly.

I am therefore relieved when Cassie's head appears around the door. She wants Laura to help her tack up Chance, and waits whilst my mother pulls on her coat and boots, chatting excitedly about where she's going to ride him first.

I wait until they go outside then, feeling like a coward, I put on my own jacket and boots and slip across the yard, past Chance's stable, where Laura is helping Cas tighten the girth on his saddle. I move quickly into the wind tunnel that is the long passage, and go through the gate and across the fields.

I head straight for the sea.

I don't know why, but it calms me. The wind clears my head, and so does the freshness of the salty air; the motion of the water is like watching a pendulum swing before your eyes, lulling you to a state of restfulness. Today I feel that I could walk off my worries, that if I march hard enough and fast enough along the coastline, they will lag behind me until they are eventually out of sight.

It is only as the scenery becomes familiar that I realise I have been this way before. I must be retracing my steps on the walk that I took from Land's End on that wild and windy day, only going the other way; any minute now and I will come to the promontory where I took shelter from the storm amidst the rocks.

It is piercingly cold, but the sky is almost cloudless. The wind has died; only the slightest of breezes ruffles the grass beneath my feet, lifting the long white-green fronds and blowing them toward the ice-green sea like streamers. The gulls circle at the cliff edge, catching the wind with widespread wings, riding the breeze like surfers catch the waves, their mournful cry echoing repeatedly above me.

When I reach the squat stone Huer's hut, I know that I have come to the right place. Sliding down the rocks beyond it, I search for the entrance to my secret hide-away. I know it's here somewhere, but it takes me far longer to find it this time, clambering over the rocks, slipping on the grass and then the mossy surface of the cliff face. I can't believe I did this in a storm, although the lack of visibility was probably a bonus. If I had been able to see exactly where I was going, I probably wouldn't have gone there in the first place.

I eventually come across the narrow opening in the rocks that leads down into the little sheltered hollow, and am glad I made the effort when I get there and sit down once more to rest my back against the smooth granite. Cocooned away from the world, with only the sky above me and the sea below, I feel my tense body start to relax a little. Protected by the peace and tranquillity of the place, the questions buzzing in my head like a swarm of agitated wasps also die down like the wind, to silence.

My hands are pushed deep inside the pockets of my jacket. There is something under the fingertips of my right hand; it is smooth, like a photograph. My hand closes around the object and I pull it out into the daylight.

It's the postcard I wrote in Trenrethen. Hidden from

Orlaithe and forgotten. I read it again.

> *Dear, Dear Rob,*
> *I wish you were here. That's the usual way to start a postcard, isn't it, but I don't think it could ever have been so heartfelt before. I feel so lonely without you.*
> *Love always,*
> *N x*

Reaching into the pocket again I pull out the two envelopes I also hid there. These are the letters I wrote to Rob in the small hours when loneliness drew me to communicate with him in any way I could. If only I could speak with Rob. If only he could read the thoughts I poured out onto these pages. Maybe I can send them to him on the wind – throw them into the air and let them be caught and carried to wherever he may be.

There is a gap in the rocks beneath me, leading into a darkness that falls deep into the unknown. Without thinking I take the postcard and the letters and slip them through it. Pressing my eye to the gap, I watch them float down into the darkness below until they become invisible.

When I return to the house, Laura has disappeared once more into her cowshed-cum-pot shop, not reappearing until just after seven.

In an effort to conciliate I attempt to cook dinner. Attempt being the operative word. Fish pie. The recipe sounds easy enough, but the reality is a little different, the end product eliciting a fearful 'What is it?' from Cas when I finally dish up. I think it's the fact that it's all white – the fish, the potato, the sauce, and the cauliflower I rather unfortunately chose to serve it with.

Fortunately, it doesn't taste as awful as it looks. And

fortunately, Laura is as chatty and friendly as usual. Halfway through dinner, however, she gets a phone call, and my fish pie is abandoned with an alacrity that I could be insulted by, until Cas hisses at me that the caller was male, and Laura is now blow-drying her hair, having had the speediest shower in the history of indoor bathrooms.

'I think she's got a boyfriend,' my step-daughter confides, as soon as Laura has shot out of the door in a smart wool suit wafting clouds of Chanel as she goes, and claiming that she's heading for a 'business meeting'.

I look up from my plate. 'Really? She's never said anything,' I reply carefully.

'Well, who do you think is going to get the benefit of that outfit if it isn't a man?'

'You know, you could be right.'

'There's no *could* about it.' Her tone is fairly harsh, but the usual animosity in her eyes when she looks at me seems to be missing.

'I wonder why she's never mentioned anything?' I say tentatively. 'It's not like Laura to be coy.'

'True. There must be a reason for her to be so secretive.' Cas bites her bottom lip in contemplation, tilting her head to one side as she looks at me. 'I know who'd probably know for definite,' she tempts me. 'And she's not discreet enough to cover up for Laura either.'

'Orlaithe?'

Cas nods. 'What do you reckon?'

'Really it's none of our business.'

'True.' Cas releases her full pink lip from between small white teeth and raises her eyebrows at me in a silent question.

Twenty minutes later, united by a common cause, we are piling out of my car and heading into the brightly lit interior of the Ship. It's Friday night, so the pub is packed with drinkers and diners, locals mingling with visitors. We look for Orlaithe, who is busy behind the bar. She spots us and waves, but I soon find that we don't need Orlaithe to spill the beans.

Laura is in the Ship.

It takes us a few moments to spot her. Cas and I are just fighting our way through to the bar and Orlaithe, when I feel my step-daughter tug at my sleeve.

'Natalie,' she hisses. 'Look over there.' She points to a table in the furthest corner of the room from the door. A secluded table. She has her back to us, but Laura's caramel curls are quite distinct. And, as Cassie suspected, she's with a man.

'I knew it,' Cas crows triumphantly. 'I just knew it.' She begins to push her way through the crowd toward them, but I hold her back.

'It's one thing finding her, Cas, but to be honest I don't think they want to be disturbed, do you?'

'Nonsense! You're her only living relative – well, apart from your Great-Aunt Daphne in Worthing . . .'

'She's still alive?'

Cas nods. 'According to Laura.'

'You know more about my family than I do.'

'Well, perhaps if you actually sat down and talked to your mother,' Cas pulls a face at me, 'you know – make an effort . . .'

*Like you do with me.*

'You still didn't know about *him*, did you?' I reply.

'So let's rectify that right now and introduce ourselves.' Smiling archly at me, Cas pulls free and marches over, plonking herself down in the seat opposite the happy couple, as Laura looks up in guilty surprise.

I feel a flood of embarrassment. Laura is pretty open, and I think if she'd wanted us to know about this man then she would have told us by now. I could try and blend into the wallpaper, but Cas is gesturing furiously for me to follow her. I look around for a means of escape, but seeing none, and knowing I have been spotted, I end up heading over to their table.

Cas grins up at me. Laura doesn't look quite as welcoming.

'Nattie darling, I was just telling Cas, this is a business acquaintance of mine, Charles Treloar. Charles, this is my daughter, Natalie.'

I hold out a hand. 'Pleased to meet you.'

Charles seems much less uncomfortable than Laura. He stands to shake our hands when Laura reluctantly introduces us. 'Lovely to meet you, my dears,' he says, and politely invites us to join them, which is a little belated seeing as we have already gate-crashed.

'I think we need more wine now that two have become four.' He smiles affably, and excusing himself, heads for the crowded bar.

'What are you doing here?' Laura immediately hisses at us. 'Are you following me?'

'Not at all!' I bluster untruthfully.

'We just fancied a drink.' Cas lies far more easily than I ever could.

Fully aware that Laura knows for a fact Cas and I wouldn't suddenly decide to go out together, I blush pale pink, and picking up a beer mat, fan myself furiously pretending my colour is down to the heat. Laura shakes her head, but I am happy to see that she is now struggling not to laugh.

'So,' Cas grins encouragingly, 'who is he then?'

'Like I said, he's a business associate.'

'Yeah, and Natalie's the Virgin Mary.' Cas rolls her eyeballs at my mother.

'Born again,' I mutter.

'Although he is very handsome, isn't he?' Laura can't resist a gloat. 'Don't you think he looks a bit like Albert Finney – younger and slimmer than he is now, of course, and darker as well?'

'Mmm.' Cas looks over to the bar, where Charles is waiting to be served. 'I suppose he's not bad for an old bloke, although I'm not sure about the cords and elbow patches.'

Laura can't help but smile at this, although it's obvious she'd rather it were a cosy twosome, despite her assurances that it's strictly business.

'Now you've tracked me down, perhaps you'd be kind enough to push off?' she says with a smile.

'Charming.' Cas grins at her.

I'm happy to leave them to it, but as Cas points out, now Charles has been kind enough to buy enough wine for all of us it would be extremely rude not to sit and drink a glass with him.

And so I nurse half a glass of red and sit and watch in mild amusement as Cas makes Laura squirm and Charles laugh with leading comments and innuendos, before I finally manage to drag her back to the farm, leaving my mother to enjoy her illicit evening in peace.

On the drive back, warmed and encouraged by this evening's camaraderie, I try to engage her in conversation once again, only to be disappointed when Cassie falls back into her usual sullen silence.

At two in the morning, I'm woken from a strange dream about talking geese by the sound of my mother returning home. She shut the kitchen door quietly enough, but the loud creak of the third step of the stairs and the equally loud giggle that ensues immediately after, are enough to pull me back from an odd conversation with a far more amiable and suddenly vocal Gertrude about which kind of stuffing would suit her best for Christmas Dinner. I hear deep laughter as Laura's bedroom door opens and shuts, and then the creak of protesting bedsprings as two bodies fall upon the mattress. Pulling my pillow over my head, I will myself to sleep.

I wake up again just after six. It's no good trying to go

back to sleep, I'm wide awake. Everyone else will be up by seven anyway.

I get out of bed, and head down to the kitchen. I'll make myself a cup of tea, go back up and have a shower, then make an early start on breakfast.

I'm just pouring boiling water into the teapot when I hear a nervous cough.

'Ahem.'

I turn to see Charles standing awkwardly behind me, shoes in hand.

'Good morning,' he says gruffly.

I'd forgotten that Laura had a nocturnal visitor.

A hushed voice calls down the stairwell after him. 'Charlie darling, you forgot your . . .'

Laura is tiptoeing down the stairs in a see-through white nightdress, an embroidered shawl thrown around her shoulders to give her a modicum of modesty. She's holding a flat cap in her right hand, and clutching onto the stair-rail with the other. She stops dead in her tracks when she spots me though.

'Ah, Nattie darling, you're up early this morning.' Her voice is strangely high.

'Looks like we're all at it,' I reply, struggling to keep a straight face. 'Getting up early, that is,' I add, as Laura goes scarlet.

Charles practically snatches the cap from Laura and sprints for the door. 'Well, must rush off, lovely to meet you . . . again,' he says as he passes me, eyes down.

'Not staying for a cup of tea?' I smile beatifically, waving my mug at him. Laura flashes me a look, but it's more amused than angry.

'Er, thank you, but no. Must dash, late for . . . well . . . late.'

'How about some breakfast? I'm cooking bacon,' I call after him, but he scurries out of the door.

Laura helps herself to a cup of tea from my pot, and sits down in the chair opposite me.

'That explains *that*,' I tell her.

'Explains what?' she asks without looking at me.

'Things that go hump in the night. I thought I heard noises, but I told myself I was imagining things.'

Laura sips her sea, and refuses to answer.

'Business acquaintance my arse.'

She stares at me for a moment and then starts to laugh. 'Okay, so you caught me out. Charles is my guilty secret.'

'Doesn't it bother you?'

'What?'

'The fact that he's married.'

'How did you know that he's married? I didn't say that.'

'It was what you *didn't* say rather than what you did.'

'From what I can gather, Charles and his wife Evelyn have what is normally termed an "open" relationship.'

'Oh, and you know that for a fact, do you?'

'That's what Charles told me, yes.'

'I suppose that's slightly more novel than "my wife doesn't understand me".'

'Yes – it's the opposite one. She understands him all too well.'

'And is he er . . . open with just you, or does he like to share himself amongst the good citizens of Trenrethen indiscriminately?'

A curious smile is playing about Laura's lips. 'Do you know, you sound just like my mother did when I was young. This is one of those role reversals that all the magazines warn you about – you know, where the child starts to take on the responsibility, and the parent becomes the child. You'll be trying to put me in a home soon.'

'I couldn't find one that would take you. You're too much of a liability. You'd be sneaking old men into your room after lights out.'

'Old men!' She laughs indignantly. 'I don't think

Charles would appreciate being called old. Do you know something though, for an old codger, he's bloody good in bed.'

'I don't think I want to know that.'

'Why so coy? You've already told me you heard the squeals of ecstasy.'

'Oh, is that what the noises were? I thought you'd brought some of the farm animals into the bedroom to keep warm. After all, it was pretty chilly last night.'

'Not in my room it wasn't,' she pouts at me. 'In my room it was steamingly hot!'

'Ugh,' I shudder. 'Stop it, you're just trying to wind me up.'

'Yes,' she admits happily. 'And it's working beautifully.'

The sound of a far from melodic horn announces that Hank is pulling up in the yard. He doesn't normally honk to let us know he's here, so we rush outside to see what the problem is.

'It's the *Return of the Triffids*,' announces a dry voice behind me. Cas is standing in the doorway in her grey wool pyjamas, watching as Betsy, who has been transformed into what looks like a moving hedge, pulls up outside the house. Closer inspection reveals a giant Christmas tree tied to the roof of Hank's car, so huge that it covers the car from the curved boot to the horns on the front of the long bonnet, obscuring the windscreen so badly that Hank has to peer out of a clear space of about three inches wide to see where he's going.

Laura, her modesty covered a little more respectably with a Barbour, dances excitedly around the car whilst he unties the ropes holding the tree there and lifts it from the roof. Puffing, he pulls it to the ground and then raises his eyebrows at Laura.

'Where do we want it?' Laura has this uncanny knack of being able to interpret most of Hank's facial expressions.

'Ah,' he agrees.

'It would be nice to have it in the kitchen, considering that's where we spend most of our time. What do you think, girls?'

I nod my approval. Cas, who is trying not to look excited, and failing dismally, nods too.

The small man carries the huge tree with ease across the farmyard, only dropping it to the ground as he reaches the kitchen door, so that he can pull it carefully through backwards, it being a touch too large to fit through without effort. He lugs it across the terracotta tiles, a trail of pine needles in its wake, and props it in the corner to the right of the fireplace.

I breathe in deeply. 'I love that smell, the smell of fresh damp pine needles.'

'It's never quite the same when they try to re-create it in loo-cleaner, is it?' Laura grins at me, as I stand in the middle of the kitchen sniffing heavily like Mac on a scent trail. Hank stays for tea and biscuits before heading out to check a pregnant cow in the far meadow.

Finally remembering her state of undress, Laura disappears upstairs to change, then heads out into the Long Barn, returning twenty minutes later with the box of tree decorations she packed away and put there last year.

'It doesn't matter how carefully I pack them, something always manages to get broken,' she complains, putting the box on the floor and starting to remove the contents. She takes out tinsel and baubles, and painted pine cones, and then begins to carefully unwrap some folded tissue paper. Inside is a battered old fairy, fashioned from a cardboard loo roll and pink feathers stolen from a feather boa. I recognise it instantly, because I made it myself when I was very small.

'I can't believe you've still got that!' I exclaim in disbelief.

My mother looks up and grins at me. 'It goes on top of the tree every year.'

'What the hell is it?' Cas picks it up by a worn feather, between thumb and forefinger, holding it away from her as though it could be contagious.

'It was supposed to be a fairy,' I murmur, 'although I was only about four when I made it.'

'You said it was a ballerina, Nattie,' Laura tells me.

'I did?'

'Yes, you were quite adamant. Your father and I had taken you to a matinée of *The Nutcracker*, just before Christmas and you were so taken with it. This was your version of the Sugar Plum Fairy. So she's a little ballerina, just like our Cas, eh?'

Cas doesn't reply, simply snorts a little derogatory *hrrumph* from her nose and returns the battered object to Laura. I look at her sour face in concern. She hasn't mentioned dancing since we came here. I've certainly never seen her practise, despite the many hours she puts in at school, the competitions, the dance recitals, the exams.

Maybe she's like me. I thought that work was my life, but I've barely missed it at all since coming here. I thought I'd be climbing the walls with frustration, but instead I have forgotten work as swiftly as a young teenager would a holiday romance.

We decorate the tree together, Laura proudly placing my battered fairy on the highest point.

It's evening. Laura is restless.

'Anybody fancy a walk?'

No one answers.

'It's a beautiful evening,' she encourages Cas.

Cas looks up from her book, and frowns. 'You think?'

'Well, it's not raining.'

'That's a first,' Cas shrugs, getting up from the rug. 'Okay – why not?'

Laura turns to me. 'Nattie?'

'No.' I shake my head. 'You two go.'

'Oh, come on. You could do with some fresh air too.'

I look at Cas. I know it's stupid, but I want her to invite me to join them both. I want to feel wanted by both of them and not just Laura. Cas looks up from pulling on her boots, and raises her eyebrows at me in question, then when I don't move, she reaches to the coat rack and lifts off my jacket, holding it out toward me without speaking.

I smile and get up from my chair, taking the coat, and an old woolly hat of Laura's that looks like a tea cosy but is so warm that I've become pretty fond of it. Laura is bending down to do up the top straps on her Wellingtons and, as I lean down to pull on my own boots, she winks at me.

'Ready?' She straightens up.

Cas is trying to clip a lead onto Stu's collar. Thinking it's some kind of game, the tiny pup is rolling around on the floor trying to eat the metal clip every time it comes near him.

'You're going to have to learn to use one of these sometime,' Cas sighs, giving up, and calling him to heel instead, 'otherwise when we get back to London you'll be flattened by the first bus you meet!' It's the first time she has mentioned going home.

'He'll learn in time.' Laura bends down and pats the puppy's head.

'You think so? I'm starting to worry that he's inherited the same brain capacity as Jasper.'

Outside, Laura comes between us, taking first Cassie's arm and then mine. We walk like this, arm-in-arm, across the narrow top half of Mile Meadow, through the thick privet hedge and into the field beyond, which slopes gently away in front of us to another hedge about a third of a mile away.

It's five o'clock, the sun is sinking slowly toward the sea on our right through a bank of black and purple clouds. The ever-present wind is softer today, ruffling the

205

dark-green sea grass on the edges of the cliff like a hand running through fine hair. The coast bends around here, dropping to the north, so if I look from the front to my right side, I can always see the sea. We pass through another field. I can see a beach ahead of us and a road in the distance leading down to it. I'm not totally sure where we are. I think Trenrethen may be beyond the brow of the furthest hill, but I couldn't say for sure.

'I don't remember half of this.'

Laura looks across at the sound of my voice. 'Well, you didn't exactly spend much time here, did you? You probably didn't *see* half of this. You should have seen her when she was younger.' She turns to Cas and grins teasingly. 'Locked away in her room with her stereo on full volume, she was just like Kevin the Teenager from Harry Enfield. "*It's so unfaaaair*".' She drops her shoulders and does a passable impression of Britain's most notorious teenager, making Cas laugh and me begin to protest.

'I wasn't that bad!'

'No, you were worse. Although I can't blame you. I wasn't exactly the world's best mother now, was I?'

I look at her in surprise.

'What do you mean, Nat wasn't here for very long?' Cas asks. 'I thought you came here when she was fifteen.'

'Yes,' Laura sighs. 'And then Nattie *left* here when she was just sixteen.'

'You left home at sixteen?' Cas asks, her mouth dropping open in awed disbelief.

I nod, but don't reply; it's not exactly a topic I want to discuss with Cassie in case she gets any ideas about doing the same thing herself.

'I never knew that.'

'There are a lot of things about me that you don't know.' I shrug.

Cas nods slowly, as though only just acknowledging

this fact, and I grapple around in my head for a change of subject.

We're through the two small fields that sit beyond Mile Meadow, and the ground begins to slope more dramatically here. I can see the beach more clearly now to my right, and ahead of us the narrow winding road that runs down to it through the rolling hills, like the cleft in a peach. Just ahead of us, about three hundred yards away from the road, a long patch of grey is showing through a small gathering of trees.

'What's that?' I ask, pointing down to it.

Laura, who was looking out to sea, follows my gaze. Nestled halfway down, out of sight of the road, is an old derelict cottage, long and low – white lime with a grey slate roof.

'That's Smuggler's Cottage,' she tells us.

'Smuggler's Cottage?' Cassie looks sceptical. She's heard too many tall stories from Laura about shipwrecks and pirates to trust her too much on local history.

'Honestly, that's what it's called,' Laura says indignantly.

'Yeah,' Cas drawls in disbelief. 'Maybe. But Bombay Duck's never had any duck in it, has it?'

As we get closer, a picture-postcard cottage comes into view. It's sadly neglected. The grey slate roof that was the first thing I spotted through the trees is, on closer inspection, full of gaps, like a child who's lost too many milk teeth. The front door stands ajar on broken hinges, the black paint rotted and peeling away from the split wood. Most of the windows are broken, their frames rotted away; the white limed walls are dirty grey with damp, or sea green with the lichen that grows profusely over the stonework. It is, however, despite the poor state of the place, one of the prettiest houses I have ever seen. Idyllic, set in an overgrown wilderness of brambles and winter-bare dog roses, and grass that is knee-high.

'What a fantastic place. How could someone let it get like this?' I murmur, stepping through what once would have been a garden gate, but is now an empty space in a tumbledown stone wall.

'Who does it belong to?' Cassie asks, following me through, Stu dancing ahead of us, intrigued by the wonderful smells emanating from the house and its garden, which only he has the heightened senses to notice.

Laura smiles strangely. 'Me.' She shrugs. 'It belongs to me.'

Cassie's eyes widen in surprise and she opens her mouth to speak, but Laura continues, 'It was already derelict when we first moved here,' she says, stepping through the front door and turning into the room on the right, so that we have to follow her to hear what she's saying. 'It wasn't as bad as this, of course, but I haven't had the money to do anything with it. Which is such a shame, since it's crying out for some attention. Of course I did think about selling it to someone who could afford to restore it, but I've never had the heart to do so. Some people were interested about eight years ago – they wanted to make it into a holiday home for them and their family, but they were so awful that I didn't follow it through. They had three children who were absolute monsters. I caught them throwing stones at the poor sheep, and they took such delight in baiting my poor old Rufus, I couldn't bear the thought of them living close to me. It really put me off selling the place, although of course it's sad to see it like this . . .'

As Laura talks I have stepped across the rubble-strewn floor of what I think must have been a sitting room of sorts.

'Oh wow! Would you just look at that view?'

Laura stops talking and follows me over. There is an empty frame where the window has rotted away, the glass once held within its confines now shattered on the stone floor at our feet. And visible through this gap is the garden, overgrown to almost a complete wilderness, but still recognisable as something once tended by the hands of men, bordered by a line of stone that was once a wall. Beyond the wall is a short meadow, falling toward a soft beige beach, and beyond that, stretching on for ever, framed by the walls like a perfect picture, is the sea.

'It's fabulous, isn't it?' my mother says.

I nod slowly. 'I never saw this place when I was here.'

'Like I said to Cas, you weren't here for very long, were you, and you spent most of that time sitting in your bedroom plotting your escape. You didn't really stop to take a look around you and see if you actually liked what was here. Then again, I don't think it was the place you were running away from, was it?' Laura holds out her hand to me, and after a brief moment of confusion, I reach out and take it. The sound of footsteps overhead tells me that Cas is exploring upstairs.

'Mind out up there!' Laura calls to her, squeezing my fingers and then letting go. 'The floorboards are a bit rotten in some places.'

'A *bit* rotten?' repeats a voice that sounds too close, and we both look up to see Cassie's grinning face peering at us through a large hole in the ceiling. 'Do you think this is a smuggler's emergency exit?' she asks with fey wide-eyed innocence, taunting my mother. 'Along come the police so you just pop out through a hole in the ceiling and make a speedy exit back to your pirate ship.'

There's nothing better than coming into a warm kitchen from a cold winter's walk, pulling off your boots, your coat and your gloves, and feeling the gentle heat of the fire soaking blood back into your fingers and toes. We also feel saintly enough, having walked at least five miles, to have something totally fattening for supper – tea, cake, and a huge box of chocolates given to my mother by a grateful neighbour, which we devour between us with frightening rapidity. A spirited game of cards follows, Chase the Ace, with Laura and Cas cheating unmercifully. At ten we all go up to bed and for once I feel absolutely ready for it. I'm tired. A good kind of tired. I actually feel sleepy.

Before I settle down though, there is one last thing I feel compelled to do. I take out my pen and paper, and begin to write:

> *Dear Rob,*
> *We had a nice evening today, full of warmth in more ways than one. I think perhaps Cas may be accepting me a little more. I hope so. I really want us to be friends. I am beginning to realise how little I knew of her – the real her, her sense of humour, her warmth.*
>
> *I think it's good for her here. I was concerned at first that I might not have done the right thing, but I can see that simply being with Laura has helped Cas immensely. I think my mother and I had a small breakthrough of our own today as well. Just a brief moment of acknowledgement, but it meant a lot to me. She understands far more than I have given her credit for. I know that she is helping Cas an awful lot, but I think if I'm honest then I'd have to admit being here with her is helping me too. Although I still love and miss you more than you could ever know. But then you do know, don't you?*
> *Always yours,*
> *N x*

I put the letter on my bedside table determined to post it when next I walk along the coast.

'Can you call Cassie in for dinner?'

I look up from my paper and smile at Laura, who is reaching into the depths of the Aga, hands protected by green striped oven gloves.

'Sure. Do you know where she is?'

'In the Long Barn, I think.'

'Which one's that? No . . .' I pause. 'Don't tell me. The *long* one.'

I head out into the chill evening. It's only the second time that I have stepped outside of the house today. It's been one of those dark, overcast days which did nothing to tempt us into anything more active than reading and watching a film together, a long, leisurely day doing almost nothing, and yet I think we have all been more relaxed in each other's company than ever we have before.

A lone owl is calling from the dense middle of a thicket some miles away. Chance moves restlessly in his loose box, hooves sounding against the bare floor where he has kicked away his bedding.

As I walk down the long passage, my footsteps echoing against the narrow stone walls, I hear something that makes me pause. It is music? I stop for a second and listen. Yes, I can definitely hear music, coming from the Long Barn. Classical music, in fact. With my very limited knowledge, I cannot claim to recognise it, but it is hauntingly beautiful and makes even me, self-confessed philistine that I am, pause for a moment longer simply to listen, before carefully pushing open the heavy barn door nearest to me.

It is as well that I slowed what would have been a hasty entrance, for I would not have wished in any way to interrupt the scene inside.

Cas is dancing to the music. Her body is muffled in torn jeans and an old Aran jumper shrunk in the wash by Laura and passed on as a perfect fit for Cas, her feet in a pair of tightly laced DMs, yet she is as graceful, fluid and hypnotic as the movement of the sea.

I watch her move with the music, entranced. She is a spirit. Not of this earth, unaffected by gravity, by the limitations of the human form. She is a breath of wind, a delicate green leaf free-falling in the breeze, as light as a spun silver cobweb, yet as passionate and red hot as fire. She is so good that it hurts to watch her. It takes me a moment to realise that the twist I'm feeling inside, that reaches from my gut to my throat, is a fierce blaze of absolute pride.

But even as I watch, enthralled, she ceases to dance. Simply stops mid-turn and falling to the ground in frustration, hugs her knees to her chest and begins to sob. Quiet, desperate tears that wrench my heart, that make me want to take her in my arms and cry with her. But I know that I cannot go to her as I want to, because for her to know that I have seen her like this would make her pain double in proportion.

And so I sink into the shadows, slide outside and close the door behind me, lean against the cold rough stone of the barn wall and catch my rasping breath. The fact that we both ache for the same person, and yet we cannot comfort each other at all, increases the sense of loneliness threefold.

*Dear Rob,*
*Blinkered by my own selfishness, I never knew. What can I do, Rob? I want to help her. I want to help her so badly because I know the pain she feels. I know how much it hurts to miss you so badly, to not have you here with us. But what can I do for her when she won't let me near her? And how could I help her – what could I do for her? Teach her to deal with this in the same blind way that I have, up to now? To lock it all away inside, to find a deep place within herself to bury the pain, somewhere she cannot feel how much it hurts her . . .*

# *Chapter Seven*

A storm ravaged through the night like an angry Old Testament God raining disapproval on His people, the wind rattling the windows like a lost soul trying to break in, rain slicing through the air with the vicious bite of a falling knife.

I'm late up, not because I couldn't sleep – I think I'm getting used to functioning fairly normally on a nightly slumber of around four hours – no, I'm late up because for once I find my bed a far more enticing prospect than anything else the day has to hold. It is so beautifully warm and cosy under my duvet. The only problem is, I've always been one of those people who feel guilty if they stay in bed. Also, it reminds me of those bleak, soulless days following Rob's death when I did little else but squat in my bedroom like something only half-living.

I get up and spend half an hour in the bath, trying and failing to soak away an unnerving melancholia with Laura's lavender-scented bubble bath. When I finally make it downstairs I find that I am alone.

Laura has left a note on the kitchen table to say that she is visiting a friend. Looking out of the window onto a cold grey day, I see a light in the end stable, and know that Cas is in with Chance. It's gone two in the afternoon, and I can't see her going out riding in this weather, but I know for a fact she'll stay out there for as long as possible whilst Laura is out, anything to avoid being alone in the house with me.

I switch on the portable TV purely for some noise rather than a desire to watch anything, then help myself to a very late breakfast of toast topped with cold bacon from the fridge. I eat half-heartedly, the food tasting dry, and end up scraping most of it into the pedal bin beneath the kitchen sink. I'm worried about Cas, but as usual I don't know what to do.

I want to make sure that she is okay. The sight of her yesterday, deflated, defeated by a desperate pain, made me want to take that pain away and load it onto my own. I knew she was hurting, but she has never shown me the true depth of her anguish. She hides it so well underneath that spiky exterior, hides her grief at the loss of her father – and, of course, her mother – behind the animosity she shows me, hides her pain so well that I didn't know how truly awful she felt until yesterday.

I want to reach out to her, but I am afraid of being rejected yet again. I know that if I *don't* even try, however, it will eat away at me, like a maggot inside a fallen apple, for being such a coward. Sighing heavily, I take Laura's huge old mackintosh from the coat stand, and pull on a pair of boots.

It's bitingly cold outside, the rain falling in slanting sheets that permeate and soak in seconds. Pulling up the hood of the old coat to protect myself, I head over to the stable and look in over the open top half of the door.

It is dark in the stable but warm, the peppery smell of horse and the sweet yet pleasantly rank scent of soiled straw somehow comforting. Cas has her back to me, and is bent down by the side of Chance, his hind leg resting in her hand as she carefully cleans the mud from his hoof with a metal pick. She hasn't heard me approach.

I can see her lips moving as she talks to Chance, and yet I cannot hear what she is saying to him. I want to talk to *her*, to reassure her, and yet I cannot find the words, and I cannot find the courage. I stand and watch her for a few minutes, hoping that she will turn and see me, that she will want to speak to me, but she simply moves on to the next hoof without looking up.

I turn away and walk quickly down the long passage, angry with myself for being so bloody useless. I pull the mackintosh closer around me, but whilst waterproof, it is heavy and several sizes too big, allowing the rain to creep in at my throat where the neck sits gaping widely.

I shove my hands deep inside the pockets, my fingers closing around the letter that sits in the left one. It is the letter I found myself writing to Rob last night, pouring my heart out to the one person who would truly understand.

I know it's madness but there's something inside me, some compulsion that won't let me rest until the letter has been sent. Cas needs help. *I* need help. If I let Rob know how much we need him, then surely he will come to our aid in some way.

I open the gate at the end of the long passage, my cold fingers slipping on the wet metal, and take the now familiar route through the fields. It's a good job I know where I'm going because visibility is beyond poor. I can see about ten paces ahead of me but no further.

I pull back the long sleeve of my coat and, screwing up my eyes against the rain, look down at my watch. It is not yet three o'clock and yet it feels as if night is already drawing in. The sky and the sea are the colour and volatility of spilt petrol, the breakers crashing against the granite cliffs, breaking the water into splintered pieces as though it were glass.

I am bitterly cold. My gloveless fingers are shoved deep inside the pockets of the great coat, and yet the unforgiving material offers little warmth. Unable to see clearly, I continue as if on auto-pilot, the sound of the sea to my right the only thing that lets me know I'm still heading vaguely in the right direction, my feet sinking into the sodden ground with every step. After over an hour on what is normally a thirty- to forty-minute walk at most, there is still no sign of the Huer's hut. Every step I take is a battle against the wind, and the only thing that keeps me moving is this insane need to continue what I now view as our communication, mine and Rob's.

The rain in my face has been joined by the salt water of the sea as my route goes from field to cliff edge. I am now so tired I could just buckle where I am, sink to my knees and rest my cheek against the cold waterlogged land. There is an ominous growl of thunder in the distance, like the ravenous belly of Hell itself waiting for more lost souls to feed it, and then I hear a deep familiar bark. Moments later, Mac is beside me.

I bend down to greet him, amazed at how pleased I am to see his friendly canine face, as he thrusts his forehead into my stomach, rear end waving frantically in his pleasure to see me. Then his paws are on my bent knees and he is licking the water from my face.

I can just make out a voice yelling to me against the wind, faint, but still unmistakably someone calling my name. Mac turns, head cocked, listening, and then starts to move toward the voice. He stops and looks back at me, and when he sees that I am not following, he returns to my side and nudges my hand with his nose as if to say, 'Hurry up, you idiot.'

The voice calls again, and a dark figure looms into view through the gloom.

'Natalie? Nattie, is that you?'

It is Connor. I peer at him through hair so soaked that water is streaming in rivulets down my face, dripping in a steady waterfall from the end of my nose and my chin.

'It *is* you! What the hell are you thinking of, walking out in this weather?'

'I needed to clear my head,' I reply, my fingers closing protectively around the letter in my pocket.

'You're more likely to lose it than clear it, trying to

cross the cliff path at the moment.'

'You're out,' I reply a touch petulantly.

'Only because I looked out of my kitchen window and saw a madwoman trying to march across the cliff head, and felt duty bound to come out here and stop her.'

'I don't need looking after.'

'No, I'm sure that you don't; you just need your head read from time to time.'

'Okay, so I didn't think.'

'Now there's something that we can finally both agree on.' His face softens. 'Come away in, for heaven's sake, Natalie, before we both go over the edge.'

We stand and stare at each other for a moment, both refusing to move, until I give in rather ungraciously, and follow him from the cliff path, across a field and through a gorse hedge, to where his muddy Range Rover is parked haphazardly in a gateway. Connor opens the passenger door and Mac pushes past me to jump in and park his large damp backside in the passenger seat, obviously relieved to be out of the wind and the rain.

'Shift over, you big oaf.' Connor shoves him good-naturedly, but he refuses to climb into the back seat. 'Sorry. Sometimes he doesn't know his place.'

'I think the problem is he does, and it's in the front seat.' I smile nervously at Connor. 'It's okay, I think there's enough room left . . .'

I squeeze in next to Mac, who good-naturedly shifts over a little so that his backside is hanging over the handbrake, and rest gratefully against the solid warmth of his body. I watch as Connor runs head down against the rain to the other side of the car, and wrenching open the driver's door, climbs hastily in. Brushing his soaked hair from his forehead, he starts the engine and pulls away, the huge car struggling to skid out of the mud-bound gateway and back onto the road, wheels spinning in the slick of liquid mud that is now the verge.

I hadn't realised how cold I was until my hands begin

to thaw out in the warmth of the car heater. I'm almost groaning with pain as the numbness turns to that horrible nerve-jangling ache that feels like it's never going to lessen.

Glancing across, Connor notices the struggle I'm having, my bottom lip white and bloodless where I'm biting into it to stop myself from crying out with pain. He doesn't actually say *fool*, but I can see it in his eyes. He pulls over to the side of the road, and silently taking my hands in his, begins to massage them in turn, rubbing vigorously until the aching pain turns to the prickling rush of pins and needles.

We are only five minutes away from where Connor lives.

Only when I see the lights of the house, do I realise how dark it's actually got in the last half an hour. Night has come prematurely, carried by the storm, daylight obscured by the dense bank of cloud stacking up in the sky like cars on a blocked and fog-bound motorway.

Connor lives in an old farm cottage, nestled in the elbow of a hill overlooking the ocean. 'The Loft' is long and low, with white limed walls – a little how I imagine Smuggler's Cottage could look, if repaired and loved and lived in.

We run through the rain from the car. Mac reaches the doorway first, pushing through our legs as Connor unlocks the heavy wooden door and ushers me inside. We step into a hallway that runs the width of the house from front to back, a set of wooden stairs to the right taking an L-shaped route via the back wall of the house to the first floor.

Silently Connor takes my heavy coat which is raining its own small puddle on the tiled floor, and throws it easily onto some coat hooks on the wall at the bottom of the stairs, along with his own jacket which is almost as soaked. I'm glad to be rid of its sodden weight, until Mac decides to dry off by shaking himself in front of us. It's like being hit with a garden sprinkler, and I find myself even wetter than I was outside in the storm.

Connor's solemn face finally breaks into a smile. 'Look at the state of you. You look like you've been drowned twice over. I think I had better get you a towel, or three. Go and wait for me inside, the fire's lit.' He indicates a door to the left, before heading up the stairs, two at a time.

Taking off my muddy boots, and leaving them carefully on the rush matting by the front door, I duck under a lintel into the room on my left. It is a large room, with a warm pinkish-grey flagstone floor, and white walls. Two picture windows look out to where, were it not for the dark and the storm, we would clearly see the rolling mass of the Atlantic Ocean. A third window, to the rear, overlooks not a garden, but the slope of the hill. It seems less a living area than a gallery. An entirely unintentional showcase for various pieces of his work.

There is nowhere to sit by the fire, so I simply stand and drip in front of it, until Connor returns with two huge towels, and one of his own jumpers for me to change into. I struggle to peel off my sodden jumper, which is sticking to the T-shirt below.

'Come here.' Connor steps up to me and pulls the jumper and T-shirt easily over my head, then immediately wraps one of the towels about my shoulders, and taking the second, begins to rub at my hair as vigorously as he rescued my hands from frostbite.

His hands eventually slow down and he rubs more gently, and then he pushes the towel back and away from my face, letting it fall to the floor behind me. He rearranges my damp hair, gentle fingers taming a stray tendril from my eyes, imprisoning it behind my ear.

'There – that's much better now, isn't it?' he says softly, smiling at me.

I am suddenly filled with a worse embarrassment than that of being found acting like a lunatic out in the thunderstorm. While Connor hangs my wet things over the back of a chair by the fire to dry out, I feel the need to make polite conversation.

'Lovely place you have here,' I smile, uneasy with the cliché.

'Thanks. I like it,' he replies without looking at me.

I look about the room. Apart from an old pine table, which has been pushed back against the rear wall, and is currently bearing the weight of a large jar full of white spirit and paintbrushes and a square glass vase full of different coloured stones collected from the beach, the room is home to an assortment of artwork in varying degrees of completion. Blank canvases are stacked four deep against the wall by the door. A large painting of what I assume must be the view from his window is stood on an easel just to the side of the original window almost like a displaced mirror image of it. There are piles of driftwood on the floor in the corner; a wooden horse as tall as my waist stands next to it, made from several pieces of wood bound together with thin copper wire. None of the wood has been cut; the pieces have been painstakingly placed together until the shape emerged from them, a wild stallion galloping across the beach below.

It must have taken him ages. It is absolutely beautiful.

'I didn't realise you were so good,' I say, without thinking how rude this might sound. He simply smiles, so I'm hoping that he's taken it in the spirit in which it was meant. Why is it that when you come across art, you want to appear to be knowledgeable about it? We're not all going to be Sister Wendy, but everybody has an opinion, some more informed than others.

I always feel slightly disadvantaged by my lack of further education. Most people within my field have a degree – something I've always battled to prove I didn't need to get where I wanted to go. I always feel slightly socially inferior. Don't ask me why, I know it's silly. I have a brain, and when I use it, it's far keener than some people I know, even though they have MAs and PhDs coming out of their backside. Still, it must be such a comfort, having a piece of paper to fall back upon.

A pile of slender branches lies next to the huge open fire that is currently burning low in the black grate. He has arranged them very artistically. I try to come up with an appropriate comment.

'This is er . . . very unusual,' I offer, hoping to sound knowledgeable.

'You think so?'

'Oh yes. The way the branches intertwine, random and haphazard, yet somehow structured.'

'Oh, really?' He raises his eyebrows at me.

I nod enthusiastically.

'That's for the fire, Natalie.'

'The fire?'

'You know, kindling for the fire.' He picks up a small axe that is leaning against the wall next to the pile of branches, and waves it at me. 'I've been chopping wood.'

'Oh,' I say flatly. 'I thought it was some kind of statement.'

'The axe?'

'Yeah.' I bite my bottom lip. 'I thought it was symbolic.'

He stares at me for a moment, while I struggle not to turn the same colour as the blood-red winter roses arranged in a vase on the window ledge. The next thing I know, he's roaring with laughter, laughing so hard in fact that tears begin to well in his eyes.

'Well, how was I supposed to know?' I mutter, before feeling that my mouth too is starting to emulate his smile, born initially of embarrassment, but then fuelled by a resurgence of my sense of humour over my sense of idiocy. 'I'm not doing very well today,' I tell him. 'Have you read any Douglas Adams?'

'Yeah,' he nods. 'I have.'

'The *Hitch-hiker's Guide* series?'

'Most of them.'

'Well, I feel like Arthur Dent. At the beginning of one of the books, I can't remember which one, he's completely on his own, because he's somehow ended up back in prehistoric times . . . and he's spending an awful lot of time trying not to go mad – you know, he's really worried that he's going to go mad. And then he just wakes up one morning, and decides sod it. What's the point of worrying about going mad, until you go mad with worry. Why not just go mad straightaway, and reap the immediate benefits of *being* mad, such as not having to worry about *anything*, and sod all the pain involved in the process of trying not to go mad until you *do* actually go mad.'

'That's how you feel at the moment?'

'Pretty much, yeah,' I reply, amazed that he followed me.

'Want to talk about it?'

'Not really,' I sigh.

He nods as though he understands. 'Okay. You'd better give Laura a call and tell her where you are, she'll be worried.'

He steps through a door at the far end of the room, and I follow, walking into a small dimly lit rear hall. There is a closed door to my left, another at the end of the corridor, and a glow of light where the corridor turns to the left at the end, kind of like an upside down L. 'The phone's in the study.' He nods toward the heavy door. 'I'll stick the kettle on. Do you want tea or coffee, or something a bit stronger?'

'Tea would be good, thanks.'

He disappears into the room on the left where the light is coming from, whilst I push through the heavy baize door in front of me.

'The light switch is on the right of the door frame,' Connor calls to me as I grope along the wall in the semi-dark.

222

I find the switch and flick it on, gasping as the room is flooded with a warm low light from three wall lamps. It seems as though every piece of soft furnishing missing from the sitting room has been crammed into this one small room. The curtains are heavy Burgundy-backed William Morris, and drawn, which explains why the room is so dark; the carpet is thick and the rug that covers this, luxurious; the two floor coverings combined are like walking on a cushion.

There are two chairs, one wing, one for the dark oak desk bound with dark tan leather. And books. Everywhere, books. You cannot see the walls for the books that line them. They are piled in haphazard towers upon the floor, upon the desk, upon the window ledge, and open in front of the hearth, where the remains of a fire glows dimly in the soft light.

Forgetting my phone call, I dive hungrily upon the nearest pile of old leather-bound tomes, holding the first one to my face and breathing in the aroma of musty paper and leather in delight, then turning it to read the cracked gold lettering along its spine.

*Wuthering Heights.* How apt. I almost laugh with the irony of it all when the book falls open at the page where Cathy is staggering across a weather-ravaged moor. Abandoning Cathy to be rescued by Heathcliff, I hover between the shelves and piles of books like a bumble bee which has suddenly found itself in a hot-house at Kew, unable to settle because the choice of nectar is simply too overwhelming.

Connor comes through the door bearing two mugs and a dust-covered bottle of brandy, to find me sitting cross-legged on the floor in front of the fire buried face down in an ancient copy of *Pride and Prejudice*. He hands me my tea, which is laced fairly heavily with brandy. I sip it gratefully, feeling the warm liquid curling down into my stomach, and then the warmth seeping through the rest of my body as the alcohol gets to work in my bloodstream.

'You like books?' he asks, smiling at the sight of me cross-legged on the floor, surrounded by a wall of bound paper that I have gathered to me like Aladdin scooping up gold in the Forty Thieves' cave.

'I love to read.' I beam up at him, 'I'm a writer – I need words, books, like . . . like a diabetic needs insulin . . . like you need paint and canvas.' I stop and smile at him, a little abashed. 'I'm sorry, I'm a total bore when I get started.'

He laughs and waves his hand around the room. 'And I'm not, you think? Books are wonderful. Think about it, when you paint, you're not just creating a pretty picture. You're giving someone a whole different world to fall into. It's the same with books.' He bends and picks up a copy of *Robinson Crusoe* from the top of one of the piles. 'This isn't just a collection of words, it isn't just a story. This is one of the things that shaped my childhood, made me who I am today.'

'I know exactly what you mean. Seeing some of these again is like being reunited with old friends. I didn't have many real friends when I was young,' I admit slowly. 'We never stayed in one place long enough for me to make any – to *learn* how to make any. It's hard always being the new girl, especially when you don't have any social graces to speak of. These, the characters within them, they were my friends – more real to me sometimes than life itself. When the Swallows fought the Amazons I was there with them sailing that boat through the rocks in the darkness guided only by the light of two lanterns. When Lucy stepped through the back of the wardrobe into Narnia, I left my footprints in the snow beside hers. The ability to transport someone to another world with just the written word . . .' I sigh in wonderment. 'That's why I started to write in the first place. I wanted to be a novelist. I kind of lost direction though – not that I don't enjoy what I do. It's just not quite what I actually meant to do when I started out.'

I falter, aware that I have been rambling on, but he's smiling encouragingly at me, no trace of condescension evident.

'Life has a way of taking off without you sometimes,' he says, settling down on the floor beside me. 'Not always in the direction you wanted it to. Have you ever read this one? It's one of my favourites.' He reaches for a book in the pile beside me and his arm brushes unintentionally against mine, the cashmere of his jumper producing a soft sting of sensation along my naked forearm that makes me shiver, despite the warmth of the room. He picks up an old blue book beyond me, an outline of a boy kneeling like a warrior on the front.

'Is that what I think it is?' I breathe in excitement.

'*Brendan Chase*,' he tells me, handing it to me as though it is precious cargo.

I take the book with a wistful smile, carefully turning the pages, yellow with age.

'This was my father's favourite book,' I tell Connor. 'He used to read it to me when I was small to send me to sleep, but it always had the opposite effect. I never wanted him to stop reading, and flatly refused to close my eyes.'

'What else do you like to do beside read?'

'That's another passion.' I gesture to a chessboard set out upon the hearth. 'Not that I'm very good, but I enjoy it. It makes me use my brain. No one at Whitsunday will play. I used to play with Rob . . .' I stop, take a breath, push the pain back down.

Connor hears the catch in my voice, watches me pause and take control. 'Do you want to talk about it?' he asks me for a second time, although this time without the trace of a smile.

'No.' I shake my head. 'He always used to beat me hands down.'

It is obvious that this is not what Connor meant, but I am grateful that he takes my somewhat glib hint. He reaches for the board, and places it between us.

'If you don't want to talk, how about we play instead?'

'Would you like to? I mean, I don't want to stop you from working or something.'

He shakes his head. 'I'm done for the day. Go on, play me. It's not often I get the chance to meet a fellow enthusiast.'

The pieces are made of marble, the white men shot through with veins of soft green, the black streaked with white, the stone smooth and cool between my thumb and forefinger. We play chess. I love playing, but that doesn't mean I'm particularly good at it. Whereas I can forward-think of the consequences of each move to about one step, he is still three steps ahead of me each time. He's almost apologetic when he beats me once more on the third game.

'Don't worry, I'm used to never winning.'

'How about we give it one more game? You nearly got me on the last. You obviously just take longer to warm up than I do.'

I shake my head. 'That's being kind, thanks, but I really should be going.'

He looks at his watch, and raises his eyebrows in concern. 'Jeez, is that the time? It's past seven already. Laura will think that I've kidnapped you.'

'Ah.' My face falls. 'I haven't actually phoned her yet – I got side-tracked.'

He hands me our empty mugs. 'Take these through to the kitchen for me, I'll give her a call for you.'

I smile, grateful that he is intuitive enough to offer to call Whitsunday for me. If I'm being completely honest I hadn't forgotten, I'd just pushed it to one side of my mind, a side where I keep things that I want to ignore for a while. It's a pretty full side at the moment. To be honest it's nice to be here; it's the sort of place, and Connor the sort of company, where you can forget your problems for a while.

To talk to my mother, and even more to talk to Cas would just bring reality flooding back in. I don't particularly like my reality at the moment.

Connor's kitchen is a beautiful place, with limed wood and washed walls, light and airy, modern yet cosy. He has all of the appliances you could ever wish for in a kitchen, and yet from their shiny-as-new appearance it would seem that they are rarely used.

Not quite sure whether one of the cupboard doors is hiding a dishwasher, and not wishing to pry, I place the mugs in the sink and begin to fill it with water and Fairy Liquid. I can hear Connor on the phone in the study talking to my mother, his tone deliberately calm and reassuring, and feel a pang of guilt. No matter what I think, she must have been worried about me.

I can be so selfish sometimes, so self-centred, turning in on myself as though only I can understand what I'm going through. I forget that Laura went through the very same thing as me when she was almost the same age. Younger, in fact, than I was. I remember how turned in on herself Laura became when my father died, how remote and untouchable *she* was, how the life in her seemed to simply die without him. I remember too mourning the loss of the vivacious, affectionate mother that I knew and loved, the person that Laura seems to be once again . . .

I hated the Laura that was – I felt abandoned by her. Her misery had stolen my mother. I used to want to scream at her to get a life, to move on, to be strong – all of the things I find so easy to ignore when others say them to me now.

Connor comes through as I'm drying the mugs on some paper kitchen towel. He's frowning. 'Laura says there's a tree down across the top of the track, and another on the A30; the radios are warning about flash floods.'

'Is she okay?'

'Now she knows you weren't underneath the tree when it fell, yes. She couldn't think of any other reason why you'd be out for so long, and so late as well. They'd been out looking for you for over an hour.'

'Oh no, they hadn't, had they?' I put the mug that I'm drying down on the side, and guiltily cover my mouth with my hand.

He nods gravely.

'Oh, I feel awful. I didn't tell anybody I was going out.'

'So I gather.'

'I'd better go.'

He shakes his head. 'You can't. The road's blocked, remember, and the track. I should imagine the Fire Brigade will be out to the main road as soon as they can, but your mother told Hank not to worry about clearing the track to the farm until the morning; unsurprisingly, she didn't want him coming out in this. I won't be able to drive you back to the farm – nothing can get through at the moment.'

'Then I'll walk.'

'Don't be insane.'

'I'll be fine, it's not far.'

'Sure – along the coastal path and across the fields, which as you'll remember is where I intercepted you earlier. If I wasn't going to let you walk out in this then, do you really think I'm going to let you do it now, when it's pitch black and the storm is worse?'

I'm tempted to point out that I don't need Connor Blythe's permission to do anything, but I know that he is talking sense, whilst I am thinking irrationally as usual.

'I promised Laura that I'd keep you here for the night.'

'Oh, but I couldn't possibly,' I blurt out a touch rudely,

suddenly horrified at the thought of spending the night here. 'I mean, I don't want to put you out . . .'

'You're not putting me out.' The tense face relaxes and he smiles at me a little. 'Besides, how many times have you had Mac for me?'

'Well, that's a little bit different, isn't it?'

'Yeah, you've got far better manners for starters.' The smile grows and my discomfort eases a little.

'How can you be so sure?' I can't help smiling back at him.

'You don't fart constantly and try to steal food from other people's plates, do you?'

'Not in public, no,' I joke weakly, grateful for his humour.

'Then that's settled – you're staying and no more argument. Now the only problem left to solve is that I have a spare bedroom, but I don't have a spare bed.'

'I can share with Mac – he normally shares with me.'

He shakes his head, ignoring the jest. 'You can take my room.'

'That's no good. Where are you going to sleep if I take your bed?'

'In the sitting room.'

'The place with all the paintings?' I ask in concern, aware that the only piece of furniture he could even contemplate sleeping on would be the table. 'No way. I won't steal your bed, and then make you sleep on a cold stone floor.'

'I won't have to.' He leads me back into the hall and opens the only remaining door onto another very small room.

The room with the paintings was a studio, *this* is his sitting room. It may be tiny, but it's beautifully decorated. It looks like somebody's taken a comfortable drawing room from a stately home, and stuck it in the tumble dryer on hot, shrinking it to a miniature perfection. There are heavy old-gold curtains and golden oak furniture to include a coffee-table supporting the weight of more books, art ones this time, thick tomes beautifully bound.

There is a TV table bearing a small unobtrusive portable television, two windows to the front, more books, lamps casting a soft glow, and the walls are literally covered with paintings, not his own, but watercolours of pretty gardens and green landscapes, a stark contrast to the bold and beautiful seascapes that he paints. But most of all there is a large velvet sofa, the sort you sit on and sink straight into.

'See? It's more than comfortable – you could sleep an entire rugby team on that sofa should you ever feel so inclined, not that I do, mind you, so will you stop worrying now?'

I nod.

'Okay, now we're settled on the sleeping arrangements, how about some food? I'd order in a takeaway, but unless they deliver by rescue helicopter, nothing's getting through tonight.'

'I'm not really hungry,' I reply, despite the fact that I've barely eaten today. I think my stomach has an *Out of Order* sign on it at the moment.

'Well, I am, and you won't let me eat alone, now surely?'

'That depends on your cooking,' I reply, still hiding my nerves behind humour.

'Oh, I can just about manage to grill a steak.'

Back in the kitchen I watch as he switches on the grill of his oven and begins to get utensils from the drawers, taking a long sharp knife from the block on the marble side.

'Can I help?'

He reaches into the fridge and pulls out a paper bag full of mushrooms. 'You can wash those for me if you like. There's a colander in one of the bottom cupboards, the one on the far right, by the side door.'

I wash the bag of mushrooms and hand them to Connor, who is wielding a sharp knife and a frying pan simultaneously with an enviable expertise. He puts the mushrooms onto a huge wooden chopping board and deftly chops them into tiny pieces, throwing them into the frying pan where he already has a chopped onion sizzling away. He adds garlic, pepper, red wine and then cream, and then leaving the deliciously aromatic sauce to simmer gently, removes the salad tray from the fridge and proceeds to wash and chop the contents until the large blue ceramic salad bowl he takes from a shelf bearing several unusual pieces – including, I note, one of Laura's ashtrays tucked away at the back – is full to overflowing.

Two huge steaks are turning rapidly under the grill; pulling them out, he puts one on each plate and adds the sauce.

'Just about manage to grill a steak,' I mock, as I help to set the small table that stands against the wall opposite the sink. Then: 'Don't tell me, you made this as well,' as he puts a fresh loaf down on the table beside the salad.

'Kneaded with my own fair hands and then rolled out on the thighs of dusky maidens,' he quips, pointing out the empty Tesco's wrapper on the side. He pours us both a large glass of wine from the bottle that he had already opened for the sauce. 'Cheers! Well – go on, eat something. It's not as poisonous as it looks.'

'It doesn't look poisonous, it looks great.'

I wish I could knock up something like this with such apparent ease. Maybe it's the artistic nature; the creativity isn't only limited to paint and canvas. Perhaps he's one of those perfect men, who can turn their hand to anything. Artist, gourmet chef, ridiculously attractive, charming, spotless house.

Intimidating.

'This is fantastic,' I murmur.

'It's also fantastically simple.'

Modest to boot.

'You could be a chef.'

'Heaven forbid!' He almost chokes on the piece of steak he is chewing. 'Shall I let you in on a secret?' He leans in confidentially. 'I'm a lousy cook, so I am. This is the only thing I can manage that doesn't taste like it's been murdered and left to rot for three weeks, apart from a fry-up in the morning, that is – but anyone can make a mess of bacon and eggs in a pan, and it still taste okay. And,' he adds, jabbing at his plate with his fork, 'this isn't even my recipe.'

I can't help laughing. At me, as well as him. I know what I'm doing. I'm finding fault in the fact that he didn't seem to have any, simply because I *need* to find fault with him. I don't want to like him as much as I do, and I have known from the picnic that I like him.

I try to relax. 'Have you always wanted to be an artist?'

He shakes his head. 'No way. Not at all. In fact, I think the very first thing I wanted to be was a deep-sea diver. Jacques Cousteau was a big influence,' he explains with a grin, as I raise my eyebrows. 'Then of course I wanted to be James Bond. I think most boys go through a stage of wanting to be some kind of Superhero.'

'Yeah – and he was the one who always got the girls.'

'Sure, but it was his cars that I wanted. I fell in love with his Aston Martins long before I saw the finer points of Honey Ryder and Pussy Galore. Although of course I did eventually notice those as well.'

'When I was a child I wanted to fly,' I tell him shyly, looking down at my plate.

'You wanted to be a pilot?'

'No. I didn't want the constraint of an aeroplane, I simply wanted to fly. Like a bird. Spread my arms and soar up into the sky above me. I sometimes dream that I'm flying just like that, swooping and diving like a swallow, way above the heads of everyone, and I always feel slightly smug about it. I can fly and everyone else is stuck to the ground with feet like cement.'

He pours more wine into my glass.

'I read somewhere that if you dream you're flying then it indicates an overwhelming desire to get away from your problems,' I murmur.

'And I suppose there are a few people that you could dump on whilst you were up there too?' he replies with a poker-straight face.

I almost spit my wine straight out again as I convulse with laughter, starting to choke.

'Is the food that bad?' he quips, as hand to mouth I struggle to regain control of my breathing.

'No, the food's great, it's the jokes.'

'Oh, my jokes are bad now, are they? Well, have you heard the one about the rabbit who goes into the butcher's shop and asks for a cabbage . . .'

And he's off. A run of jokes so awful, they're funny beyond belief. I spend the next half an hour laughing so hard that I find I cannot eat any more. Connor finally stops reeling them off like a comedian on stage at Jongleurs, and looks at my half-eaten meal in concern.

'You've barely eaten a thing. Would you like a pudding? Some fruit or something?'

I shake my head, my hand nursing my already full stomach. 'I couldn't possibly. That was great though, thank you.'

'How about a glass of brandy then?'

The wine was strong; my head already feels a little dizzy, light and heavy at the same time, as the alcohol gets to work on my brain. It has given me a taste though.

'Please. That would be good.'

He takes our plates to the drainer by the sink, and pulls a bottle of Cognac from one of the cupboards, whilst I carry the rest of the things over. There's a framed photograph on the wall by the kitchen window.

An old black and white of three people standing in front of a cottage not dissimilar to the Loft. A dark-haired woman is flanked by two men.

'Who are they?'

'My folks. Ma's the one in the dress in case you were wondering, and the old fella on the left is Uncle Vernon. He's the only one still alive of the lot of 'em – eighty-seven and still going strong, so he is. Swears it's all down to drinking three pints of Guinness every night since he was fourteen years old.'

'This was taken in Ireland?'

'Yes.'

'Have you lived here for very long?'

'England or Cornwall?'

'Both.'

'I came over from Ireland when I was nineteen, lived in London until I was about twenty-seven, twenty-eight, and then decided I'd had enough of it and moved down here.'

'You didn't want to go back home?'

'Home?'

'To Ireland?'

'That's where I was born – it doesn't mean it's home. Home is wherever you make it. Wherever you feel comfortable.' He sits back down at the table and pours us both a large measure of Remy into two tumblers. I sit back down opposite him.

He pushes one of the glasses across the table to me, and raises his own. 'Good health.'

'Your health,' I echo. I drink too deeply, coughing slightly as the smooth liquid burns a fiery course over the soft flesh of my oesophagus. 'Do you have any family here?' I ask when recovered.

He nods. 'A brother. He's five years younger than me, but he's married with about eighteen children.'

My eyes widen at the thought. 'Eighteen children?'

'Well, five really, but it feels like more when they all

get going. The youngest is two and the eldest is ten, so you can imagine it's bedlam in their house.'

'And do they still live in Ireland?'

He shakes his head and smiles. 'Durham.'

'And what about you?'

'What about me?'

'Have you ever been married?'

'No.'

'Oh?' I wait for more details, but he says nothing, simply refilling our brandy glasses and sipping slowly, watching me over the rim of his glass with an amused expression on his face.

'Girlfriends?' I ask, immediately wishing I hadn't because it sounds like I have an interest and I really don't want him to think that.

'I was living with someone when I was in London. We were together for about six years.'

'And what happened?'

'I moved down here.'

'And that was it?'

'It turned out she loved life in London more than she loved me.'

'I'm sorry.'

'Don't be. Everything happens for a reason. And it wouldn't have been fair of me to expect her to give up everything she wanted, to follow *my* dream, now would it? I wouldn't stay in London with her. She wouldn't come to Cornwall with me. Neither of us are to blame, we just wanted completely different things from life, things that were more important to us than each other.'

'And since then?'

'I've never found anybody that's important enough,' he replies, looking down into his drink. 'Although,' his eyes flicker up at me, their blue-grey surface sparkling with mischief, 'Orlaithe and I have been having a passionate affair right under Hank's cowboy boots for some time now.'

'Yeah,' I flash back at him, 'and I'm madly in lust with Daveth Brann.'

'Really. He's married with about eighteen children of his own, so I wonder he has time for seducing you. Then again with all of those children he must be doing something right in the bedroom department.'

'More children? How do people cope with so many? I have enough trouble trying to look after one.'

It's a jokey comment, but Connor stops laughing and studies me seriously. 'Maybe you're trying too hard with the one that you do have.'

'What do you mean?'

'Children are like animals, Nattie, they can sense when you're uptight and it makes them nervous. With Cas it's almost like she's living down to your expectations.'

'What do you mean?' I repeat.

'She knows you expect her to play up and give you a hard time, so that's what she does.'

'So you're saying it's all my fault,' I reply, fighting back a feeling of indignation.

'No, that's not what I'm saying at all. I'm not saying it's anybody's fault. You've just got into a bit of a vicious cycle, that's all.'

'I thought it was supposed to be a vicious circle.'

'That too,' he replies, smiling in a conciliatory way. 'I'm not having a go at you, Nattie. I think the way you've dealt with . . .' he pauses, obviously hunting for the right word, '*everything*, has been incredible considering the circumstances.'

'My mother talks too much,' I mutter. 'Is there anyone in the west of Cornwall who doesn't know about *everything*?'

'Probably not. She really cares about you, you know, Natalie.'

I look back at him blankly.

'Your mother. She talks about you all the time.'

'She does?'

'Yes, she does. All the time. Why do you never come to see her?'

I could tell him to butt out and mind his own business, but for some reason I want to explain to him how it's been. I don't want him to think ill of me. It's important to me that he understands the relationship Laura and I have had over the years, or rather lack of relationship, from my perspective as well as hers. But where to start?

'We haven't been very close, since my father died,' I begin carefully.

He nods encouragingly.

'She changed, literally overnight. I mean, of course she would, you can't have something like that happen and it not affect you. I know that . . . now. But it felt to me as if I'd lost my mother as well as my father. She became so cold. Unloving. She just shut me out completely. And I needed her. I was six years old, I'd just lost my father, and I needed her . . .'

I trail off. This is the first time I've really voiced these feelings to someone else. I never even really talked about it to Rob. He tried to talk to me about why I so rarely saw Laura, but I always used to fob him off, to change the subject somehow, as though I was embarrassed or ashamed to admit that I felt that way about my own mother. That I understood completely as an adult why she changed so radically when my father died, and yet as an adult I could still not come to terms with the hurt I had felt over it, the rejection.

I felt it was a part of my personality that was flawed, and I wanted Rob to think that I was perfect. I don't need Connor to think I'm perfect, but I don't want him to think I'm still wallowing in the upset of my six to sixteen-year-old self. I smile at him. A hearty smile that is meant to convey that I'm over it all now.

'That was a long time ago now. You understand more as you get older.'

'Yes, but you have to forgive, as well as understand.'

'But I do – forgive her, that is. As you get older you realise that life is what *you* make of it. You can't rely on other people to ensure you have a happy life.'

'You can't rely on other people, but you should be able to rely on your own mother, that's what you really think, isn't it, Natalie? Do you forgive her – *really*? Come on, be honest with yourself. You're telling me that you've forgiven her for not being there when you needed her, but you've still only managed to visit her about five times since you were sixteen.'

'I thought you said you wanted to be James Bond, not Sigmund Freud.'

'I know. I'm sorry. It's always so much easier to advise other people on their problems than to sort out your own, isn't it? But I know what it's like to lose someone you care about deeply, and *you* know what it's like to lose someone you love. It makes you want to push everyone you might possibly care about out of your life, as far away as possible, so you can't feel that pain again. If you don't care, then you can't get hurt. If you have nothing to be taken away, then you have nothing to lose. The only problem is, you may be able to pretend you don't care to other people, but the hardest part is fooling yourself. Then on top of that there's the fact that you feel like a jinx. Maybe it was your fault that person died. Maybe if someone else gets too close then the same fate will befall them. Look at Cas. Look at how she pushes you away.'

'That's because she hates me,' I mutter crossly, sipping quickly at my brandy.

'That's utter rubbish and you know it.'

'I do? She never gives me any indication otherwise, in fact she practically revels in finding new ways to make me understand exactly how little I mean to her.'

'If you mean so little to her, then why make so much of an effort over you?' He puts his glass down on the table and sits back in his chair, eyebrows raised in question.

'I'm not sure what you mean,' I lie, wanting him to go on.

'If Cas really hated you, she'd ignore you, she wouldn't keep trying to get under your skin so much. Anyway, you must be hating me for it's none of my business, only in so far as Laura is a good friend. A good friend and a good person.'

I nod. 'I do realise that. She's been amazing with Cassie, they really seem to have bonded.'

'And isn't that the absolute pits?' he prompts me.

'It's great that they're friends. Heaven knows, Cas needs someone she feels she can talk to . . .'

'You just wish that someone could be you?'

'Yeah,' I finally admit. 'Is that wrong of me?'

He shakes his head. 'Not at all.'

'Don't get me wrong, I'm really pleased they hit it off so well—'

'Cas needs your friendship as well, Natalie. Oh, she'll deny it till she's blue, but it's true. I just think she expects more from you than from other people.' He pauses and we are silent for a moment. 'Is she like her father?' he asks carefully.

'In some ways, very much so. In others, not at all.'

'What was he like?'

'He was my best friend.' I put my tumbler down on the table.

'You miss him, don't you.'

It's not a question, he is too intelligent for it to be a question – it's a prompt, an opening for me to unload my feelings onto a gentle ear. And it's tempting. It's so tempting to tell this man how much I miss my husband, to pour out all of the feelings I have been bottling up inside of me for nearly two years now, all of the pain, the loneliness, the frustration, the anger even, and yet I cannot lose control. Control for the moment is my only motor, and my only salvation. I cannot talk about Rob, and yet I want to share something of him with Connor.

'I have a picture,' I reply eventually. 'Would you like to see?'

He nods, and I stand up to get my wallet from the back pocket of my jeans.

He studies it quietly for a long time. 'I can see Cas in him.'

'You can?'

'His eyes – and around the mouth.'

'I wish she were more like him in nature.'

He hands me back the photograph, and both aware that this subject is closed for now, we clear up together in silence. There is no dishwasher. I offer to wash whilst he dries. It is only ten and yet I am truly weary. Connor notices my ever-increasing yawns over the soapsuds and suggests that I turn in for the night.

'Come on, I'll show you up to your room.'

He leads the way through the house and up the stairs to the first floor. Here there is a bathroom, a small bedroom stacked full of painting equipment, and boxes, hence no bed, and Connor's room.

Connor's bedroom is huge. Apparently he converted the Loft himself from an empty shell and took advantage of the change to redesign it to suit himself. Three walls of the room are painted soft terracotta, the paint a ragged and stippled effect, like light on moving water. The fourth wall opposite the window is for some reason a different colour, the gentle shade of the sand on Sennen beach. The floor is bare polished boards, the warm rich brown of treacle toffee. There is another open fire, bigger than the others, so large you could almost stand inside it without having to duck.

Again, the furniture in this room is fairly sparse. A large wooden bed is positioned straight in front of me, bed head to the wall, sat between two uncurtained sash windows looking directly out to sea. To either side of the bed is a small wooden table, each bearing a brass lamp, the right one also housing a hand-held phone, and a man's watch, and the left a digital alarm clock.

A tall, handsome chest of drawers sits opposite the bed, and there's a wooden chair in one corner with a shirt thrown across it, a large paint-stain streaked across the front of the white linen. It's a going-out shirt, a smart, expensive shirt, a shirt that needs cufflinks and a silk tie to finish it off, but nonetheless it is a shirt that is now soiled with a huge streak of Vermilion across one sleeve.

I can just imagine him arriving home from a smart dinner-party, and being taken completely by the mood, by the muse, and without a thought for his expensive clothes, throwing paint onto canvas in an orgy of abandonment, until not only the canvas, but he too is covered with paint, but satiated.

His voice breaks my reverie.

'Right – the linen's clean, I only changed it this morning. Well, to tell the truth, my cleaner changed it this morning – yes, I have a cleaner,' he admits with a sideways glance. 'I tend to get a bit lost in my work and just forget sometimes, so your mother sorted out Loveday for me. She's a wonderful woman, so she is. You just happen to have come at the right time, because she's spent all of the day sorting my mess out for me. If you'd come yesterday you would have *had* to sleep with Mac, because his bed was the only one that was made! Right – the bathroom's next door and there are fresh towels in the linen cupboard, so I'll leave you to get some rest. If you need anything, just shout – okay? Or bang on the floor,' he jokes. 'I'm right below you so that should get my attention.'

'Thank you,' I tell him quietly as he turns to leave. 'For everything.'

He hesitates at the door for a moment as though

wanting to speak again, but in the end he simply smiles and says good night. I wait until I hear the door of the sitting room close below me, and then take off my clothes, and aware that I shall have to wear them again tomorrow, fold them neatly over the chair along with his paint-stained shirt.

The bathroom is sited between the two bedrooms, a door from Connor's room leading into it as well as one from the landing. I take a quick shower, and return to the room wrapped in one of the towels he told me I could find there. There is no hair dryer and so a little reluctant to get into his bed just yet, sit in front of the fire to dry my wet hair.

It is strange to be here. In Connor's bedroom.

Despite the warmth of the fire it makes me shiver with discomfort. And it is not a discomfort born of not wanting to be here, of feeling uncomfortable in this most personal of places. It is a discomfort born of the recognition that I *want* to be here, that is the problem. I am full of sadness to be alone in this room, and guilt, because right now, for this one moment, the person I want to be here with me is not Rob, but the man I know is only a few short steps or a broken call away. A man who, without invitation or insinuation, has reached through my protective layer to a heart I thought had ceased to function. A man who, if I was brave enough to reach out to him, would meet my touch with real flesh, living emotion, tangible hope.

And I am drawn tight into myself with longing, and frustration, with ignored want. My mind is so full of thoughts that scream at me like a rabble, that I feel I will never find peace again. And yet, the warmth of the fire, the soft crackle of burning logs, the faint sound of music coming from downstairs, the wine and the brandy, are all a lullaby to a tired mind.

I climb into Connor's bed, feel the soft cream linen

wrap around my naked flesh, and shiver involuntarily, then close my eyes and despite the fact that I'm certain I won't, drift straight away into a sleep that is for once peacefully dreamless.

# *Chapter Eight*

I wake up the next morning with none of that sense of bewilderment you feel when opening your eyes in a foreign place. I am ashamed to admit to myself that I know exactly where I am, and exactly whose bed I'm sleeping in.

Naked, my head resting where his usually lies.

Despite the fact that the linen is clean it still smells of him, the room smells of him, a lingering scent of Connor Blythe, a heady erotic scent that sends my stomach spinning. I stretch out my hands, ploughing the linen with my fingertips, stretching in an almost sybaritic release of tension.

It is early; the clock on the side table tells me that it's not quite seven. It is still raining gently, but the storm has broken, the black clouds are no longer, and the sky is a mist of soft grey, through which I think I see the yellow glow of the sun trying to break through. First a finger of light, and then two, forcing the clouds apart like someone trying to squeeze through a narrow gap.

When the sun has pulled apart a bigger curtain of cloud through which to peer, I suddenly see the sense in his décor. The paler wall is there to reflect the light that streams through the windows either side of the bed, filling the room with sunshine, light reflecting from the sea in waves that wash and ripple across the wall like a moving picture show. I could lie in bed all morning and just watch the hypnotic movement of light, like a therapy to a tired mind.

It's so quiet here. The only noise is the sound of the ocean, a gentle constant rhythmic rush, almost like the sound of someone breathing. No farm animals scuffling or squawking in the background, just the whisper of the sea lulling me back toward sleep again. A door opening then closing nearby makes my eyes blink open. The sound of the shower tells me that Connor is in the bathroom. Try as I may, I cannot stop myself from picturing him in my mind as I listen. I almost see the water running in rivulets down his naked body, his face turned upward to meet the flow . . .

And then the door from the bathroom is pushed open and the face that filled my imagination is peering apologetically round it. I feel a sudden rush of shame.

'Hi, you sleep okay?'

I nod slowly, drawing the duvet from my breastbone to my chin as though to cover myself completely, as though my thoughts are embarrassingly displayed for him to see across my pink flushed skin.

'I just need to get some clothes. I'm sorry, I should have thought of it last night.' He walks across the room to the chest of drawers, a white towel slung about his hips, his hair wet, his back and shoulders still damp, dusted with drops of water.

Connor takes clean clothes from the tall set of drawers and then almost hurries from the room, calling back over his shoulder that breakfast will be ready when I am. I can hear him downstairs in the kitchen, the flick of the switch on the kettle as it reaches boiling point, the metallic click of the springs on the toaster ejecting its load of charcoaled bread, the soft sound of music in the background.

I want to run away. To throw on my clothes and slip quietly out of the house, tiptoeing until I reach the boundary wall, from where I will run like the wind to hide away amidst the rocks that line the cliff head. Instead I rise and dress and go downstairs to share the breakfast Connor has made, both of us a little stilted, too polite.

After breakfast, Connor takes me home. Although the rain has stopped and the main roads are clear of debris, some places are still drowned under several inches of rainwater. When we reach the track to Whitsunday, it is so close to slurry I fear that we may not make it down, but the four-wheel drive of the Land Rover keeps us moving through the river of sludge and loose stone and pot holes full of water.

Halfway down we meet Hank brandishing a chainsaw. He is wearing a long brown Barbour coat, the kind with the cape about the shoulders, and a black stetson with a gold-linked chain around the crown, part country gentleman, part country and western.

He has made short work of the half-dead tree that had fallen across the roadway. It is now sliced and stacked, no doubt ready to be put in the Long Barn until dry, and then used to fuel the fires in the house. He raises his stetson as we pass by him, stepping backwards to avoid the wave of water thrown up from the road by the wheels of the Land Rover as we continue down to the farmhouse, the faded jeans housing his short bow legs already dark in patches from the wet.

Cas is in the yard, Chance tacked up and ready to ride out. She spots us coming in, I know she does, I see her look, but for some reason she pretends that she hasn't seen us, pausing to check some imaginary problem with Chance's girth, whilst Connor pulls the Range Rover to a halt and we climb out onto the slippery mud-coloured cobbles.

The kitchen door pushes open and my mother emerges into the sunshine wiping her floury hands on a tea towel, all smiles and friendly greeting, and yet still Cas ignores us.

Mac jumps out of the car and trots over to Laura, sniffing in anticipation, the smell of baking cookies following her through the open door, lingering on her hands, and the flowered apron she has slung about her waist.

Cas puts a foot into the left stirrup, swings her right leg over the saddle and, gathering up the reins, forces Chance into a fast trot across the yard, heading for the main gate and the track up to the main road. Her eyes are set determinedly forward, her face as hard as granite; she looks at neither me or Laura. She doesn't even acknowledge Connor, simply tapping Chance sharply with her heels to get him past us as quickly as possible.

Her dramatic exit is ruined by the fact that a far more amiable Chance recognises a friend and stops to snuffle my pockets for mints. Cas's face is as black as thunder as she kicks the indignant animal on past me, forcing him into a slow canter as they hit the track, his hooves kicking up little arches of mud in their wake.

I look at my mother in surprise, hoping for an explanation. She simply sighs, and shakes her head. Connor too is watching Cassie leave with a puzzled expression creasing his forehead.

'Well, I'd better get a move on, I've a deadline to meet on a commission,' he says, still looking after Cas.

'Okay. Thanks for everything.'

He turns back to face me. 'It was a pleasure. I should be thanking you really – you're good company, Nattie. If you ever fancy a re-match on the chess front.'

'If I ever fancy a good thrashing, you mean.'

The double entendre is unintentional, but glaringly obvious. Either of us could lighten the moment by continuing the joke, but we don't, we simply look at each other, and I know. I know that he sees how I feel about him, despite the fact that I've been trying to hide it not just from him, but from myself. The flicker of emotion that falls beyond the boundary of friendship;

that fleeting something that passed between us in the sea on the day of the picnic. In this moment, although not in words, but in this one look, we both finally acknowledge that recognition to each other.

And I see something else. *I see the same emotion echoed in his own eyes.*

'I think I'd better go.' He finally speaks, and not trusting myself to answer I nod vigorously.

Laura waves him off then turns to me and hugs me tightly. 'Am I glad you're back.'

'Yeah.' I smile half-heartedly at her. 'I'm sorry I didn't call.'

'We were worried.'

'I know. It was really thoughtless of me.'

'Cas went up to the main road four times looking out for you.'

'She did?'

Laura nods.

'What's the matter with her?'

Laura looks down at the floor, her face colouring up with embarrassment. 'She was really worried about you, not that she'd admit it to anybody, and then you did stay the night with Connor, which was perfectly understandable given the circumstances but I'm afraid she's drawn her own conclusions. She thinks you've been out . . . you know . . .' Laura looks at me.

'Shagging,' I say bluntly.

'And were you?' my mother asks, barely managing to hide her enthusiasm.

Tetchily brushing my hair out of my face, I shake my head and copying Cas, push past her angrily without answering. Laura hurries into the house after me.

'I'm sorry, Nattie.' She puts a hand on my shoulder to stop me moving forward. 'I shouldn't have said that. I know it's not my place, it was thoughtless, but I just want you to be happy.'

Shaking off her hand I turn to face her. 'And you

think jumping into bed with someone I barely know is going to put me back on the right road to happiness? You think if I get a good seeing-to, a bloody good fuck, then that will make me less uptight? Why not offer Connor up as a sexual sacrifice to the born-again virgin that is Natalie Forester, High Priestess of Getting Nowt.'

Laura's face falls, crumples in fact like a screwed-up tissue. For a moment I think she's going to cry. I sigh and run my hand agitatedly through my already unruly hair.

'Look, I'm sorry I flew off the handle but—'

'It's okay,' she replies quietly, looking away from me.

'No, it's not okay. I'm sorry.' I slump down into one of the wooden kitchen chairs, and bury my red face in my cold hands.

Laura comes and kneels before me, pulls my hands from my face and smiles up at me encouragingly.

'I got no more than I deserved. What I said to you was thoughtless, it was wrong.'

'Is it?' I snap at her. '*Is* it really so wrong?'

She pulls back, startled. 'What do you mean?'

'Is it wrong for me to find someone else attractive?' I persist.

Laura doesn't answer.

'The thing is, I haven't just switched off, but I feel that I should have done. The man I love is dead. There, I've finally said it. But it still doesn't ring true, and the fact that I can say it aloud doesn't mean I can accept it. He still feels so alive to me, in here,' I push my white knuckles against my chest, feel the faint pulse of my heart under my breastbone. 'And yet I *know* I'm never going to see him again. Never. Rob is dead. But how can I feel even the slightest flicker of emotion for someone else, when the love that I have for him is still living so strongly inside of me?'

Laura takes my hands again. 'Oh Nattie love, it's so hard, isn't it? Rob's gone, and believe me, I do know how painful it is to lose the man you love, but he wouldn't expect you to stop living, to stop feeling, would he? If Rob had just switched off when Eve passed away, he would never have met and loved and married you, now would he?'

I shake my head. 'I know, but although I *will* admit that I like Connor, I know for a fact that I can't act on it. And what about Cas? You saw how she just reacted . . . How do you think she'd cope if I suddenly started seeing someone else? It wouldn't be right. It really wouldn't. And how could I be with anyone else when I still love Rob?'

Laura wraps her arms around me, resting her chin gently on the crown of my head. 'Give it time, darling, give it time. I'm sorry – I shouldn't have pushed you.'

'No, *I'm* sorry. I shouldn't have snapped, and I should have phoned to let you know where I was far sooner last night. I'm the one who's thoughtless.'

'As long as you're safe,' she murmurs, rocking me like a baby. 'So long as you're safe, that's all that matters.'

An hour and a half later the clatter of hooves on cobbles tells me that Cas is back. Laura is knitting in the corner, the same red mohair 'something' she has been working on since we first arrived here, and which has yet to form anything tangible or recognisable. She looks up, rises slightly in her seat to look out of the window, and then glances at me and raises her eyebrows in question. I know what she's getting at. She wants me to go out and talk to Cas. I know that I should. But what do I say to her? Her emotions are already tangled and complicated enough without the added confusion of my feelings regarding Connor.

Laura gets up and puts down her knitting. 'I'll go, shall I? See if I can calm her down a bit – tell her nothing happened.'

'If you don't mind.'

'And will you come out in a minute?'

I sigh and nod an affirmative. It's more like fifteen minutes however before I can find the courage to get out of my chair and act as peacemaker. By the time I walk outside, Cas has removed Chance's tack and is grooming him before putting him back in the stable, her back to me as she bends to clean out his feet with a hoof pick. Laura has a Dandy brush and is gently detaching the mud from the paler golden hairs of his chestnut belly.

Laura looks up as she hears the kitchen door closing, and grimaces at me. Her chat with Cas obviously isn't going as well as she hoped. A bit more frantic signalling, and a fair bit of lip reading, and I work out that Laura has tried, but Cas won't listen, and she suggests I give it a go myself. Cas has finished Chance's hooves, and goes to take the saddle, which is resting over the bottom half of the stable door, back inside the stable next door which is used as a tack room. I wait until she comes back out, and then walk slowly over to her.

'Cas . . .'

She ignores me completely, simply walks straight past me across the yard and into the kitchen, shutting the door pointedly behind her. Laura looks from me to the kitchen, and back again, obviously desperately torn. In the end she shrugs apologetically and follows Cas inside the house. I suppose it's better that way, at least she normally manages to calm Cas's ruffled feathers quite well. Far better than I ever could anyway.

I'm tempted to do my own disappearing act now, to simply sod off and stare at the sea for an hour, but I know in my heart that I ought to clear things up with Cas as soon as possible. Apart from that, poor old Chance has simply been left, tied by the rope from his head collar to the stable door, half groomed, still sweating from his run out, but beginning to shiver as the sweat turns cold in the cool of the day.

I pick up Laura's abandoned Dandy brush, and finish what she started, getting the mud from his belly and his flanks, and the soft feathers around his hooves. I then pick up a body brush from the box of grooming equipment, and give him a vigorous brush down, before fetching a Jute from the tack room, and rugging him up.

The exercise has done me good. I am now sweating as much as Chance was before I cleaned him up, but it's lifted my adrenaline levels to a point where I feel able to face Cassie. I put Chance back in his loose box and go back into the kitchen.

Laura and Cas aren't speaking as I thought they would be. In fact, when I go in, Laura shakes her head, and then tilts it toward the stairs, to ask if I'd like her to make herself scarce. Cas is at the kitchen table still in mud-splattered jodhpurs, her face resolutely turned down to the table.

I nod my thanks, and Laura heads swiftly and silently up the stairs, the sound of her bedroom door closing behind her. Mac, who stayed behind when Connor left, is in the kitchen watching Cas eat a sandwich. Normally she'd be sharing it with him, but today she simply ignores him, as she does me, flicking through a magazine with her spare hand far too fast to actually be reading it.

I know that in order to make things right I cannot simply push Cas away as she has me. The root of our problems is the massive insecurity she must feel right now. She lost everything dear to her and is left with the one person she has been insisting she doesn't want in her life.

Taking my time, I wash my hands in the big sink; unbeknownst to her, I can see her reflection in the sloping silver side of the kettle next to me. She's watching me, but when I turn to face her she has looked away quickly so that I don't catch her eye.

'There's nothing going on.'

She looks up at me blankly as though she hasn't a clue what I'm talking about.

'Between me and Connor. There's nothing going on. We're just friends, that's all.'

She says nothing, simply looks expectantly at me as though waiting for me to carry on. There is a nagging voice at the back of my head, a voice that is calling me a liar. But how on earth can I admit my feelings to Cas when I haven't even come to terms with them myself, and so I stick to the literal physical truth, once more ignoring my emotions.

I take a deep breath, try to keep my voice as level and calm as possible. 'We are not seeing each other, I swear to you. If I ever started a relationship with someone else I would talk to you about it from the very beginning. I wouldn't lie to you, and I wouldn't try to keep it a secret.'

I am tempted to add more, to say that I shouldn't have to justify myself to her, but I bite my lip, both physically and proverbially and wait for her reaction. She says nothing, but I notice that two minutes later, Mac is happily chewing on the remainder of the bacon sandwich; the hand that she was using to eat it, now rests gently against the top of his head.

The telephone is ringing. Laura answers it in her room. I can hear the faint sound of her voice and then her footsteps on the stairs as she comes down to join us, peering hesitantly around the door frame, waiting for my signal that it's okay to come back in.

'That was Connor. He asked if Cas would mind walking Mac back up to the Loft?'

I look at my mother in silent question but she simply shrugs to show that she too is unsure of the reasoning behind his request. Mac usually finds his own way home, but to my surprise Cas seems more than happy to do this, despite the fact that it's at least a two-mile walk. She instantly shrugs on her jacket and heads out into the winter sunshine, Mac hugging her heels and sniffing at her pockets for the chocolate he knows she sometimes keeps there.

'How did it go?' Laura queries in concern as soon as Cas has gone.

'Well, she didn't say much, but I think I got through to her.'

'And you?'

'What do you mean?'

'Has someone got through to *you*?' She comes and sits beside me, her eyes keenly searching my face. 'What you said to me about Connor . . .'

'What about him?'

'You said . . .' She pauses, obviously trying to phrase the question carefully. 'How *do* you feel about him, Nattie?'

I look at my mother's concerned face and search inside of me for an answer. 'I don't know,' I reply slowly. 'I really don't know.'

*Dear Rob,*
*I'm so confused. I don't know what I should do any more. I never thought I would meet someone again who made me feel this way, who made me laugh, who made me feel happy and who made me forget, someone who, with just a look, takes away the constant dull pain that has been beating away inside of me like a second heartbeat. To be with him feels so right, and yet I feel so guilty. Guilty that I am letting Cassie down, guilt about you. Did you feel this way when you first met me? That in some way loving me, wanting me, was a betrayal to Eve?*

*I don't know what I should do, Rob. And therefore knowing me I shall do what I do best, and pretend that I feel nothing. More emotions for me to try and ignore as best I can.*
*Love*
*N x*

Cassie returns several hours later. To our complete

surprise her mood is more upbeat than it has been for some time. In fact she's smiling broadly, a vast difference from the scowling girl who sat in this kitchen this morning. She is chattering away to Laura about the time she has spent up at the Loft with Connor.

'He showed me his paintings. He's amazing! I didn't realise he was so good.'

Laura is nodding and smiling indulgently, pleased to see Cassie so cheerful.

'*And* he offered to teach me to paint. Isn't that great?'

Laura nods again and glancing over at me raises her eyebrows.

Connor has sent Cas back to us with a sketch book and an assortment of drawing pencils. She spends the afternoon trying to do sketches of little Stu, which isn't an easy first subject as he rarely keeps still unless he's asleep, but her enthusiasm doesn't wane. I wonder how long this positive mood will last, but then something else happens that afternoon that guarantees her smile will remain for at least the rest of the day, if not beyond.

I know something has occurred when Cas waltzes into the kitchen after the evening feed, grinning like a lunatic, and falls to her knees in front of Laura's chair, her eyes shining, face flushed.

'Luke's asked me out. Can I go?' The words tumble out of her mouth in a breathless rush.

Laura looks over at me questioningly.

'Can I go?' Cas repeats, this time to me. She's smiling so hard that she's almost bursting with pleasure.

'I don't see why not.'

'Great – because he said he'd pick me up at seven thirty!'

'So you'd already agreed?'

'I didn't think you'd refuse,' she replies almost insolently, but I don't want to burst the bubble of happiness she's currently floating in.

Instead, wary of the intentions of a hormonal twenty-year-old male, I ask: 'Where are you going?'

'We're going to meet some friends of his in the Ship, to play pool. Is that okay? Can I go to the Ship?'

'You may, yes,' I reply cautiously, 'but I want you to bear in mind that you're too young to drink.'

'But . . .'

'No buts, Cas, you're under age. It wouldn't be fair on Orlaithe for one thing. She's good enough to let you in there, don't take advantage. Besides, Luke will be driving, won't he. He won't be drinking so you won't feel like the odd one out.'

She digests this for a moment. I can see by her face that she's having an inner struggle at the moment, to defy me, to argue, or to accept what I'm saying. In the end, to my surprise, she nods.

'You're right.'

'I *am*?'

'Yeah.' She says it as if she, too, finds this fact surprising, and then the grin returns and she jumps to her feet again. 'I'd better go and sort out what I'm going to wear.'

'But it's only half past three,' Laura calls after her as she charges toward the stairs.

'Exactly – I've only got four hours!'

'That's nice, isn't it, Nattie?' Laura's fishing. 'It will do her good to spend some time with people her own age, won't it?'

'Mmmm,' I reply, unconvinced. 'What's he like?'

'Luke? He seems like a nice boy.'

'Yeah, but is he?'

'What do you mean?'

'Appearances can be deceptive. Just because he *seems* like a nice boy doesn't mean he is. I mean, how well do you *really* know him? What if he messes her about?'

'Nattie, they're kids, they're going out on a date for heaven's sake, that's all.'

'I know, but she's had too much hurt to cope with any more at the moment.'

'You're worrying too much about it, Nattie.'

'Yeah,' I reply in surprise. 'I am, aren't I?'

'It's called being a mother.' Laura smiles wryly.

I blink at her in surprise.

'Why don't you go and see if she needs any help choosing something to wear?' she adds hopefully.

'Are you sure that's a good idea?'

Laura shrugs. 'You won't know unless you try.'

I tread nervously up the stairs, feeling silly that I have butterflies in my stomach for a feat so trivial as going into Cassie's bedroom. I knock on the door, but she has her portable CD player on, attached to some mini-speakers that Laura found her from a drawer in the study, and doesn't hear me.

I'm tempted to just turn around and go back downstairs, but instead I take a deep breath, push down on the latch handle, open the door and walk straight up into Cassie's room before I can change my mind. This is the first time I've been in here since the day we arrived. I don't go up to Cassie's room; I look upon it as trespassing on her territory, the enemy in the camp, too confrontational.

There are clothes everywhere. On the bed, on the floor, hanging out of drawers. Cassie has her back to me. She is rifling in a panic through the remaining clothes in her cupboard.

'Are you struggling?'

She turns and looks at me, almost jumping at the sound of my voice. She seems a little bewildered to see me, and for a moment a little hostile, but then to my relief she smiles, looks at the clothes strewn everywhere, and then laughs.

'Shall I let you in on a secret?'

'If you're sure you want to,' I reply.

'It's my first date.'

'Really?'

'Yes.'

'And you can't decide what to wear?'

Cas looks about the room at the clothes thrown all over the place. 'How did you guess.'

'Do you want some help?' I venture hesitantly.

She looks at me for a moment, appraisingly, and then she nods. 'Yeah, why not.' She turns back to her wardrobe and for a moment I remain rooted where I am, unsure of what exactly to do, but then without turning to face me, Cassie begins to speak again. 'Can you remember your first date, Natalie?'

'Or was it too far back in the Middle Ages?' I add, laughing nervously.

She looks over at me and smiles briefly.

'Yeah, I can remember it, although I don't know if that's a good thing or not. It actually doesn't seem that long ago when I think about it. I was older than you – I was eighteen.'

'Eighteen!' she exclaims, putting down a top she was considering, and staring at me in astonishment.

'I was a late starter. I was always working or studying when I was your age. I didn't have time to meet, let alone date boys.'

'Who was he? What was he like?'

'He was an estate agent from Putney called Wayne.'

Cas sniggers.

'I know, awful name – that was only the start of it as well. I thought he was totally sophisticated because he was twenty-three, wore a suit to work, had a mobile phone like a brick, and drove a brand new Ford Fiesta. Admittedly it was a little 950 with the agency name emblazoned down the side, that went about forty miles an hour at top speed, but it was still a brand new car, and boy, was I impressed. Oh and he had a mullet.'

'A mullet?'

'You know, hair that's short at the top and sides, and

then long down the back. They were all the rage then. A bit like wearing a Davy Crocket hat you can't take off.' Cas's eyes widen in horror at the thought.

'It was an awful haircut.'

'I can imagine,' she answers. 'How did you meet him?'

'I used to sell advertising space for a free newspaper, and he used to deal with the agency's adverts. Not that I ever spoke to him, of course; he dealt with one of the other girls, Heather, but she finally confessed that I used to drool from afar, and he ended up asking me out. With much prompting from her, I might add. You know, I think he only did it because he actually fancied *her*, but she wouldn't touch him with a bargepole, which should have told me something, shouldn't it really?'

Cas giggles. 'And what happened?'

'It turned out he was a complete arse, of course. We only went out the once. He spent the whole evening talking about himself, whilst I got steadily more and more drunk because I was so bored, and then I ended up throwing up in his company car, just when he was trying to kiss me good night.'

'Oh no, you didn't!' Cas's mouth falls open in horror at the thought. 'You must have died of embarrassment.'

'Absolutely, especially as I threw up mostly all over him. Naturally, I never saw him again. He even stopped coming into the offices to place the adverts. They sent another guy after that – Edmund, I think his name was – who funnily enough Heather ended up marrying, would you believe.'

'Oh crikey.' Cas is still cringing at the thought of my embarrassment. 'I hope tonight isn't a total disaster.'

'Oh, I think you made a much better choice of man for your first date, which is a good start. Don't worry, everything will be fine.'

'Yeah, I suppose so,' she suddenly smiles at me. 'If I can decide what the hell I'm going to wear!' She holds up another top from her wardrobe for me to inspect. 'What do you think of this?'

It's the first time I've seen Luke close to. He's only been up to the farm a few times since Cas and I have been here, although she has met him several times whilst out riding. I have only seen him from a distance helping Hank with some of the more laborious and heavy repairs, or perched on one of the barn roofs filling holes with tarpaulin.

He's a healthy good-looking lad. He has tousled blond surfer hair, and a lean toned surfer's body, and the even, coffee-coloured tan of someone who spends most of the twelve months of the year outside. And bright against this tan are eyes of such a piercing violet-coloured blue they don't look real, like those spooky contact lenses you can buy in vivid colours. Although Laura assures me that they are his own.

My mother answers the door to him at seven thirty on the dot. Cas is still upstairs having taken over an hour to finally decide what to wear. Luke doesn't appear to have prevaricated too long over *his* choice of clothing. He is wearing tattered trainers, a slightly off-white T-shirt, torn jeans and scuffed leather jacket, hardly dressed to impress, but then I suppose the 'James Dean *Rebel Without a Cause*' look would impress Cas far more than 'smart' ever would.

He raises a hand in greeting to Laura, and nods at me, but doesn't say a word. I don't suppose working with Hank is very good training for speaking in public. He brightens perceptibly when Cas comes downstairs though, managing a slightly breathless, 'Hello,' at the sight of her in the slash-neck top, knee-length denim skirt and long boots we finally settled on between us.

Laura and I follow them outside to see them off. I look around the yard, and then catch Cas by the arm.

'Where's his car?' I ask.

261

'His car?' Cas echoes me innocently.

I look at Laura, who shrugs. 'Come to think of it, I don't even know if Luke's got a car. He's always come in with Hank in Betsy.'

Laura calls after Luke. 'Where's your car, Luke?'

'I haven't got a car. I came on my bike.' He points to just beyond my own car. There is a Kawasaki parked up next to it, just visible behind the bonnet of my BMW. I eye the vivid green machine with some concern.

'Take my car,' I tell him.

'What?'

'I said, take my car.' I hurry back inside and get my handbag from the dresser, rummaging inside it for the keys. Cas has followed me. I thrust them at her before I have a chance to change my mind.

'I'm not having you roaring across the countryside on that thing. They're dangerous, motorbikes.'

She looks at me oddly for a moment, and then a small smile slides across her face. 'Are you serious?'

I nod, offering her the keys again. 'But you *love* your car,' she announces, managing to question and ridicule at the same time.

'I know. Just tell Luke to be careful with it, okay?'

'Yeah, right. I will.' She reaches out and takes the keys, as though expecting me to snatch them away at any minute. She gets to the door before she turns back to me. 'Nat?'

'Yeah?'

She hesitates for a moment, and then her frown relaxes into a smile. 'Thanks.'

I was determined not to wait up for her.

I tell myself that I'm not and it's just my usual insomnia, but here I am sitting in bed, covers pulled up to my chin, ears on elastic for the sound of a returning car, or the sweep of the headlights arcing across the wall opposite my bed as my BMW pulls into the yard.

When my clock says eleven-forty I start to get agitated. I know it's last orders at eleven, so even giving them twenty minutes to drink up and be kicked out, she should be back by now. The Ship is only a fifteen-minute drive away at most. I should have given her a time to come home by, she's only sixteen for heaven's sake, but of course that never crossed my mind, did it. I am a complete novice at this parenting thing.

Despite telling myself that I don't mind what time Cas gets in, that I'm not at all worried, and I could close my eyes and sleep like a baby if I really wanted to, I stay firmly awake until I hear my car return, until I hear Luke's motorbike roar off ten minutes later, and until I hear the key being turned in the kitchen door lock. And I don't close my eyes until I hear the click of the latch on the stair door, and Cas humming softly to herself as she climbs up the stairs to her room.

Cas is the last one down to breakfast next morning. I'm determined not to grill her for information on her date, but Laura has no such reticence. She pounces on her the minute she steps through the kitchen door.

'Did you have a good time then?'

'Yes, thank you.' Cas smiles happily.

'What did you do?'

'We went down to the Ship to play pool, like I said. He beat me every time though.' She picks up a piece of toast from Laura's plate, and takes a small bite. 'Laura, can you play pool?'

'Can I play pool?'

'Well – can you?'

'Can a eunuch sing soprano?'

Cas looks at her quizzically, a little unsure as to whether this means yes or no. She needn't have worried, Laura soon enlightens us.

'When I was touring with the Metropolitans, we were doing a version of *Fiddler on the Roof*. John Lansford –

you remember the man from those TV ads in the seventies, the one with the beard selling Ford Escort cars? – well, he was playing the part that Topol took in the film version, and I was the eldest daughter, and you should have seen this man and me play pool together. We were like something out of *The Hustler*, although he, of course, looked nothing like Paul Newman . . .'

As Laura rattles off on one of her 'when I was an actress' stories, Cas shakes her head indulgently, and then looks across at me and smiles, a genuinely easy friendly smile of camaraderie, and my heart pulses with pleasure, as though she has just bestowed upon me something very precious indeed.

An hour later, we are in the Ship, playing a game of doubles. When it came to choosing teams Cas plumped for my mother straight away. I wouldn't have expected any different, of course, but I think things were swayed a little by Laura's excessive boasts about her pool prowess. I am paired with Orlaithe, but the fact that she's the only one behind the bar today means that I am practically playing solo.

We win the toss, so Orlaithe breaks, a passable break, which whilst it downs nothing, leaves the yellows decidedly easier to play than the reds. Laura, despite the stories, doesn't notice and opts for an easy red, impressing Cas by downing the first two balls she goes for. Cas smiles proudly and gives her the thumbs-up when she comes away from the table, then they both watch keenly as I approach.

'She's trying to look professional,' my mother teases as I chalk the end of my cue.

I flash what I hope comes across as an enigmatic smile at them both and play for my first shot, praying fervently that I didn't waste my entire youth. The ball goes down, closely followed by another, then the next, and the next, until I spot Cas's face, and miss an easy shot, so that she can get a chance on the table. Unfortunately Cas also misses an easy pot, which has her swearing crossly under her breath.

Orlaithe misses as well, but leaves Laura on a snooker that she misses completely, giving me two shots to follow, which I use to sink my remaining three balls, and then the black.

'*Trying* to look professional, eh?' I taunt Laura as I put my cue back in the rack, and sit down at the bar.

'You never told me you could play,' Cas tells me almost accusingly.

'You never asked,' I tease her.

'It's a sign of a misspent youth,' Daveth announces from across the bar, swaying slightly on his stool, as he waves his fifth pint at us as though to add emphasis to his opinion.

'What is, Davey?' asks Orlaithe, who has gone back behind the bar to serve the growing number of customers.

'Being good at pool. It's a sign of a wasted youth.'

'I wouldn't have thought being good at something was a sign of wasted time,' Orlaithe snorts at him. 'I'd have said spending the past forty years glued to the same bar stool with a pint pot in your hand might be, though.'

'Ah, sure, but what would you do without me, Orlaithe my lovely? I'm your best customer.'

'Frequency doesn't automatically give ascendancy, Daveth Brann,' she chides him, but taking his almost empty glass she fills it and hands it back to him with a wink. 'On the house, m'darling,' she tells him. 'A little loyalty bonus for ya. And you,' she turns to me and does a double thumbs-up, 'deserve one on the house as well. That was an amazing win you had there, well done, especially as you practically had to play single-handed without me, so you did.'

Cas is agitating for us to play again, but the pub is now too busy for Orlaithe to leave the bar unmanned. Our match is saved, however, by the timely appearance of Charles Treloar, whom Laura immediately beckons over to join us.

'We need a fourth for pool, do you fancy a game?'

Charles' strong handsome face breaks into a broad beam, and he rubs his hands together in anticipation. 'Lovely, yes, definitely. Whose team do you want me on?'

'I'll play with Nat, Charles can play with Laura,' Cas suggests. She leans in and whispers in my ear, 'He should be used to that by now.'

'Cas!' I can't help but laugh, surprised by what she has said, but more surprised by the fact that she said it to me. I don't know what Connor said to Cas in the time that she spent up at the Loft, but I decide that he is a miracle-worker. I have never felt this easy with her.

Charles is obviously more than happy to make a match.

'Why don't we make this game a little more challenging?' he offers, having kindly bought us all another round of drinks.

'What do you propose?'

'How about a little wager?'

Cas and I look at each other, she nods. 'Okay. How much are we talking here?'

'How about fifty?' Charles offers.

'Fifty pounds?' Cas exclaims in disbelief.

'Not enough?' Charles queries. 'Then shall we make it a proper bet and double it, say to a hundred?'

'He's joking, isn't he?' I ask Laura.

She shakes her head gravely. 'Oh no. Charles never jokes about money.'

Cas turns pleading to me. 'Nat, can we? You'll beat them easily.'

'Well, I don't know that it's right . . .'

'I'll stand you a hundred for the girls, Charles,' cuts in a voice.

We turn to find Connor seated at the bar behind us. I hadn't seen him come in, concentrating too hard on Cas and the game, and feel a sudden rush of pleasure mixed with embarrassment to see him there.

'You'll take the bet then, Connor.' Charles smiles broadly at him. 'I hope you're ready to lose.'

'Oh, I reckon the girls are good for it.'

'No, it's okay,' I cut in. 'We'll take the bet.'

'If you're sure?' Charles raises his eyebrows again, this time in question.

'Absolutely,' I reply determinedly. 'Thanks,' I turn to Connor, 'but I wouldn't want to lose you that much money.'

'I don't for a moment think that you will.'

'You saw the last match?'

He shakes his head. 'No. I've only been here a couple of minutes. But I reckon you're not the kind of girl to make a bet like that if you don't think you can win. Especially as it would disappoint Cas a great deal more now if you lose.'

'We won't lose.' I am ashamed to find myself boasting.

As if in recompense for my arrogance, it's not a fortuitous start. We lose the toss, and Charles chooses for them to take the break, with Laura slamming the white into the colours impressively hard. I'm next on the table and aware that I'm being watched when I miss an embarrassingly easy shot.

Charles, who is next up, apparently has a full-size snooker table at home. This proves to be a disadvantage, however, as he is finding his angles are slightly out on a smaller table. This is fortunate for us as Laura seems to have regained a little of her lost form, having cleared two of the reds on the break.

'His technique's good,' she tells us teasingly, as Charles also misses a relatively easy shot. 'He's just used to playing with larger balls.'

Cas practically chokes on her Diet Pepsi, as my mother

267

winks hard at me, and following the next miss by a still giggling Cas, saunters up to the table to pot three more balls in succession, before leaving me on a snooker with no balls down at all for our team. She swaggers away from the table blowing the chalk from the end of her cue as though it's a smoking gun.

I can see Cas watching me as I head for the table next, no doubt wondering at the wisdom of her sudden change in allegiance. I have this overwhelming urge to play the game of my life; unfortunately, when I want to play well, that's when I usually play pretty badly. It becomes too important to me, I need to relax to make my shots. I make a pretence of chalking my cue, and sneakily knock back my own drink as well as the rest of my mother's then, filled with a little Dutch courage, I head back to the table and clean up.

Tom Cruise, eat your heart out. My heart gets lighter, and Cas's smile gets wider as I sink every single one of those little yellow balls with a satisfying thud as each one hits its target, until I get to the black.

It's a tricky shot; I've managed to almost snooker myself, and I've got to play it off a side cushion, something I've never been particularly good at. I bend to study the angle, and feel a hand on my elbow. It's Cas, and she's holding out a large measure of brandy.

'I thought you might need this. It's okay, I didn't buy it. Orlaithe said it's a freebie being as technically you're still on the same team.'

I look over to Orlaithe to mouth my thanks, and realise that our little game is being watched by the entire pub. The only person not enthralled by the competition is old Davey, who has fallen asleep face down on the bar, but apart from him, all eyes are upon us. Or rather, me.

Talk about off-putting.

I bend back down to the table again, measure the distances and the angles with my cue, and then fighting the urge to close my eyes, take my shot.

There's a collective groan as the ball misses the pocket, heads for the side, rebounds and then heads straight back across the table, disappearing into the pocket opposite the one I was originally aiming for.

'*Yes!*' Cas leaps off her stool, runs up and grabbing my hands, swings me around the table in a victory dance. The huge smile on my face is due more to Cassie's joy than any triumph at our victory. She's completely elated that we won. She lets go of my hands so that I come to a rather giddy stop at the bar, and transfers her energies to singing, 'We are the champions!' at the top of her voice, right in Charles's left ear.

Charles is sporting enough to laugh good-naturedly, and then he pulls a roll of notes out of his pocket and peels off five twenties.

'It's okay.' I hold my hand up to stop him. 'We don't really want your money. It was hardly a proper bet, now was it?'

'No,' he says. 'If I'd won, would you have honoured it?'

'Well, yes of course I would have,' I reply.

'Then you can't tell me not to.'

'But—'

'I insist.'

'Okay,' I nod. 'If there's no turning you – but why don't you put it behind the bar?' I look over at Cas, seeking her agreement, and she nods enthusiastically.

'The drinks are on us!' she yells. 'Thanks, Nat, I've always wanted to do that.' She comes back to my side, still smiling like the cat that got the cream and a large dish of Gravadlax on the side for good measure.

'Can you teach me how to play like that?' she asks enthusiastically. 'You were amazing.'

'I think someone's impressed,' Laura murmurs.

'There's a first time for everything,' I reply sarcastically, but I can't help smiling at the fact that for once Cas seems to be affected by something that I've done in a positive way.

Connor too is smiling broadly. 'See now, that's a mean game of pool you played there. I take it you've had a fair bit of practice in your time?'

'Nah.' I raise my eyebrows at him. 'That was just beginner's luck.'

'Sure, and this is the first pint of Guinness that's ever passed my lips,' he lies, winking at me as he raises his glass in salute.

'In that case, you must let me and Cas buy you your *second* pint ever.'

'No need. I've already got them in.' He gestures to Orlaithe who, grinning broadly, places a bottle of champagne down on the bar in front of Connor. 'In anticipation of your victory. Cas, do you want to do the honours?'

As Cas, beaming even harder, pops the champagne Grand Prix-style, Connor turns back to me. 'So, where *did* you learn to play like that, young lady?'

'I lived in a YWCA for a year when I first moved to London,' I tell him, sitting down on the stool next to him and accepting a glass of champagne. 'I think I played pool every night I was there. There wasn't much else to do and it was a way of relaxing after college and work. And I *had* to win; I couldn't *afford* to lose. It's been a long time since I last played, though. I was a little worried I might have forgotten how, but I suppose it's a bit like riding a bike; you never forget the knack, it just takes you a while to warm up to it. Talking about warming up . . .' I glance over at Cas to make sure she's not listening in, but having dished out glasses of champagne, she has now been challenged to another game of pool by Charles, Laura showing her how to take the shots and hopefully beat him.

'What did you do to Cas yesterday? She came up to you as miserable as sin, and came home in the best mood I've seen her in for ages.'

'That's what happens when you spend some time

with Connor Blythe, you can't help for fall about laughing,' he smiles. 'Oh no, that's when you see me naked for the first time, isn't it – and I certainly didn't show young Cas my bits and pieces.' He grins broadly at me, and I smile gratefully back at him, well aware that he is trying to make sure there is no atmosphere between us after yesterday's awkward goodbye. 'No, seriously, I just spent some time with her, talked to her. I'm not knocking you or your mother but I think she's a little lonely, you know.'

'Yeah, I can see that would easily be true. It's been hard for her to meet people of her own age down here, but she went out on a date last night, so hopefully she'll get to know a few people now.'

'A date, was it?' he queries with a smile.

'Yeah,' I nod. 'I think she had a nice time.'

'That's good news.'

'Did you say anything to her about me?' I find myself asking him.

'Now why would you be thinking that then?' he counters elusively.

'Because she's treating me like a human being!' I tell him, turning back to face him.

'I might just have pointed out the fact that that is indeed what you are . . .'

'Instead of a monster,' I add.

'Yeah,' he replies, looking a little shamefaced. 'You're not angry with me for interfering again, are you?'

I watch as Cas jumps up and down with excitement as she finally pots her first ball, and then catching me watching her, grins and gives me a thumbs-up.

'Far from it,' I reply, smiling softly to myself. 'Far from it.'

# Chapter Nine

'I'm going shopping,' Laura announces the next day. 'Anybody coming with me?'

'I only went yesterday,' I reply from the sink, where I'm washing up the breakfast dishes.

'Not the supermarket. Clothes shopping,' she explains.

Cas is in front of the fire playing with Stu, rolling a shiny red bauble that has fallen from the tree to him like a ball. She looks up in interest. Despite the fact that my mother has more clothes than a couturier in Paris Fashion Week, she hasn't actually bought anything since we've been here.

'I need a new dress for the Christmas Ball.'

'Christmas Ball?' Cas and I query at the same time.

Laura nods enthusiastically. 'We have one every year. Either on Christmas Eve, or New Year's Eve. We alternate each year to give people a chance to do something different. Not your kind of ball, ladies. I suppose, it's more of a hop really.'

'A hop?' Cassie sneers, but it's a fairly good-natured mockery. 'You make it sound so . . . so *provincial*.'

'There's nothing wrong with being provincial,' Laura chastises her. 'We can't all be city slickers you know.'

Cas ignores her, rolling her eyes to the ceiling in mock horror.

'I can just imagine it now,' she continues, warming to her theme. 'Check shirts galore, scrumpy on a hay bale, vast excitement at the chance to line dance your polished plastic cowboy boots off.'

'Oh, you've been to one before then?' Laura replies earnestly, but I can see the mischief gleaming in her eyes.

'You're not serious.' Cassie's eyes are wide. 'That's not really how it is, is it?'

'No it's not, you snob.' Laura cuffs her softly round the head with her skein of bright red mohair wool, the fluff of which attaches itself to the static in Cassie's hair, giving her faded pink a fuzzy red edge in parts. 'It's more of a grand *après Christmas* barn dance, except it's held in the great hall of Cadogan House instead of some draughty old barn.'

'Cadogan House – isn't that on the Treloar Estate?' Cas enquires innocently.

'Home of the magnanimous Charles?' I prompt.

My mother does not rise to the bait. 'We had it on Christmas Eve last year. We even had a Santa: Charles kindly dressed up for us.'

'Yeah, and I bet he let you sit on his knee and ask for something interesting to come in your stockings,' I chuckle.

Laura doesn't blush, she simply says, 'Nattie, I'm your mother. You're not supposed to say things like that to me.'

'Most mothers don't have a better sex-life than their daughters,' I reply, winking at her.

'Not difficult when your daughter's practically celibate,' she hisses back, so Cas can't hear her.

'Take out the practically.'

Laura smiles sympathetically, then the smile turns into a laugh. 'Talking of Charles, poor man, I made him a beard from untreated lambs' wool and he had the most awful allergic reaction to it. I couldn't kiss him for a week – not on his face anyway.' She grins wickedly at me.

It's my turn to look shocked.

'Thought I'd get that one in before you could,' she says. 'Anyway, I need a new dress. I'd wait for the sales, but you can guarantee there won't be anything decent left. How about it, then? Anybody want to come shopping with me?'

'Well, I do have some Christmas presents to buy.' I sigh reluctantly.

'Cas?'

'Okay, nothing better to do I suppose.'

We pile into my car and head up the coast and inland to Truro, a haven of enough high-street stores to keep Laura and Cas happy whilst I wander around the more unusual shops, trying and failing to find Cassie something for Christmas that she might actually like.

After two hours of trudging round shops I wouldn't normally step inside, I eventually wander into a second-hand bookshop, tempted by a copy of Frank Sinatra's autobiography that I think Laura might like. The shop is quiet compared with the noisy hubbub of Christmas shoppers on the streets outside, the only sound the solemn tick of a grandfather clock sitting regally in a dark corner. The place is dimly lit and vaguely reminiscent of those Victorian emporia you see in period dramas, with double-bay windows crammed full of curiosities. A refreshing change from the neon-lit, consumer-charged atmospheres of the modern stores.

I pick up the autobiography and then begin to browse, mainly for my own enjoyment but with the idea at the back of my mind that I might spot something horsy perhaps for Cas, or arty for Petra. I'm wallowing happily in the nostalgia of the children's section when I come across an old copy of *Treasure Island* by Robert Louis Stevenson. It's in immaculate condition, and the colour illustrations are absolutely beautiful. I find myself thinking how much Connor would like it. But it's quite expensive, and I'm not at all sure how appropriate it would be for me to buy it for him. I'm also taken aback by how much I want to buy it for him. *Really* want to.

I feel that old familiar pit of guilt begin to swim around in my stomach, like a spoon stirring sugar into bitter coffee. I'm just about to put it back on the shelf when Laura appears at my elbow.

'Found you at last!' she says. 'How did I know you'd be in here, eh? It's chaos, isn't it, an absolute nightmare. We're nowhere near finished but Cas and I are just about ready to call it a day. I'm just popping over to the chemist's, so do you want to meet us in there...' She trails off. 'What's that you're looking at?'

I show her the book. She reaches out and takes it from me, her eyes lighting up with pleasure. 'Oh wow. You clever girl. I've been looking for a lovely second-hand edition of that for a friend. You weren't thinking of buying it for yourself, were you?'

I shake my head.

'Will you get it for me then?'

I nod, and putting it with my own purchases, take them all to the counter, feeling strangely disappointed that I'm not buying it for Connor.

Nobody has found everything they wanted, although my mother has her new dress – a scarlet, vampy velvet thing in which she no doubt looks sensational. Cas has also bought a new outfit to wear to the ball – a tiny dress made of what looks almost like gold chainmail, and a pair of gold sandals with Roman-style laces that wind their way up each leg almost to the knee, and dangerously sharp four-inch heels that would go straight through the foot of any man who dared to dance with her.

'We got them from a little designer shop in the Mews,' Laura tells me enthusiastically. 'You should see her in them, Nat, she looks absolutely fabulous.'

Although I'm certain Cas does look fabulous in her

new outfit, personally I think it would be more appropriate for hanging round a street corner in Soho, but I'm not going to say or do anything to shake the state of harmony that we have lived in since Cassie's visit to Connor two days ago.

The next morning, I meet Cas in her riding gear as I'm coming our of the bathroom.

'Morning.' She smiles cheerily at me, before heading down the stairs at great speed, the kitchen door slamming as she goes straight out to Chance.

I feel as if I've just won the lottery. Maybe Connor has encouraged her to give me a chance, to try to get to know me a little better. In response, I too have taken a little bit of time to push past her boundaries, and have been rewarded far more than I could ever have expected. Other people have encouraged us to open doors that we both had firmly closed for fear of further heartache.

Laura is seated at the kitchen table reading the morning paper. Whilst Cas seems far happier, my mother's face looks as grey as the morning sky outside.

'Are you okay?' I asked in concern that she may be feeling ill.

'Yes. No. Well, not really. It's just a bit of a shock, that's all.'

'What's the matter?'

She pushes the newspaper across the table toward me. 'Ralph Billingham passed away this morning.'

'Really?' I pick up the paper and look at the front page.

*END OF AN EROS* screams the headline. *Britain is today mourning the loss of a man who was described in his heyday as the Valentino of English theatre* . . .

Ralph and Molly Billingham were the Posh and Becks of English theatre in the 1960s and 1970s. Living legends. Until now, that is.

'I knew them, Ralph and Molly, a long time ago.'

My mother's quiet sad voice makes me look up from the paper in surprise. 'You never told me that.'

'I thought you knew. You met up with them a fair few times when we were living in Brighton, although I don't suppose you would remember as you were still very young then. They were very good to me after your father's death. We all started out together, you see, treading the boards as young hopefuls. Although they obviously went a lot further than I ever did.' She sighs. 'I haven't seen them for such a long time.'

I'm obviously still looking blank.

'Roll and Moll,' my mother reminds me, 'that's what you used to call them. They had a fluffy white poodle that they used to have clipped – you know, so that it had all the tufty bits in the right place. Weird-looking thing – a French poodle. I think it was actually called Frenchy if I remember correctly. Funny animal, bit of a leg shagger.' She grins and cringes at the memory. 'I remember a party they had once where it practically fell in love with a pair of tweed slacks I was wearing. I ended up pouring a large gin and tonic over it.'

Her smile widens at my shocked expression. My mother the animal lover assaulting a dog with a loaded drink!

'It was the only way to dampen its ardour,' she chuckles. 'Do you remember? You should: that dog adored you because you used to feed it all the time. Whenever we went round for tea Molly would give you a cake, and you'd give it to the bloody dog. It was quite embarrassing, really. I'd spend the whole afternoon surreptitiously picking cake crumbs out of the Axminster. I'm surprised you don't remember, you loved old Frenchy so much.'

'I do remember, I just didn't realise who they were.' I'm a bit flabbergasted that, without my knowing, the kind lady with the funny dog was one of the most well-known actresses in the country.

'They were a lovely couple, Nattie, totally devoted to each other. You rarely hear of a marriage lasting so long in the business, but they were truly everything to each other. I must send my condolences to Molly – she'll be inconsolable.'

'Would you like me to find out an address for you?' I offer. 'I'm sure I can get the name of their agent if you'd like me to use my contact at work?'

'No need.' Laura stands up and goes over to the cluttered dresser. Pulling open a drawer stuffed full of papers, old dog leads, and assorted boiled sweets, she rummages for a few moments before pulling an envelope from the back.

'They still send me Christmas cards. I've got twenty-eight years' worth of these. They're still in Brighton – in the same house, believe it or not. Well, at least Molly is.' Laura's eyes are sad.

I want to hug her, but for some reason hesitate, and the moment passes. How little I know about my mother. How little I know about myself. Or should that be how little I *choose* to remember? I've been blocking out my childhood as if it was some nightmarish existence I'm better off forgetting, but when I think about it, when I really think about it, I could have had a far worse time than I actually did.

I think it was the before and after comparison that was so extreme; this made things feel far worse than they probably were. My father was taken from a wonderful loving close-knit family that never recovered from his absence.

My thoughts are interrupted by the sound of a horn as a van pulls up to the gate. It's the blue-painted van of Audger & Sons, the local butchers. Jowan Audger, a little wizened man, must be in his eighties, and he has been running his chain of shops since he took over from his father at the tender age of fourteen. I recognise the bow-backed figure of Jago Audger his eldest son, who must be at least in his late sixties, behind the wheel of the van. He used to run one of the smaller shops in Trenrethen that has now closed down. Four generations of Audgers work the remaining five shops between them, from Jowan down to the youngest Jory, who is only eighteen, but already in charge of the largest shop in Truro.

They've come for the geese. Laura has arranged for them to take all three, returning the largest one to us, in other words Gertrude the Grim, plucked and prepared for Christmas day, with the other two, her henchmen, taken in payment for this service.

Laura's face falls even further. 'Oh no, I'd forgotten they were coming. It had to be today, didn't it.'

'Do you want me to tell them to go?'

'No, no, I can't mess them about like that. Jago's come all the way over from Helston. We better go out and help him.'

Cas is outside, sitting on a hay bale outside of Chance's loose box, cleaning the leather of his bridle with an amber block of sweet-scented saddle soap. The metal bit, which is caked in dried grass, is soaking in a bowl of water at her feet. I can hear her talking to him as he leans out of the box, blowing affectionately into her hair as she works, telling him what a slob he is, and how he gets everything so absolutely filthy, and seeing as she has to muck out his loose box every day, then why for once can't he come in and clean the bathroom. And perhaps after she's finished polishing his tack, he'd like to come in and iron her clothes. She doesn't know I can hear her, and I smile in appreciation of her humour.

As my mother enters the yard, Meggie appears silently from the long passage to walk by her side, a wet nose thrust into the palm of her hand in affectionate greeting. Laura is talking away to herself as she walks over to greet Jago Audger, and the grey-haired man who's accompanied him.

'The geese are good guard dogs but I have Meggie for that anyway, don't I, old girl? Besides, I only breed them for Christmas. And they're such hell hounds, they really are. I mean, if they were nice-natured I couldn't even consider . . .'

It's as if she's trying to justify the slaughter to herself. I go to stand beside her, linking my arm through hers in reassurance.

Gertrude is not happy to be herded out of her domain by strangers.

'I'm sure they can smell it on him, you know,' Laura mutters to me. 'The stench of dead meat.'

'Why don't you just change your mind and keep them?'

Laura shakes her head determinedly. 'She's a nasty piece of work, you know it yourself only too well. If I wasn't keeping them for Christmas, I'd have got rid of them quite a while ago. If I send them somewhere else, they'll only go the same way in the end.'

Even though I love animals, I'm not cut out to be a vegetarian. I like eating meat. But it's so much easier when everything's pre-cut and packaged; it's very hard to associate a piece of bacon or a pork chop with a living breathing animal.

Gertrude is snapping waspishly at the man herding them away, ruffling up her wings like a haughty grand dame rearranging her shawl about her shoulders. Cas doesn't stay to watch, she puts Chance's tack away, and whistling for little Stu, announces that she's taking him for a walk.

Despite having been on the wrong end of Gertrude's wrath (and beak) myself, I find that I too am upset to see them go. I wanted to be here for Laura, especially after the news she received this morning, but I find that I am weak where death, and imminent death is concerned, and offering stumbling apologies, which Laura thankfully understands, I gather my bits together, jump into the car and drive into Penzance. I've ostensibly gone there to try and finish my Christmas shopping, to fight my way once more through the marauding crowds of present-hunters. Yesterday's trip made me realise just how much I have left to do. I can't find anything I want though.

Apart from my own lethargy, the shelves have been stripped in a last-minute frenzy of panic buying. Some of the shops have already started their sales, and all is chaos, merchandise spilling off shelves and onto floors, new goods damaged in the crush of people.

In the end I go back to the car park and climb wearily into my car, and drive up to Truro again. It's only two o'clock but it's one of those days when it feels as though evening is already drawing in. There's a heavy mist descended upon the land, like smoke in a crowded bar.

I have more luck in Truro. I find Petra a beautiful pair of antique earrings in a jewellery shop in a quiet back alley. They are shaped like little crooked stars, the many tiny diamonds in them twinkling like real ones in the shop lights, which are switched on to their full-strength, headache-inducing neon due to the dull grey of the day. The owner offers to wrap them for me so, feeling very organised, I march them straight to the post office and send them to her Registered Post, so at least she'll have them to open on Christmas Day.

I miss Petra. We talk on the phone, but it's not been the same without her. I hadn't noticed quite how much I'd come to rely on her over the past year or so as a constant source of comfort, of entertainment, of levity in heart-sinking moments. I wish she were with me now.

If there is any time of year guaranteed to make a lonely person feel even more alone, then it is Christmas. Everywhere I turn I see couples hand in hand, arm in arm, laughing, chatting, laden with bags. Every shop I go in I see so many things that Rob would have loved, and that I would have loved to have bought for him. I don't know why I thought I could do this on my own. If Petra were here now I wouldn't feel so lousy. Actually, if Petra were here now, she would have dragged me into the nearest pub or bar for a well-earned glass of wine or two. I may be on my own, but that's still a pretty good idea.

I head into the nearest pub, order a large glass of white wine and a baguette, and find myself a recently vacated table in a corner of the packed room. The pub is full of people taking a respite from their shopping; some youths are playing a rowdy game of pool, shouting to each other above the sound of jazzed-up Christmas carols coming from the speakers positioned at intervals about the place. Gaudy decorations hang from the ceiling, a tree in the corner flashes its coloured lights. While I'm waiting for my sandwich, I dial Petra's mobile.

'Hello,' rasps her low sexy voice. 'This is Petra, I'm tied up at the moment,' typical tease, voice full of innuendo, 'so if you want me, leave a message.'

I suddenly don't know what to say, so I leave a message wishing her a Happy Christmas, and trying not to sound too melancholy. If I thought calling into a pub for a drink would make me feel better, then I was very much mistaken. It feels worse, being in here amidst so much merriment, being the only person in the pub on my own. I'm tempted to knock back my glass of wine and then order another, but halfway down the glass I remember Cassie's pained, almost fearful expression as she informed me that I drink too much, and abandoning my glass and untouched food, I head back out into the cold wintry streets, determined to finish my shopping, and go as soon as possible. I have a splitting headache. My feet ache, my arms and my shoulders ache from carrying too many bags, and my stomach aches, simply I think because it feels the need to join in with the rest of my body, and would feel left out if it wasn't in some kind of pain.

To cap it all, I can't remember the way back to the car park.

I walk down an alleyway I think I came out of earlier, looking for an antique shop where I saw a bracelet for Cas that wasn't quite perfect enough to make me buy it on the spot, but now I think merits a second look. I am, however, once more lost. Instead of the antique shop, I find myself outside Truro Cathedral.

I look around, trying to get my bearings, and to my relief see the main pedestrian shopping street beyond it, but as I head toward the bright lights of the street, I somehow find myself turning instead toward the open front doors of the Cathedral, drawn inside by the light and warmth streaming through them.

It is a beautiful building, a hidden jewel, its three spires reaching skywards like hands stretching upwards in search of mercy; the fact that it is almost tucked away from sight, an Angel of God kneeling amidst the distraction of commerce, belies the beauty that sits inside.

I look around me in awe at the great stone arches towering above me, lit by the soft golden glow of a hundred or more candles, their light fading into the darkness of the ceiling so far above my head. A notice inside the door tells me that the architect's aim was to build a place of worship that 'will bring people soonest to their knees'. Voices are hushed with awe, even children silenced by the dramatic power of the place. If you look for God then surely you will find Him here.

I walk forward, pulled into the vast belly of the building by the knots in my own stomach. I wander round slowly until I find myself standing in front of some stone figures in the north transept by the memorials; the figures, a notice informs me, apparently depict *Time* and *Death*.

*Time* and *Death*.

These are my enemies, the things that have turned my world upside down, my heart inside out. I feel as if I

284

could easily reach out and slap the cold stone face of *Death*, take a chisel and gouge out his cruel hooded eyes. I move quickly on, coming to a halt in front of a carved stone statue of a man with a benevolent face. Such a kind face. I am drawn to read the plaque alongside of him. It is Saint Nicholas, shown with three boys whom, according to legend, he brought back to life.

Could Saint Nicholas give me back a life for Christmas, if I light a candle, say a heartfelt prayer? Or perhaps he could explain to me why that life was taken. Is there some sort of reason or logic to it that I have yet to find? If there *is* a God then why do we suffer so? Why do we lose the ones we love?

I do not question the existence of God. I see Him in the beauty, and not the savagery of the world around me. I see Him in the kindness and decency of humanity. I see Him in the gift of life – a life that can be taken away at any moment, but is given nonetheless. I did not have a wake. I did not want to celebrate Rob's death. But I should have celebrated his life.

I leave the Cathedral and continue my shopping filled with a new determination.

I get back to an empty house. Laura has left me a note saying that she and Cas have gone to the cinema. They tried to phone me but my mobile was switched off, and if they'd waited for me they would have missed the start of the movie.

The dogs are out. Meg will be somewhere on the farm. Cas must have taken little Stu with her, although I can't see them letting him in the cinema. He is often quite happy to fall asleep on a blanket in the back of the Landy and wait for her wherever she may be.

I try to get in the Christmas spirit by putting on one of Laura's tapes, pouring myself a large glass of sherry, and switching on the lights on the Christmas tree. A re-run of Morecambe and Wise is on the television, and although I have the sound switched off, the light it's casting and the figures dancing across the screen make the room less empty somehow.

I sit on the floor in front of the fire to wrap my newly purchased presents, fighting with the sticky tape. I know that I have bought too much for Cas. I must be trying to compensate for the one thing she truly wants but cannot have. I should have learnt from her birthday that no amount of material things can make up for this, but my reasoning is that if she has so many presents to open, it may at least give her mind something else to focus on – a bit like me and work really.

Work. I've certainly found that easy to forget. An occupation for my mind that I no longer have. And yes, I do think about Rob more, but even though it's very hard and very painful, I am also starting to learn that it's a pleasure as well, to think about him. A pleasure I have been denying myself through fear.

The memory of him or something that he did can still make me smile – even make me laugh out loud sometimes. He left me a wealth of happy memories, and no one and nothing can ever take them from me. For instance, at Christmas once, instead of hanging up the mistletoe, Rob insisted on carrying it everywhere with him, demanding kisses constantly, saying that the price of it was a complete rip-off, so he was going to get his money's worth before it shrivelled up and died. I even pulled back the duvet to climb into bed that night to find him lying there in a pair of boxer shorts with the mistletoe pinned to the elasticated waistband.

I love giving presents, and I think I've found Laura the perfect thing. A new stereo system. It's small and unobtrusive, but it has everything a music-lover might need, including a CD player. At the moment she only has her old tin-pot radio cassette player, and an assortment of well-played tapes, which she loves with a passion, but now she can have her favourite songs on tap. A press of a button and Helen Carr will sing for her over and over again without the agonies of rewind. Some might say I'm a glutton for punishment, because it means I will have to listen to Judy Garland on repeat play as well, but the price is worth paying for the pleasure it will produce. I bought her some CDs to go with it – jazz, mainly, some classical, a Glenn Miller. *No* Judy Garland.

The man in the shop even carried it to the car for me, which was very helpful, especially as I had no idea where my car was. I think he thought I was a little mad. However, an insane woman with a platinum credit card finds tolerance where others may not.

I have bought Orlaithe a baby-doll nightie in her favourite shocking pink. It's completely see-through and trimmed at the edges with the softest most feather-like fur. It's totally outrageous and I know that she'll adore it.

I couldn't resist the gift that I found for Hank, a pair of brand new cowboy boots, displayed in the window of a strange shop that sold a range of eclectic designer wear, situated down one of the many back alleys that twist and turn their way through the town. They are beautifully black and shiny, made of a patterned leather that looks like snake, and entwined around each heel, curling up the leg of the boot as though ready to crush your ankle, is a bright red boa constrictor.

For Connor I have bought a bottle of good brandy to replace the one we drank during the thunderstorm. I couldn't think of anything more original. I remember a little longingly the book I found when Laura, Cas and I went shopping, and wish in a way that I *had* bought it for him. It would have been a more thoughtful gift.

For Cassie I have bought everything I saw that I thought she might like, fool that I am. I finish my wrapping with a tin of Quality Street I have ostensibly bought for the dogs, who both love chocolate, and a multi-pack of mints for Chance, placing my gifts under the tree with all the other brightly wrapped boxes that are gathering there in ever-increasing numbers. Like rabbits left alone to breed, each time you return there are more of them than before.

I then tidy away the debris of the past two hours, the odd ends of brightly coloured wrapping paper, the inevitable sheets of Cellophane that won't compact no matter how hard you try to screw them up, emerging from their rumpled balls like flower petals in sunshine as soon as you put them to one side. I push the tape and the scissors back where I found them in one of the dresser drawers, and sit down at the kitchen table, marvelling at how quickly the sherry bottle has plummeted in level considering I haven't drunk that much of it, have I?

There is another bag on the table containing my Christmas cards. I pull it over and begin to sort through them, trying to remember which one I bought for which person. There is a card slightly smaller than the rest at the back of the bag. Inside it, the message reads: *To the one I love*. I still love you, Rob, so it's still valid, I tell myself, sticking my chin in the air in defiance at the rational side of me that is chiding me for mild insanity.

It takes me almost as long to write my cards as it did to choose them. I always feel that I must put something witty, or something appropriate, can never settle for a mundane but easy *Happy Christmas* like most people. To Petra: *Lie back and think of England*. A joke we've both used a thousand times before but it still always makes us laugh. To Hank and Orlaithe: *Hope you have a great Christmas instead of a Blue Christmas*. Is that too obscure? Will they get the Elvis reference? Hank will, I'm sure, being such a fanatic, and Orlaithe will forgive me if she doesn't as she's such a nice person.

To Cas:

I pause and chew thoughtfully on the end of my Biro. What can I put to Cas. *New Year, New Start?*

Talk about clichés – but then isn't the whole thing just

a jumble of clichés? Christmas clichés? Putting Cas's card aside, I move on to my mother and find I am just as stuck with her, so in the end I give up, pushing everything back into the W.H. Smith carrier bag, to come back to at a later date.

Unable to face another glass of sherry, the previous four large glasses of which keep sending nauseous bursts of taste back up my throat and into my mouth, I flick on the kettle for a cup of tea, and take my other purchases from the fridge. Slowly and carefully, I begin to prepare dinner. Rob's favourite meal, Beef Wellington.

I don't normally agree with recipes, preferring to add a bit of this and a bit of that until I think that whatever I'm cooking tastes good. But as this was his favourite dish I thought it only right that I should be able to do the recipe justice.

When everything is ready, the Beef Wellington cooking nicely in the oven, the potatoes, peeled, parboiled and roasting away above it, the vegetables washed, cut and placed in pans on top of the Aga, I turn my attention to the table. Taking the huge bunch of white roses that I placed in the sink when I first got home, I cut them carefully from their Cellophane wrapper, put them in a large glass vase full of water, and place them in the centre of the kitchen table.

Rob always used to buy me roses. Every week without fail. I bury my nose in the centre of them and am disappointed to find that they don't have any scent at all. It's the wrong time of year. Nonetheless they are still beautiful – a perfect centrepiece to a table that I have set with the best I can find of the crystal, linen napkins, and the old gold-rimmed porcelain dinner service that used to belong to my grandmother.

Two bottles of good Burgundy are left open to breathe. And upon Cassie's plate sits an extra present that I wrapped along with the ones for Christmas Day.

★ ★ ★

Just after eight, I hear the rumble of the old Land Rover engine as Laura and Cas pull up in the yard outside. Suddenly uncertain, I take the gift-wrapped parcel from Cassie's plate and put it out of sight by the side of my seat. The door pushes open and Laura and Cas step through, bringing with them a rush of icy wind which threatens the guttering candles on the table.

Now that Laura is back, Meg appears as if from nowhere. Slipping through the door before it shuts, and between their legs as they pull off shoes and coats, she takes up her station by the fireside, eyes closing within a matter of seconds. She is soon fast asleep, worn out by a day patrolling the winter-ravaged farm.

Cas unwinds her scarf and throws it onto a chair, and then stops in surprise at the sight of the carefully laid table. 'What's the occasion?'

How do I explain? How do I say that in a way I am having a wake for her father, that it has taken me this long to realise that I missed that chance to celebrate his life with people who loved, cared for and respected him. I don't know if Cas would understand, or if it would just upset her, turn her back in on herself. I suddenly find that I don't want to explain.

'I just felt like cooking,' I reply unconvincingly.

'You never feel like cooking,' Cas replies suspiciously.

'Well, I did this evening.' I force a smile.

'Whatever Nattie's reasons, it smells divine!' Laura hangs her coat on the stand, 'I'm starving – when will it be ready?'

'Whenever you are.'

She immediately sits down at the table and picks up her knife and fork.

'I take it that means you're ready?'

'We missed lunch.' Laura grins. 'All we had in the fridge was cold meat, and this morning kind of put us off that, didn't it, Cas?'

She seems a touch too bright, as if forced. I wait until

Cas goes upstairs for the loo to ask: 'Are you okay?'

'I suppose so.' She rubs at her eyes tiredly. 'This morning was a bit rough. And of course the shock of Ralph passing away like that – so near to Christmas as well.'

'Have you spoken to Molly?'

Laura shakes her head. 'I tried to get through on the telephone but I couldn't. She'll be absolutely besieged by journalists at the moment, bless her. I'll try again tomorrow, but Cas and I popped a condolence card in the post on the way to the cinema so at least she'll know I'm thinking of her.'

Cas comes back down and Laura falls quiet. We sit down to eat.

'What was the film like?' I ask as Cas cuts enthusiastically into her beef.

'Good,' Cas mumbles through a mouthful of food. 'Even though Laura picked it.' She stops chewing and looks mockingly at my mother. 'She didn't know what it was about, she only chose it because it had Brad Pitt starring in it.'

'Call me shallow,' Laura shrugs jokingly, 'but I'm a sucker for a pretty face. This is really good,' she adds, pointing at her plate with her knife. 'Isn't this nice, Cassie?'

Cas mumbles a reply that I don't catch, but I've noticed that she is eating steadily, instead of picking at her food like she usually does if I ever cook.

'I didn't know my daughter could cook.' Laura winks at me.

'She can't,' Cas replies through a mouthful of beef, without looking up from her plate. 'Well, only this.' Her eyes finally flicker upwards, and I'm surprised when she half smiles at me. 'This was Daddy's favourite.'

'Ah.' Laura catches the smile, and puts down her fork. 'I see.' Reaching for the wine, she fills all our glasses, and then raises hers toward us. 'I think we should have a toast.' She waits for us to lift our glasses too. 'To absent friends.'

'To Daddy,' Cas says softly, her eyes filling.

I look at the full wine glass in front of me. At the blood red of the Burgundy within it. Rob and I used to toast every virgin bottle. 'To us,' he would always say.

I lift my glass, to join Laura and Cassie's. 'To us.'

The meal is finished. It is late. Cas, full of food and drowsy from the wine, is yawning and suggesting bed. I reach down to the side of my chair and pick up the parcel that is sitting there, and tentatively pass it over towards her.

'I've got something for you.'

'It's not Christmas yet,' she replies in confusion.

'I wanted you to have this now.'

When Cas reaches across the table to take it, I can see that she is embarrassed. I don't normally buy her surprise gifts, and she is obviously struggling to come up with a reason for this one, especially so close to the gift-fest that was her birthday. Glancing up at Laura as if for reassurance, she pulls away the paper to reveal a photograph in an intricate gilt frame.

I found the frame in the same shop where I bought Petra's earrings. The photograph is of Cassie and her father. It was taken just after New Year when she was home with us for our first Christmas as an official family. Cas was just fourteen and she is perched upon her father's lap, her head thrown back, and they are laughing, his hand resting gently on her knee, her fingers about his wrist. She didn't know I was taking the picture, and for some reason I never showed it to her.

I think it was a private moment, and I wasn't too sure that she would have welcomed the intrusion that I made upon it, the photograph clear and graphic evidence that I was there when she thought they were alone: when she was relaxed and happy with him.

Cas simply stares at it, unspeaking, her face turning

redder with every slowly passing second. For a moment I think with horror that she is angry, and then she turns to me, and I see that tears are slipping down her pink cheeks. Leaning across, she brushes the merest whisper of a kiss across my face.

'Thank you,' she whispers, and getting up from the table, slowly makes her way upstairs, clutching the photograph in its gilt frame to her chest.

I'm not surprised to wake up and find that it's still black outside. I'm like an alarm clock that's constantly set for certain times throughout the night. I have almost forgotten what it is like to get a straight night's sleep. I look at the clock beside my bed, knowing in my heart that it will be twenty past two in the morning; for some reason I always seem to wake up at twenty past two every morning. Ooh, a little variety for once! The neon digits tell me that it's two o'clock. I'm early today.

Sighing, I turn away from the clock and bury my head in the pillow, willing myself not to wake up any more than I already have, so that returning to sleep will be easy. Seconds later, however, I am sitting bolt upright, straining to listen. I heard something. In the yard. I know I'm always hearing things – the noise of a restless animal, the creaks and murmurs of the old house – but over the time that I have been here I have come to recognise them for what they are.

This is something new, something foreign, not of Whitsunday. There it is again! This time I know for definite that I heard something. And this time I know that it is the unmistakable sound of voices. I scramble quickly from my warm bed into the cold of the room, treading carefully across the creaking floorboards, paranoia that I will be heard making me more careful than I need to be.

I peer out of the window. There is a light in Chance's loose box, the thin, constantly moving beam of a torch.

Yesterday's clothes are thrown over the chair in the corner of my room, I reach for them in the darkness, pull them on without underwear, kicking my trainers onto my sockless feet without untying the laces.

Not daring to switch on the light, I feel my way down the staircase. As I reach the kitchen, my hand falls on the wooden-handled brass bedwarming pan that hangs as a decoration just inside the stair door. I take it from the wall, holding it like a tennis racket, and, looking far braver than I feel, inch my way across the kitchen and as quietly as I can, unlock and open the door into the yard.

There is definitely someone in Chance's loose box. I wonder for a moment if it's Cas, unable to sleep; she often chats away to Chance as if she's having a real conversation with him, but when I stop and listen again the tone is too low and masculine, and definitely receiving a response from a second. As I step away from the door toward the stable I freeze and my heart jumps out of my skin as the bottom half of the stable door swings open, and someone emerges leading Chance in his head collar.

It's a boy, no more than seventeen or eighteen. He freezes in his tracks and looks at me from dark hooded eyes, his mouth falling open, but remaining silent.

'What the hell are you doing?' hisses another voice from the stable. 'Get a move on, boy, and shift your hairy arse, you stupid animal.'

The boy and I remain at a distance, our gazes locked like pistoleers waiting for the signal to begin their duel.

Chance shifts uncomfortably, eyeballing the stranger next to him unhappily. His hooves are tied with muslin, presumably to muffle any sound as they led him away across the cobbled courtyard. Oh my God. They're trying to steal him. They're trying to steal Chance.

'What the hell do you think you're doing?' I squeak indignantly. I want to sound authoritative and strong, but the adrenaline of fear and injustice has tightened my throat, as well as heightening my senses.

On hearing my voice, the second figure pushes past a nervously tap-dancing Chance, and steps from the shadows.

I swallow. 'I said, what the hell do you think you're doing?' I repeat, more firmly this time.

'I suggest you go back inside, lady,' returns a calm quiet voice. 'You don't want any trouble now, do you?' His tone and his demeanour are more than menacing.

My head is telling me to turn and run, but there is something inside of me that is outraged by the tone of his voice, appalled by the sight of poor old Chance, whose eyes are now rolling with fear, nostrils flared as though he can smell danger.

'Oh, I think it's a bit too late for that now, don't you?' I reply in a tone that is far calmer than my churning insides will allow.

The second man steps out of the doorway, pushing Chance sharply in the ribs with his elbow to move him out of the way. Chance squeals in protest.

'Leave him alone!' I hiss, stepping forward again. 'I know what you're doing, and I'm not going to let you get away with it. I'm not going to let you take him.'

The younger of the two looks from me to his companion; although it is dark, I am now close enough to see the panic in his eyes.

'Yeah? And what are you going to do to stop me?' the older man sneers.

The other lad speaks, his voice quavering. 'Come on, Danny, she's only a girl.'

'Exactly,' the second man murmurs, raising the heavy torch menacingly in a clenched fist. 'She's only a girl. What can *she* do to stop us?'

'Danny, please.' The younger man's voice is fearful, his eyes darting from his companion to me, in sheer panic.

'Stop saying my name, you moron,' Danny snarls.

The younger lad turns pleadingly to me. 'Please, lady, just do as he says and go inside. I don't want nobody to get hurt.'

'You heard what the lad said, lady. He wants you to go inside 'cause he don't want nobody to get hurt.' The older of the two steps closer to me, his face twisting maliciously. 'The lad's a bit squeamish, see. Now personally, me, I don't mind using a bit of force to get what I want.'

I think he expects me to turn and run, but I don't. He steps forward again, his face becoming clearer as he gets closer to me. It's not a pleasant face, with its narrow hooded eyes and broken nose – it's the face of a pugnacious man.

Unexpectedly, he shakes the torch at me, making me jump. I think he expects me to melt onto the ground in a puddle of frightened female, but again I don't. Nor do I think he expects me to step closer to him – and he *certainly* doesn't expect me to swing my warming pan like Tiger Woods at the Ryder Cup. But this is what I do.

With a roar of pent-up frustration, the Vesuvius inside me that has been building up since that damned day in February nearly two years ago finally erupts and I swing that pan like a Viking wielding a hammer on a battle-ground. I hear a sickening crunch as brass connects with flesh, and Danny roars with shock and pain, dropping the torch with a loud clatter. Lights flick on inside Whitsunday, panicked voices erupting across the still cold air of the night.

The younger lad drops the lead rope of Chance's halter and throwing a petrified glance toward his companion and then the house, he sprints away and out of the yard down the track, mud flying from his heels.

I am left alone with my opponent. He is down, but definitely not out.

'Bitch! You f—ing bitch!' The profanity rises in volume as he hauls himself upwards from his knees, rising once more like the vanquished villain at the end of a horror movie. I wait for him, shaking like a leaf, but poised and ready to swing again with my now rather dented weapon. And then I hear a faint metallic click, and see that in his hand he now holds a knife; the full moon is glinting against the hard silver of the blade.

'Oh shit.'

'Yeah, you said it, lady,' he mocks me, repeating, '*Oh shit.*'

This time I step backwards, my eyes fixed by fear onto the blade, which he switches from his left hand to his right and back again in a steady threatening movement, all the time moving forward as I move backwards.

'Oh my God!' I hear Laura's cry behind me as she reaches the kitchen door. 'Nat!'

He is momentarily distracted by my mother screaming out my name, and for a second I can see him hovering between fight and flight, but then he lunges toward me. I don't know if he's trying to scare me more than harm me, but I'm not taking any risks, especially as I see Cas dart from the doorway skirting widely around us to take hold of an abandoned Chance's halter rope, which is threatening to tangle dangerously around his nervously darting hooves.

I wave my warming pan in front of me like a light sabre, and tell him as commandingly as I can to step back.

'I've already called the police!' Laura's voice is high-pitched.

He simply laughs at me and steps forward.

'Leave her alone!' Cas's tearful cry is overshadowed by the loud throaty growl of an angry animal, and the next moment I see a huge body hurl itself out of the shadows.

The man turns at the sound, and shouts in fearful surprise as, teeth bared, Mac flies at the hand holding the knife. There's a scream. A blood-curdling scream

297

that is neither human nor animal, and then the man is gone, running, holding his wrist and crying out in pain, the knife abandoned on the ground, no longer silver, but flecked red with blood, and Mac is lying before me as still as death, a long trail of scarlet running from his body across the stones.

At the time I was aware of another voice screaming, but it was only later that Laura told me it was mine. I must have had some kind of 'head fit', as Cas would so succinctly put it. I didn't quite pass out, but everything after that became a bit dazed.

Apparently, Connor was called down from the Loft, and arrived in a cloud of wheel-spin dust just as the vet, summoned by a tearful Cas, was kneeling beside Mac. And then the police arrived in a confusion of sirens and flashing blue lights – the last to arrive, despite the fact that they were the first to be called, my mother having been straight onto them as soon as she was woken by the sound of me battering my assailant with a warming pan.

Although it only takes Connor and the vet fifteen minutes to reach us, it's thirty minutes before the police handbrake-turn into the yard like the cars in the opening credits of *The Sweeney* and dive from the two squad cars as though still expecting the criminals to be there.

It was at this point that Laura swore at them briefly, told them they were too bloody late, and gently led me inside and sat me down at the kitchen table with a cup of hot sweet tea which is still sitting in front of me three hours later, cold and untouched, a thin grey skin forming on the chill surface.

The police are still here. Although there are only four of them, they are everywhere, like over-excited puppies, giving the illusion of a whole army of boys in blue, running around with their notebooks and plastic bags, looking for evidence, fingerprint-dusting the stable, even removing Chance's head collar as evidence. The Detective Inspector in charge, a dead ringer for Rowan Atkinson in *The Thin Blue Line*, only with a moustache that Hercule Poirot would have been proud of, is so excited when he bags the flick-knife that I think he's going to pee his dark-blue pants. It's still dark, but the yard is illuminated by the police cars parked side by side, the two sets of headlights on full beam.

The noise and the light have fooled the ducks and chickens into thinking that morning has come early today, and there is a cacophony of sound coming from the pens. Chance, thoroughly fed up at the indignity he feels he has already suffered, and the intrusion he is now suffering, has already savaged the peaked cap of one of the officers, whisking it firmly from his curl-covered head with strong teeth, and shaking it as a terrier would a rat, before tossing it contemptuously to the ground to be trampled on with hooves now free of muslin.

Cas is standing at the kitchen window, looking out at the French farce in the farmyard with growing agitation. She has been banned from the yard by the police for fear of 'tampering with police evidence' after calling one of the young officers a 'bloody idiot' for his less than nimble-fingered removal of a dancing Chance's head collar, and pushing him out of the way to do it herself.

She is now muttering insults about 'incompetents', having finished a lengthy diatribe about how even the thickest moron would know they're not going to get much evidence from a length of rope covered in horse saliva and dried grass. Laura, as always needing to be busy, is making tea and bacon sandwiches for everyone, great thick doorsteps of bread spread thickly with fresh butter. She places the first one in front of me, tempting me to eat, but I feel no hunger, just a heavy headache-making nausea.

I'm trying to concentrate on what's going on around

me, but all I can see is Mac lying in front of me, a trail of blood leading from his inert body. I can't get the picture out of my head. That lifeless body, and that crimson pool of blood slowly seeping across the cobbles . . . And then another picture emerges out of the dark shadows of my mind where it had been pushed in the hope that it would never resurface to haunt me again. *The mangled wreckage of Rob's car in the police compound.* My mind switches agonisingly from Mac to the car, Mac to the car, Mac to the car again, like a sick slide-show stuck on two pictures.

'Natalie?'

*Mac to the car, Mac to the car.*

'Natalie?'

My mind snaps back into focus on my surroundings. Connor has pulled out a chair and sat down beside me. He carefully pulls my own chair round to face him.

'Nattie?' He takes my chin in one gentle but firm hand and forces me to look at him, staring me straight in the eyes, until he is sure that he has my attention. And then he shakes his head, and letting me go, momentarily covers his own eyes with the same hand, then reaching out to me curls his fingers around the back of my neck and pulls me to him so that for a moment our foreheads rest together, his eyes connecting so closely with mine, brimful of anguish, disbelief.

For a moment I rest against him, my eyes closed, drawing comfort from his touch, and then the kitchen door slams shut as one of the police officers comes through from the yard, and I snap back into my seat, as though suddenly stung instead of soothed.

'How's Mac?'

'He's okay – still alive.'

'Oh, thank God!'

'He's just dazed, but he's fine, honestly. He must have hit his head hard on the handle of the knife and knocked himself out temporarily.'

'But the blood?'

'It's not his – most of it isn't, anyway. He lost a small piece of flesh just above his left eye, there's some of his hair caught on the knife's handle. He must have taken a huge bite out of the other focker though.' He laughs dryly. 'Apparently the police could follow the trail of blood right up to the road.'

'But he's okay? Mac's all right?'

'He's fine, I promise. He'll have a scar to be proud of, but he's fine.'

'Thank goodness.'

'In fact,' Connor adds, 'the only thing we'll have to worry about now is his ego. He already fancied himself as a bit of a bruiser, a dog about town,' he's trying to make me smile, his own lips curling in encouragement, 'so from now on he'll be the "dogfather" – of the canine world. He'll insist we call him *sir*, and let him sit in the front seat of the car whenever he wants.'

I let out a laugh that's almost a sob of relief. 'He's a hero. He saved me.'

'Well, don't tell him that or he'll get even more big-headed.'

I manage a faint smile.

'That's better.' Connor encourages. 'You look pale, Nat. Do you want a cup of tea, or maybe we can persuade Laura to let you have something a bit stronger?'

I shake my head. 'Can I see him?'

'Mac? If you can get past the army of fans feeding him chocolate, sure you can.' I get up from my chair, but he catches my wrist and pulls me back to face him. 'Why didn't you just let them take the horse, Natalie?'

I look for Cas. She has left her post at the window and, having retrieved Mac, is now kneeling on the hearth-rug in front of the fire, Mac's huge head cradled in her lap.

'How could I? Cas needs him. She's grown so fond of

301

him. I sometimes think he's the only thing she has left that she really cares about.'

'More than you or your mother? They could have killed you, Nat.'

I shake my head. 'He was trying to scare me, but he wasn't trying to kill me.'

'You don't know that.'

'He was a horse thief, not a mass murderer. I just wound him up, that's all. I played it wrong.'

'That's exactly my point.' Connor shakes his head in frustration. 'You shouldn't have played it at all. What on earth made you go out there? What on earth possessed you to try and take them on, and on your own as well? You're not bloody indestructible, you know.'

I close my eyes slowly and then open them again. 'I had to,' I tell him quietly. 'I've had too much taken away from me. The most precious thing in the world snatched away, stolen from me. If you think I'm ever going to let anything, or anybody do that to me or the people I love again . . .'

'But you could have been killed.'

'Death doesn't scare me.'

'I know,' he replies, gently squeezing my wrist before letting go, 'and that's what frightens *me*.'

Mac has several thick black stitches above his left eye, which are pulling up the usually droopy skin to give him a kind of permanently surprised look. He seems completely unconcerned by this, however, enjoying the attention he is receiving from Cas, the younger of the four policemen, my mother and the vet, with a slightly bemused and indulgent acceptance, like a King among his fawning subjects.

I push my way through the throng, and throw my arms around him, burying my face in the thick warmth of his furry neck. 'Thank you, thank you, thank you,' I tell him, as Mac returns my kisses by curling his tongue wetly and affectionately into my ear.

★ ★ ★

The police have finally finished. Tracks they found at the end of the drive show there was a car there, pulling something, probably a horsebox. Apparently we're not the first place in the area to have had animals stolen; we're just the first where it turned into a scene from *West Side Story*.

I can tell that the DI doesn't know whether to hug me or harangue me for being a 'have a go' idiot. In the end he does the latter, giving me a full-blown lecture on the dangers of not leaving the police work to the professionals. It's at this point my mother kicks them out, stating furiously that if the professionals did their job properly then we wouldn't have to act like vigilantes in the first place.

The news has spread like wildfire on the local grapevine and even though it's not one of his days to work, Hank is the next to appear. It is the most animated I have ever seen him; he is puffing with outrage like a little red-faced steam engine. He spends twenty minutes running his hands up and down Chance's legs, checking for non-existent swelling, or the heat that signifies an injury, picking up his hooves to check the tender soles, and feeling behind his ears. Cas is hovering behind him like a blue bottle, repeating, 'Is he okay?' every few minutes in the hope that he'll answer her eventually.

Finally satisfied that Chance is still in ruddy good health, Hank nods an affirmative. He then disappears into the back of the Long Barn, to emerge fifteen minutes later, his horny hands swathed in thick gloves, carrying a huge roll of razor wire, only to have a stand-up row with my mother who's adamant that she wouldn't have any of 'that horrible stuff' up on her land even if the German army had invaded again and were at this very moment bearing down on us in fully armed Panzer tanks.

You can't argue with Hank; you simply shout at him,

whilst he stands his ground. If, when you've finished shouting he simply walks off and carries on with whatever it was he was going to do in the first place, then you know you've lost the argument. This time, however, it would appear that Laura has won, because he takes the razor wire back to the Long Barn, and stores it once again wherever it was that he had hidden it in the first place, disappearing instead to buy security lights from a hardwear store in Helston. The shop will be open by the time he gets there, as the night has flown by.

'Horrible stuff,' I hear Laura repeating to Connor about the razor wire. 'It may keep people out, but look what danger it can do to the animals. They don't have the brains to stay away from it – not the first time anyway. I saw a young Jersey once who'd stumbled into some razor wire, and struggled like hell to get out. She was cut to ribbons – horrible sight.'

'You can understand his reasoning behind it, though.' Connor smiles grimly. 'You're a little bit of an easy target here, aren't you?'

'If you mean that we don't live in a fortress then yes, but that's not how I want my life to be. I'm not going to let some petty criminal make me live in a permanent state of siege.'

'What about a lock on the gate?'

'What – and have to go to the trouble of unlocking it every time you want to go in or out?'

'You can't just do nothing,' Connor states reasonably.

'I don't intend to,' Laura mutters angrily. 'Maybe next time they stroll through the open door of somebody else's place, they'll get more than they bargained for.'

When Hank gets back, Connor announces that he has to leave, to travel up to Portsmouth – a meeting he cannot cancel. As Mac seems disinclined to move from his position in front of the hearth, Connor suggests that the big dog stays with us until he returns later in the evening. Although he keeps saying that he's got to go, Connor seems reluctant to leave, even suggesting that he try to cancel his appointment, an idea that is quickly vetoed by my mother.

'Don't be ridiculous. You've already said that you can't. We shall manage quite well on our own, thank you.'

Connor is finally hustled out of the door and on his way by an agitated Laura. As soon as Connor's car pulls out of the gate, she is at the door, pulling on her coat.

'I've got to go out,' she mutters, when challenged. 'I won't be long.'

Now that the police have finished in the stables, and Hank has pronounced him none the worse physically for his ordeal, Cas is itching to spend some time with Chance. I follow her outside, keen for some fresh air, since the kitchen is a mix of cigarette smoke, sweat born of fear and adrenaline, the lingering smell of fried bacon, tea and antiseptic.

Cas turns as I step after her, and looks at me for a moment. 'You were really brave, Nat.' She moves forward and to my complete amazement, hugs me. 'Thank you. I don't know what I would have done if they'd taken him.' Then she lets go and practically sprints over to the stable.

Chance, who barely uses his equine voice, whickers in relief as he recognises that it is his Cas, and not one of those stupid men who have since the early hours of this morning made it their business to so thoroughly unnerve him.

'You stupid old thing,' I hear her chastise him affectionately. 'Jeez, you're anybody's for a handful of mints, aren't you?'

Hank, who has checked the small herd, and counted the chickens and ducks three times over to make sure none are missing, is on a ladder, fixing a security light just above the kitchen door.

I don't want to go back inside. I walk down the long passage and lean on the gate, breathing in the fresh salty air, listening to the soft whisper of the sea at the end of Mile Meadow. Despite the fact that I keep trying to push them out of my mind, last night's events are running through my head like a movie on a rerun. I see the knife coming for me over and over again, and feel the bile rising from my churning stomach to my throat, and leaning against the gate-post for support I slump forward and begin to throw up, on and on until I am empty inside.

Laura returns an hour later, the asthmatic rattle of the Landy announcing her arrival several minutes before she drives into the yard. Cas and I are there to greet her, and watch as she climbs from the driver's seat, then reaches back in to pull a long soft leather case from the seat beside her. She leads the way into the kitchen and puts the case down on the table, looking for all the world as if she has an announcement to make and yet saying nothing. She simply switches on the kettle, lights her fifth cigarette of the morning, despite the fact that she swears she gave up weeks ago, and leans back on the counter, waiting for the kettle to boil and for us to speak.

'Well then, what is it?'

Laura pulls on the cigarette, smoke curling from her crimson lips, and then exhales heavily before answering me. 'It's a shotgun.'

'What the hell are you doing with a shotgun?'

'I borrowed it from Charles.' She looks from me to Cas, and then back to me again almost challengingly, obviously aware that my first reaction to this news will not be one of pleasure.

'A shotgun?' I repeat stupidly.

Laura nods. 'I want to make sure we're . . .' she pauses for a moment. 'I think the right word would be *protected*. Just in case – and I'm not saying it will happen

– but just in case they decide to pay us a return visit.'

I frown at Laura in annoyance. Of course this thought had crossed my mind, but I'd hoped she'd have sense enough not to say it in front of Cas. I'm angry at her for putting this idea into my step-daughter's head. It would appear it's something she's already thought of for herself, though.

'It's quite common for criminals to return to the scene of the crime.' She nods as if in agreement with my mother.

'But a gun!'

'I think it's a good idea.' Cas goes over to the case and begins to unzip it. 'In fact, if someone tries to take Chance again, I'll shoot them myself,' she states coldly. So much for Cas being traumatised by the gun or the thought of the guy from last night making a reappearance. From the tone of her voice she'd actually relish the chance to fill his backside full of gunshot. She pulls the gun from its leather sleeve and pretends to take aim out of the kitchen window.

'Put it down, Cas!' I snap.

'Don't worry,' Laura reassures me. 'It's not loaded. Not yet anyway.'

'Can you teach me how to use it?' Cas strokes the long metal gun barrel in fascination.

Laura silences my exclamation of protest with the fairly sensible argument that Cas will be far safer knowing how to handle the gun properly, than being completely ignorant of it, but I'm still not happy.

'I don't know about feeling safer with that thing here – I think I feel worse. Don't you need a licence for them anyway?' I protest as she begins to show Cas the rudiments.

'I've only borrowed it.'

'But you still need a licence.'

'Charles has got one.'

'Yeah, for his use. Not ours.'

Laura turns to me, her face resolute. 'Nattie, last night a man broke into my home and attacked my only child with a knife. If it hadn't been for Mac, heaven knows what would have happened to you. Which do you think is the bigger risk? Having an unlicensed gun in the house for a week or so, or facing that man again with nothing more than a dented bedpan to fend him off? I'm not taking any chances. Don't worry, I shall keep it locked in the cupboard in my bedroom, and yes, I hope I never have to bring it out again except to give it back to Charles, but I for one shall feel an awful lot safer knowing it's there if we need it.'

We continue the day in an uncomfortable silence. I am angry with Laura for bringing a gun into the house. I understand her reasons, but this still doesn't make it right. I mean, what's she going to do if someone does break in again? I can hardly see a woman who won't put up razor wire for fear of hurting animals, taking up a shotgun and shooting somebody, and to simply threaten with it would surely aggravate a situation.

If I'm being totally honest, I'm also angry with myself for being so reckless. I may not be scared by the thought of death any more, but what on earth would be the effect on my mother and Cas if something happened to me?

On the pretext that I have some work to do, I go to my room but as always I just sit and stare at an empty computer screen, unable to think of anything other than my own situation. How can I possibly write about the lives of other people when I'm so wrapped up in my own? I go and lie on the bed, close my eyes for a moment, and hope that a rest will kick-start my weary brain.

After about ten minutes, I open my eyes again, and my gaze comes to rest on top of the wardrobe, and the shoebox I discovered there on the day of the picnic. I'd forgotten all about that. Curiosity overcomes me.

Moving the chair across I climb up and fetch it down, and return to my bed to open it, carefully removing the ribbon that has been tied with such care. A dog-eared manuscript is in the box. It takes me a moment to recognise the handwriting as my own. I thought I'd lost this years ago, but Laura must have kept it. I wrote it when I was living here. It's a story about a girl who heads for the city from the country in order to find fame and fortune. No guesses as to who it was based on.

Fascinated, I sit back and begin to read. It is so odd to read these words again, to remember how I foresaw my life then, and be able to compare it with what actually happened to me when I finally made it to London. The thing that strikes me the most, however – no matter how immodest it may sound – is how good it is! A little childish maybe, but then I was only young; it is none-theless well written, absorbing even. Perhaps with some work . . .

I finally finish writing four hours later, and only then because I suddenly realise how late it has got. Revising the novel I started in my teens has taken my mind off absolutely everything. I feel more refreshed than if I'd slept a whole night through. But then again – they do say that writing is therapeutic.

I press the save icon, close up my laptop, and go down to the kitchen to find that Cas has made dinner in an attempt to induce some harmony back into the house-hold, which is kind of ironic seeing as she is normally the source of most discord, and not the peacemaker.

To give her her due, she has tried really hard. She's made a lasagne that looks and smells delicious; the mixed scents of tomato and garlic, melted cheese and oregano hang heavily in the kitchen air. She has also opened two bottles of red wine to go with it.

Laura is called in from the Long Barn, where she is

ostensibly checking the feed bins, but in reality I think she is avoiding another confrontation over the shotgun. When she comes in, she doesn't look at me first and noticing, Cas quickly pours us both a large glass of Chianti.

A bottle and a bit later, we are all decidedly more relaxed, but we're still not speaking much. Each person's head is filled with the events of this morning, but not one of us really wants to talk about it. The silence is eventually broken by the sound of the phone ringing.

It's Connor. He's checking that we're okay, and apologising for the fact that he's been held up and is staying in Portsmouth overnight. He wonders if we can keep Mac for him. I tell him that we'd be happy to. Knowing that my mother has a shotgun doesn't make me feel any safer, but I am more than grateful to be sharing my bed with Mac, even though he is the biggest duvet hog I have ever known. When I wake as always several times in the night, my mind full of intruders, I am reassured to see him sleeping peacefully and undisturbed beside me.

Three days later and the events of that night now seem more like a dream than reality. All remains quiet at Whitsunday. The only visitors are Hank and Connor, who keep finding one excuse or another to come and check up on us. I personally believe that Danny the Desperado is long gone by now, and all that we are left with is a bad memory, some bloodstains on the cobbles and an Incident Number that will remain lodged in the police databanks for many years to come under *Unsolved*.

We also have something else to take our mind off everything. It is Christmas Eve. I greet this day with mixed emotions. Laura is excited, Cas is quiet, no doubt thinking of her father, as I am.

We spend the day working steadily together, the morning clearing up, cleaning, feeding animals, and the afternoon preparing tomorrow's lunch.

Taking up the entire bottom half of the fridge, lying in chilled state is Gertrude, pale, plump and plucked. I thought I'd take pleasure in stuffing something that once wanted to eat my arse for breakfast, but it's very strange knowing that the lifeless carcase in the fridge was once an animal with attitude. In the end I leave the stuffing to Laura and peel what seems like eighteen tons of Brussels sprouts instead, whilst Cas takes her turn with the potato peeler.

'Are we going down to the Ship tonight?' Cas asks hopefully, as she places her peeled and chopped potatoes into a bowl of cold water and then puts them into the fridge for tomorrow.

To Cassie's obvious disappointment, Laura shakes her head. 'I hadn't planned to, no.'

'But they're having a bit of a party. Orlaithe has been cooking mince pies all week, and Denzel's going to play the piano.'

'In that case we're definitely not going down,' I joke, winking at Cas. I turn to Laura. 'Seriously, how about it? Could be fun.'

'Well, I had planned on us just staying in together – you know, an old-fashioned family night with games and mulled wine . . .' She trails off at the sight of our less than enthusiastic faces. 'Okay, okay, I give in. We'll go down to the Ship.'

The first person we see when we enter the Ship is Luke, uncharacteristically smart in seal-grey cords and a dark-blue shirt.

'Now I see why Cassie was so desperate to come down here,' Laura whispers to me, as Cas immediately rushes off to join him at the pool table.

Orlaithe is wearing a fitted red chiffon dress, and a shiny, pointed princess-style party hat with a piece of mistletoe attached to the very tip. She is greeting

all-comers with a glass of sherry and a kiss from her
crimson painted lips.

'Laura! Nattie! Lovely!' she calls in pleasure to see us,
waving to Cas as she rushes past her, threading her way
through the full bar to meet us. 'First drinks on the
house.' She offers me a sherry from her laden silver tray.

'No thanks, I promised I'd drive back.'

'Good – that means I can have two then, doesn't it?'
Laura grins, helping herself to two glasses.

The pub is full of revellers. Hank is wearing tinsel
slung about his neck in place of his usual bootlace tie.
The small bald wizened Denzel is already at the piano
playing a mellow version of 'Winter Wonderland', a
gap-toothed grin fixed permanently on his twisted
chamois leather face.

It is obvious that Laura is hoping to see Charles in
here. Her eyes are scanning the crowd, the hope fading
to disappointment as she doesn't spot him, her smile
turning resolute as she determines to enjoy herself
anyway. She follows Orlaithe back to her position by the
bar, the two glasses, one held in each hand, already
empty. I watch her as she orders more drinks, her
disappointment concealed.

My mother is an admirable woman. The strength I see
in her now in so many things . . . she is so different from
the person I thought I remembered. But then with time
comes change.

I think back to where I was this time last year. Seven
o'clock and still sitting in my office, kidding myself that I
needed to be there. The only person apart from Security
still in the building, everyone else gone home to their
families, to their Christmas.

On Christmas Day, I visited Louisa-May in the morning, and then went back home to work again. Paid little
thought to my own mother or where she might be,
whom she might be with. It warms me a little to know
that she was probably here, with these good and

generous people. I know I miss Rob, and I feel sad, and scared, and scarred, but I can't help but feel privileged that this year I am here too.

'Hi.' The soft, unmistakable voice of Connor draws me back into the present.

'Hello,' I reply quietly, trying to slide my mouth into a smile that doesn't look too forced.

'Are you okay?'

I nod slowly.

'You look a little sad. Missing the bright lights and sophistication of the city?'

I shake my head. 'Would you believe the opposite? Besides, we've got the bright lights . . .' I point to where Orlaithe has hung a string of coloured fairy lights along the brow of the bar. 'And as far as I'm concerned they can keep the sophistication, this is much more fun.'

'You're warming to us, aren't you?'

I raise my eyebrows in question.

'The Cornish, our way of life,' he explains. 'It gets us all in the end, seduces you with its easy charm until you can't imagine life anywhere else.'

'I think I could be,' I answer thoughtfully. 'Why did you move from London?'

'Me?' he asks, as though surprised by the question. 'Oh, I had to get away before it ate me alive.'

'What do you mean?'

'I suppose I didn't so much move away from London itself, but what London represented to me as an artist. When I was working there, the art world became hi-jacked by sensationalism and a desire for celebrity, and I had to leave before it got to me as well. I just wanted to paint, and it seemed like this medium was no longer considered to be art. Do you know that most art schools are so convinced that drawing and painting are dead that they no longer automatically teach them? It seems like such an insult. I mean, delve into the history of art, and you come up with such beauty. The High

Renaissance, Leonardo, Michelangelo, Raphael, Titian, Bellini, Bramante, Lombardo, Torrigiano . . .'

The names fall from his tongue like honey spilling from a knife. '. . . That was, that *is* what I call art. I know it's only my opinion. I'm not arrogant enough to claim that everyone should think the way I do – after all, art, like beauty, is in the eye of the beholder – for me, the London art scene was no longer a pool I wanted to swim in; it is full of sharks.'

'You sound very cynical.'

'That's just the thing. That was how it would have made me if I'd stayed in London. I didn't want to lose the joy. What is anything, without the joy? Look at young Cas and her riding, now there's dedication for the love of it.'

'Yeah, she's good, isn't she? She's coming along really well with her drawing and painting too.'

'That she is.'

'She rarely practises her ballet though.'

'Maybe she's lost the passion.'

'Maybe,' I reply, thinking back to the day I saw her in the Long Barn. 'She's amazingly good though, frighteningly so.'

'She has a lot of willpower, a lot of determination. Cas would be good at anything she turns her mind to, and she wouldn't want to admit defeat on something simply because she no longer enjoys it, especially with her dancing. What with her mother and everything.'

'Has she spoken to you about it?'

'Not in any great depth, but it's been mentioned, yes.'

'What did she say?'

'It wasn't really what she said, it was just an impression that I got. I think the dance is not so much for her as for an obligation that she feels, which is a shame. But she will find the right path in the end, she just lacks direction at the moment. Then again, it's a rare sixteen year old who knows what they want to do with the rest of the life that seems to stretch before them like a never-ending road. Especially one who's been through what Cassie has.'

'It's been hard for her since Rob died.'

'I can imagine,' he replies with feeling.

'You once said to me that you'd lost someone close to you?'

'My brother Colm was always a mammy's boy. Da' and I were close. It hit me hard when I lost him, even though I was expecting it to happen. He'd been ill for some while.'

'You miss him?'

'Sure, but he wouldn't want me to spend the rest of my life wallowing in the misery of it. He'd want me to be out there making my mark. He'd want me to make him proud.'

'He would be . . . very proud.'

'Oh, you think so, do you?' He replies. His voice is tinged with his usual mirth, but when I look up at him, the eyes that look back at me are searching, reaching almost inside of me with an intensity, a need, a desire almost.

I am flustered; the heady feeling that consumes me cannot be attributed to alcohol since I haven't touched a drop.

'Would you like a drink?' My voice is trembling like the sea grass clinging to the cliff outside, unsettled by the breezes that scurry in across the Atlantic.

He shakes his head and when I look at him again it is only the easy friendly humour that I see there within him.

'I'd love one, Nat, but I only called in to say hello to everybody. I've got to be going any minute.'

'Party?' I ask, feeling a faint flush of disappointment, which I instantly dismiss as ridiculous.

'No, I'm away up to London. I promised to spend Christmas morning with my brother and his family.'

'I thought you said they lived in Durham.'

'That they do, but it's Christmas at my sister-in-law's parents this year.'

'You don't sound too keen.'

'Oh, yes and no,' he sighs. 'I want to see them, and it's always a joy to watch the nieces and nephews opening their presents, but it's a little awkward being a guest in the house of someone you don't know very well.'

I nod in sympathy.

'And although Mac's name is on the guest list I'm not sure how well they'll take to having such a large dog in their house. I've been there a couple of times before and they've too many cream carpets, so they have.'

'You could always leave him with us.'

'That's kind of you, but to be honest he's a fairly convenient escape route should I be needing one.'

'That bad, eh?'

'No, I'd just rather be spending Christmas here this year.'

I know this time that it is not my imagination. He is searching my face, looking for some kind of response. But I cannot speak; I am tongue-tied and idiotic.

He sees my embarrassment. I'm not sure how he interprets it, but it is enough to make him back away, to say his goodbyes, to turn and leave. And yet despite my reticence, my confusion, I cannot let him go without at least acknowledging both to him and to myself what I see and feel, even if as yet I don't quite understand.

'Connor.'

He turns back to me.

'Drive carefully.'

To my surprise, he comes back to me and briefly, gently touches my face. 'I always do, I promise.'

The heavy front door closes behind him. I feel hot; a flush of colour and confusion is spreading over me. I look around for Cas but she is playing pool with Luke, and Laura is watching them. I am thankful that neither were witness to a moment of intimacy that I find at once intimidating and yet strangely comforting.

But we didn't escape scrutiny entirely.

'Connor's gone then.' It is Orlaithe. I can tell by the tone of her voice that she was a witness to our goodbye.

I breathe out, compose myself, turn to face her. 'Yes,' I reply brightly. 'Gone to spend Christmas with his family in London.'

'Sure, and that will be nice for him.' She winks at me as though we are sharing a secret, making me feel at once reassured, but embarrassed.

'What are you doing tomorrow?' I ask in an attempt to change the subject.

'Lunch with Hank's old ma, and then, as you know, over to you for supper.'

'Hank's mother's still alive?' I ask in surprise.

'Ninety at the end of January so she is, and could still drink Hank under the table. Big party we'll be having then, huge party, and sure you and little Cas are invited.'

'We'll be back in London by then.'

'Oh, now that's a shame. But you'll be coming back to see us again soon no doubt.'

'Yeah,' I say. 'We will, definitely.'

I suddenly realise that the strange twist in my throat and stomach is a stab of feeling almost bordering on disappointment that at the end of January, I will be back in London, back at my desk in the *Naked* offices, and Cas will be sent back down to Cheal.

Both of us so far away from . . . everybody.

It is nearly midnight when Orlaithe finally locks the door behind the last of the customers to be sent home. A select group of regulars are still seated at the bar – Laura, myself and Cas, Daveth, who can barely keep his eyes open, Denzel and his third wife Agnes, who is originally from Islington, a tiny woman, like a little brown Cockney sparrow. Agnes is talking to Cas.

'Did you know that all of the animals are supposed to kneel at midnight, in honour of the birth of Christ?'

Cassie is looking over to the fireplace where Old Shep and Jasper are both fast asleep, basking in the soft glow of the burnt orange embers.

'Well, they're not kneeling, but they're definitely prostrate – does that count?'

Hank is looking at his watch. He coughs gently and nods toward an old German wall clock, its brass pendulum swinging rhythmically, a little like Laura swaying gently on her barstool. As we look over, its melodic chimes sound the first strokes of midnight.

'Happy Christmas!' Orlaithe choruses, immediately flinging her arms around Hank and planting an affectionate kiss on his forehead.

I look around me at the happy smiling faces and once more give thanks that compared to the bleak loneliness of last Christmas, I am now surrounded by love and affection.

And I try to think of Rob, to see if the pain of bringing him deliberately to mind has lessened any. But as my mother and Cas and my newfound friends turn to hug each other in celebration, I find that my overwhelming thought is not of Rob, but whether Connor has completed his journey in safety.

# Chapter Ten

I awake on Christmas morning and for a brief moment almost feel that Rob is here with me. If I open my eyes I will break the spell, because that is surely what this is. I can almost feel his arms around me, his cheek resting against my hair. He promised he'd always be here for me.

'Happy Christmas!' A twin chorus, my mother's voice and Cassie's, the notes bursting through my listless body.

Laura comes hurrying into my bedroom, Cassie close behind her. To my surprise, Cassie rushes to the bed and throws back the covers, and then clasping both of my cold hands, hauls me upright, tugging me out of the bed, with a smiling haste. 'Look, Natalie – look and see.'

Cassie's eyes are wide with excitement, her cheeks flushed, a smile dancing about her lips like sunlight on water. I stumble to my feet, her hands still firmly clasped in mine as she leads me over to the window, where Laura is busy pulling back the floral curtains to let in a brilliance of light that is dazzling in its purity.

'It's snowing!' Cas cries enthusiastically. 'It's Christmas Day and it's snowing!'

I gaze out onto the white world outside my window, pupils shrinking to pinpricks. Great white flakes of snow are falling heavy and soft and silent onto the ground below, covering everything as far as the eye can see. The roofs of the barns, the fields beyond, the trees, the hedges – all are white; the sea alone is not, and yet it has somehow been watered down from its usual dramatic hues to a muted grey that reflects the sky above.

'Snow at Christmas,' Laura sighs, then adds with typical Laura humour, 'I wish I'd put a bet on.'

I look at the two faces one either side of me, both smiling, both shining with an inner light from the promise and the pleasure a white Christmas brings to them. Without Rob I thought Christmas Day would have no meaning, no feeling.

'I've always wished for snow on Christmas Day,' Cas murmurs, more to herself than us. 'This is my first gift.'

She feels it too. That he is here, that this is somehow *his* doing.

Cassie has uttered Laura's magic word.

'Gifts, yes – presents!' Laura exclaims, but then to my surprise adds, 'We've work to do first. Animals don't suddenly learn how to feed themselves, just because it's Christmas Day. Come on, Nattie, hurry up. Shower and change – let's get everything done as quickly as possible then we can open our presents!'

I go downstairs to find the lights blazing on the walls and on the tree, the oven on, the fire soaring high into the blackened chimney, but the kitchen door wide open: a strong contrast of excessive heat and the purest cold that only snow can give. Laura and Cas are already outside, both wrapped in scarves with woollen hats pulled down over their pink ears, long thick pink socks peeping from the top of Laura's Wellington boots.

Cas is changing Chance's jute rug to a hardier New Zealand one, in preparation for turning him out into Mile Meadow for a couple of hours of freedom, as she won't be riding him today. Laura is attempting to entice the ducks from their home with a bucket of corn.

Little Stu is in raptures. His first snow. Not quite sure what has happened to the world as he knows it, he sits half in and half out of the kitchen door, excited and yet sorely afraid. Then Meg dives straight out of the door, her nose working through the two inches that already lie, like a snowplough as she crosses the yard, head down, plumed tail swaying from side to side like the conductor's baton at a Vivaldi concert. Encouraged by this bravery, Stu dips in one small paw, retracts it swiftly as though burnt, tries again, and then like a high diver taking a deep breath, he plunges in, and is soon body surfing across the yard, the baby fur on his belly being tied in dirty knots by the cold water.

Laura has Christmas hits blasting from the kitchen whilst we work, the animals serenaded by Bing Crosby singing 'White Christmas', Dean Martin with an apt 'Let It Snow', Doris Day, even Cliff Richard gets his chance as we're not close enough to fast forward.

It's amazing how soon the pristine white snow turns to wet grey slush as we wade through it in our Wellingtons with hay nets and feed buckets, and jugs of hot water to melt the ice that has formed on the water troughs. I'm surprised that Laura has enough willpower to do anything before she attacks the pile of presents waiting for us under the tree. When I was a young child she used to be the first one up on Christmas Day, chivvying my father and me to follow her as early sometimes as five in the morning. She could never wait. Has she matured, or does the magic just fade as you get older? Either that or she has finally developed some willpower.

Laura looks up and waves to me as I step outside of the kitchen door. 'Hurry up, we're nearly done here. There's just the girls down in the pasture to take care of – would you do that?'

I found it hard to know what to put on this morning. Apart from last year when Christmas was just another day to be endured, I've always dressed up for Christmas. I think everybody does, but knowing I won't have time to change before my mother descends upon the presents like an eager vulture on roadkill, I am now feeding cows in a cream cashmere jumper, and a very expensive pair of grey wool Joseph trousers. Hardly sensible attire for pushing your way through a herd of hungry Friesians. I'm not quite sure how I managed to land up with this job, whilst my mother and Cas see to the slightly less clothes-threatening Chance and the chickens.

I finally make it back into the house in fairly decent condition, although my wellies are far too disgusting to bring inside with me, and have to be left outside the door. This must be the first morning we have stayed here when Laura hasn't insisted on making a full cooked breakfast. Instead, she and Cas have unsurprisingly finished their chores well before me and are sitting on the floor by the huge tree, its lights twinkling merrily in the unlit room, impatiently waiting for me to come back. So impatient in fact that although they haven't opened any presents yet, they have divided them up into separate piles, giving them an opportunity to have a good squeeze on the sly.

As a reflection of his growing status in the household, and more importantly in Cassie's heart, the biggest pile of all apparently belongs to Little Stu. He has a new collar from Laura, which he desperately needs, having thrown off his status as 'runt' by having a mad spurt of growth in the past two weeks. He has a new bowl from me, presumably so he can eat more food and continue said growth spurt. From Cas there is a dog-bed more luxurious than any of the old bone-shakers in the bedrooms upstairs that we have to sleep in, and enough squeaky rubber toys to annoy us until Easter. She has also bought him a little plaid puppy coat, which he doesn't want to wear, but thinks is edible, and a new lead to replace his remarkably flimsy puppy one, which he also thinks is edible and has chewed to the consistency of a frayed shoe lace. His final present is a stocking crammed full of treats and sweets and chews, supposedly from Meg. He has by remarkable coincidence sent her the same gift and Meg's handwriting is remarkably similar to Laura's.

'You're mad,' I tell my mother, but she simply smiles happily and urges Cas to start on her own gifts.

I'm surprised that Laura hasn't even touched her own pile, until watching her, watching Cas, I finally realise what the change is in her. The greatest pleasure she now gets from Christmas presents is watching other people open the ones she has bought them.

With a surge of fresh guilt I realise that this is only the third Christmas Day I have spent with my mother since I left home. I know she usually spends Christmas Day with friends – at least, that's what she always said over the years when I've made my usual tentative enquiries about her plans for the festive period. I never knew whether to believe this, but it was easier for me to take it at face value, so I never pushed the subject.

I found Cas hard to buy for, especially as I went a bit overboard on her birthday. I've got her the usual stuff – underwear, make-up, CDs – but in the end I actually found her main present in the same place as Laura's. I saw it in the window, surrounded by tinsel, big black cardboard arrows, much hype from an overexcited copy-writer, and a price tag that took your breath away.

It's an all-singing, all-dancing, laptop computer. It really is an amazing piece of equipment, so sophisticated you could almost just plug it in and leave it to type up a novel for you on its own. I know I'm spoiling her again, and I know that money is no substitute for the things she really needs in life, like love and guidance and good care, but to be honest I was totally running out of ideas.

I just hope she likes it. I could have bought her a small car for what it cost, but as I learnt from her birthday, expense isn't everything. I'm more than nervous that my Christmas gifts will receive the same reception as those I bought for her birthday. She's ripping the paper off the box now, whilst I stand by and watch and chew my nails in nervous anticipation of her reaction.

'Oh, my God!' she exclaims, immediately covering her mouth, as though this will excuse the blasphemy.

'I take it that means she likes it,' Laura whispers with a grin.

'Oh my goodness, this is amazing.' Cas looks up at me, blue eyes shining like headlights.

Despite the fact that she looks more than pleased I find myself starting to make excuses. 'I know you've got one at home, and you've probably got hundreds you can use at school, but this one you can take anywhere, like when you go on holiday, or go to a friend's, and we'll hopefully be spending a bit more time here as well, so you can bring it down with you.'

Laura's eyes widen. 'Really?' she asks me quickly.

'What?'

'You'll be spending more time here,' she prompts.

'If you'll have us, yes,' I nod, looking over at her. To my horror her previously grinning face begins to go red and crumple like a used tissue. 'What's the matter?' I ask.

'That's the best Christmas present I've had so far,' Laura sniffs, pulling a paper tissue from the box on the dresser and blowing her nose rather violently.

Cassie looks at Laura, then at me, and then her face breaks into a broad smile. 'In that case you'd better open Nattie's present to you then, hadn't you?' she urges her.

Laura stops sniffing and she and I both look at Cas in surprise.

'You know what it is?' We both query at the same time.

'Hey, I'm still just about classified as a kid, aren't I?' she excuses herself. 'It's my job to sneak a look at the presents.'

I watch my mother open her gift from me, waiting for her to tell me off for spending too much money with a smile of pleasure on my face. It's the first time in ages that I have bought her a proper Christmas present; in fact, for several years after I first left home, she was lucky if I even sent her a card. Thinking back now, she always managed to find me, wherever I was – and sometimes I must have been difficult to trace, because I often moved on without bothering to let her know where to – but she always caught up with me, and she always made sure I got a Christmas present.

Birthdays, too.

I feel bad about this now and yes, I will admit that there is a little bit of guilt gone into the purchase of something so extravagant, but only a very little. I feel I have a lot of missed presents to make up for.

Laura rips off the expanse of wrapping paper. 'Such a huge box,' she murmurs, her eyes flicking up to me and then back to the task in hand, with more than a hint of chastisement to come if I have indeed, as she now suspects, spent too much money on her.

The stereo is finally unveiled, and Laura immediately enlists Cassie's help to set it up on top of a chest of drawers in the corner. She puts on one of her CDs, and the two of them do an impromptu dance routine across the flagstone floor, before flinging themselves back in front of the tree again breathless and laughing.

I look at their flushed, smiling faces and feel my stomach twist with pleasure and with pain, and then it's my turn. Laura realises that I have been standing back to watch instead of getting stuck into the wrapping paper.

'You haven't opened any!' she yells, immediately getting down on her knees and sorting through the remaining gifts. 'These are from me,' she thrusts a pile of gaudily wrapped gifts into my arms, 'and these,' she adds, putting two more on top so that I can't see where I'm going, 'are from Cas.'

I put the pile back down on the floor and pick up the

first one. *To Natalie love from Cassie*. With three kisses as well. But I'd recognise my mother's handwriting anywhere. Lifting the gift tab, I raise my eyebrows at her.

'She chose them for you,' Laura whispers, smiling encouragingly. 'She just didn't have the patience to wrap everything.'

I open the dark blue gift wrap covered in little fat red jolly Santa Clauses to find a pair of big fluffy slippers in the shape of monster's feet; the second contains a beautifully soft, bright red cashmere scarf, and matching gloves.

'Because you're always cold.' I almost jump as Cassie speaks, she is standing so close behind me.

'Thank you. They're great.'

She shrugs.

I think the monster's feet are more of a statement than anything. Monster feet for the monster stepmother. I put them on the floor, where they are promptly pounced upon by Stu, who starts to pretend he's actually wrestling a real monster, his growls muffled by a mouthful of brown fake fur.

Laura is opening her gifts from Cas. She has bought her nail varnish in copious amounts, reds and pinks, luminous glitter, acid greens, violent purple. There is also a strange cigar-shaped electric device with different detachable heads for giving yourself a pedicure.

'What on earth!' Laura exclaims, holding it up to her face so that her eyes are almost crossing in an effort to work out what it is.

'It's for pedicures.' I grin at her.

Laura looks at the thing in her hand and starts to giggle. 'For a moment there I thought Cassie had been under-age shopping in Ann Summers.'

'Honestly, you've got such a dirty mind,' I hiss at her, thankful that Cas's attention is firmly focused on opening her remaining presents. Laura has bought Cas clothes, Petra has sent perfume.

Chanel for Laura. Poison for Cas. Angel by Theirry Mugler for me.

Cas immediately douses herself in the stuff before deciding she's not actually too keen on the cloying scent, and goes upstairs to wash it all off again.

Laura waits until Cas smells like soap again, and then tells her, 'I've got one more thing for you, but I just need to fetch it – okay? Wait there a minute, and promise no peeking out of the window.'

Cas and I exchange intrigued glances as Laura disappears outside. She is gone for quite some time and then a door bangs, followed by muffled noises, a strange shuffling sound as something comes across the yard, and then a few minutes later we hear her calling us to go out.

We go to the kitchen door and pull it open once more. Laura is standing just outside, holding the lead rope of Chance's halter. Chance is looking puzzled but very festive. His New Zealand has been changed to a day rug trimmed with white fur like the lining of Santa's red suit, his halter is adorned with tinsel, and he is patiently wearing a pair of plastic reindeer antlers attached to a plastic Alice band, which have a little string of working fairy lights strung between the tips, that blink green, yellow and red, like malfunctioning traffic lights.

'Happy Christmas!' Laura cries as Cas laughs in delight at the sight of him. Reaching out a hand, Laura takes hold of one of Cas's own small ones, and putting the halter rope in her palm, closes her fingers around it.

'I don't understand.' Cas's eyes narrow as Laura smiles broadly at her.

'He's your gift – Chance. I'm giving him to you for Christmas.'

'But . . . but . . .'

Laura laughs out loud with pure pleasure. 'Do you know, I think that's the first time I've ever seen you speechless, darling,' she bellows gleefully, before throwing her arms around Cas and hugging her so hard that she couldn't speak even if she wanted to.

'But you can't.' Cas finally finds her voice, as Laura lets go. 'He's *your* horse, you can't give him to me.'

'I can and I have,' Laura tells her determinedly. 'Although of course if you don't want the old sod . . .'

'Don't want him?' Cas breathes incredulously. 'Don't want him?'

'I take it that means you're pleased?' Laura tilts her head and waits for Cas's answer. In response, Cas goes quiet. And then the smile begins. It starts off slow and careful, and then erupts across her face with the magnitude and rapidity of a particularly virulent computer virus, until her whole mouth cracks open in one glorious yell of happiness.

'*Yeeeessssssss!*'

Chance jumps backward in rolling-eyed surprise as Cas leaps forward and grabs my mother's arms in excitement.

'Thank you, thank you, thank you, thank you,' she shouts, jumping up and down like a madwoman, still holding onto Laura's arms so that they too are swung up and down like the handle on an old water pump, the shock echoing through Laura's body, and echoing in the bemused yet delighted smile on her face.

'I think that means she likes it.' I echo Laura's own words from when Cas opened my own gift.

As Cas finally lets go to fling her arms around Chance's neck, Laura turns her attention to me. 'I know I should have asked you first, darling, but—'

I silence her with a kiss to each cheek as Cas begins to fuss around Chance who, bewildered at first, soon catches his young friend's good mood and begins to nudge her pockets for treats.

'Look at her – look at how happy she is,' I say. 'Of course it's okay.'

'I thought she could take him back to school with her

– apparently they have the facilities, and then if you come to stay he can come here for a holiday too.'

'Won't you miss him?'

'Yes, of course I will, but she takes far better care of him than I ever have, so you see he would miss *her* far more, and she has grown to love him so much...'

By two o'clock, lunch is ready.

Breakfast was an orgy of Christmas chocolate, which was wonderfully indulgent at the time, but has now left us all feeling slightly sick and ready for some proper food. Cas and I have set the table with the best china, crystal glasses, linen napkins, and an old cream damask tablecloth that has been in my family for at least three generations. The lights are turned off, all except for the Christmas-tree lights, and the table and room are lit with as many candles as we can find.

The Robbie Williams Swing CD that has been blaring out of Laura's new stereo for the past twenty minutes, has been changed for a little dinner music of the sweetest jazz.

Just as Gertrude is coming out of the oven, a scratching on the door announces the arrival of Old Shep closely followed by Jasper. They either have an incredibly finely tuned sense of smell, or perfect timing.

Old Shep, Jasper, Meggie and Stu are now in a row in front of the fire, like an unusual canine matrioshka doll, ranging down in size, Son, Mother, Father, Puppy, flank to flank, bottoms roasting happily in the heat from the logs. Four pairs of eyes are fixed firmly upon the kitchen table, whereupon sits, in pride of place amidst the garlands, crackers, candles, and piles of steaming veg, the roasted carcase of Gertrude, the Goose with Attitude. I have to admit that stuffed with chestnut, sage and onion, brandy glazed and in roasted rigor mortis, she is a far more appealing prospect than she was when ruling the yard with her vicious temper.

Laura is at the head of the table, Cas and I seated to either side. My mother is poised over Gertrude with carving knife and carving fork. She has been standing like that for a fraction too long.

I put down the fork I have been tapping against the tabletop. Cassie is obviously struggling with the same battle of conscience – I can see her throat descending and rising like a fully occupied lift, as she swallows repeatedly. Julie London stops singing to an imaginary lover that he is 'Blasé' and Chris Connor begins to croon 'Lullaby of Birdland' . . . We all burst out laughing.

'Gertrude doesn't need a lullaby.'

'No, she's well and truly out for the count.'

Laura puts down the carving knife. 'We can't do it, can we?'

Cas and I shake our heads in unison.

'I'll see what we've got in the freezer, shall I?'

Christmas Dinner: roast potatoes, parsnip purée, roast shallots, Brussels sprouts, glazed carrots, purple sprouting broccoli, chestnut and sage stuffing, sausagemeat, gravy, cold ham, pork pie and Pepperoni Pizza.

'I can't believe we haven't even got any frozen chicken or anything,' Cas sighs, as she bites into a piece of crust.

'I assumed we'd be eating goose for at least a week,' Laura shrugged. 'It seemed a waste to get anything else in.'

'Oh, at least we've been spared that then,' Cas sighs with a smile.

'What do you mean?' I ask, offering her more vegetables.

'Goose pie, goose sandwiches, curried goose, pickled goose, goose pâté.'

Later, Cas and I share the washing up, while Laura, who did most of the cooking, sits down with a glass of port, and the leather belt of her camel-coloured slacks undone, so that she can squeeze in one last mince pie.

My step-daughter, who has been over-talkative throughout dinner, has suddenly fallen ominously silent. I turn and carefully ask a question I wouldn't have dared to ask her only a week or so ago. 'Cas, are you okay?'

'I wish he were here, Nat.' She looks up at me, her big blue eyes threatening tears.

'Yeah,' I reply quietly. 'So do I.'

We are both silent again for a moment. Then Cas picks up the tea towel and starts to dry the dishes once more. After a moment she speaks again. 'He probably is, isn't he?'

'Here?'

'Yeah.'

'I think so.' I smile at her gently. 'I really think so.'

She returns my smile.

We finish the rest of the dishes, the two of us working together quietly and methodically, a team almost. And when I smile at Cas again, she smiles back, and it feels so good to be so much more at ease in each other's company.

Laura is fast asleep by the fire, mouth open, snoring softly, red paper hat slipping down over her face. I dry my hands, applying some of the moisturiser that Laura always keeps next to the sink.

'Are you all right if I go for a walk?' I whisper to Cas. 'I need to burn off some of that pizza.'

She nods. 'I'm going to go and get the fur off of Chance's rug before he decides it's edible.'

We head out into the yard together, Stu following Cas closely. She unlatches Chance's stable door, and I go past, down the long passage and into the hayloft, taking out the bunch of red and white roses I left there yesterday in a bucket of water, and then make for the field. Rob's smiling handsome face is fixed firmly in front of me, shielding all else from my view. My mind is empty of everything except him, his face, his voice, his touch, the smell of him, the feel of his lips on mine, how it felt to be held in his arms.

And then halfway down the snow-ridden field, another face comes to mind. I stop and turn back. Cas is still in the stable. She looks at me and then at the flowers. I find that for once I don't need to explain. I simply hold out my hand and Cas runs down and takes it, and we walk together down to the cliff's edge, where we stand silently for a few minutes, before sharing the roses between us, and throwing them one by one into the sea.

The sun is setting as we return to the house, sitting bold and low in an ice-blue sky, casting long shadows ahead of us as we walk across the expanse of white that is the meadow. Cas is suddenly a little distant again, walking two paces behind me, as though she's deliberately taken a step back to survey this new feeling of silent camaraderie.

Back at Whitsunday, Laura is awake and has started laying the table again for Christmas tea. Its centrepiece is a huge Christmas cake so heavily laced with brandy the smell is overpowering. My stomach groans at the sight of so much food so soon after such a heavy lunch, but I know that Laura has invited people round for afternoon tea. I start to make sandwiches – ham and cheese and pickle – and for the first time ever lament the absence of a turkey.

At four o'clock, Connor arrives. Mac pushes through the door in front of him, wearing a new leather collar trimmed at the back with a small sprig of mistletoe. Laura and Cas rush to greet him, faces flushed with pleasure. Cas takes his coat and hangs it on the laden hat stand, whilst Laura takes the bags he is carrying. I stand back, but then he is walking towards me, unwinding the black cashmere scarf from around his neck, running fingers through his tousled hair.

'Happy Christmas, Nattie.'

'Happy Christmas,' I reply, absentmindedly stroking the bristled head of Mac, who is thrusting his face into the palm of my hand in search of attention. 'How was London?'

'Good. It was nice to see Colm and the kids.'

'You must have driven like a maniac to get back here so early,' I find myself saying, aware that I sound as if I am chastising him.

His mouth twists into a smile that is hard to read. 'To tell you the truth I made my excuses and left before lunch, which was really terribly rude of me.'

I want to ask him why but Laura is beside us offering Connor a glass of champagne and then Cassie is wanting him to look at her new computer.

Connor has brought gifts. For Cassie, there is a small figure of a horse carved out of driftwood. A perfect replica of Chance. And a beautiful set of paintbrushes that Cas proudly explains to Laura are made of sable, and are therefore the finest paintbrushes an artist could ever wish for. For Laura there is a framed painting – well, more of a cartoon – of a man in hunting pinks astride a fat-bottomed horse. Whilst the main body of the hunt are heading east after a rapidly disappearing fox, he is heading west toward where a buxom woman in a diaphanous pink nightdress is hanging out of her bedroom window. It is easy for those who know them to see that the man is Charles, and the house is Whitsunday. The cleavage and caramel curls are instantly recognisable too.

Laura begins to laugh. Cas, who is peering over her shoulder to see, joins in the laughter.

'That is absolutely brilliant,' she breathes, looking at Connor in bright-eyed admiration.

'Yeah, it's *really* good, isn't it?' Laura agrees. 'But I'll have to be very careful where I hang it though!'

Connor is beside me as I watch them exclaiming over Laura's watercolour. I feel his fingers touch mine as he slips a gift-wrapped package into my hand.

'Don't open it yet,' he whispers, folding my fingers around the small parcel, as though sealing a lock.

I feel hard edges underneath the paper. And strong warm hands holding my cold shaking fingers for a fraction of a second too long.

Then Cas is beside us, keen for Connor to open her gift to him. To my relief his fingers slip from mine. I move away, fetch my gift for Connor from under the tree.

'Don't forget the other one.' Laura nods toward another present still under the tree.

I peer at the upturned label. *To Connor love from Laura, Natalie, and Cas.*

Laura pats my shoulder, and reaching for the gift, takes it over to Connor, with a kiss and a smile, watching as he unwraps it carefully.

It's the book that I found in Truro. *Treasure Island.*

'Oh wow,' he says in delight. 'Laura, where on earth did you get this from!'

'Natalie found it.' Laura smiles knowingly at me.

'You did?'

'Well yes, I . . . but.'

'Clever girl. Thank you so much. You would not believe how long I've been hunting for a decent copy of this.'

I smile half-heartedly. How can I explain to him that when my mother asked me to buy it, she never actually told me whom it was destined for. Laura wants me to take the glory. Knowing her reasons for this, I find myself feeling faintly angry with her. She intended to give pleasure to both parties, but I will not be pushed.

Laura can see that I am not best pleased, and is just suggesting her usual panacea for all things, a drink, when the tension is broken by the sound of Elvis Presley in the yard. This could only mean the arrival of Hank and Orlaithe, but I didn't hear the usual mechanical asthma of Hank's clapped-out Capri.

It is they, however, as thirty seconds later Orlaithe bursts through the door, her red curls damp with melting snow, her arms full of carrier bags, which she practically drops on the floor in an enthusiasm of greeting.

'Happy Christmas, everybody! Would you believe this weather! Not that it's here to stay though, it's melting faster than an igloo in the desert so it is.' She rushes forward to hug everyone in turn, first Laura, then me, then Cas, then she spots Connor, and swoops down on him, planting a kiss on each cheek which leaves two perfect crimson lip prints.

She then gallops back to the centre of the room, and begins to twirl like a catwalk model. 'Look what I got for Christmas,' she crows with a pleasure that she's dying to share with all of us, as she wafts around in the vast leopard-print fake fur coat she is displaying with such pride. 'Don't I look just gorgeous, don't I look so posh! Liz Taylor, eat your heart out!'

Hank is nowhere to be seen.

'Where's Hank?' asks my mother.

'Francis? He's still out in the yard, so he is. I think I might need a bit of a hand getting him inside though.'

Cas goes to the still open door, and peers through the snow. 'Oh my God!' she cries, stepping outside. 'Come and look! Quickly – come and look at this.'

Intrigued, we follow her out into the cold evening. I'm the last out of the door, bumping into Laura as she suddenly stops in her tracks in front of me, stunned into silence like the rest of us by the sight that greets her.

Cas finally speaks the question on everyone's lips. 'Where's Hank's car? Where's Betsy?'

'Car? You call that bag o' rusted metal a car? I couldn't bear to see him driving round in that thing any longer! So I cashed in me life insurance and bought him a little Christmas present.' Orlaithe is so pleased with herself, she's beaming like a Cheshire cat.

Parked in the middle of the yard, like a huge exclamation mark at the end of a short sentence, is a pink Cadillac. An alien vessel landed amidst a farmyard. Hank is still sitting in it, hands glued to the steering wheel, a strange, almost dazed expression on his face.

'He's been like that all day.' Orlaithe hails us from the doorway, shaking her head in delight. 'He would've missed Christmas Dinner if I'd have let him, and just sat in it all morning. Stroking it and everything, he's been. At least I know what to get him for his next birthday – a giant tin of car polish! Francis, you old git, get out of that car this instant and say hello to your hosts.

'You gotta love 'im, doncha.' She turns to us and beams, as Hank makes no effort to move, simply stays where he is, stroking the top of the steering wheel over and over again.

I thought it would take death or destruction to make Hank part with his beloved Betsy, but he has evidently been seduced and bewitched by this wanton pink lady. The only remnant of Betsy is her cow horns, now proudly set on the long pink bonnet of the new arrival.

'We could just leave him out here,' Orlaithe suggests with a mischievous grin.

'He'd freeze to death,' Laura says with a shiver.

'Oh well, at least he'd die happy.'

Hank finally gets out of the car, and wanders over to us. His ruddy weathered face is wearing the supremely satisfied if slightly dazed smile of a man who's just been attacked then left for dead by a horde of nymphomaniacs.

'At last!' Orlaithe chastises him good-naturedly. 'I was beginning to think that someone had stuck your arse to the seat with Superglue.' She ushers Hank inside.

'Now then, let's get this party swinging,' she announces, pulling a bottle of Bushmills from one of her bags. 'Laura, darlin', get me six glasses. Connor, be an angel and fetch the ice.'

I let Cas drink a little wine with dinner – well, more than a little on special occasions, but I certainly don't think it's a good idea to introduce her to hard liquor at her age.

'Not for Cas,' I tell Orlaithe.

Orlaithe pulls a face at me. 'So and the girl's sixteen now so she is. I always say that if you're old enough to kiss a man then surely you're old enough to have a wee drop of whiskey?'

Cas colours pink at this, but still finds her voice to plead her cause. 'Please, Natalie, can I just try some?'

'Go on, Nattie, it *is* Christmas.' Laura adds her voice.

'Okay, okay.' I hold up my hands in submission. I'm not going to be the one who puts a damper on the occasion.

Connor notes my concern and puts a comforting hand on my arm. 'Don't worry, Nattie, she probably won't even like the taste of it,' he says as Orlaithe makes a big show of pouring Cas her first whiskey. 'You know what teenagers are like. If you tell them they can't have something then they just want it more.'

Sure enough, Cas's nose wrinkles in distaste at the first sip. She looks over at me as if it's my fault she doesn't like it. As though I've deliberately soured it for her.

'How about another glass of champagne instead?' I find myself offering.

She looks at me in surprise. 'Really?'

'Why not.'

'Okay then.' She's obviously concerned that I'll change my mind if she doesn't snap up the offer.

I go to the fridge and pull out one of the bottles that I bought in Truro, tearing off the foil, and twisting the wire. I think about opening the kitchen door, and firing the cork into the cold clear darkness of the evening, but I'd probably end up mowing down one of the chickens or getting Chance right between the eyes. And then I remember how Rob used to like to shoot the cork as far as possible into the distance, before proposing a toast.

Rob.

On my mind so much this morning and yet when Connor walked through the door, all other thoughts flew straight from my mind like rooks startled from their tree-top resting places by gunfire. Should I feel guilty? Should I feel bad that even as I was walking back from the cliff edge with Cas, I was wondering where Connor was, if he was travelling, if he was safe?

I find myself shooting the cork at my mother instead, and then, having filled everybody's glasses, I stand away from the others and raise a toast to my dead husband. 'Happy Christmas, Rob,' I whisper.

Laura's jazz CD is on repeat play. Connor is sitting between Orlaithe and Cas, all three perched on the edge of the kitchen table, as Hank and Laura dance together across the room. Hank is a surprisingly good dancer for someone with such bow legs, and such an odd gait. Connor's arms are about Cas and Orlaithe's shoulders, swaying as they sing along to Carmen McRae.

Orlaithe is still wearing her fur coat, refusing to take it off for one minute despite the warmth of the room, and Cas is smiling so hard her small straight nose crinkles up as well as the corners of her raspberry pink lips.

'You'd be so easy to love . . .'

Cas, who didn't know the words first time around, insists that they play it again. In fact it finally gets repeated about eight times until they're all singing along like professionals, my mother's fine soprano, and Orlaithe's powerful lungs lifting them well above the others. Connor is a surprisingly good baritone; even Hank is humming away. Cas's voice is sweet and true.

On the final play, Connor hops down from the table, and walks over to me, says nothing, but simply holds out his hand and smiles. I look over at the others. Hank is now dancing with Orlaithe, her red hair glowing brightly in the candlelight, fur coat twirling gracefully around her like the full satin skirts of a *Come Dancing* finalist. Laura is spinning a grinning Cas around the room, the two of them dancing beautifully together, feet moving with practised ease.

I look back at Connor. His beautiful blue eyes are inviting, a half-smile on his lips teasing me, reassuring me. I take his outstretched hand, and as he pulls me laughing into the fray, I feel a sudden lift of spirits and a surge of gratitude that, although I cannot share this Christmas with Rob, I am truly blessed that I get to share it with the people in this room.

The party doesn't end until nearly four in the morning. We're having such a good time, nobody wants to break up the gathering. Hank and Orlaithe have both had far too much to drink to drive anywhere and are housed in my mother's room, whilst she goes up with Cas into the attic. Connor is offered the huge sofa in the drawing room we never use, but opts to walk the two miles home to clear his head.

I follow the others up to bed, and sit on the wide window ledge of my room, whilst I wait for the queue to the bathroom to die down. The land as far as I can see is white and the sky has darkened to a deep shade of purple. It's like an alien landscape. Far in the distance, I can just make out the tiny dark silhouettes of Connor and Mac as they walk back to the Loft. I watch them until they disappear from my view, and then I suddenly remember Connor's gift to me, still unopened. Pulling my robe around me, I pad barefoot down the cold wooden stairs to the kitchen.

I left the parcel on the dresser, but the first things I spot are Cassie's monster slippers underneath the kitchen table. I tread on tiptoes across the cold flagstone floor, and gratefully slip my feet into their furry warmth, giggling at how ridiculous I look. I take the parcel and return to the warmth of my bedroom, sliding underneath my maximum tog duvet.

It's beautifully wrapped in thick paper the golden colour of tumbling autumn leaves, tied with thin silver ribbon. I pull off the paper to find a beautiful silver frame, and within that frame is a painting, a painting taken from the photograph of Rob that I have in my wallet. This time, Rob is no longer alone. Connor has painted me into the scene, so that Rob and I are smiling out at the world together, the arm that was thrust into his pocket, now circled protectively about my shoulders.

I don't know whether to smile or cry. I think I'd cry, only I know that's something I can't do. Connor only saw the photograph for a few moments, but he couldn't have captured Rob more perfectly if he had studied him for a lifetime.

Pulling my dressing-gown closer around me, and pushing my feet into the ridiculous, but heavenly soft slippers, I slide from the bed and go to the desk, then pad back over to sit on the window seat once more. The moon is full and bright, reflecting on the vast landscape of snow stretched out before me, making the still night with its dark purple sky seem strangely light and luminate.

I touch the picture. Trace the outline of Rob's face with the very tip of my finger.

*Dear Rob,*
*Happy Christmas. See what Cassie got me?* I wiggle my feet in the air as I'm writing. *I think she's trying to tell me something. Do you remember what she got me the Christmas before last? You gave her one hundred pounds to buy me a present and she bought me three padded coat hangers, a bottle of mouthwash, some granny pants, and a nose-hair clipper. You wanted to tell her off but we were laughing too much. Things didn't seem so bad then, did*

*they? I always thought that I'd win her round eventually. I don't think I'm doing a particularly good job at the moment, although like today's snow, things between us seem to have thawed considerably, which is the best Christmas present I could have hoped for this year.*

*It was a lovely Christmas Day, Rob. I never thought I'd say that again, never thought it would be so again without you. I can't believe how great it was to be with my mother again today. I've been a fool, Rob, an idiot to push her away for so long. I've wasted so much precious time, but now I'm determined to make up for that. I only wish it hadn't taken losing you to make me find her again. I wish you could have known her a little better. I wish you could have been here today, met the people who are slowly helping me, helping Cas, piece our lives back together again.*

I put down my pen, lean forward and press my lips against the miniature of Rob's face, feeling them push against the cold glass that covers it. I pull back and look at the painting, an imprint of my lips superimposed like a halo around Rob's head.

A halo for an angel.

If God is love, Rob, then I know you're with Him, because I still love you so much.

# *Chapter Eleven*

Nobody manages to get up until well after ten on Boxing Day morning. By the time we feed the animals it is nearly midday. They are all waiting impatiently for us to emerge from the house, a cacophony of different voices raised in a somewhat indignant greeting. Chance even manages a wicker as Cas emerges pulling on her boots and rubbing sleep from her eyes, and he barely ever makes his feelings vocal.

I feed the chickens, which flap and squawk around my ankles as if rebuking me for bringing them their breakfast of corn so late in the day. Orlaithe borrows the Landy to drive hurriedly back down to the Ship to open up for her lunchtime regulars. Hank stays to help us out by lugging the heavy sacks of cattle feed down to the meadows.

Once finished we all collapse back into the kitchen for a very late and welcome breakfast of sausages and scrambled egg, despite the fact that I vowed passionately when I first woke up that I couldn't face a single morsel of food – *and* that I'd never drink again – but how many times have we heard that one?

We've nearly finished breakfast, when there is a knock on the door. Cas and I both look at Laura.

'Are you expecting anyone?'

She shakes her head and frowns slightly. 'Not this morning, no.'

The old black iron fox's head that is the door handle is

rapped once more. As I'm the only one who's finished eating I go to answer it, cautiously pulling the door open, eyes narrowing as I look from the gloom of the kitchen into the brightness of the day outside. The figure standing on the doorstep has the sun behind it, but even in outline only, it is unmistakable.

'Surprise!' She flings out her arms dramatically.

'Petra!' Hurling myself forward I throw my arms around her and hug her tight, hearing the sharp intake of breath she's forced to take as I squeeze.

'Oh my goodness! What the hell are you doing here?'

'I take it that means you're pleased to see me?'

'That's the understatement of the decade. You don't know how wonderful it is to see you.'

'I thought you might like a visitor.'

'You make it sound like I'm in hospital or something.'

'Prison?' Petra offers. 'Permanent solitary confinement.'

'Rest and relaxation, honestly . . . But you're not supposed to be here. I thought Peter was still with you. What happened – did he have to leave early?'

'I'll tell you all about that later,' Petra sighs, her smile fading. 'In the meantime,' the sad face turns to one of mischievous glee, 'I brought gifts.'

'More?'

'Of course. Never turn up somewhere uninvited if empty-handed, that's what I say. I even brought something for *you*.' Petra turns to Cassie, her gaze challenging, but not unfriendly.

Cassie eyes Petra suspiciously, like a nervy horse on road training, rolling its black eyes at a hedgerow it is sure contains all sorts of boogie monsters, and dark horse-eating demons.

'I'll need a little help bringing it in from the car though.'

Hank has been scrutinizing Petra like a greyhound that has just spotted a very tasty-looking rabbit. To my amazement he leaps to attention.

'I'll be giving you a hand there if you like,' he offers. 'Getting your things from the car.'

Laura and I exchange glances of disbelief. That is the longest sentence either of us have ever heard him utter.

'That's very kind of you.' Petra flashes Hank the whitest smile, and he follows her outside like a puppy.

'I think Orlaithe had better watch out,' I say. 'If that wasn't a case of love at first sight then I've never seen one.'

Laura laughs. 'Hank must have a thing for red hair.'

Minutes later they are back, Petra flinging the door open with a flourish. 'Tada!' she announces dramatically, sweeping her long velvet coat aside like a curtain in a theatre as Hank follows her in, pushing a wheelchair.

The next moment, Cassie is screaming with delight. 'Granny!'

'I slipped Matron fifty quid for an early parole,' Petra jokes.

'Louisa! I thought you were somewhere off the coast of Spain!'

'Actually I think she flew home on her own.' Petra pats the padded grey arm of the wheelchair. 'This thing's jet-propelled, you know.'

Cassie is up from her seat and across the room in seconds, throwing herself at her grandmother with joyous abandon. Louisa's pale lips have cracked into the hugest smile, her thin white hands patting at her grand-daughter's slim back.

'Heavens, child, there's nothing of you, and where on earth has all of your beautiful long hair gone? Oh my, it's *so* short! What would your mother say?'

'You should have seen it a few weeks ago,' I tell her. 'It was bright pink.'

Louisa-May smiles nervously over Cassie's shoulder at the assembled group, her hesitant gaze ending up on my mother. They have met only twice before. At the wedding, and then . . . I shake my head to take away the images.

'I do hope you don't mind me coming.' Louisa is addressing my mother. 'I tried to phone Natalie's mobile phone from the airport before my flight, but I'm afraid I couldn't get through. Petra persuaded me that it was a good idea to surprise you all, but I do so hate to turn up unannounced and uninvited.'

'Don't be ridiculous. It's absolutely lovely to see you, it really is.'

Louisa-May looks frailer than when I last saw her, her soft face more lined, her silver hair thinner. There are bruised dark circles underneath sunken eyes, which are the same bright blue as Cassie's, only faded a little like a delicate flower that has spent its life in too-bright sunshine. But her smile, though weak, is warm. I can see her assessing me in the same affectionate concerned way that I am appraising her.

'How are you, Nattie?' She reaches up with slender arms to hug me. 'You're still too skinny by far, that's not good. Not good at all.'

'At least I can fit into my jeans now.' I laugh lightly.

'I think we could all fit into your jeans!' Louisa looks disapprovingly at my belt, which is now down to the first hole and still loose. 'At the same time.'

The light laugh turns into a brittle cough, and there is an instant flood of people descending to take care of her. Petra pushes her toward the fire, Cassie fetches a rug to tuck around her knees, Laura offers her tea; even Hank is hovering in the background with a plate of biscuits, which he alternately thrusts toward Louisa and then Petra with an awed expression on his weathered face.

'So what happened to the holiday of a lifetime?' I ask, as Louisa-May gratefully accepts a steaming mug of tea from Laura.

'I got back sooner than expected. I must confess I took a plane from Gibraltar in an effort to make it home for

Christmas Day, although things didn't quite work out as planned. Your lovely Petra picked me up from the airport at midnight last night, bless her heart.'

'So you had this all planned?'

'Well no, not at all. At this precise moment in time, I'm supposed to be attending the Captain's Boxing Day luncheon, followed by a game of shuffleboard on deck – well, I'd only have been watching of course, with Mary, Donald and Esme Campbell, and the Leamingtons from Lymington. Unfortunate place to live with a name like that, but such a lovely couple. I didn't want to let Mary down, but I did so want to be with you both. My sister had made a lovely bunch of new friends on board so in the end it didn't seem like such a horrid thing to leave her there. In fact, she'll probably be able to have a better time without having to take care of me. That's what I've been telling myself anyway. I do feel a touch guilty, but I so wanted to see my little girl. Not that she seems so little any more.' She looks affectionately at Cas. 'I swear she's shot up at least an inch since I saw her last.'

'So what happened? How did you get here in the end?' Laura asks, offering Louisa a glass of port and a mince pie, before she's even a quarter of the way down her tea.

'As a last resort I phoned the house in Hampstead, hoping you might have left a message with another telephone number, and I was lucky enough to get Petra.'

'Fish feeding,' Petra explains.

'On Christmas Day?'

'I'll tell you about it later,' Petra murmurs with a pained look.

Laura is beaming in anticipation of a party. She loves visitors, especially unexpected ones, insisting that you get all of the pleasure without the chore of having to tidy up first. It's only polite that unexpected guests must take one as they find one.

My mother also loves Petra. They are kindred spirits

really, both remarkably upbeat, both appearing a little scary and fierce if you don't actually know them well, but both, as I am learning about my mother, with a heart as big as Africa.

Cassie too is smiling broadly, not one of her usual sarcastic or sad smiles, although I will admit they have been rare in the past week or so, but a big happy beam. She is obviously delighted that her grandmother is with us.

'I got a present for you as well,' Petra tells me.

'You made Cas smile. That's the best present ever.'

'So you don't want this, then?' she teases, waving a bottle of premier Cru Champagne at me.

'Ooh I love you, Petra James.'

'Only because I bring you champagne.'

'What other reason could there possibly be? Is it pre-chilled?'

'It was. Now it's positively frozen.' She pulls her coat closer around herself, and shivering moves toward the fire, gently pushing a reluctant Meggie out of the way with the toe of her Chanel boots. 'I'd say this was Bleak House, Laura darling, except that anywhere with you in it can't possibly be so. Your present is in the boot of my car,' she tells her. 'It's the rest of the case.' She indicates my bottle with a flick of her red hair. 'One for Nattie, five for you. That's fair, isn't it?'

'Oh, absolutely,' Laura grins. 'Perfectly fair. Hank will bring the rest of your things in. How long are you staying? Do tell me it's for ages. I hate it when people hit and run. You must stay for as long as you possibly can.'

'We have only come here on a flying visit. We wouldn't want to impose at all. In fact, I was going to see if you could recommend a hotel or B&B nearby, just for the night.'

'Nonsense!' Laura cries, rushing forward to take Petra's bag from Hank, as though holding it for ransom to make Petra stay. 'You'll stay here! You can go in with

Nattie, and Louisa can have my room.'

She silences Louisa's protestations by assuring her that there is more than enough room for another person to go in the attic with Cassie.

'If you're sure we're not putting you out . . . I've got to be back in London by Friday, but we can stay down here for a couple of days, if that's okay with you?'

'Not long enough!' Laura winks at her.

Laura and Hank take Petra's bags up to my room, and Louisa-May's to Laura's, and then Cas helps Laura move a few things up to the attic, chattering away excitedly, obviously over the moon that Louisa is with us.

Although breakfast seems about two minutes back, I start to prepare lunch, more for our visitors' sake than ours, whilst Laura heads back down to the Ship with Hank to pick up the Landy.

'I'm not really hungry,' Petra peers over my shoulder, looking doubtfully at the ham and egg pie I'm cutting into slices, 'but I'd kill for a drink.'

'Tea?' I offer.

Her eyes open wide in mock surprise. 'Tea? Come on, Nattie, we're in Cornwall not purdah. How about a glass of champagne? I brought enough to float the *QE2*.'

'Now?'

'Why not? It's past midday, and I reckon it's still officially Christmas enough to warrant champagne with lunch.'

We open one of Petra's bottles.

'So how's Cassie?'

I glance over to where Louisa-May is installed in the shabby but comfortable wing chair by the fire. Cas is kneeling before her, her hands on her grandmother's knees, her face shining with pleasure as she shows Louisa-May her new laptop. I feel a strange stab of envy at how close she is sitting to her grandmother, at the look on her face as Louisa rests a gnarled hand against her smooth cheek for a few seconds.

'She has her moments,' I say.

'Good ones or bad ones?' Petra smiles sympathetically.

'A vastly uneven balance of both. Although things have got better in the past few days.' I try to smile at my friend. 'One good thing is that she and my mother have hit it off really well.'

'Nice,' says Petra, smiling wryly, and patting my hand in sympathy. Petra is the one person who could possibly understand the mixed emotions my mother and Cas's easy friendship evokes. The one person, apart from Connor, whose insight is uncanny.

'I'm glad you're here,' I tell her, leaning in and taking comfort from her closeness.

'I knew you would be.' Petra smiles smugly at me.

'So go on. Why *are* you here? What happened to your cosy Christmas for two then?'

Petra stops looking smug and sighs heavily instead.

'I might have known it was too good to be true. He flew out to America on the twenty-third with his wife. He said he wouldn't but he did. Apparently they brought the wedding forward to Christmas Eve instead of New Year's Eve, and it wasn't fair to miss it. That was his excuse anyway. But he can't call me before he flies, can he, oh no. He has to wait until Christmas morning, so I'm sitting there in my best undies, bright red, very festive, like an idiot, waiting for him to turn up first thing like he said he would, and the clock's ticking away, and I know in my heart what's going to happen . . .' She tails off and shakes her head.

'But why? Why did he leave it so late to call you? He must have known at least a couple of days beforehand about the change of plan?'

'Of course he knew, but I suppose he was too bloody scared to face me, the coward. There's not a lot I can do when he's already three thousand miles away, is there?' She pauses and frowns. 'Do you know what else I think?

350

I think he didn't want to give me a chance to make alternate arrangements.'

'Whyever not? Selfish bastard.'

'Likes to think of me at home on my own pining for him, instead of being out and about having fun, I suppose.'

'Why didn't you phone us? You know you'd have been more than welcome here. More than welcome. I knew I should have phoned you. I wanted to, if only to say Happy Christmas, but I didn't want to disturb you both. I had this picture in my head of a cosy little twosome . . .'

Petra shrugs. 'You and me both. Pride, I suppose. I couldn't face the "I told you so's".'

'You'd rather spend Christmas Day on your own? So what were you doing at my place?'

'Ooh, raiding your chocolate drawer, drinking your alcohol,' she jokes. 'I didn't want to stay in the flat because Peter said he'd call later and I really didn't want to answer, you know, let the old bastard wonder where I was for a change, but I knew if the phone rang, I'd just have to pick it up, sad case that I am, so I was trying to think of somewhere I could go, and maybe someone else who'd be alone on Christmas Day.'

'And the only one you came up with was Meryl?'

'Exactly. Sad, aren't I? I spent Christmas Day evening with a fish. You know, you're my only friend, Nat.'

'Correction. I'm your only friend in England.'

'Petra no mates.' She sniffs, pretending to feel sorry for herself.

'Correction to the correction, I'm your only *female* friend in England. You have plenty of other buddies, they're just all male.'

'Yep, and they're all married.'

'Exactly, and what self-respecting wife would want you hanging around her husband, especially on Christmas Day, when whatever she filled his stockings with certainly couldn't match up to what you fill yours with.'

'Why don't I have any other female friends, Nattie?'

'Because women are usually far too scared of you to make contact. Either that or they're too scared that their husbands or boyfriends will like you more than they like them.'

'Oh, what it is to be gorgeous,' she sighs self-mockingly. 'How come you weren't scared of me?'

'Oh, I could see right through you.'

'Thanks a lot!'

'No, not like that. In a nice way. I could see that underneath the hard bitch exterior, was a—'

'Hard bitch interior?' Petra jokes.

'—was a lovely cuddly bunny,' I tease, rubbing the end of her nose affectionately with a finger. 'So how was Meryl anyway?' I ask, trying to change the subject. Despite her jokes, Peter's behaviour has obviously hurt her a great deal.

'Doing swimmingly, thank you. She sent you a big wet kiss.'

'Would you ever get another kind from a goldfish?'

'Nope, but I'd like to give a Glasgow kiss to a cold fish,' Petra quips back smartly. 'Have you ever tried stuffing a twenty-pound turkey complete with sage, onion and sausagemeat down a waste disposal unit?'

'I can't say that I have, no.'

'Well, that's what I was doing yesterday during the Queen's speech,' she tells me curtly. 'Never mind. As far as I'm concerned, Christmas starts right here, right now. Cheers.' She bangs her glass against mine, and then drains it in one go. 'Ready for another?'

By the time Laura gets back, Petra and I have finished one of the bottles between us, and are more than happy to crack open another at Laura's instigation. Then we all settle down to watch *The Wizard of Oz* for about the eightieth time in three decades.

Louisa-May is asleep, her grey head nodding in the warmth of the fire.

'She doesn't look well, does she?' Petra whispers.

I shake my head in concern. To me Louisa-May is a skeletal leaf on an autumnal tree.

'We were hoping the cruise would do her good, but it seems to have had the opposite effect and worn her out completely. She needs a lot of care, and I don't think her sister has been coping that well.'

Although she is not completely reliant on a wheel-chair, Louisa cannot walk very far and therefore has spent most of the day confined to the kitchen. Worried that our visitors might be bored, Laura has been making phone calls.

'Right, that's all sorted,' she announces happily.

'What is?' Cas looks up from the rug. *The Wizard of Oz* has finished and she's now watching *Carry on Camping*.

'We're going out.' Laura goes to the boiler in the corner by the sink and flicks on a switch. 'Right, give it half an hour for the hot water to kick in and then please form an orderly queue for the bathroom. I want you washed and changed and ready for inspection by seven fifteen, okay? And no jeans,' she tells me sternly. 'I've barely seen you wear anything else since you got here.'

Petra's bags are on my bed. She bends down and unzips her huge overnight bag. 'I brought some post down for you – oh, and a message from Elaine.'

'Which is?'

'Well, not that she expects you back soon or any-thing.' Petra laughs and launches into a frighteningly good impression of Elaine's Janet Street-Porter style voice. 'Basically it's up to you how long you want to have off, but they've got an interview coming up with somebody frightfully important, and she thinks it might be just up your street.'

'Yeah, who's that then?'

'Molly Billingham.'

'As in Ralph Billingham?'

'The one and only. You heard then?'

'Of course I heard – it was front-page news. We're in Cornwall, Pet, not Outer Mongolia.' I think about telling Petra that the Billinghams are old friends of my mother's but something stops me. 'So when is this interview lined up for?'

'Well, there's the rub, they haven't actually got one. She's refusing to see anybody.'

'Oh right,' I reply, suddenly angry as I see the intent behind Elaine's choice of interviewee. 'I see: Elaine thinks that I can sell her a sob story in order to see her, worm my way in using *my* husband's death as a comparison for her own.'

Petra pulls a face. 'Hey, I know it's crass, but don't shoot the messenger, okay?'

'Crass? I'd have put it a little more strongly than that.'

'I hear what you're saying,' Petra shrugs, 'but that's the way it is in our line of work, Nat – you know that.'

'And I'm not the kind of journalist who'd sell my soul for a story, Pet – *you* know that.'

'Yes, you've got far too much integrity for someone in your position. Heaven knows how you got as far as you did carrying around *so* much integrity.'

'I'm beginning to wonder myself . . .' I take a deep breath. 'I'm thinking of handing in my notice.'

Petra stops unpacking and looks at me in shock. 'You're what!'

'You heard me.'

'Since when?'

'About two minutes ago. No, oh I don't know, it's like it's just come into my head, but now I've actually said it, I realise it's been on my mind for a little while.'

'But . . . what else would you do?'

'I have other plans, vague ones I admit, but the

prospect of going back to work is becoming less appealing by the day.'

Petra's eyes are still wide with shock. 'But you *live* to work!'

'No.' I shake my head and reach out to take her hand. 'That's the thing, you see, that's what being here has finally made me realise. I don't live to work, I work to keep living. At least I did – and that's not right. Come here, I want to show you something.'

I take my manuscript from where it is now hidden, underneath my knickers in the top drawer of the chest opposite the bed.

'I want you to read this, not now, but soon, and let me know what you think. I've started revising it, but it still needs more work.'

Taking the manuscript, Petra zips it into her overnight bag. 'Of course I'll read it, Nat, but . . . quitting your job – is that really what you want to do?' Then, noting the stubborn look on my face, she changes the subject. 'And how are *you* getting along?'

It's a loaded question.

'Not bad,' I chirp as brightly as I can. 'I've got something else to show you.'

Petra pulls a face at me for avoiding the issue, but is distracted when I leap from the bed and lift out the painting that Connor gave to me. She studies it intently, her mouth falling open in wonder.

'Hell, that's fantastic!' she breathes.

'Isn't it just?'

'Who painted it for you?'

'A friend. Well, more a friend of Laura's. He's an artist.'

'An artist?' Petra smiles in delight. 'Ooh, come up and see my etchings.'

'It's not like that,' I frown at her. 'We're just friends – if that. I hardly know the man.'

'Maybe you *should* get to know him. What's his name?'

'It's Connor. His name's Connor. He's Irish.'

'Ooh, don't tell me – he's tall, dark, with brooding eyes and a velvet voice.'

'He's got brown hair.'

'Okay, tall, brown-haired, with brooding eyes.'

'And he's about five eight, five nine.'

'Okay, medium, brown-haired and brooding.'

'And he definitely doesn't brood – in fact, he's got quite a good sense of humour.'

Petra holds up her hands in defeat. 'So I'm wrong on everything.'

'Not totally – he does have the velvet voice.'

'Is he attractive?'

'I hadn't really noticed,' I lie.

'Oh, come on!' she cries in disbelief.

'Yes, I suppose he's attractive.'

'Coming from you, that means he's bloody gorgeous,' she murmurs, starting to wriggle out of her clothes. 'What's Connor's surname, darling?'

'Oh blimey, now that's a question. I'm sure Laura told me . . . Booth? No, that's not right. Bright? Nope. Oh yeah, I remember – Blythe, it's Connor Blythe.'

'Blythe?' Petra's neatly plucked eyebrows shoot up her smooth forehead.

'Yeah, that's it.'

'Connor *Blythe*?' She repeats it as if she doesn't believe me. '*The* Connor Blythe? You didn't tell me it was *the* Connor Blythe, Natalie. That's like finding the Holy Grail and then keeping it in a box in your garden shed.'

'What are you on about?' I turn back to her in exasperation.

'You mean you really don't remember the name? Call yourself a journo?'

'Are you telling me you've heard of him?'

'Nattie, *everybody's* heard of him – except for you, it would appear. He was one of the YBA's – you know, Saatchi, White Cube; like Damien Hurst's nicer kid

356

brother. Just as famous, without having to use dead animals. He had three pieces in the Sensation Exhibition in 1997. Photographs. Which is odd, because that isn't his usual medium – he is a painter first and foremost. But you should have seen those photographs, Nattie. They were a set of three, quite small,' Petra waves her hands in the air as she describes them, 'about A5 size I think, and he had them displayed in a row, three pictures side by side, under one title. *Despair*.'

She pauses and takes a breath. 'Do you know, they actually made me cry. It makes me fill up just to think about them now.' She takes another breath, her hand fluttering to her chest in angst as she relives the memory.

'He'd found a picture of a child in a concentration camp, another of a little boy from the Vietcong during the war in Vietnam, and then he'd taken the third one himself; a little girl rescued from the genocide in Africa. Just their little faces looking out at nothing. Oh, and the eyes. Those eyes, they'll haunt me for ever.'

She pauses, biting her bottom lip hard between her teeth.

'I'd never seen him do anything other than paint before that. He was shortlisted for the Turner Prize for that one though – took the art world by storm – and then he just disappeared from the scene. It was as if he wanted to make a final statement or something. Nobody has really seen him for over four years. Of course, the odd painting turns up in galleries here and there every so often, to be snapped up for a ridiculously exorbitant price, but nobody actually gets to see the man any more.'

Petra stops speaking and picks up the small painting of Rob and me.

'My goodness, girl, you actually own an original of Connor Blythe. That puts you up with the Saatchis and the Tate Modern. This must be worth at least four or five.'

'Hundred?'

'Thou, darling. Although of course to you it's price-less.' She smiles softly, putting the painting down on the bedside cabinet.

Reaching over, I pick it up and put it back safely in the drawer.

Petra slips off her trousers, and falls back against the pillow in just her red lace lingerie, her long curls falling haphazardly across her face and the linen. 'Can you introduce me?' she asks.

'Oh, you'll probably get to meet him anyway if you're staying for a few days.'

'I wonder if he'd let me interview him for the magazine?'

'Well, if he came down here to get away from all the publicity then I very much doubt it.'

'It's all very well saying you hate publicity when you're famous, but you probably miss it when you don't get any more. He might have thought he wanted it all to go away when he was under such a heavy spotlight, but now he's had some time on his own, he might actually be missing the attention.'

'That's a screwy kind of logic, Pet. People who want publicity, court publicity. Connor does nothing of the sort.'

'Look, it's worth a try. It's also worth a huge pay rise. It would be a real coup to get an interview with him. In fact, I might just do a little one on the side. Think of the syndication fees.'

'Emphasis on the *sin*. You'll be committing the cardinal one if Elaine finds out. She'll sack you.'

'She can't sack me, I'm freelance. Besides, the board would kill her. I'm their biggest fish, Nat,' she grins at me immodestly. 'They'd sink without me.'

'Thank you!'

'Not you, darling, you'd survive without *Naked*. It's they who would not survive without us. So what do you think?'

'What – about life beyond the magazine and a regular pay cheque?' I reply, deliberately misunderstanding her.

'No – about my interview with Connor Blythe.' She says it as if it's already a reality.

I shrug. 'I'm not the one you need to ask, am I? You'll have to speak to him.'

'There's no harm in asking, is there? He can only say no.'

'I suppose so.'

Two taxis arrive at seven thirty to take us all out. We pile into the back of them scrubbed up, made-up, perfumed and kind of excited. I haven't had a good girls' night out for ages. Petra has even persuaded me into a dress. It's the first time my legs have seen daylight in ages.

'So where are we going then?' Cas finally asks a tight-lipped Laura.

'We're going out for dinner.'

'Where to?'

'You'll see soon enough.'

My excitement turns to confusion however as the taxis drive down past Trenrethen, and then start to wind down the cliffside road to the Ship.

'The pub?' I exclaim to Laura in consternation. 'After all the fuss you made about us getting dressed up, I was expecting something a bit more glamorous than that.'

Laura merely smiles mysteriously.

Orlaithe is waiting for us. She makes a huge fuss of Louisa, even moving some regulars from a particular table so that she can sit comfortably, not too near, and not too far from the fire, and then fetches our drinks to the table.

Petra and I are just discussing the logistics of five people eating at a knee-height drinks table, when Orlaithe comes back over.

'Do you want to come through now? Your table's ready?'

'Come through?'

Laura's smile widens.

We follow Orlaithe along a corridor tucked away to the right-hand side of the bar, that I thought simply led into a private area. She opens a door at the end, however, onto a small room that I didn't realise was there, with wooden flooring, elegant furniture, hunting prints around the terracotta-painted walls, dried flowers, and William Morris print curtains at the windows.

This is Laura's surprise. A romantic little bistro you would expect to find in London, not tucked away at the back of a pub in the tail end of Cornwall.

'I never knew this was here.' I turn to Orlaithe in surprise.

'Oh, we're very exclusive back here so we are – invitation only,' she jokes. 'Actually this is the paying guests' dining room. But we open this bit to the public on weekends as well.'

'And don't tell me, Hank does the cooking?'

'Oh no,' Orlaithe beams. 'I have a young man who only comes at weekends.'

'I used to go out with someone a bit like that,' Petra quips, winking at me. 'Except his speciality was lunchbreaks.'

She shows us to a table set for five. Louisa-May is seated at the end with Cas to her left and me to her right. Laura sits beyond Cas, and opposite Petra who sits down next to me. The menu is very different from the food served up in the bar; there's no shepherd's pie or ploughman's lunches in here.

'They're very good for fish,' Laura is telling Cassie.

Petra is ignoring the menu and reading through the wine list instead. I hand Louisa-May a menu, which she takes with a shaking hand.

'How are you, Natalie?'

'I'm fine.' When Louisa raises her eyebrows at me, I admit, 'Oh all right, I'm not fine, I'm far from fine. But

I'm okay, honestly.' I take her hand. 'Please don't worry about me.'

'It's an old lady's job to worry, and you and Cassie are all that I have left to worry about, so please don't ask me not to care, Natalie.' She gently squeezes my hand.

'And you?' I return the question.

'Tired, but I'm still holding on in there.' She smiles weakly. 'Do you know, I'm actually looking forward to getting back home, which shows you how shattered I am. Greenwich, an apt place to wait for the rest of your time to run out.'

'Oh, don't say things like that, please.'

'No, you're right. I'm sorry, Nattie, this is a party, isn't it?'

Cassie has disappeared, ostensibly to go the loo, but the amount of time it's taking her, I have a feeling she may have bumped into Luke in the bar. Louisa takes advantage of her absence.

'How has she been with you?'

'Better.'

'Oh, I'm so glad to hear it. Do you think she's finally coming round?'

'I don't know about that, but she's definitely more tolerant of me than she used to be. We even have a laugh together sometimes.'

Louisa-May smiles, but there is a sadness to it.

'Please know that Cassie needs you – she just won't admit it to you, and more so, she won't admit it to herself. You're an angel, Nat. I love Cassie dearly, with all my heart, you know how precious she is to me, but despite the fact that I'm old and weak, I'm not blind. I've seen the way she's treated you, and I also see that you so clearly don't deserve it. It's about time Cas realised that too.'

'Well, I understand Eve was a pretty tough act to follow in Cassie's eyes.'

'She idolises her mother, because she never really

knew her. She just remembers the perfect, beautiful ballerina. A little girl's fantasy mother. She doesn't remember the real Eve at all. Or if she does, she chooses not to.'

'Tell me about the real Eve, Louisa, please.'

Louisa sighs as she searches through her mind for the right words.

'She was very wilful, I can tell you that much. I suppose in a way we were all blind to her faults because she dazzled us so much. Always the performer. But she was also a very selfish girl. You gave Rob more in the time that you were together than she ever did in all their years together – apart from Cas, of course. Don't get me wrong, Natalie, she was my daughter and I loved her more than anything, but she wasn't the easiest person in the world to live with. She was so spoilt by the lifestyle, by the adulation. She was the prima ballerina, and I'm afraid she often acted accordingly. You're a good person, Natalie. I couldn't wish for a better person to bring up my grand-daughter. If you only give half of the love and support to her that you gave to Rob then it would be more than she could ever need. Please, promise me you won't give up on her. She needs you more than you or she could ever comprehend.'

Her pale eyes are searching my face, pleading with me for tolerance, for understanding, I want to reassure her, but Cassie returns to the table and I can do nothing but smile and squeeze her hand, and hope that I can communicate in looks what I cannot say in words – that I have every intention of being everything Cas needs in a parent if only she will let me.

A rowdy dinner follows, full of fun and laughter, which ends only after dessert and coffee, when Orlaithe whispers to Laura that Charles is in the bar, and she is keen to take the party through so that she can see him. Charles is playing a game of pool with another man who, although I can only see him from the back, and bent over the pool table at that, I instantly recognise as Connor. I feel a prickling sensation across my skin.

'Mmm, *very* nice.' Petra is standing beside me, her head tilted as she examines the curve of Connor's backside, which is presented to full advantage by his position. 'I don't suppose you know who that delicious arse belongs to, do you?' she asks, slipping her arm through mine.

Five minutes later, Petra is talking to Connor, having engineered an introduction via Laura, who has taken Connor's place at the pool table. Connor is leaning against one of the upright wooden beams that support the low ceiling; Petra is standing in front of him, blocking him from the rest of the room. Her body is bent toward his, a smile playing about her lips as she talks, her eyes every so often flickering up to his flirtatiously.

I watch Petra the manhunter in action.

She looks so beautiful. How could any man not want her? Would it worry me if Connor found her desirable?

And then, although she is still talking, Connor looks over her shoulder and sees me; he looks me up and down, notes the soft grey jersey dress, and the kitten heels, the make-up and the chignon that my usually wayward hair is pulled into, and he smiles slowly. Petra turns to look at me and smiles also, and I step towards them, drawn into their conversation.

'She looks wonderful, doesn't she?' Petra says proudly, aware of Connor's gaze.

'You've got legs!' he says, pretending to be shocked. 'I knew you had an arse, but I never knew about the legs.'

'I should have worn trousers,' I sigh. 'I might have guessed this would be too good an opportunity for you to make fun of me.'

'I'm not making fun. You look absolutely gorgeous.' And then the spark of mischief flicks back into those blue eyes. 'Although it's nothing of course on the outfit you were wearing when I first met you. Now *that* was spectacular.'

'Oh yes, and what was that?' Petra asks innocently.

Hank proudly drives us back to Whitsunday in Betsy II, as his new pink car has been lovingly christened. Louisa-May is parked safely in the front, Laura, Petra, Cas and I are squeezed into the long back seat, rowdy, singing and laughing, nobody really minding that we are sort of overlapping each other, legs and arms flailing awkwardly every time we round a bend, spines jangled painfully by the car's non-existent suspension every time we hit a pot hole or bump in the road.

When we get back to Whitsunday, despite the fact that it's nearly midnight, no one shows any inclination to kill the party and go to bed. In fact, Laura is rummaging in one of the dresser drawers for a pack of cards, whilst Petra gets more chilled champagne from the fridge, and Cas fetches five glasses in the hope that she'll be allowed to carry on drinking at least a little.

'Where are the blasted things?' Laura grumbles. 'Ah, here they are!' She pulls a new pack of cards from the back of the drawer with a pleased smile, and begins to unwind the Cellophane. 'Now – who's for a game of Poker?'

'Strip?' Petra jokes.

'Only if it's in reverse,' I shiver.

In our absence, the fire has burned low. The log basket is empty so I head across the yard. I realise that I am smiling as I collect new logs from the Long Barn, for no particular reason. It's a long time since I smiled for no reason at all. Although if I'm completely honest there *is* a reason, just not one that I want to admit to myself.

When I get back everyone is seated around the table, my mother shuffling the cards like a croupier at Monte Carlo.

'Right,' she announces. Cutting the pack, she licks her

thumbs and begins to shuffle. 'Aces are high, Flush beats a straight, and Deuces are wild.'

I stoke up the fire, put the spare logs in the basket on the flagstone hearth, and sit down next to Petra who has saved me a seat.

'Thank heavens we're only playing for chocolate!' she whispers in my ear as my mother divides the pack into two and proceeds to slide the cards together again with practised dexterity.

'*Only* chocolate?' I joke. 'We're talking Terry's chocolate orange here, and a Christmas one at that. I don't know why but the Christmas ones always seem to taste better.'

Despite the fact that I have an awful lot of chocolate to bet with, I seem to have very few poker skills in comparison and I've soon lost my entire stock between Laura and Cas, who has a little too much natural card-playing ability for my liking. Petra too, is currently down to her last bar of Bournville, and is casting concerned looks at the intent faces around her.

'I'll match your Matchmakers and raise you five After Eights.' Laura sends a challenging look over to Cassie.

'Somebody's getting serious here,' Louisa-May is seated beside me on the sofa, having come out of the game just after me.

'Okay.' Cassie slides down in her seat, looks at her cards, and then back at Laura, her eyes bright. 'I'll meet your five After Eights, and . . .' she pauses dramatically, and then reaches down the side of her chair '. . . I'll add a selection pack as well!' she cries, thumping it onto the middle of the table.

'Not the selection pack!' groans Petra. She throws her cards down on the table, kisses the Bournville goodbye with a sorrowful look, and then balances it on the rapidly increasing pile in the middle of the table. 'That's me well and truly broken.'

Pushing her chair away from the table, she comes and

joins Louisa and me on the sofa to watch the remaining battle.

'Nat, give us a sniff of your Black Magic box,' she wheedles.

'It's empty. I lost them all to Cas.'

'I know that, I just want to smell the lingering aroma.' She grins.

I notice that despite the fact that she's just lost at cards, Petra keeps on grinning – smiling too hard, in fact.

'Why are you looking so pleased with yourself?'

'Ah, I was wondering when you'd notice. I've got a hot date.'

'You have?' I ask in surprise.

'A very hot date – steaming hot, in fact.' She pauses for effect. 'Tomorrow night I am having dinner with Connor Blythe.'

'You mean he agreed to let you interview him?'

She nods ecstatically.

'How did you manage that then?'

'Oh, I have great powers of persuasion, as you know.' Petra glances up at me. 'You don't look very happy for me.'

'Oh no, I am – of course I am,' I stutter. 'I mean, I'm just surprised he agreed, that's all.'

'I'm not,' Petra pouts. 'Like I said, I can be *very* persuasive when I need to be.' She carries on, chatting away happily about how she plans to take him to this gorgeous little seafood restaurant she's heard of further up the coast in Newquay, and how he's so amazingly attractive that if he plays his cards right, he might get more than just dinner. She's even asked Laura about hotels in that area in case they decide to stay the night – after all, 'it's quite a long drive.'

'There's the Narrowcliffe, which is right on the front opposite Tolcarne Beach. I've stayed there a couple of times, and it's been really good – the food's fantastic, but then again you've already got a table booked somewhere, haven't you? I have the phone number somewhere if you want it, but you're right – it *is* a long drive for one evening.' Not noticing the relish in Petra's voice at the prospect of having a good excuse not to drive back, my mother starts suggesting other restaurants closer by that are 'rather good', but Petra is happily determined to ignore any recommendations.

I know Petra is predatory. When she sees something she wants, she goes all out to get it regardless of circumstance. Something I've admired her for in the past. It would appear from the way she is talking that Connor has just been added to her list of desirables.

I know Connor is a free agent, and technically speaking so is Petra. Peter isn't exactly in a position to induce devout loyalty, now is he? So why does it bother me so much?

Deep down, I know exactly why it bothers me. I can deny the feelings that I have for Connor, I can argue that they're not real, that they are born of loss and loneliness, or confusion, but I cannot ignore them. Especially now, hearing Petra talk about him as though he is already a conquest; I feel the first lick of the sinuous snake-tongue of jealousy.

To feel like this about someone else is strange. It feels almost as if I'm betraying Rob. A small seed has been planted. A precious seed. Instinct and Mother Nature say that I should nurture it, help it grow and blossom.

And yet I cannot hold even this small seed within me without feeling that I am betraying Rob – and therefore I choose to ignore it as best I can.

And yet, like the princess and the pea, it will bruise and agitate me. I know it will.

# Chapter Twelve

Laura is going out for dinner with Charles. Mrs Charles is apparently visiting her elderly mother in Town, and the lovers are taking the opportunity to spend a rare evening together at a restaurant that is far enough afield to avoid the gossips. My mother looks spectacular in a silver bias-cut gown that falls from one smooth brown shoulder, leaving the other bare, skimming alluringly across the top of her right breast. It is a special evening, their first alone since Christmas. The statue of lovers entwined has been carefully and beautifully wrapped and Laura even more so. Full war-paint seductive perfume, and killer silver heels to match the dress.

'Wow!' says Cas, looking up from her magazine, as Laura pauses at the bottom of the stairs and strikes a pose.

'Do you think Charles will like it?'

Petra is seated at the kitchen table in my dark blue towelling dressing gown, one of her long legs propped up on the chair beside her as she paints her toenails deep crimson with one of Laura's new nail varnishes. She looks up at my mother and wolf whistles.

'I think he'll like it so much you won't be wearing it for very long.' She grins. 'You haven't got another one I could borrow, have you? You look spectacular.'

Laura smiles happily. 'Nat?' She turns to me, her eyebrows raised in question.

'It's great. Total knockout.'

A car pulls up in the yard, the lights sweeping through the window and across the far wall.

'That'll be him,' says Petra, as a car door slams.

Laura shakes her head doubtfully. One thing I have noticed in my time here is that Charles Treloar never comes in. At least not unless we've all gone to bed first.

'I wouldn't have thought so, it's probably Connor,' she says.

'Connor! But I'm not ready yet!' Petra shrieks. 'Stall him for me. I need to change!' She shoots up the stairs, my bedroom door banging behind her as she hurls herself through it.

Cas rushes to the door to let Connor in. Laura remains in her pose, hoping for compliments, which she immediately receives.

'Wow! You look fabulous, Laura,' Connor says, taking her hands and stepping back so that he can admire her. 'Treloar is a lucky man.'

'I don't know what you mean.' Laura pretends to be coy. 'I'm just going out with an old girlfriend.'

'Old and friend, yes,' he winks at her, 'but the only girl in the equation is the very glamorous one standing here in front of me.'

A horn sounds as another car pulls into the yard. 'Well, that's my cue.' Laura is glowing like a schoolgirl. 'See you later, guys.'

'Have a good evening,' I call after her.

Cas is agitating Connor to look at one of her latest paintings: a watercolour of Chance, leaning out of the top half of the door to his loose box, one of the collies, I can't tell which one, curled in a ball at the bottom of the page, asleep in a patch of sunlight. I like it, love it even; it has a lovely light quality to it, kind of like a young Tintoretto, but Cas doesn't believe my praise.

Out of the window, I can see Laura and Charles still lingering in the car; the engine is running, and the outline of Laura is pressed to Charles, their heads together in a long kiss. I think she's missed him over Christmas. Yesterday in the Ship was the first time she had seen him since the day we played pool.

'The world's worst kept secret love affair, eh?' Connor is standing behind me. Cas has gone to her room to fetch more paintings to show him.

'Does his wife know, do you think?'

I can see him thinking carefully before he answers.

'I think she knows what, but not who,' he finally says.

'Oh, what a shame. As much as I love Laura, I do feel sorry for Charles's wife. It must be hard for her.'

A fleeting smile transforms Connor's pensive face. 'To be sure and Mrs Treloar doesn't care – she has a young man herself up in London.'

'But I thought she'd gone to visit her sick mother? Don't tell me she hasn't got a sick mother!'

'Between you and me she *did* have a sick mother, very sick indeed. So sick, in fact, the poor soul is no longer with us.'

'And she lied to her husband about something like that?'

'I don't think she lied, exactly, not that I know every detail of course, but I think there's one marriage where an awful lot of things are left unsaid for the sake of ease and convenience.'

'How awful.'

'Not an ideal relationship in your eyes?'

I shake my head.

'Although everybody has different ideals, don't they? What would you be looking for in an ideal relationship, Natalie?'

I turn sharply away from the window to face him.

'Found them!' Cassie thunders back down the stairs clutching a handful of paintings. She spreads them out on the table, and beckons eagerly for us to go and look at them. Connor is full of praise for her work, which even I, art philistine, can see is something special.

'I told her they were good,' I tell him, as a beaming Cassie gathers the paintings together, more carefully now that they have Connor's seal of approval, and goes to store them in Laura's study, 'but I don't think she believes praise for her painting unless it comes from you. She thinks that Laura would insist she was excellent even if she stank, and that I'm just trying to humour her to avoid confrontation.'

'Well, she should believe you. She's really very good. She has a marvellous eye for detail. I think she has the talent to make a career of this if she ever wanted to.'

'You think she's that good?'

'That I do, yes.'

The click of high heels descending the wooden staircase tells us that Petra is finally ready. She's obviously been inspired by Laura, showing off her endless legs in a chocolate-brown skirt that could be described as a pelmet, yet still has a slit that reaches even further up her left thigh. Her top is made of a heavy gold material that almost looks like chainmail, and swoops so low between the two high golden orbs of her breasts that you can almost see her belly button. She has set and polished her red mane into a cascade of silken temptress curls that falls to well below her shoulders, and shines like the flesh of a ripe horse chestnut.

As Cas watches her tread carefully down the narrow stairs in delicate gold sandals that are more strap than shoe, her mouth falls open in awe and admiration. I look over at Connor; he too is open-mouthed but I am surprised to see that the expression on his face is more one of fear than fascination. He's wearing ripped jeans, splattered with paint, a cosy old navy jumper, and a slightly concerned expression, and is obviously expecting nothing more than a shepherd's pie and the Spanish inquisition over the kitchen table.

Petra's already gruff voice is smoothed to a low seductive husk. 'Connor, lovely to see you again. I hope you're hungry – I've booked us a table at this fabulous restaurant further up the coast.'

Connor laughs nervously and indicates his own rather scruffy attire. 'As I'm sure you can see, I wasn't expecting to go out.'

'Never mind, we can stop at your place on the way and get you out of those clothes and into something a little more . . . suitable.' The pause, like her voice, is heavy with innuendo.

Connor looks around the room as though searching for an escape route or a fire exit. His eyes light on me hopefully.

'I promised to take Nattie and Cas down to the pub for a few jars after the interview, so I did.' He looks beseechingly at us, hoping that we'll take up the line and cover for him.

Cas nods enthusiastically, only too happy to fall in with Connor's lie and no doubt be taken to the pub as her reward. I, however, know what a coup this is for Petra, and look from one to the other, my loyalties torn. They are both looking at me pleadingly.

'Why don't we all go out together?' I find myself saying.

Petra's face falls in disappointment, Connor's in mild relief; although ultimate escape has been denied him, at least he will not be left to face Petra alone.

'But I've booked a table – for two.' Petra makes signals with her eyes at me, winking madly as though she has something quite irritating in one of them.

I sense the only irritation is my refusal to take her heavy hints and act upon them. She cannot understand why I am so clearly ignoring her desire to have an evening alone with Connor. I can't blame her, for I cannot understand it either. I tell myself it was the sheer panic in Connor's eyes. I tell myself that if it weren't for my intervention, he would probably have bolted back to his studio to hide behind the largest canvas in his spare bedroom, and I have therefore saved Petra's interview.

I am being altruistic. I have made the situation more comfortable for both. And highly uncomfortable for me.

'That's a great idea, so it is,' Connor says a touch too heartily. Cassie obviously agrees.

Before Petra gets a chance to talk Connor out of the idea of dinner for four instead of two, Cas rushes upstairs to change. It's the quickest I've ever known her move. She's back downstairs in five minutes flat, in full warpaint, and a black mini-skirt, knee boots, and an orange sleeveless polo neck. She promptly plonks herself down on the sofa between Petra and Connor, her jumper clashing horribly with Petra's hair and ruining the carefully co-ordinated look of my friend's outfit so badly that I wonder if the sabotage was deliberate.

It takes me a little longer to change out of my jeans and jumper into a plain black dress I keep for those occasions when I don't know what to wear, pull a brush through my hair and put on lipstick and mascara. I now fervently wish I'd kept my mouth shut and just let them get on with it. I'm hoping that if I take too long something might happen whereby I can graciously back out of playing gooseberry for the evening.

For once my prayers are answered.

Just as we are leaving, the raw and angry growl of an oil-starved motorbike announces the surprise arrival of Luke. They have a date, and Cassie has forgotten. To my surprise she looks more disappointed than happy to see him. It's with something verging on reluctance that she climbs out of Petra's Mercedes, to speak with him. I can hear her talking, making excuses, then, expression unreadable, she returns to the car to make her apologies.

Once again I insist that Luke leave his old Kawasaki behind and take my car.

'You let him drive your car?' Petra asks incredulously as Luke manoeuvres carefully out of the yard, driving as though he has a man with a red flag walking in front of him, only to hear the telltale sound of the revs being pushed up as they round a bend and are finally out of sight.

'I'd rather that than Cas go on the back of that filthy death trap,' I reply, looking over to the empty stable where Luke has parked his old green motorbike. I turn away from watching the lane and smile feebly at Petra and Connor. 'Well, now Cas has gone I think perhaps I should just leave you to it. You know the saying: two's company—'

'Well, if you insist,' Petra says immediately. 'But you know you're more than welcome to join us.'

Yeah, about as welcome as a puritan at a swinger's party.

'Come with us, Natalie.' Connor tries again.

I shake my head.

'But what are you going to do for the rest of the evening? We can't leave you here on your own.'

'Oh, I'm a big girl now. I'm sure I can survive a night on my own. It'll be quite nice actually,' I add truthfully. 'I'll get first choice of TV channel, and I won't have to share my chocolate. Maybe I could even go for a spin on Luke's motorbike,' I joke weakly.

'Don't wait up!' Petra whispers as she leans across to kiss me goodbye before I can change my mind.

I stand and watch as Petra's sleek and expensive silver Mercedes coupé speeds up the drive in a cloud of wheelspin dust, then turn and slowly go back into the house and up to my room, collapsing onto my bed. I stare at the ceiling for a while, study the crack that runs from the furthest corner across the room toward my bed and then forks in two different directions, like the long flickering tongue of a snake, and pretend to myself that I don't think or feel anything. Concentrate on the mundane visual instead of the abstract emotional for a change.

I write for a bit, but can't concentrate enough to really

get going. Then I get up and flick through my wardrobe pretending that I care what I'm going to wear to the New Year's Eve party.

Despite my protestations that I would enjoy a rare evening on my own, the place feels terribly empty without Laura and Cas, and instead of my indulgence-fest of junk food and junk TV, I suddenly find myself kicking my heels. Drifting aimlessly from room to room in an effort to know what to do. Louisa has retired early, saying she's tired after our night out. Eventually I go back to my room and change into jeans and a sweatshirt, and pulling on a pair of Wellingtons, go out into the yard and check the animals, filling Chance's water bucket, and checking his hay net. I throw the snoozing birds some extra corn but, already stuffed to the beaks by the careful attentions of Cas, they ignore it. The goose pen stands glaringly empty. Despite the relief at not having to face Gertrude's bad temper at every morning feed, the place seems strangely quiet without them.

Having done everything I can in the yard, I cut through the long corridor between the barns, and through the gate into Mile Meadow, and walk the sloping land down to the cliff edge. When I was young, I used to sit on the edge of the cliff at the end of Mile Meadow and look out to sea and dream what my life would be like when I finally made it to London. Like Dick Whittington without the cat. I hardly made Lord Mayor, but I still managed to make myself a life there, and a good one at that. It was difficult, but I always refused to give up, surprising even myself with my own strength of will. I still have that life to go back to, but without Rob there it no longer seems so attractive.

It's dark, but it's one of those nights that is lit by a million bright stars in a black velvet sky, where everything shimmers silver, from the grass beneath my feet to the lichen on the winter-bare branches of the trees. The moon is almost full, hanging heavy in the sky as though it's just been flung there by an unseen hand, and is now threatening to fall back down towards the earth. It looks so close you feel you could reach out a finger and touch it, hold out your hand and catch it in your palm.

The snow has nearly gone, the wind a soft warm breath blowing gently on the frosted surface until all has melted. I turn and walk along the cliff path, heading down towards the beach road, and before that, Smuggler's Cottage.

It doesn't take me long to reach it, walking swiftly through a night that is almost silent except for the gentle whisper of a quiet sea. In darkness, the house looks more ruinous than ever, but it also looks welcoming. It's not creepy or scary like most tumbledown buildings, harbouring as many ghosts as your imagination will allow. When I look at the cottage I simply imagine how it would have been when it was someone's home. Then I imagine how it could look now with a little care and attention. I stand and stare for several minutes, listen to the soft sound of an owl hooting in the distance, and then turn for home.

To my surprise, Laura is there when I get back. She is sitting by the fire in the kitchen, like Cinderella after midnight, still in her evening dress, sparkling silver shoes kicked off by her feet, all five dogs – Meg, Shep, Jas and Stu, and even Mac – lined up in a row next to her. The small portable is on, and she is watching a repeat of *Parkinson* whilst eating a bowl of tomato soup.

'You're home earlier than I thought you'd be,' I tell her as I kick off my wet boots, and unwind the red scarf Cas gave me from around my neck.

'Charles had to get back. Evelyn called and said she was on her way home.'

I raise my eyebrows. 'What about dinner?'

Laura waves the bowl and spoon at me. 'This is it.'

'Oh, I'm sorry, and you all dressed up as well.'

Laura shrugs. 'Care to join me? There's more on the Aga.'

I help myself to some Heinz, and go and sit down next to her. The face that was practically luminous with excitement earlier, is now dragged down with disappointment.

'So not a great evening, eh?' I sympathise.

'Not the best, no,' she sighs. 'I know,' she cuts in as I open my mouth to speak. 'It's the perils of dating a married man.'

'I was just going to say I'm sorry your evening was ruined, that's all.'

'Oh right. Connor and Petra get off okay?'

'Uhuh,' I nod, warming my hands on the bowl, and tell her about the last-minute change of plan.

'So Cas ended up going out on another date with Luke then.' Laura puts her empty bowl down on the table, and begins to pick at a hunk of brown bread she has left on her plate. 'That must be their fourth one.'

'Yeah, but she didn't seem too happy about it though.'

'No, well, she wouldn't have done, would she?'

'What do you mean?'

'She likes Luke well enough, but given the choice between him and Connor.' She tails off as though expecting me to know what she's implying.

'I still don't know what you mean,' I shrug.

'Cassie likes Connor,' she replies bluntly.

'But what about Luke?'

'Oh, she likes him well enough, but I sometimes wonder if the prospect of getting out and about without the two old ladies cramping her style is more attractive to her than the actual boy.'

'Old ladies, thank you so much.'

'Luke could take her to places where she might get to see Connor.'

'To see Connor?' I query in surprise.

Laura nods slowly.

378

I think of Cas's disappointment when Luke turned up this evening, and the amount of time she's been spending up at the cottage, and what I had been completely blind to before suddenly becomes as plain as daylight.

'She's likes Connor, doesn't she?'

'That's exactly what I said.'

'I know, but I wasn't sure what you meant. Poor Cas.'

'It's just a crush. She'll get over it.'

'Maybe.' I shake my head in despair. 'But I think there's more to it than that.'

'Hardly, Nattie, he's old enough to be her father.'

'*Exactly*,' I reply pointedly.

'Oh.' Laura's face falls. 'I see what you mean.' She sighs heavily, before adding, 'So there you have it – now we're all a little bit in love with him. It's all his own fault for being so lovely,' she adds quickly as I throw her a glance that could easily scorch a hole in that gorgeous silver dress of hers. 'Of course, if I were twenty years younger I'd have married him several years ago myself and we wouldn't have such a problem.'

'If he'd have had you.' I smile grudgingly.

'He'd have had me like a shot. I was quite a catch in my youth.'

'Do you know, that's what Dad always used to say to me.'

Laura stops grinning, and looks at me quickly. 'He did?'

I nod. 'All the time. Repeatedly.'

A slow, deeper smile returns to Laura's face, as does a little of the glow that was there earlier before her evening got ruined.

'He was a wonderful man, your father.'

'I know.' I nod. 'I may only have been six when he died, but I remember him so clearly – well, more the things he used to do, the things we used to do together.'

'He adored his little girl, didn't he? He adored both of his girls. He would have been so proud of you, Nattie.'

She puts an arm about my shoulders and hugs me to her. 'I wish he were here now to see you.'

'I wish they both were. Do you know, I really wish that Rob could have met Dad. They'd have got on, wouldn't they?'

'Like a house on fire. Too well probably. We'd never have seen them – they'd have been off playing golf together all the time or fishing or the other things that men insist they like doing.'

'Dad never played golf.'

'I know, but it's something he always said he'd like to do if he had the time and the money.'

'That's funny. Rob always said the same. He used to remind me of Dad sometimes, the things he said, his mannerisms.'

'Well, they do say that girls are always trying to find one as good as their father, and your father was a good man, Natalie. A very good man.'

'One of the best,' I agree.

Laura tightens her hold about me, bringing her other arm up to encircle my waist, and I rest my head on her bare shoulder.

'I think that's why I'm seeing a married man, you know, Nat. That's the hard part about losing your husband. It didn't end because you fell out of love. I still love Eddie, and I always will. And so it's hard to commit yourself to someone else. I know my relationship with Charles seems far from ideal, but it suits me. Even after all this time, I still only feel that I have a *part* of me to give him, but fortunately because of his situation, that's all he wants.'

I listen quietly as Laura confides in me, the two of us so close, breathing in time. She has changed over the years. I suppose it was inevitable that she would. Time changes everything.

I have been running away from the person that she was when I was sixteen, but I now know she is no longer that person. The sad part is, I have a feeling she hasn't been for a great length of time. I have missed a huge part of my mother's life, and she mine, by my desire to hide from someone who no longer exists.

In a way it's like meeting Laura Dunne for the first time. Although the reality is that I'm getting to know my mother all over again. The good part is, I am slowly realising that I actually like this new Laura. I enjoy her company – she is, as many of her friends have said to me, a good person.

I don't sleep well that night. In fact, I watch the clock work its way through from ten p.m. until three a.m. before I finally fall asleep, only to wake just after six the next morning.

Surprisingly, after such a rotten night, I don't feel tired, and knowing that my mother will be up in just under an hour anyway, I decide to get up and surprise her with a cooked breakfast.

I've been in the kitchen for ten minutes, when I hear the sound of a car pulling quietly into the space next to mine. It's Petra. I open the door for her.

'Morning,' she mutters, walking straight past me. She has changed clothes and is now dressed in a pair of ridiculously flattering Burgundy wool trousers, beautiful polished leather boots, the softest grey cashmere jumper, and a leather flying jacket with a fur collar. She looks like she's just stepped straight from a magazine advert for the Ralph Lauren Winter collection.

'What happened to the little crotch-hugger number you went out in?' I ask her wide-eyed.

'I had these in the car, just in case.'

'Don't tell me, and a toothbrush, and your heated rollers, and a whole arsenal of make-up . . . just in case,' I tease her.

Petra doesn't laugh; she simply sighs, sits down at the kitchen table and pours herself a cup of tea from the fresh pot I placed there a few minutes ago. She adds milk and two sugars, stirs, then doesn't sip, simply stares morosely into the depths of her mug.

'How did it go with Connor?' I finally ask, having realised she's not going to offer any information.

'He was the perfect gentleman,' she replies without looking at me.

'Well, that's nice.'

'I know.' She sighs again in disappointment, then looks up at me. 'I plied him with alcohol, then when I said I'd had too much to drink to drive he insisted that we stay – and then he booked two rooms. *Two rooms*,' she repeats bitterly. 'Is there something wrong with me, Nat?' She holds her hands out in question. 'Am I that unattractive? I practically throw myself at the man, and he turns me down. Maybe that was it – maybe I came on too strong. Some men can't handle that, can they? They like to chase instead of being chased. Maybe that's what I did wrong. Connor's a pretty macho kind of guy, isn't he? Perhaps I should have played hard to get, and let him do all the running. Then again, I kind of have the feeling he might have run in the opposite direction. Oh, I don't know, Nattie, can you help? How should I play it with Connor?'

'I don't know that you should *play* it at all,' I reply after a long hesitation. 'It's not a game, Pet. You don't have to play a role. Connor seems to be a pretty open kind of guy. What you see is what you get, so maybe you should just be yourself.'

'Mmm,' Petra murmurs, unconvinced. 'Or maybe the problem is I need to be someone else.'

'What do you mean?' I ask her, puzzled.

Petra sips broodingly at her hot tea, her large eyes staring almost accusingly at me over the rim of the mug.

'He spent the whole bloody evening quizzing me about you.'

'He did?' I drop the piece of bacon I was peeling from

the plastic pack onto the floor.

'Oh, don't get me wrong – it was nothing creepy,' she assures me quickly as I get down on my hands and knees to retrieve it. 'Just general questions, nothing desperate, or sick, like what kind of panties you wear, or which side of the bed you like to sleep on, but questions nonetheless, not about me, about *you*.'

She falls silent for a moment and then asks, 'Why didn't you tell me there was something between you?'

'Because there isn't,' I reply sharply, feeding the offending piece of bacon to the nearest dog.

'Oh come on, Nat, I know you. You didn't look very happy when I told you we were going out. I should have realised then—'

'There's nothing to realise, Petra,' I tell her.

'Maybe you should tell Connor that then, because I get the distinct impression he was a damn sight more interested in you than he was in me. Come on, Nat, what's going on? Why didn't you say anything to me?'

'What could I have said? We're friends. Okay, so if I'm totally honest I do have feelings for him and maybe he reciprocates them a little . . .'

'There's no maybe about it,' Petra tells me, shaking her head. 'I just wish you'd said something before I made such a big idiot of myself.'

'But that's the thing, nothing's actually going on between us.'

'Nothing physical maybe, but up here . . .' She taps the side of her head with her forefinger, 'I get the feeling it's busier than the M25 on a Friday evening. Tell me I'm wrong.'

I take a deep breath and let it out in a sigh as Petra watches me, waiting for an answer. 'I can't. I'm sorry.'

Petra looks at me keenly for a moment and then eventually shrugs. 'It's no big deal, he's a lovely guy, but if I'm being completely honest I suppose I just wanted to get my own back on Peter somehow.' She pauses for a moment, looks down at her hands, studies the back of her immaculately painted nails. 'I'm going to finish with him, Natalie,' she says quietly.

'You're going to finish with Peter?' I repeat incredulously.

She nods, catching her bottom lip between her teeth. 'My momma always used to say that when the good times in a relationship outweigh the bad times, then you hang on in there, but if it ever turns itself around, then you run as fast as you can to get out.'

'And the bad times outweigh the good times, do they?'

She nods. 'You know they do. The scales are definitely uneven,' she replies flatly. 'Either that, or they've just suddenly fallen from my eyes.'

'And this sudden de-scaling, is it something to do with Connor?'

Petra shakes her head vigorously, but then changes her mind and starts to nod instead. 'No . . . well, yes . . . yes, I suppose it is. It's taught me one thing, Nat: there are other men out there I could easily fall in love with – if only they'd let me,' she adds with a wistful laugh. 'What I'm trying to say is that Connor was the non hump that broke this camel's back.' She pauses and clutches her head. 'You know, I really shouldn't mix my metaphors. I've got the mother of all hangovers.'

I go to one of the dresser drawers and hunt for the Alka Seltzer I know Laura keeps there.

Petra is still talking. 'Connor's something special, and maybe he did open my eyes to the fact that there are far better men out there than Peter bloody England, but this has been coming for some time now if I'm honest. I used to think my relationship with Peter was convenient, you know, to both of us. Now I realise he just uses *me* like a convenience. Pays his twenty-pence worth, dumps on me, then washes his hands and leaves until the next time he feels an urge. I'm worth more than that, Natalie.'

'I know you are – I've been telling you that for years.'

'Yeah, I know, and now I'm finally listening.'

'All I can say is thank goodness for that.'

'So you think I'm doing the right thing?'

'I *know* you are,' I tell her, dropping the tablets into a glass of water and handing it to her.

Petra waits for the fizzing to subside then knocks back the white liquid as quickly as she can.

'I know it's not my place to interfere,' I go on, 'and I wouldn't normally, but I think Peter is such an arsehole that I for one will be totally over the moon if you finally kick him into touch.'

'You would?' she asks me, pulling a face at the bitter taste.

'Yeah,' I nod. 'You know I'd never try and tell you what to do, Pet, but if I'm going to be a good friend to you I have to say it. Get shot.'

She nods thoughtfully. 'So a good friend would tell another friend something even if they don't think it's what they want to hear at that moment?'

'Yeah,' I reply slowly.

'In that case, can I say something to you?'

'I suppose.'

'Connor likes you, Nat, it's obvious, and the more I think about it, the more I see that you like him too. Hell, you've practically just admitted as much. A girl would be lucky to find herself a man like Connor Blythe. Don't get me wrong, Rob was a good, good man, and I know you still feel it's too soon for you to let someone else into your heart, but at least let him into your life, Nattie. We all need as many true friends as we can get, and unfortunately they always seem to be few and far between . . . I know only you will know when the time is right, if ever, but please don't let Connor pass you by for the wrong reasons. Promise me you'll think about it, okay? I'm not asking you to do anything, just think.'

★ ★ ★

Petra has asked me to think – to do the one thing I have done far too much of in the past few weeks. But she is right. She has seen something I have known but tried so hard to deny since the picnic.

*Connor.*

I want him. I want to be with him, to spend time with him, to talk, to laugh. I have even found myself fantasising about what it would be like to sleep with him, feel him naked beside me – inside of me. Oh, the guilt.

*Dear Rob,*

*I have met someone I think I could love. A strange, strange thing to be telling you, I know, to tell the husband that I still love that I think I could love another. But I hope that you will understand.*

*Forgive me, Rob. I shouldn't feel like this. Should I?*

*Sometimes I wish you weren't so bloody perfect. How am I supposed to get over that? If only I had something to hate you for, something that irritated the hell out of me, something else to focus on instead of how much I miss you.*

*It wouldn't be fair on Connor to start a relationship when my heart still feels so full of you, would it? He might always feel that he came second to you. And are these feelings I have for him real, or are they just a symptom of my loneliness?*

*I know that you, Rob, my best friend, would want me to be happy. It's not rational to hold myself away from the thought of happiness with someone else because of you. You wouldn't want that. If you were here, you'd be telling me to go for it. To grab every chance of happiness with both hands.*

*And I do think he could make me happy, Rob.*

*Yes, I think I could love him.*

I walk down to my private place and slip my letter through the gap in the rock and, as always, feel a little better for having done so. It is as if, with each letter, I am sending away a little bit of my sorrow, and this time absolving myself of guilt through confession.

I don't stay as long today, choosing instead to walk back along the cliff path, enjoying the soft cool breeze on my face, listening to the gulls call to each other, cries carried on the back of the wind. Streamers of gossamer thread sail from the bushes, not spiders' webs, more spider motorways, running in straight lines like roads, from bush to bush, catching the light of a low yet brilliant sun.

The frost-stiff grass breaks beneath my feet like glass as I walk. The sky is an ice blue, streaked with dark grey clouds haloed with the golden glowing orange of the sinking sun.

As I get closer to home, the low wall marking the bottom of Mile Meadow clearly visible some fifty yards away, I stop and walk carefully down the sloping land toward the steep bank that stretches between field and beach.

I can see a figure down below. A man is playing with a large dog, throwing a stick into the sea; the animal hurls itself into the rolling waves, soaking its owner each time it returns with a vigorous shake from head to tail, before dropping the stick to be thrown again. The man is laughing, the melodic sound carried up to me on the lightest of breezes. He is shoeless, a pair of Timberlands abandoned in the sand just behind them, and the hems of his jeans are trailing in the sand and the water so that they are far darker than the rest of the denim. He is wearing a thick Aran jumper, and his short golden brown hair is bright in the sunlight.

It is Connor.

I sit and watch him for a while, lost in the perfect beauty of the day and the world around me, and the fact that I am numb to it all in some way.

Then Connor too sits down, cross-legged in the sand,

looking out at the sunset. Mac comes to lie beside him, resting his heavy head in Connor's lap. One of Connor's hands comes to rest on the animal's huge head, to stroke it, a subconscious gentle repetitive movement, as automatic as breathing.

He sits as I do, lost in the beauty that surrounds us, the sound of the waves and the touch of the wind, the gentle breath of a lover sleeping beside you. I look down on him, still and quiet. I am intruding on a private moment. Feeling like a voyeur, I stand up, and make my way back up the bank. When I reach the top I turn back.

He is still there, seated exactly as he was. Only Mac has moved and is watching me quietly and thoughtfully, as quietly and thoughtfully as his master watches the sun slowly sink into the sea, its bright orange brilliance slowly extinguished by the cool dark green of the deep ocean, the two colours mixing like paints curling a path through moving water.

# Chapter Thirteen

I return to the farmhouse to find Louisa-May packed and ready to leave. Her suitcase is standing in the kitchen and Louisa is sitting on the bed in Laura's room, looking weary, struggling to pull up the zip on her hold-all.

'You're going?' I exclaim in surprise. 'I thought you were staying until tomorrow?'

'I'm sorry, Natalie.' She smiles apologetically. 'You've probably noticed I'm not quite myself at the moment. I feel very drained, which is silly because holidays are supposed to revitalise you, aren't they?'

'Yes, they're supposed to, but it doesn't always work out like that, does it?' I sit down on Laura's bed beside her.

'No. I think I overdid things a little. I feel as if I've been away from home for ages. Your mother has been so kind, but to be honest there's nothing worse than feeling ill in somebody else's home.'

'You need your own bed,' I nod in agreement. 'Don't worry, I know how it is.'

'Oh, I'm so glad you understand, Natalie.'

'It's Cassie you've got to convince, not me.' I close the zip on her bag, squeezing in the sides so that the metal teeth can slide more easily together.

'How can I tell her without her realising how dreadful I feel?'

'Maybe she should know. Maybe you shouldn't hide it from her.'

'I only want to protect her.'

'I know. But she's fully aware of the fact that you're not well. She's very bright. If you try and hide things from her, she'll notice and think things are worse than they actually are.'

Louisa sighs. 'I suppose you're right.'

'Well, that makes a nice change as far as Cas is concerned.' I laugh softly.

Louisa-May reaches out and pats my hand. 'You shouldn't put yourself down, darling. Trust me, you'll soon learn that there are always plenty of other people ready to do that for you, so you should never do it to yourself. You've got a wise head on young shoulders. You've just got to learn to trust your instincts.'

'Considering my instincts are normally to bury my head in the sand, or my face in a wine glass I wouldn't say they were particularly trustworthy,' I joke feebly.

Louisa-May smiles, her lined face creasing like the back of the knee on a pair of old velvet trousers. 'I'll talk to Cassie, but will you do something for me?'

'Of course, what is it?'

'Petra has kindly volunteered to chauffeur me back to London, but I'd be so grateful if you'd check that she actually *wants* to go back now, and isn't just leaving for my sake.'

I nod. 'I'll go and talk to her now.' I get up from the bed, but Louisa calls after me.

'Nattie, it's not very easy to accept the fact that I can't be as active as I used to be.'

I pause and turn back to her. 'It must be difficult,' I reply quietly.

She sighs and slowly nods her grey head. 'It is, especially when you don't want to waste a moment of the life you have left . . .' She pauses and reaches out to me. We embrace.

'I hope in time you'll forgive me for what I am about to say, and one day understand why I felt I had to say it,' she murmurs, and then pushing me away from her, she says: 'I know you loved my son-in-law, but please, for me, for him, don't waste your life grieving for what could have been. Rob would have wanted you to be happy, Nattie. He would have wanted you to find someone who made you as happy as you once made him. The best way of honouring Rob, my dear, would be to live your life as fully as you can.'

Petra is in my room, packing.

'Are you doing a moonlight flit without paying your bill?' I ask her.

She looks up and grins. 'Yeah, but don't tell the management. I've heard they're worse than the Mafia.'

'Why don't you stay for the party on Saturday?'

She flicks a half-smile at me, and shakes her curls in refusal. 'Thanks, but no. I won't stay.'

'What are you going to do?'

'Don't worry, honey, I won't be on my own. I made a decision and a few phone calls yesterday. I'm going home for a few days.'

'Home?'

'New York.' She nods happily. 'I've booked a flight for tomorrow night from Heathrow. I'll be counting down to the New Year with the crowds in Times Square.'

'Wow,' I reply. 'Sounds kind of exciting.'

She looks up from her bag, her eyes narrowing. 'It will be. Hey, I've just had an idea. Wanna come with me?'

I shake my head slowly.

'Does that mean you don't *want* to come, or you *can't* come?' she queries, hands on hips.

'Do you know, I think it's a bit of both.'

'You mean you can't leave Cassie?'

I sit down on the bed and start to fold a shirt she's thrown there. 'I can't and I don't want to. And my mother as well. Do you know something? I actually like

391

it here, Petra – I've been happier here than anywhere else in the past twenty-one months or so. You wouldn't believe it, would you? After everything I did to get away when I was younger.'

'Things change,' Petra replies simply. 'People change. Especially their priorities. Things that you thought were important . . .' she tails off and for a moment looks wistful, then she shrugs matter-of-factly, and starts to get the rest of her clothes from my wardrobe '. . . well, you suddenly realise that they're not any more.'

'Like Peter?' I look up at her in question.

'Yeah, like Peter.'

'What are you going to do?'

'Well, Peter's flying in the same day that I'm flying out – with luck we'll pass each other going in opposite directions in Terminal Three or something, although if Peter's put on more weight over Christmas they'll have to ship him in through Four.' The smile that accompanies this jibe is not as wistful as her smiles of late. 'When I'm not here waiting for his return like an eager and obedient pet Labrador, I think he'll get the message.'

'Are you sure about this?'

'Absolutely.' She nods resolutely. 'I'm fed up with being his lap dog. And I mean to say, Petra and Peter? The names don't even sound right together, do they?' I still think that Petra is hiding a heavy heart behind humour. She has been seeing Peter England for a long time now, at least three years. I know this isn't easy for her.

The last of her things is folded into the overnight bag, and I pull up the zip. 'Give me a ring, yeah? Let me know that you're okay.'

'Of course I will, honey.' She loops one arm around my neck and plants a red-lipped kiss on my forehead. 'You too, right?'

For a moment we rest together, foreheads touching,

nd then we pull apart, looking more cheerful than we
eel.

'Now, I wonder if my favourite grandma's ready for
ier lift home yet?'

'etra and I help Louisa-May down the stairs, one in
ront, one behind, each holding a frail wizened hand
arefully, as though carrying the finest, most fragile bone
hina. Cassie is lurking by the door, looking as if she
vould like to lock it and hide the key, and stop her
,randmother from leaving. Her face is twisted with
nguish.

'Why won't you stay? Please stay,' she begs.

'Oh darling, I'm sorry, but I really need to go back
iome for a while. I'm terribly tired after gadding about
or so long.' Louisa is trying to keep her tone light, but
ier anxious face belies the voice.

'But we'll look after you here, won't we, Nattie?' She
ooks pleadingly at me.

'I know you would, sweetheart,' Louisa-May cuts in,
but to be totally honest, I really do *want* to go home. It
eems that I've been away for such a long time. I tell you
vhat – why don't you pop down and see me when you
,et back to London?'

I looked from one to the other. 'Better still,' I suggest,
why don't we detour a little on our way back, pick you
ip, and take you back to Hampstead until Cas returns to
chool? What do you think?'

Cas looks at me and then back at Louisa, a small
;limmer of hope lighting up her miserable face.

'Would you? What do you think, Granny, would you
ome? Do you think you'll feel better by then?'

Louisa too begins to smile again. 'I think that's a
narvellous idea. Give me a few days to rest up and then
'll be back on full throttle and raring to go again.'

Cassie helps Louisa-May into the low-slung body of
'etra's silver Mercedes, whilst Laura and Petra struggle

to fold the wheelchair into the boot alongside their luggage. We stand and wave until they are no longer visible.

Cas has slipped one arm through Laura's, and the other through mine, a fragile rose supported between two canes. As the Mercedes disappears from view into the night, she smiles up at me, a tight, brave smile, and then heads over to the safe haven of Chance's loose box. I have come to realise that she goes there for comfort, found in the warm sturdy neck of the horse himself or the work that caring for him brings.

I myself feel a little flat. Christmas is over, the New Year is nearly upon us. Very soon, it will be Cassie and me who'll be packing up our things and heading back to London. I follow Laura into the house.

'I thought we could go out tomorrow night,' I say, 'just the three of us. Maybe we could go down to the Ship again and play pool? Cheer Cassie up a little now that Louisa-May has gone back home.'

Laura slips off her Wellington boots, bending to rub at her toes which are stiff with cramp. 'That's a lovely idea, darling, but I'm afraid you're busy tomorrow.'

'I am?' I turn to her in surprise.

She hops over to the table and parks herself in one of the chairs, smiling at me a little sheepishly. 'I have a confession to make. I've been interfering again on your behalf, but please don't be cross with me.'

'What have you done?' I sigh, picturing further attempts at well-meant but unwanted matchmaking.

'I had a long chat with an old friend today.'

'Oh yes?'

'Yes.' She nods.

'I wondered why you were in your study for so long this morning,' I offer, as she pauses, obviously for effect. Determined to say no more I reach for a tea towel and begin to wipe the lunch dishes, which are still stacked on the wooden drainer next to the sink.

'Yes,' she repeats. 'I was talking to Molly – Molly Billingham.'

I stop pretending to dry an already dry plate, and turn to face her. 'You were? Really?'

Laura nods. 'How is she?' I ask cautiously.

'Tired.' Laura sits down at the table, her elbow against it, her chin resting in her hand. Her other hand goes to her neck, where the fingers interlace with the heavy silver chain she wears there, thumbnail flicking at the safety bar which sits across the catch.

I nod in understanding. 'Sleep never seems to come when you need it most.'

'They were very close, Molly and Ralph.' Laura looks at me keenly. 'I hope you don't mind, but I told her what happened to Rob. I thought . . . I thought perhaps it might help her to know that there are some people out there who understand how she feels at the moment.'

I sigh heavily, the hair of my long fringe flicking lightly upwards as I exhale.

'I hope you don't mind too much?' she repeats.

'No.' I shake my head. 'No, it's okay.'

'I think it helped her to talk about it all. In fact, she asked a favour of you.'

'Of me?' I ask in surprise.

'Yes. She's getting a lot of unwanted press attention at the moment. Of course, her press office have given out a formal statement on her behalf, but Molly hasn't spoken to the media herself; she really doesn't feel up to it. The shame is they simply won't leave her alone. Do you know, she had a young man turn up on her doorstep only yesterday pretending to be from her insurance company. Turned out he was from some scurrilous rag trying to get an exclusive.'

'Sounds about typical,' I mutter. 'It's the story everyone wants – even Elaine's been angling for it big-time.'

'So you see, you'd be doing her a huge favour.'

'What do you mean?'

'If you interviewed her.'

'You're serious?' I finally put down my tea towel and turn to face her.

Laura nods vigorously. 'She felt that if she gave you an interview, then it would get the papers off her back. It wouldn't be an exclusive any more so it would hopefully be old news.'

'She wants me to interview her, and thinks that I'd be doing *her* a favour?' I repeat incredulously.

'That's about it, yes. Although you must know that wasn't why I called her, but when she told me the hacks were circling like sharks, well I thought . . . it was mostly her idea, darling, I didn't hint too heavily. You're not cross with me, are you?'

'Cross with you?'

'For interfering.'

'Do you know, I'm learning something?'

'What's that then?'

'That if you do *interfere*, as you put it, you normally have the most altruistic of reasons.' I walk forward and embrace her, placing a gentle kiss on both of her cheeks.

'Does that mean you'll do it?'

'Of course I will, and thank you.'

'Oh, I'm so glad. I think it will help Molly as well, just to talk to someone else who knows what she's going through right now. I'll go and give her a ring, tell her you'll be there in the morning.'

The next day I leave early, hoping to miss the morning build-up of traffic that normally slows the A30 to a painful crawl. I've got a long drive, only a small part of it on a motorway, the M27. In the end it's past lunchtime when I finally crawl through the traffic into a sunshine-filled Brighton.

Molly Billingham lives in a huge old Victorian house near Queens Park; set back from the road, it is surrounded by a high stone wall, iron railings and massive beech trees, their naked branches sweeping a bright grey sky.

I have been told to park in a side road, and go round to the back of the house, where I will be met at the rear gate at precisely one thirty. All very cloak and dagger, but when I see that her front gate is besieged by press paparazzi, I realise the need for this precaution.

The garden gate is opened by someone I presume to be Molly Billingham's housekeeper – a plump woman in her early fifties, with grey hair swept back from her head in a tidy chignon, sensible shoes, and a pristine white apron covering her tweed skirt. She takes me into the house through a side door. We pass into a large kitchen with a vaulted ceiling, and then through to a parlour at the back of the house, a quiet room with green silk Chinese wallpaper, and striped silk chairs. It is full of antique furniture, and overlooks a beautifully mature garden, which even in winter looks as green and fresh as a spring meadow.

Molly Billingham is waiting for me here. Seated in a wing chair by the fire, she is elegant in a simple black dress, a string of grey pearls at her slender throat. She looks tired, weary in both mind and body, and yet she is undeniably, unmistakably beautiful. Breathtakingly so, with charcoal hair, and eyes the translucent green of the purest jade.

I'm embarrassed to find myself staring at her, but she doesn't seem to notice. She's probably used to this reaction from people. She doesn't rise as I enter the room, but holds out her hand to me instead.

'This has to be Natalie. I haven't seen you since you were seven, but you have a look of your mother about you.'

I cross the room and take the hand that's offered me, not quite sure what to do with it, as it is placed as though she is Queen Elizabeth, and I Raleigh, who should kneel and kiss it.

'How is your mother?'

'Well, thank you. She sent her regards, and these.'

I hand her the huge bunch of roses and lilies that Laura sent with me, and she takes them with a smooth elegant hand and holds them to her face, breathing in deeply.

'Beautiful. Thank you.'

The housekeeper comes back in bearing a tea tray.

'Natalie, take a seat, please. This is Miss King, my companion and very able assistant. It's a little early for afternoon tea, but I thought you might need some refreshment after your long drive.'

'Thank you, that's very kind,' I reply, accepting a cup of tea from Miss King, and wondering what her first name is. She looks like the kind of person who has never had one, or never ever used one.

Miss King pours our tea, and then leaves the room, taking Laura's flowers with her. I'm perched on the edge of my seat like a nervous schoolgirl, waiting to start asking the questions I have sketched out in my notebook, my tape recorder set to play, but as soon as Miss King has closed the door behind her, I see Molly Billingham relax as though someone has just unlaced her corsets.

She looks over at the door as if checking that the woman's definitely gone, and then leans in conspiratorially. 'Would you like a drop of something stronger in your tea, my dear?'

I shake my head nervously.

'Very well, but I'm sure you won't mind if I add a little something.'

She reaches down behind her seat cushion and pulls out a slim half bottle of Cognac, almost sighing with pleasure as she pours a large measure into her teacup. Then screwing the lid back on tightly, she pushes the bottle carefully back into its hiding place.

'Just between you and me, of course . . .'

I know exactly what she means. I'm not to mention this to Miss King, nor must it find its way into my article.

'Of course.' I nod reassuringly.

'Miss King is a little, shall we say, *over-protective* at times. I know she only has my welfare at heart and really I'd be lost without her, especially at the moment, but I do think I'm a touch too old and world-weary for a chaperone, don't you? Now, where were we . . . ah yes, I was saying how much you remind me of your mother. You don't happen to have a cigarette, do you, my dear? Miss King keeps hiding mine so that I can't find them.'

'I'm afraid I don't smoke,' I start to reply, but then spot a packet of Dorchester tucked away behind a vast ceramic lamp on an occasional table. I fetch them for her, and she lights a cigarette with shaking hands from a heavy green onyx lighter, inhaling deeply as though it is smoke and not oxygen she needs to breathe.

'Thank you, darling.' She stops and stares at me intently. 'You really *do* look like Laura, you know. It's so odd, you never used to as a child. I always thought you were the spitting image of Eddie, but then we all change, don't we?' She laughs. 'Everything changes eventually.' She takes another drag on her cigarette, and then suddenly looks more cheerful.

'She was a star, your mother. She could have been someone, but your father's death knocked all the stuffing out of her. She seems happier now, but it took her a very long time. Yes, a very long time . . .' Her mind goes somewhere far beyond me and this room. Something tells me not to interrupt her, so I sit quietly and wait for her to come back to me.

'There was never anyone else for me but Ralph,' she says suddenly. 'Do you know, I was sixteen when we first met, and seventeen when we married. We eloped. My father wouldn't give us permission to marry, he thought I was too young, so we ran away to Gretna Green. How much more romantic can you get than that, eh? Of course my father was absolutely furious when he found out. He didn't approve of Ralph, you see – he was an actor, which was terribly frowned upon then. My father wanted me to marry a bank manager, or a surgeon or the like, somebody with a *proper* career, who could provide me with a good lifestyle.' She laughs at the irony, glancing about the opulent room. 'So of course he shouted and ranted and threatened to cut me off, and told me it wouldn't last – but we proved him wrong, didn't we, Ralph darling? We proved them all wrong.'

I get the feeling she isn't talking to me any more, but then her eyes suddenly snap onto mine with a frightening clarity.

'We were together for forty-seven years, married for forty-six, would you believe that? Out of everything that we experienced in our lifetime, we used to say that our marriage was our greatest achievement. And now he's gone . . .' The eyes go misty again.

'I was lucky,' she tells me. 'We had a long time together. A long and happy time. Your mother told me about your husband – Robert, wasn't it?'

I nod.

'I'm so sorry.'

'Thank you. And I for you. What happened to him?' I probe gently.

'It was his heart, or so they said. He went to sleep in that chair and simply didn't wake up again.' She points to the chair that I am sitting in. 'She named you after Natalie Wood, you know.'

'I'm sorry?' I reply, confused yet again by the sudden subject change.

'Your mother. She named you after Natalie Wood, didn't you know that?'

'I didn't, no.'

'Yes, she had quite a thing about Natalie Wood. So funny then that you married a man called Robert.'

I obviously look confused as she continues to explain.

'Natalie Wood married another Robert, Robert Wagner, but it was she who died in tragic circumstances. Although of course he went on to remarry. I always think it's easier for a man to move on; their emotions, I think, are slightly more detached than those of a woman. Ralph and I, we made a vow to each other that if something ever happened to one of us, then we would find someone else. I couldn't bear the thought of him being alone and lonely – that would have been far more painful to me than the thought of him being with and loving someone else. Your mother tells me that your husband was married before you?'

I nod.

'And he found love again. Do you have children?'

'We didn't together, no, but I have a step-daughter, Cas.'

'And are you close?'

I shake my head. 'Not really, but I wish that we were.'

'My one regret is that we never had children. Too wrapped up in each other, you see, and we were always so busy, so in love with each other and with our work. By the time I realised I wanted children it was far too late for me to have any.'

'Your promise to Ralph: do you think you could love again?'

She shakes her head. 'I'm too old now. My life is over.' She is only four years older than my mother!

'Oh but no, you shouldn't think like that,' I protest. 'I know it's difficult to ever imagine yourself with someone else at the moment, but believe me, it does get easier.'

'Does it?' she replies hopefully. 'Does it really get easier? Please, Natalie, tell me it does.'

'You never think it will, but yes it does. People keep telling you to give it time, and you just want to scream at them to shut up, but it's true. In time things *will* get a little easier; the pain will still be as awful, but I promise

401

you it won't be quite as agonising.'

She smiles again and holds out her hand to me. 'You see that photograph, there, the one on the mantelpiece in the silver frame? Would you fetch it to me, darling.'

I rise and get her the photograph, stand beside her as she touches it gently with her fingertips.

'My Ralph,' she tells me. 'He was so handsome. I want you to use this picture in your article. It was taken on our wedding day . . . have I told you about my wedding day? We eloped, you know. I was only seventeen . . .'

It is only when I leave the house and get back into my car that I realise we have been talking for over three hours.

There are five messages on my mobile phone, one from Laura, and four from an over-excited Elaine who wants an immediate brief. I phone Laura first to tell her I'm just setting off for home, and then I phone Elaine.

It is so odd talking to her. The world that was my salvation for so many months, now seems so unreal, so irrelevant. Elaine's eagerness, normally so infectious, is now simply an irritant. She is chatting about what she wants me to do when I get back next week, her enthusiasm for my return obviously fuelled by the coup of the interview with Molly. Normally I'd be as excited as she is, but I really did mean what I said to Petra.

I feel like a different person now. I'm not totally sure what I want to do any more, but I do know that *Naked* is no longer my lifeline.

I play back the tape recording of our interview as I drive back down to Whitsunday. I feel that Molly really opened up to me, but in return she made me talk about things that I have tried very hard to ignore.

Like the future.

Like children.

Rob and I had talked about children only in so far as we agreed we would discuss it at a later date. Too wrapped up in each other, I suppose, like Molly said she and Ralph were, and if I'm honest Cas had put me off. Of course, no child of mine would ever behave the way that she did, I vowed, but she was a short sharp shock in the restrictions and strains a child can put on a relationship, no matter how healthy. I had Rob and my work, both more than enough to take up my time and keep me happy.

Now I ache for the child I could have had with the man I loved. The child I'll never have.

For a while after his death I thought I might be pregnant. I clung onto this hope like a drowning man being thrown a lifebelt, nursed it to me, a secret hope, only to have my heart broken again when I found out my body was simply reacting to stress, the fact that I had stopped eating, and my weight had plummeted.

I wasn't pregnant, I was ill with suppressed grief. Grieving badly, like Molly is at this very moment. Convinced, like her, that without the man I loved, my life was suddenly void.

What shocked me most was the fact that I wanted to tell Molly that her life wasn't over, that she was still young and beautiful, she could still live. That she was still a person in her own right, and that her life had not ended, it had simply changed – in the most monumental, heartbreaking way – but a change nonetheless. That after the blind grief there would eventually come acceptance.

All of the things that my friends and family have been saying to me, and I have steadfastly refused to hear.

It has taken me a while to realise that my life did not end when Rob's did. And although my love for him still lives on inside of me, I know now that I do want to feel a tangible love again. A love that I can touch and hold, one that fills me with warmth instead of an aching sense of loss.

And I want to have children. I know that now.

To do so, I shall have to move on.

Laura is waiting up for me, half-asleep at the kitchen table. 'How did it go?' she yawns.

'It went really well.'

'Good.' She sighs with relief. 'I was worried that it might be difficult for you, might bring it all back to you.'

'Is Cas all right?'

'She seemed okay, a bit quiet perhaps. She was waiting up for you, but fell asleep so I sent her to bed. I think she's missed you today.'

'Really?'

Laura nods. 'Yes. Really.'

'Well, you sometimes don't realise what you have until it's not there any more.'

'You mean Rob?' she asks me softly.

I shake my head. 'I always knew that Rob was special.'

'Then what?'

'Life,' I reply simply.

I'm just about to switch off my light when I think I hear a noise downstairs in the kitchen. I'm always hearing noises. Whitsunday is an old house, with a loud voice, but this is different. It takes me a moment to realise that it's the sound of the switch on the kettle flicking off when it hits boiling point. Somebody is making themselves a hot drink.

This isn't unusual in itself, except for the fact that I know it's not Cas, because you can always hear when she comes down from the attic. The stairs creak, especially the penultimate one, then the latch on the door is a little stiff, and always makes a noise when you open it.

I look at the clock. It's two in the morning. My mother is never normally up at this time; she's usually tucked up in bed, snoring gently. I get up and put on my slippers and dressing gown, then creep across my room and out to the head of the stairs.

There is definitely someone down there. I can see a faint light coming through the door where one of the old warped wood panels has pulled away from its neighbour to leave a gap of about half an inch. I tiptoe down the stairs and peer through the gap into the dimly lit kitchen.

Laura is seated at the kitchen table in her dressing-gown. She has a desk lamp from the study next to her. The main lights aren't on and this is the only light in the room, casting a strange blue glow that makes her look almost ghostly. Laura is bent over the blue ledgers that house the Whitsunday accounts, pen in one hand, the other rubbing at her tired eyes.

A pot of tea sits at her right elbow, along with a cup containing the dregs of what she has just drunk. She has ink on her hands and on her face where she has brushed them across it. She looks shattered, which isn't surprising given the time, but more ominously she is smoking a cigarette – something she only does now in times of stress.

I push the door and it swings open with a slight creak, making Laura look up. 'Is everything all right?'

My mother mumbles something that sounds like an affirmative.

'What on earth are you doing?'

She indicates the books with a gesture that smacks a little of despair. 'What does it look like?' she replies a little tersely.

'Accounts?'

'Right first time. Give yourself a gold star.'

'In the middle of the night?'

She looks over at the clock on the wall. 'Ooh, right again. We are on form tonight, aren't we?' Then Laura puts down her pen. 'I'm sorry, Nattie. I'm just struggling here.'

'To add up?' I ask, knowing full well that this isn't what she meant at all.

'As you know, maths has never been my forte, but sometimes it just seems harder than others.'

'So you thought it would be easier at two in the morning when you're obviously totally knackered.'

'I just thought now would be a good time to do them, whilst it's quiet.'

'When no one would catch you, you mean.'

Laura tries to look offended and fails.

'You don't have to pretend to me, I know things could be better.' I've overheard the hushed telephone conversations, I've spotted the ominous red bills that are hastily shoved to the back of one of the dresser drawers when she thinks I'm not looking, the constant stream of letters from the bank. Our row because I dared to pay a bill for her.

'That's a polite way of putting things.'

'They're pretty dire, huh?'

'Yes, they're dire all right, but definitely not pretty.'

I go and sit next to her at the kitchen table. 'Want to tell me about it?'

She doesn't reply. I try again.

'I know it's a cliché but a problem shared is a problem halved.'

Laura picks up the pen and begins to tap it in agitation against the book she is leaning on.

'I'm not blind, you know, and I collect the post every morning.'

'Okay,' she sighs. 'Okay. To keep it nice and simple, we've got more going out than we have coming in, and the bills are just mounting up.' She picks up a pile of printed papers beside her, and goes through them. 'Gas, electricity, water rates, council tax, the blacksmith, the vet, the insurance company, the garage . . . they're all outstanding. Although somebody,' she picks up the feed merchant's bill and waves it accusingly at me, 'seems to have paid this one off now.'

I smile guiltily. 'I know it looks as if I was interfering,

but you won't take anything for our keep.'

'It's okay,' she holds up her hands. 'I've already told you off for that one, I'm not going to do it again.' She tries to look stern, but fails. 'If I'm being totally honest, I'm grateful you did that, Nat. This is the one that I felt the worst about. We hadn't paid the feed merchant for six months, he only still supplied us because we're very old friends, and he didn't have the heart to cut me off, but he was nearing the end of his tether, I can tell you. I was even down to giving him my useless bloody pottery as a thank you for being such a saint. My pottery!' She snorts in derision. 'What good is that to him when he's got bills of his own to pay? And he doesn't even smoke.'

'Your pottery is not useless.'

She looks up, raising her eyebrows in disbelief.

'It's . . . er . . . it's unique.' I try and smile brightly at her. 'It sells.'

She accepts this and nods slowly. 'It helps,' she agrees. 'No one can deny that, but it's not enough. It used to be, but everything seemed to go wrong last year. The central heating went, the roof needed fixing, every time it rained we couldn't feed the animals because all of the buckets were in here catching rain drops.' She shakes her head and tries to laugh but fails dismally. 'And then we got hit by Foot and Mouth. They took the whole herd, Nat. We had sheep too then. You didn't know that, did you? But we only replaced the cows, we haven't replaced the sheep. Don't have the money. I sold everything I could, but I don't have much of value. The painting that was in your bedroom . . .'

'The waterfall?'

She nods. 'I'm sorry, I know how much you loved that painting, but I was desperate, and it was the only thing I had of any value. I got a few thousand for that which kept us going for a while, but in the end I had to take out another mortgage. That's one of the reasons I did up the attic. I was thinking about going into B&B, anything . . .'

'Why didn't you tell me what was going on? I'd have tried to help.'

'Nat, in case it's escaped your attention, we haven't exactly been close confidantes in the last sixteen years, have we? Would you have come to me if *you* needed help?'

I don't answer her.

'Exactly.' She takes my silence as a negative.

'And the mortgage? Is that what the bank have been writing to you about?'

She looks at me sharply. 'You don't miss much, do you?'

'I'm a journalist,' I reply dryly. 'Not a very good one at the moment, but if I'm anything, it's observant.'

Her face takes on a curious expression. 'About everything except yourself it seems,' she mutters.

She's trying to side-track me, but I won't let her. 'The letters,' I persevere, 'from the bank.'

Laura rubs agitatedly at her bloodshot eyes. 'It's only a small mortgage, but we've still been struggling to keep up the payments. At the moment I'm four months behind. They're threatening to foreclose if I don't pay the arrears.'

'I can help.'

Laura rises so quickly she startles me, pushing her chair back so violently that it wavers unsteadily on its rear legs for a moment, threatening to fall to the floor, before it settles back on all fours.

'This is *exactly* why I haven't told you!' she thunders, her back to me, hands in her hair tugging in exasperation. 'I don't want you to think you have to bail us out.'

'I don't think I *have* to, but what if I want to?'

'Well, I don't want you to,' she repeats insistently.

'But—'

'No buts, Nattie, just leave it, will you!' She turns back

to me, her face apologetic. 'Please don't think that I don't appreciate the offer, but it's not right. This is something I have to sort out for myself. You do understand, don't you?'

I nod slowly. 'Okay. If that's what you want, I'll butt out for now, but will you do something for me?'

'If I can.'

'Go to bed.'

She starts to protest. 'But I've simply got to finish these . . .'

'Then we'll do it together tomorrow. Please, at least let me help you with that.'

She hesitates and then seems to give in, her shoulders sinking a little. 'Okay. You're right, I *am* shattered, and I probably couldn't add two and two at the moment. It's best to leave it till the morning. I'm getting nowhere fast tonight.'

I hold out my hand to her, for fear that if I leave her down here she will simply return to the ominous task in hand, and when she takes it, I tug her up the stairs and gently push her through the door into her room.

Returning to my own room, I sit and wait until I can hear the sound of her gentle snoring and knowing that she is asleep, I slip silently from my bed and head back downstairs to the kitchen table and the big blue ledgers she has left there.

Despite the fact that I don't get to bed until four, I'm the first up the next morning. I use the phone in the study rather than the one in the kitchen, so that I don't get disturbed, perching on the red leather-bound desk, breathing in the musty smell of a room that is never used except when someone wishes to exchange a read book for a new one.

It takes forever for someone to answer, and I can hear movement from upstairs in Laura's room. 'Come on, answer the bloody phone,' I breathe.

I'm just wondering if I'm too early for London office hours, now that I am so out of sync with the place, when a receptionist finally answers in a slightly breathless voice, 'Good morning, Freeland, Quinn and Joseph, how may I help you?'

'Hello, good morning, could I speak with Anthony Joseph, please?'

An idea had been forming in my head. It was there from a very early time, from the second week to be precise, but back then it was just a little daydream of an idea, the sort of thought you have when you're just drifting off to sleep and don't take anything that seriously.

As time has moved on, however, this idea of mine has taken up a more permanent residence in my head, moving from vague to actual possibility. The conversation I had with my mother last night was the very thing I needed to spur me into turning this idea into reality.

It wouldn't be such a bad thing to have somewhere near my mother, somewhere away from London, somewhere of my own. A home. Cas and I *need* somewhere we can really call home.

Phone call finished, to my mind very satisfactorily, I set out from the house to walk the length of Mile Meadow, and return an hour later. My mother is seated by the fire, shoes kicked off in front of her, mid-morning pot of Earl Grey on the table within reaching distance.

She looks tired. Weary in body and in spirit.

I am flooded by an overwhelming urge to wipe that worried look from her face, and this all simply adds to my determination that my recent decision is the right one.

'Where's Cas?' I ask.

'Out. She's taken the dogs for a walk into the village. I promised I'd show her how to make thyme dumplings, but we'd totally run out of suet.'

'I'm glad you're alone, we need to talk.' I take the seat

next to her at the kitchen table, turning it so that I am facing her.

She frowns. 'Sounds serious.'

'It is.'

'You'd better hang on a moment then.' Laura drags herself from the chair and goes over to the dresser. She takes a bottle of Jamesons, and two glasses from the top shelf, and returning to the kitchen table sets them down in front of us. 'I was going to offer you a cup of tea, but I have a feeling we might need something a little stronger.'

'Why?' I ask her.

'I've only ever seen you look this determined once before, Nat, and that's when you told me you were leaving, the day after your sixteenth birthday.' For a moment she looks sad, and then she takes a deep breath, sitting upright as though the air has inflated her sunken shoulders, and looks at me. 'Fire away then.' And then as I hesitate: 'You're going home, aren't you?'

I shake my head, and am a little gratified to see how pleased and relieved she looks to find that this isn't what I wanted to tell her.

'No, not yet anyway. Is that okay? We've not out-stayed our welcome yet, have we?'

'Far from it. It's been lovely having you here. I don't know what it's going to be like once you've gone back to London. Funny isn't it, I've been here on my own for nearly sixteen years. You've been here for nearly five weeks now, and I'm wondering how I'm going to cope when you go back to London.'

Is my mother crying? Laura pulls a handkerchief from her pocket, and wipes the corner of her eye.

'Are you okay?'

'I think I've got something in my eye,' she tells me unconvincingly. 'An eyelash, blasted thing.' And then: 'Oh Nat, I'm just tired, that's all. Tired and over-emotional.'

'Too much stress,' I tell her, 'which is what I wanted to talk to you about. I've been thinking about the problems you're having with the bank, and I've come up with a solution.'

'Yes?' She pulls the white linen handkerchief away from her face.

'I've put my London flat on the market. I should make a really good profit from it.'

Laura throws back her head and groans. 'Nattie, this is what I meant last night when I said I didn't want to tell you what was going on. I don't want your money.'

'I'm not going to give you my money,' I assure her, 'but I do want to make a solid investment with it.'

Laura laughs, a dry cracked sound that makes Meg look up from the hearth rug in question. 'We're not exactly a sound investment, Nattie. I can't see you ever getting any back for your money. Let's see now,' she muses sarcastically, 'ten per cent of the yearly egg sales, now what would that be? Ooh, all of twenty pounds!'

'That's not what I'm talking about.'

Laura opens her mouth to protest again.

'And I'm not talking goats' cheese or pottery or organic veggies or anything like that,' I interrupt her. 'Just hear me out, okay? That's all I'm asking. If you don't like what I'm going to say, then we'll forget the whole thing.'

Laura closes her mouth again.

I take a deep breath. 'I'm not *giving* you anything. I want something in return.'

Laura looks at me blankly.

'I want the cottage.'

The blank look turns to one of bewilderment.

'I want to buy Smuggler's Cottage.' Laura goes to speak again, but I keep on talking so that she can't interrupt. 'I'm deadly serious. I've thought about it an awful lot, and if you'd be prepared to sell it to me, then I really want to buy it.'

'But Nattie, it's just a shell!'

'At the moment, yes, but that means you'll sell it to me for a reasonable price, doesn't it?' I laugh, encouraging her to join me, and for the first time this morning, I see a smile begin to form on my mother's face.

'From my profits on the place in Notting Hill I'll have enough to make it into something fantastic. Because it *could* be fantastic – we both know that. It's a good investment – I'll make my money back and more. And once it's done I can always let it to holiday-makers. I can even pay you to manage it for me,' I add teasingly, knowing full well what sort of reaction this will induce when her pride is already on overtime.

Although she is looking less dubious, Laura shakes her head.

'I'm sorry, I can't let you. You don't really want the place. You'd just be doing it to get me out of a hole, and that's not a good enough reason.'

'Yes, it would help you, which is great, because despite what you say I'm determined that I'm going to help you somehow, but the best thing about it is I really want to do this.'

Laura unscrews the cap on the whiskey and refills our glasses, knocking back half of hers in one swift needy slug.

'This will all be yours when I go anyway, so how can I possibly justify selling you something that in a way you already own?'

'Don't you see that if you *don't* let me buy the cottage, then this place won't belong to any of us for very much longer?' I reply gravely.

I think it's finally sinking in. She's not happy about it, I can tell by her frown, but she cannot fail to see the logic behind my argument.

'Besides, it'll give me somewhere to go to when Cassie inherits the house in Hampstead and promptly kicks me out of it.'

413

'You're serious, aren't you?'

I roll my eyes and pretend to smack my forehead in frustration. 'At last she realises!' I cry in mock drama.

Laura takes another sip of her whiskey, looking at me curiously over the rim of her glass. 'And you'd want to have somewhere that close to your mother, would you?' she asks quietly.

We look at each other. We are silent, a thousand buried emotions resurfacing to crash between us like the waves in the distance plunging against the shoreline.

'I think I'd like that,' I reply softly. This time the smile is genuine.

'I think I'd like that too,' she whispers, and reaching out takes my hand in her own, squeezing it tightly, before letting go.

'So now we're agreed?'

She nods. 'If you're absolutely positive . . .'

I take a sip of my own whiskey, studying her carefully. 'It's got to be worth a hundred and thirty thousand alone just for the view.' I throw this in casually, hoping she doesn't work out that to offer her exactly twice the amount of her outstanding mortgage means that I've had a rather sneaky peek at the books.

'It's worth nothing of the sort, Nattie, and you bloody well know it,' she replies, puffing up with indignation.

'I'm pretty certain that would be an approximate market value, and that's what I would want to give you for it.'

'I won't take it.'

'I want you to.'

'Oh, and that means I've got to do it, because *you* want me to.'

'No, but it makes sense. Property around here is hideously expensive. In fact, thinking about it, the cottage would be a bargain at that price. I'm probably not offering you *enough* money. How about one hundred and thirty thousand for the house, and then another forty for the second meadow next to it?'

'You're not giving me that much for that heap of rubble, and you certainly didn't say anything about buying the meadow.'

'You mean you don't want to sell me the meadow,' I tease. 'I want a big garden. Come on, you've got plenty of land that you don't use. Surely you can sell me one small field. Don't be a meanie.'

The tactic seems to work. Laura looks bewildered, but she's nodding.

'Okay, if you really want it that badly, the house *and* the field, but I won't take any more than what it's worth. In fact, you probably qualify for a family discount.'

I'm relieved to see the smile return at this.

'Fair enough. How about if I arrange for a Chartered Surveyor to come down and value it – will you agree to abide by whatever they say?'

Laura thinks for a moment and then nods. 'If you're absolutely serious about wanting the cottage. And you swear to me that you're not just doing it . . .'

'I'm not doing it because you're in debt!' I butt in. 'I really want the house. If I'm being totally honest . . .'

'And I think you should be,' she says sternly.

'If I'm being honest then I probably wouldn't have thought about it as seriously if I hadn't found out what's happening here, but I had been thinking about it, and now that I've looked into it some more, I know for certain that it's definitely what I want to do. It's not some mad whim, I really do think it would be good for me – *and* Cas. She likes it here – Whitsunday is good for her. I know we can always come and stay here, but if we had the house . . . well, we'd be able to spend a lot more time down in Cornwall without feeling that we're putting you out.'

I know it's almost a bribe. If my mother lets me buy the cottage, then she'll get to see more of us. It's hardly fair, but it achieves my purpose.

'Okay, that's fair enough, as long as you agree to abide by whatever the surveyor says as well.'

'Oh yes.' I nod. 'Whatever they say it's worth, is what I'll pay – agreed?'

She hesitates for a second, and then a slow smile spreads across her face. 'Agreed.' She grins.

And we clink our glasses together, the solid crystal singing a note of finality to the deal, Laura smiling broadly, blissfully unaware that by hook or by crook I will get her to take enough to pay off the mortgage on Whitsunday, and get her well and truly back on her feet . . . and if I'm clever, perhaps a little bit more as well.

# Chapter Fourteen

Cas comes back from the village, chattering non-stop about the New Year's Eve Ball. She has gone from being bored about the whole affair, and mocking it, to being excited instead. I have a feeling that there may be a certain person behind this change. Despite my mother's warnings about Cassie's feelings for Connor being a little more than friendship, I am convinced that, at the moment at least, what little of her heart she wants to give, she gives to Luke.

Although at first I was worried that Luke was a bit too old for her, I have decided now that if he can make her smile again then I approve wholeheartedly. The changes he has induced in her have only been good ones. I've seen her smile more when she's with him than I have in the whole time I've known her.

I cannot deny, however, that Connor seems to have a big influence on her, but I agree less and less with Laura's theory of a teenage crush on Cassie's part. Since she has been working with him up in his studio she has become much calmer somehow, easier, lighter. She has been spending a great deal of time there, learning to paint, and his patience seems to have greatly lengthened the very short fuse of her temper.

She is easier with me too. The acidic comments, the snide asides have died down; she will occasionally have one of her digs at me, but more often than not it is in good humour. She is like a different person.

Unrequited love would not have this effect upon her, surely? Unrequited love is a fuel for insecurity, heart-ache and misery, not happiness. I think the part that Connor is playing within Cassie's heart is to fill a little of the gaping hole left there by Rob. Luke, however, is something different for Cassie – not a replacement, but someone to care about in a new way.

Your first boyfriend, no matter how serious, or casual, is the first person from whom you find love that is totally separate from anything to do with your family. And with this new relationship comes a completely new set of feelings. It helps you open up to the possibility that there is more love for you out there beyond the bound-ary of parents or siblings. That people can and will love you for yourself in a way that is deeper even than good friendship, despite the fact that they are not blood relatives.

I think Luke makes Cassie think about the future, instead of the past, a big step forward for her.

And for me.

Mac has come for a visit. It is a beautiful day – no trace of snow left at all.

I sit outside on the step and feed Mac leftovers whilst he leans companionably against my knee, then when he goes to leave I walk with him back up to the Loft. When I get there, the front door is wide open. I follow Mac through it, calling Connor's name.

He's in the studio, working on the painting of the studio window and the view beyond that I admired the first time I came here. The last time I came here. Despite the fact that he has left his front door wide open, a fire is blazing ferociously in the hearth.

Connor is perched upon a stool, bare-footed, wearing jeans and a coffee-coloured V-neck jumper that looks expensive, but is covered in splashes of blue paint. He swivels around on his seat as I step into the room, and smiles broadly. 'Nattie, good to see you. And to what do I owe this pleasure?'

'I just brought Mac back,' I reply, well aware that we both know Mac is perfectly capable of finding his own home.

'And,' I add quickly, 'I wanted to see you because I realised that I never thanked you . . .'

'For what?'

'For my painting.'

'Ah, yes. The painting. Did you like it?' I nod slowly, and his face relaxes with relief. 'I was worried. When you didn't say anything about it, I wasn't sure whether I'd done the right thing or not.'

I continue to nod. 'It was a good thing. A very good thing.'

'I'm so glad.'

'And I also wanted to thank you for something else.'

'Two thank yous in one day? Fire away.'

'Thank you for looking out for Cas, for taking her under your wing. You've been a good influence.'

He laughs and puts down his paintbrush. 'Do you know, that's the first time I've ever been called a *good* influence by anybody.'

'There's a first time for everything,' I shrug.

'Clichéd but very true,' he grins. 'Well, now that you're here, how about being an angel and making the good influence a coffee. I've been gasping for a drink for about two hours, but I'm stuck to this stool so I am.'

'Oh yeah?' I raise my eyebrows in disbelief.

'Sure, glued to it by the ninety per cent perspiration of genius.'

'More like glued to it by spilled paint, but yeah, I'll make you a coffee.'

'Thank you. You know where everything is.'

I make two mugs of Nescafé, and take them back through to the studio.

'Has your friend gone home now?' he asks, gratefully

419

taking the hot mug, and sipping slowly.

'Petra?'

'Petra the Petrifying, yeah.'

I laugh in horror at such an insult. 'You can't call her that! She's lovely, really sweet.'

'No, Nattie, puppies are sweet and lovely, babies are sweet and lovely. She was Tyrannosaurus Rex in a designer dress. I thought she was going to eat me.'

'She probably would have done if you'd asked her nicely,' I tease him, taking a sip from my own coffee. 'Don't tell me you were scared of her.'

'She's very er . . .' he searches for a suitable word.

'Predatory?' I offer.

'Yeah, that's a good word, a very good word.'

'Thanks for giving her the interview, it was kind of you.'

'Yeah, it was, wasn't it? Very kind of me, throwing myself into the lion's den like that for you.' He stops and looks at me uncomfortably. We are both aware of the admission he has just unintentionally made.

'Do you know, I think that deserves something in return, don't you?' He raises his eyebrows at me, once more smoothing over our awkwardness with humour.

'It does?'

'Yeah – a biscuit to go with the coffee!'

I come back into the studio from the kitchen once again. The sun is low in the sky, fingers of golden light spreading across the pure white room like a slow-burning caress. Connor has left his stool and is leaning on the window ledge, staring out at the sea; he hears the door and without turning calls to me.

'Nattie – quick!' His voice is an urgent whisper. Without question, I hurry to stand beside him. 'Look.'

He points to our right, at a place just before the horizon, where the sparkling sea meets the pale cerulean blue of the sky.

'What? What is it?'

And then I see them. The dolphins. Twisting and leaping, dancing and playing, grace and beauty. I gasp with delight and surprise.

He turns to me, his face sparkling like the sunshine-dappled sea with pure pleasure, his blue eyes a reflection of the water. Our eyes and smiles meet, a silent communication of rapture and privilege. And then our lips meet and we are kissing. He lifts his hands and captures my face gently between them, drawing me in, drowning me in longing and need. And all the time our eyes stay open, locked, focused so intensely on each other that I swear I can see inside of him, that I could fall inside of him.

I lie beside him, our bodies intertwined, warm flesh against warm flesh, my head resting upon his chest, held close and safe in his arms, and I listen to his heartbeat. Rise and fall with the rhythm of his breath, until I feel he is breathing for me. And then I realise that *I* am breathing, that *I* am living, that *I* can feel; a myriad emotions are prickling in me, like the sting of pins and needles when the blood starts flowing freely through your body again.

As though in our coming together he has flooded me with new life.

It is late before I can bring myself to leave. I shower and stumble down the stairs with wet hair, my clothes still in disarray. Connor meets me in the hallway with coffee, which is placed to one side as he pulls me back to him, his arms drawing me close, and our lips meeting again, my eyes flickering half-shut as we kiss a long and lingering time. And I rest my cheek against his neck and savour the feel and the smell of him and the delicious comforting warmth of him holding me close as we say a long goodbye.

★ ★ ★

I find that I cannot go straight back to Whitsunday. Having refused Connor's offer to drive me back to the farm, I choose instead to walk back slowly along the coastal path. It is dusk, the light is beginning to fade as the sun sinks quickly below the churning black waters of a now cold sea.

I walk until it's dark, and the lights of Whitsunday are ahead of me, and then instead of cutting toward them across the far meadow where the cattle are huddled together, I go down toward the end of Mile Meadow, crossing the path to the cliff edge. Finding as dry a place as possible to sit, I stare into the tumbling grey depths of the sea below me. I must try and get a hold of myself and collect my thoughts, which are churning inside my head like the water swirling madly in an eddy below me, a small whirlpool sucking the debris from the surface of the water to the very bottom.

I feel that I have betrayed Rob. I am like Judas, betraying with a kiss the one that he loved above all others. And yet . . . And yet, it felt so right, so perfect, so warm, and so real.

Does the fact that I could feel this way about someone else take something away from what Rob and I had together? Anything that could make me question my loyalty to him must surely be wrong. What if he were still alive and I had met Connor – would I have . . . could I have even contemplated . . .

I shake my head to try and clear the thoughts, to allow rationality a space within a crowded mind.

I'm not sure exactly how I feel at the moment. The one thing that I am certain of, however, is that I don't for one minute regret what happened. I also know that I *have* to question the feelings I have for Connor. Not just for my sake, but far more importantly, for his.

Do I truly care about him as I think I do, or is it just my sadness, my loneliness? Would I seek comfort from another, from any other – or is it just Connor? Just he who has slipped so quietly and yet so intrinsically inside of me?

Even as I ask myself these questions I find the answer coming to me with such a piercing clarity it makes me jump to my feet.

Night has fallen when I return to the farm. The security light is on in the long passage so someone must have walked this way only moments ago, unless it was one of the dogs, slipping like a silent friendly ghost amongst the shadows.

Chance is dozing in his loose box, hind legs lifted alternately to rest them as he slumbers. The yard is empty. In the kitchen, Laura is setting the table for dinner, a casserole in the Aga saturating the air with the rich aroma of slow roasted meat steeped in herbs and red wine. Meg is asleep on the rug, Stu is beside her. She opens one tired sleep-filled eye as I enter, and thumps her tail briefly in greeting. Stu opens both eyes when I enter the room, and then stretches, pointing small toes in a long yawn of muscle, before dragging himself to his feet to wander over and say hello properly.

'Ah, so one of you has finally deigned to come home then?' Laura's voice is heavy with a sarcasm that I know is only there to hide her concern.

I stoop to stroke Stu, his tongue curling coldly on the inside of my wrist, and as her words sink through my distraction, I look up at Laura in concern. 'One of us? Where's Cas?'

She stops placing knives and looks up at me sharply. 'I was hoping *you'd* be able to answer that one. I haven't seen her for a couple of hours at least.'

'Did she say she was going out?'

She shakes her head. 'The last I saw of her, she was out in the Long Barn. Luke was out there trying to repair the blasted hedge-trimmer, but I think he left at

423

SARAH HARVEY

about five. When I think about it, I haven't seen her since.'

'Maybe she's still out there,' I reply. 'She goes there to practise sometimes.'

'I know. And I don't like to interrupt.'

'I'd better go and check she's okay though. It's nearly seven.'

'Tell her she's to help with dinner, that *I* sent you for her.'

I hurry outside filled with a deep sense of unease. There is a strange nagging voice at the back of my head that tells me Cassie is not at Whitsunday. I don't feel her here. I know that sounds remarkably odd, but I have somehow come to know when Cas is nearby – like a sixth sense, I suppose.

I hurry back down the long passage cursing my own self-indulgent distraction that I didn't notice whether the light was on in the Long Barn when I passed it only minutes ago. The security light, which had gone off, flicks back on as I step into the passage, but the Long Barn is in darkness. No Cas.

Chance was safely tucked up with his hay net when I passed, so I know she's not there.

'Cas!' My voice echoes against the walls on either side of me. 'Cassie!'

I wait, my ears straining. No reply.

When I go back into the kitchen Laura has pre-empted me and is on the telephone. 'Oh okay, right, thanks, Orlaithe . . . yeah, if you would, thanks. Take care . . . bye!' She turns to me. 'She *was* there. Apparently she and Luke went in there just after five o'clock, and stayed for one drink. Don't worry,' Laura adds quickly as my face turns pink, 'she only had a Pepsi – Orlaithe was quick to say she hadn't served her alcohol – and then they left. Orlaithe said she just assumed we knew she was there.'

'Well, she'd have no reason to think otherwise, would she?'

'She must have gone with Luke when he left.'

'Without telling us?'

'I know – I don't understand it myself. She's not done anything like this before. You haven't had a row, have you?'

I shake my head. 'Not that I'm aware of.'

'I must admit, she did seem a little agitated this afternoon. She wondered where you'd wandered off to, that's for sure. I told her you'd probably just gone for a walk and lost track of time.' Laura pauses. She doesn't ask me where I've been but the question in her tone is obvious.

'I certainly lost track of time, that's for sure,' I reply evasively.

Laura looks at me oddly for a moment, and then she smiles slightly. I have a feeling both Laura and Cas would have a good idea where I have spent most of the day. I have a sudden urge to tell Laura everything. To confide, to seek approval even. But I don't. I stay silent.

'Perhaps she just wanted to get out, to get away from us,' Laura finally offers, breaking the silence. 'Being cooped up in the house for the past few days hasn't helped. I daresay she just wanted to get out for a bit.'

'Yeah, but not telling us she was going . . .'

'I know.' Laura nods her agreement. 'I'll swing for Luke when they get back, I really will. I'm surprised at him. He normally has such lovely manners. He should know better.'

'Maybe he didn't realise she hadn't told anybody she was going off.'

Laura considers this possibility. 'True. There's no point in worrying about it. She'll be safe enough with him.'

'On the back of that bloody motorbike? She knows I don't like her going on it.'

'That's probably why she didn't ask.'

Laura's picked up the phone again. 'What are you doing?' I ask.

'You've worried me. I'm phoning Orlaithe again.'

'But—'

She puts up a hand to silence me, as the call is answered. 'Hi, Orlaithe, yeah, me again. Just wanted to know was young Luke on that bloody death-trap of a machine of his? . . . Well, thank heavens for small mercies.' She says goodbye again and turns back to me in relief. 'He's in his father's van.'

'That's good news at least, but she must have left on the bike to start off with, and I didn't see a spare helmet, did you?'

We exchange loaded glances. Concern, anger, fear. But all we can do is wait.

Waiting for what seems like so long that the beat of my heart has stilled to nothing and the hands on the clock, the image of which is burned into the back of my eyes, stop and start to go backwards, taking me back, reminding me so painfully of the night I was waiting for Rob to come home.

And he never came.


At eleven thirty we hear the sound of a car coming up the mud and gravel track, the throbbing tick of an old diesel engine, and we're both up like a shot and out of the kitchen door into the yard, the security lights Hank installed after the break-in, blinking on to blind the driver of the vehicle now pulling into the yard. It's a little white Fiesta Van, and to my relief I see that it is Luke behind the wheel and Cas sitting next to him. The van pulls to a halt, the engine spluttering a little before dying of its own accord even before Luke can turn the ignition to off.

The passenger door swings open and Cas falls bodily out of it from the waist up, head down, retching so hard you'd think her lungs are going to pop out onto the cobbles if she doesn't stop herself very soon.

Luke gets out of the car white-faced and looks briefly

at me, then back at the ground before hurrying round to help Cas up and out.

'Where the hell have you been!' Laura bursts out angrily.

'I'm so sorry,' Luke pleads. 'I tried to stop her drinking but she just wouldn't listen to me.' His face is drained, eyes wide with anguish.

'Why didn't you bring her home sooner then?' My mother rounds on him. Going to Cas's other side, she takes her arm, and puts her own around Cas's waist, leading her away from Luke and toward the open kitchen door.

'She wouldn't come, Natalie,' he pleads. 'You know what she's like, she's so headstrong, she wouldn't listen to me, and the other lads kept egging her on, buying her drinks. They thought she was funny. I asked them to stop but they wouldn't . . . and she wouldn't come home. I couldn't just walk out and leave her. I did try to phone you twice but it was engaged both times.'

'I know, Luke,' I try to reassure him. 'Don't worry, I know what she's like.'

'Natalie!' Cas sings out my name as if she's ecstatic to see me, and pulling away from Laura she staggers back over, holding out her arms as if she wants to embrace me.

I hesitate, unsure of what to do, then she sways again and I step forward to catch her. To my surprise she bursts into tears, thrusting her small face into my shoulder. 'Oh Nat, I'm so sorry, please, I'm so sorry for everything, for absolutely everything,' she sobs, clinging to me like a child. 'You do care about me, don't you? I know you do. You do love me, don't you?'

But before I can answer, she wrenches herself away from me, her mood swaying as unsteadily as her body.

'Of course you don't love me, you don't even like me – why should you? I'm a complete cow to you, aren't I, a complete and utter cow, and you just let me get away with it – you let me walk all over you like a doormat. You're spineless!'

'Cas, please.'

'You don't want me. Why would you want somebody else's kid dragging along in your lovely little life? You've got your job, your friends, you wish to hell that I didn't exist. Just a problem to you, that's all I am, a bloody hassle, Cas the Hassle. You've inherited a hassle. Bet that's not what you thought Dad would leave you in his will, eh?'

'It's not like that, Cassie, you must know that.' I reach out for her and she shakes off my hand, and starts to cry hysterically.

'Bitch, just get away from me, you . . . you bloody bitch!' She staggers backwards, the sobbing turning to high-pitched hysterical laughter. 'I hate you, you know, I don't care about you. I don't care about you at all. You're nothing.' She clicks her fingers together. 'Nothing. Nothing. Nothing.' She hisses the last, her eyes rolling back, even as her chin sinks forward, and her head lolls to the side. The next moment her knees have gone and she's pitching sideways to lean against the wall, elbow to the crumbling stone, head down, tears dripping directly from her eyes onto the cobbles below. A pathetic figure.

I kneel down beside her, take her face in my hands, force her to look at me. 'I know what it's like, Cas. I'm there, too. Please, let me help you through it.'

Cas looks at me, her drink-dulled eyes suddenly focusing with a clarity her mind is struggling to maintain.

'How can you help me,' she says simply, 'when you can't even help yourself?'

I let go of her face and sit back on my heels, stunned by the truth in those quietly spoken words. Laura darts forward, squeezing my shoulder reassuringly as she passes me to kneel down beside a sobbing Cas.

'Let me take her. Come on, darling, let's go inside. I'll take you to bed.' She helps Cas up and leads her inside.

Luke is still standing behind me. He looks excruciatingly embarrassed, his handsome face drained of its healthy tan, pale and pinched.

'I'm sorry,' he stutters again.

'No, *I'm* sorry,' I reply, not looking at him. 'You shouldn't have had to see that.'

'I . . . I think I'd better go.' He starts to walk back to the van, but then stops and turns back to me. 'She didn't mean that, you know – any of it.'

'That's the thing, Luke,' I sigh. 'I think she did. I think she meant every word.'

He shakes his head. 'No. She likes you. We've talked about, you know, her dad and stuff, and you, and she's never said anything like that before. It's just the drink. She thinks you're cool.'

'She does?'

He nods slowly. 'Yeah, cool. That's what she said when I asked her what you were like.' He opens the van door, but then hesitates again before stepping inside. 'Will you tell Cas it's okay, tomorrow morning? Just in case she's worried about me seeing her go off her head?' he asks me.

I nod numbly. 'Yes, of course – and Luke?'

'Yeah?'

'Thanks for looking out for her, not leaving her.'

He shrugs. 'Couldn't leave her like that, could I?'

Laura is in the kitchen when I go back in. She looks warily at me as I close the door and kick off my slippers, which are damp from being worn outside.

'Where is she?' I ask.

'I put her in my bed. She's fast asleep.'

'You mean you couldn't get her up the second flight of stairs because she was too pissed, and now she's passed out?'

Laura looks cagey and doesn't answer me, as always

429

trying to protect Cas. 'She didn't mean it, Nat.'

'Oh, didn't she?'

'No.' Laura shakes her head vehemently.

'And you know that for a fact, do you?'

'I truly believe that, yes. You two have been getting much closer recently, you know you have, we've all seen it.'

'Everyone except Cas herself maybe,' I reply sadly, sinking into a chair. 'I've let her down so much. She doesn't think I care about her because I never bloody well show her that I do.'

'That's not entirely true,' Laura replies softly, sympathetically. 'Cassie is your responsibility now and it's that way because that's how *Rob* wanted it. He made you the legal guardian of his only child, Natalie. That's a huge amount of trust to place in someone, a *huge* amount. Rob knew exactly how Cassie treated you, how you didn't get on, and yet he still wanted you to have her. Do you think he would have given her to your care if he thought for one minute you'd give up on her? Rob knew you, Nattie. He knew what a kind and loving person you really are; he wanted Cas to have the same kind of love and loyalty that you gave to him.'

She's right. I know she's right. I think of what Luke said, 'she likes you'. I feel the frustration subside a little, and rub my hands over my face in agitation. 'I know, I know. I should keep on trying if only for Rob's sake.'

'No, not for Rob's sake, for *Cassie's* sake. And your own. Please don't give up on her, Nat. She needs you. She loves you, you know, but she's so like you, stubbornly refusing to show it, to acknowledge it to herself even.'

I can't stop the dry bitter laugh that wells in my throat. 'She loves me?' I repeat incredulously.

Laura nods. 'You may not be able to see it, and heaven knows she tries not to show it, but it's quite clear to me that she does. You think if you don't care, then you can't get hurt. Nobody can take away someone you love, if you don't love anybody. Trust me, I know. I shut myself off from everybody, especially you. I'm not saying I never loved you, Nattie, please believe me. I always loved you – but I couldn't let myself feel just how much. Cas is the same. When your father died, I thought that I'd died too. It broke my heart, Nattie, and I vowed I would never let anybody get inside of me so deeply again. Even my own daughter.'

She has finally admitted it to me. An admission, if I am completely honest with myself, I have been wanting to hear since I was a child.

I turn to her, my helplessness and frustration deflected. I stand and stare at her for a long and silent moment, finally confronting a hurt far deeper and of a much longer standing than my struggle with Cas.

'But I'd just lost my father. I needed you more than anything in the world.'

'I know, I know, and I'm so, so sorry. You wouldn't believe how sorry I am.' She comes to me, holds out her arms, enveloping me in the warmth of her embrace, stroking my hair, pressing her cold cheek against mine, eyes tight shut as though her whole body is holding onto the sigh that sits inside of her.

She finally lets it go, a long breath of release, and then steps backwards, sinking into a chair as though suddenly too weak to stand.

'It's very easy to be selfish in our grief, Nattie,' she says softly, looking at the floor instead of at me. 'To get wrapped up in how hurt we are, how we feel, how nobody could ever come close to knowing what we're going through. But that's wrong. Death touches everybody at some point in their lives. When your father passed away all I could feel was myself. I couldn't even begin to see that someone else could ever know the hurt I was feeling. But I was wrong, so very, very wrong, because there was a little girl who felt the same pain as

431

me, twofold even because instead of just losing her father, she lost her mother as well.' She looks up now, her eyes full of unshed tears and sorrow. 'I wasn't there for you when you needed me the most. Don't give up on Cas in the same way. Don't make my mistakes all over again.'

'But Cas doesn't need me like that. She doesn't want me – I'm not her mother.'

'No, but you're the closest thing she has. I don't think it's a case of her hating you any more. I don't think she ever really hated you, she was just jealous that her father loved someone else as much as he loved her. And now I think she's just scared to get too close to you in case she loses you as well. I was like that, Nat. I couldn't let myself feel how much I loved you because I was scared that I'd lose you too. That you'd go too eventually. Which you did. And the fact that it was me who'd driven you away made it ten times worse. You only realise these things when it's too late, Nattie. Do you know, you reminded me so much of your father; every time I looked at you, all I could see was him, and it hurt so much, Nat. So badly. Everyone said we were the odd couple, but he was my rock. I was the gaudy kite sailing jauntily high above without a care in the world, but without his strong hands to guide and hold me steady, I would have been tossed, broken to the ground. I think we Dunnes are like swans, we mate for life. But what happens if one of those lives is ended? Love, companionship, marriage, happiness – I felt that I had no right to those things without your father, and so I just shut myself off, closed my mind to any thought of ever falling in love again, because I didn't believe I could. As much as I adored your father, as much as I still love him, I regret that now. I know now that I could have moved on, maybe fallen in love again, maybe even married again. I say that I'm with Charles because of the lack of demands on a limited heart, but my only limitations are the ones that I have put upon myself.'

She looks down at her hands and sighs heavily, sorrowfully, and then almost whispers, more to herself than to me, 'To think I could even have had more children.'

She looks up at me, and I can see the tears sliding from her eyes, even though she's struggling so hard not to cry. 'And perhaps I could have kept the child that I had.' She reaches out to me beseechingly. 'Please, please forgive me, Nattie.'

I stumble towards her, sinking down to my knees in front of her, taking first her hands, and then wrapping my arms about her neck, holding her to me as she cries into my collar bone. And as I hold my mother, sobbing in my arms, I feel a strange sense of calm, almost of peace, and a release of the hurt that I have held within me for so long. For too long. And I stroke her soft hair as she did mine, quiet her, comfort her, until the sobbing ceases.

'It's all right, Mum. *We're* all right,' I tell her over and over again, and I know at last that we are.

# Chapter Fifteen

It is New Year's Eve. Cas is sitting on Laura's bed, watching in fascination, just as I used to when I was a child, as my mother applies her make-up. She has just come from the shower and is wrapped in a big white towelling dressing-gown that is one of Laura's cast-offs, a navy blue towel around her freshly washed hair. She doesn't look up as I enter the room.

Things had become far warmer between us recently, but now we seem to be back to the big freeze. She hasn't spoken to me all day, avoiding me studiously. I have tried to talk to her, to tell her how I feel, to find out how *she* feels, but she will not listen. She is quite dogged in her refusal to discuss last night.

Laura says that she is embarrassed, but I think there is more to it than that. I promised to talk to her if anything happened between Connor and me, and yet I have kept things from her. Despite the fact that until yesterday, nothing physical had happened between us, there were still plenty of emotions flooding between us like salt water in a tidal river. Cassie is far from stupid. I know she has seen the growing affection between us, no matter how much I tried to deny it firstly to myself and then to her.

I also think she has her own opinion of where I spent yesterday afternoon, and that this was the trigger for her behaviour last night.

Laura has finished her make-up, and slipped into the

new crimson velvet dress. She twirls on the spot. 'What do you think?'

'A vast improvement on the slacks,' Cassie grins, mouthing the word with distaste. Laura spots me in the doorway, and turns to me in silent question, striking a pose, hands on hips so that I may admire the outcome of her self ministrations.

'You've still got great legs,' I offer.

'What about the face?' she asks, pouting heavily.

'Well, you can't expect everything to survive the years intact.'

Laura's mouth drops open in outrage. 'Ooh, I bet you wish you look like me when *you're* forty-eight,' she taunts me.

'No, but I wouldn't mind looking like you when I'm *fifty-eight*.' I smile, as my mother knocks ten years off her real age.

'You're fifty-eight?' Cassie asks incredulously.

Laura looks at Cas for a moment, then nods reluctantly. 'A woman should never reveal her true age,' she adds quickly.

'Wow, I didn't realise you were *that* old.'

'I think there's actually a compliment in there somewhere.' I can't help but laugh as Laura's eyebrows shoot up her head in consternation. Then she looks me up and down, my scruffy jeans, my unwashed hair. 'Shouldn't you be getting ready too?'

I look over at Cas. 'I don't know if I'm going to come.'

'What do you mean, you might not come!' my mother exclaims in outrage. 'You've got to come – it's New Year's Eve. It's not a choice, you know, it's obligatory. Now go and sort yourself out, for heaven's sake put a skirt on!'

Charles's house is the sort of place you should roll up to in a carriage and four, not a car. With its sweeping circular drive and columned entrance, Cadogan House is majestic old lady, sitting high on a peninsula on the edge of the sea, like a queen upon a throne of granite crafted by the violent caress of the sea.

We are very late; the house is already full of people, the enormous ballroom filled with women in their most expensive dresses, and men looking uncomfortable in starched shirts and ties that only get an airing on special occasions. The room is huge and yet people are packed into it like cattle in a transporter, the noise of talking and laughing almost drowning out the twelve musicians playing on a raised platform at the end of the room.

I feel slightly underdressed in black evening trousers with boots, and an off the shoulder top, which at Whitsunday looked casually elegant, but here, looks somewhat out of place amidst the long sweeps of velvet and voile. Cassie was met at the door by an eager Luke who had apparently been standing sentry for over an hour. I'm not surprised he is so keen. She looks amazingly beautiful tonight, her fragile, elfin features enhanced by the gold dress, a slender, mythical nymph, heads turning to look at her as she walks into the room, Luke's hand proudly on her arm as if to prove to himself and others that this gorgeous creature is actually with *him*.

Whilst Luke takes Cas onto the dance floor, Laura and I head straight for the bar. A swift neat double to calm her nerves, and she sets out to look for Charles, in the hope that she can catch a moment with him whilst his wife is on the dance floor in the arms of another man.

With Laura gone, I look for Cassie, but cannot see her. I do, however, spot Orlaithe and Hank, dancing up a storm. Orlaithe looks stunning in a kingfisher-blue dress that twists elegantly around her as she and Hank dip and move to the music. She spots me and waves enthusiastically, signing that they'll join me for a drink when the music stops.

And then I see Connor. He is standing on the far side

of the room in the middle of a group of chatterin
people, and yet he is silent and somehow apart fror
them, his own eyes scanning the room as mine are.
know that he is looking for me, and his was the face
was searching for, too.

I haven't seen or spoken to him since that almo
dreamlike time we spent together yesterday. He appar
ently called the house this morning, but spoke wit
Laura only. I know that he was phoning for me too, bu
some fear held me back, and I left the house befor
Laura could call me to the telephone. I tell myself I hav
been too preoccupied with Cas, but I know in reality
am afraid. Afraid that somehow, by speaking to him,
will be forced to spoil with regret an afternoon that wa
for me a precious gift, a turning point.

I have no regrets myself, apart from the turmoil tha
our relationship may cause Cas.

Our eyes meet.

He half smiles at me, until I return the smile, and the
he begins to move across the room towards me. I know
for certain when I see him, when I look into his eyes
that it is still there – that link, that connection – that *nee*
which sets our feelings apart from simple friendship.

'What are you doing here propping up the corner o
your own?'

'Just watching,' I reply quietly.

'Well, you shouldn't be just watching, you should b
out there enjoying yourself.'

'Oh believe me, if I was out there, I wouldn't b
enjoying myself.'

'And why not?'

'I can't dance.'

'And you think these people can?' The strained fac
breaks into a smile and he gestures expansively at th
dance floor. 'Nobody knows what they're up to; they'r
doing eight different dances out there and they don'
give a flying fig, because all they're intent on is having

438

ood time, and enjoying the evening.' He emphasises
ie *enjoying*, indicating that this is something I obviously
aven't been doing this evening, but certainly should be.

'It's difficult,' I reply.

'Sure but it isn't,' he answers, deliberately misunder-
anding me. 'You just move your feet from side to side,
nd try not to tread on anybody's toes.'

I can't help but laugh.

'Dance with me?' he asks, emboldened by my smile.

I don't reply.

'Come on, Nattie – dance with me.'

He holds out his hands and I find my own rising to
ieet them. His thumbs lock over the back of them as if
) keep me from backing away or backing out. Then he
raws me onto the dance floor into the middle of the
ughing, breathless crowd. And we dance.

We dance Blaydon Races, Strip the Willow, the Gay
ordons and the Cornish Six-Hand Reel, where we find
urselves dancing with Laura and Daveth, and Hank and
rlaithe, Cas and Luke in a group of youngsters in the
iird set on the other side of the dance floor. We can't
ilk because the music is too loud and the movement
)o fast, but his eyes and his smile and his touch say
verything I need to know.

And then, just as I think I can dance no longer, the
iusic winds down. A lone violinist begins to play a love
ong, a waltz. He draws the sweetest music from the
rings as his bow glides across them like a lover's finger
ently caressing.

We slow. Instinctively, Connor pulls me closer, to rest
gainst him. My cheek is pressed to the hollow between
is neck and his collarbone, the soft yet rough warmth
f his shirt against my skin.

I can feel his heart beating almost in time to the
iusic; my eyes close and I let him lead me. We move
uidly together, as though his body is so familiar to me
iat we are almost as one, and it is finally obvious to us,

439

and not only to us but to any onlookers from the intimacy with which we hold each other, that we are at last together.

As the music ends, we break apart. My eyes glowing breathless I look about me in self-conscious and embarrassed pleasure and find my gaze met by smiling approval, until it comes to rest upon a familiar frown. Here I see no pleasure, I see no approval; I simply see a pain so wretched it tears this new happiness from my body like a tidal wave crashing across the earth ripping the roots of all things living from the ground.

And then the tears begin to slide down Cassie's cheeks, before she turns and bolts from the room.

I pull away from Connor, run after her, push my way blindly through the crowd. Across the other side of the room, I can see my mother. I can't hear her but I can see her lips move as she calls out my name, but I keep on running, out of the vast front doors of the house stumbling down the stone steps and onto the gravel drive.

It has started to rain. The sky is black above me, a rumble of thunder in the distance, the threat of a storm riding in from the ocean.

Cas is nowhere to be seen.

I lean against the wall and catch the breath that's rasping in my chest. As my breathing quietens, I begin to acknowledge another sound coming from nearby. The sound of someone sobbing as though their heart were breaking.

Just ahead of me another figure is leaning against the stone wall, silhouetted in the darkness by the lights from the many windows, oblivious to my presence, lost in the pit of her own heartache.

'Cas?'

At the sound of my voice, she looks up, startled, then promptly begins to hurry away from me, down the drive, and across the lawn.

'*Cas!*' I call again. 'Please, wait!'

I catch her up, reach out and put a hand on her shoulder. She snaps around to face me, her eyes black and hollow with misery and anger.

'I saw you in there – I saw you with *him*.'

'I know you did and—'

'Don't try and tell me there's nothing going on. It's so bloody obvious everybody else could see it – everybody!' Her eyes are blazing with anger. 'How could you? You said you loved Dad. If you loved him you wouldn't, you wouldn't . . . You never loved my father. You certainly don't love me! You promised me that you'd tell me if . . . if you and him . . . you *promised*. I know you were with him yesterday afternoon – I know it! But you never said a word. You lied to me. You don't care, you don't give a toss about me, do you?'

'Don't say that, Cas. You can't believe that!'

She wrenches herself away from me.

'Cassie, wait!'

But she is running away from me across the lawn, blinded by the rain in her eyes, feet slipping on the soaked grass in those ridiculous heels. Panicking, I run after her, calling out to her, as she runs ever closer to the boundary of the garden, where the smooth lawn of Cadogan House gives way to unkempt grass and scrub, where the land falls away to nothing, down into the crashing, churning sea below.

I scream out at her to stop, and to my relief she does – just as she reaches the edge, turning back to face me, the tears streaming down her face, indistinguishable from the rain that has soaked her to the skin.

'Cassie, please!' I hold out my arms to her. 'Please, Cas, don't give up on us, we need each other – *I need you*.' I take a deep breath. 'I love you, you idiot. God knows you've tried so hard to make me not, but I do.'

She watches me for a moment, breath coming in gasping sobs, eyes wary, and then slowly, very slowly, she reaches back toward me.

'Oh Nattie, I'm sorry.' She steps forward, our finger touch, intertwine, and she is a breath away from me and then suddenly she is wrenched backwards; the lan beneath her feet gives way, and she is falling backward downwards.

'*Cas!*'

My scream falls after her, and then a split second late I too follow. The breath is forced from my lungs as I h the ground and realise with heart-lurching relief that m hand is still tight about her wrist, her fingers claspe around mine. Tightening my grip, I inch forward an peer down into the darkness. Cassie is an arm's stretc below me, her face looking up toward mine, white wit fear, eyes black and bulging, mouth open, breathin quickly, too quickly. The adrenaline of fear taking ove her body, forcing her towards hyperventilation.

'Stay calm.' I struggle to speak, my mouth dry, m voice harsh.

Our eyes meet, Cassie's full of fear and panic, he mouth opening up to gasp for air again, like an alcoholi gulping whiskey. Her position is precarious. She is hel only by me, and the very tip of her stupid gold sandal which are resting, but only just, on what is really to small to be called a ledge. Below her I can hear th restless tumble of storm-ravished sea, but it's too darl and the rain is too heavy for me to be able to se anything but the terrified figure below me.

I hunt around madly for something, anything tha will help me. A small but fairly sturdy tree is growing o the cliff edge. If I shift my body sideways then I can hoo my feet through a cleft in its trunk enough to lowe myself down a little closer to Cas. I carefully inc towards it, calling out to Cassie not to be afraid.

'I want you to climb up, Cas.'

'I can't,' she sobs.

'Yes, you can. You have to.'

442

'But how?'

'You have to climb up me. Take a hold of my belt and ull yourself up.'

'I can't do that.'

'You *can* do it,' I urge her.

She closes her eyes.

'You can do it, I know you can,' I repeat more rgently as her left foot yet again slips from its precari- us hold.

'But I can't.'

'You've got to, Cas. Don't worry, I won't let go of you, promise. I'll help you do it.' It's so hard trying to keep er calm when inside I'm panicking myself. Our eyes ock. 'Please trust me.'

She hesitates for another moment, then she blinks owly, and I see her literally forcing her right fingers to let o of the small shelf of rock onto which they are clutching.

I brace myself as she reaches up and takes a hold of y leather belt, and slowly begins to pull herself up me, ventually letting go of my left wrist to take a firm hold f the small tree trunk instead. Who would have nought her delicate frame could ever feel so heavy, as ne slowly and tortuously inches her way upwards, but ventually she is on solid ground, and reaches behind to elp me as I haul myself back up beside her.

We lie together side by side, trembling violently, Cas's and still clutching mine.

Slowly we stand up.

'Oh Nat, thank you. I'm so sorry, thank you.' Cas wallows and puts her hand to her mouth as the awful ealisation of what has just happened hits her.

'Don't you ever run away from me like that again!' I cream at her, then grabbing her by the shoulders I pull er against me and hold her so tight I can feel her heart eating overtime behind the ribs of her thin chest.

'I can't lose you, too, Cas,' I mumble into her hair. 'I an't lose you, too.'

And slowly she lifts her arms from her sides and put them around my waist, her grip tightening as her hea falls forward and she begins to sob into my alread soaked shoulder.

'I'm so sorry,' she mumbles against my neck. 'I'm s sorry, so, so sorry.'

I hold her to me for what seems like an eternit neither of us wanting to let go, until the clouds abov us give an ominous low rumble of thunder, and th rain that was already falling heavily turns into torrent.

There are panicked voices calling us.

My mother. Luke yelling for Cas.

'Natalie!' It is Connor.

'We're here,' I try to call back but the wind rips awa the sound and carries it out to sea. 'I think we'd bette go back,' I tell her.

Cas nods and holds out her hand to me. As I ste forward to follow her, the earth beneath my left foo disturbed already by Cassie's fall, gives way, crumbles t nothing, throwing me backwards.

Have you ever dreamt that you're falling? That awfu moment where your foot reaches toward the groun only for it not to be there? That physical rush, an almos electric shock of free falling, before you are jerke awake, back to reality. My reality, and also my salvatior albeit a dark angel, is a ledge of rock twelve feet below. would imagine this is what it feels like to be hit by a ca All the breath is catapulted from my lungs, as my rib and the cliff face connect.

Something has to give.

Granite isn't very giving.

I hear and feel the crack and the punch of pain leave me gasping like a landed fish. I don't know if it's a flas of lightning or a white light of pure pain as my head i next to hit the rocks below, but whatever it is, it is th last thing that I see.

The last thing I hear is Cassie's voice screaming my name.

I am lying in our bed at home, Rob's arms warm about my waist and neck, his body pressed against my back, curved where I curve, bent where I bend, fitting me and warming me like a second skin, protecting me; his breath against my neck, his voice soft and full of love, repeating my name, over and over, like the gentle sound of rain against a window, as silent as snow falling.

'Natalie.'

'Nattie, can you hear me?'

'Natalie!'

'Careful.'

'Easy now.'

'Rob?' My mouth is too dry for the word to come out.

'There, quiet now. It's okay, Nattie. We'll have you out of here in a minute. Just keep still, try not to move.'

Strong arms, holding me . . . a voice, gentle and familiar. 'Connor?'

'Hush now.'

A rush of blackness.

Gradually I become aware that I am not alone. Hushed voices carry from across the room, and opening my eyes I have a moment of sheer panic. I can't see! Everything is white.

And then my blurred vision begins to clear, and I see two people in the doorway half in and half out of the room, and it is the room that is white, the walls, the floor, the ceiling, the bedclothes; one of the figures in the doorway is even wearing a white coat. And then the events of the night before come flooding back to me, and I realise where I must be. The figure in the white coat is speaking.

'She's a very lucky girl. Apart from some bruised ribs, there doesn't appear to be any major damage, but we still want to keep her in for a couple of days just to be on the safe side. Do a few more X-rays, make sure there' nothing I've missed.'

'Keep her in? But what's the point? You've said yourself she's fine. No, I want to take her home.'

'I know that, Laura, but it's better to be safe than sorry.'

'I can give her better care at home than she'd get in any hospital.'

'I'm sure that you can, but it's always better to err on the side of caution with trauma cases, you should know that.'

'But I don't want her to be here. She wouldn't want to be here either. Nattie hates hospitals, she'd be better off at home with me.'

'I know, but we've got to think of what's best for Natalie, and right now—'

'Damn it, man, she's my daughter! Don't you think I want the best for her?'

The man in the white coat smiles gently and places a soft, long-fingered hand on my mother's shoulders.

'Mum?' I try to speak. It comes out as a dry croak, but it is enough.

Laura rushes over to me. 'Nattie, you're awake, thank God. Are you okay? How do you feel?'

The man in the white coat comes to the other side of the bed.

'Natalie,' he smiles gently at me. 'I'm Dr McCardale. You've had a bit of a fall, I'm afraid, but apart from bruised ribs, everything seems to be in full working order. Can you tell me how you feel?'

'I'm okay,' I say, struggling to get up.

'You must let me be the judge of that. If you'd just lie still for a moment, I can take another look at you.' He begins to examine me, long fingers probing my neck and chest. 'I need you to tell me if this hurts.'

I smile wryly. I ache everywhere. But I'm hardly going

admit it. Mum's right. I hate hospitals. I hate the
mell, I hate the atmosphere, I hate the threat that I feel
angs in the air. My father spent the last few days of his
fe in a hospital bed, and I vowed then that I would
void them at all costs.

'Here?'

'No,' I lie.

I see my mother wink at me encouragingly from over
r McCardale's shoulder as he bends to press a palm into
he tender flesh of my abdomen.

'And here?'

I try not to wince. The last thing I want is to be told I
ave to stay.

He straightens up again. 'Well, everything certainly
eems to be all right. We carried out a series of X-rays
vhen we first got you here, although I'm sure you don't
emember any of that, now do you,' he smiles patronis-
ngly at me, 'and you'll be pleased to know that apart
rom a couple of badly bruised ribs, there doesn't seem
o be any other permanent damage.'

'Then can I go home?'

'Natalie, you've had a nasty fall,' he tells me, as
hough I'm a schoolgirl who is failing to grasp the
udiments of her lesson. 'You've been unconscious for
everal hours. We need to keep you in for observation.'

'Observation?'

He nods. 'You've had a pretty nasty bang to the
ead.'

'My mother can watch me.'

'Oh yes, I can watch her,' Laura adds quickly.

'I'm sorry, but I feel you should stay here at least for
nother night. Trauma damage is an unpredictable ani-
nal, Natalie. It's better to be safe than sorry.'

'But I'm fine.'

He holds up a hand to silence me. 'One more night at
east, and then we'll reassess the situation.'

He turns to Laura and dismisses her with a curt smile.

'It's best if you all go home now. My patient needs some rest.'

'But Cas, I mean her daughter's waiting outside to see her . . . her friends are outside, too. They've been here all night.'

'Well, if they've waited patiently that long already, I'm sure they won't mind coming back tomorrow. Tell them Natalie needs her rest now.' And he ushers a furious Laura out of the door, leaving me alone in the stark room.

A few minutes later the door goes again and I jump with relief, thinking that Laura has defied him and come back, but it's only a nurse, who cheerily force-feeds me a Diazepam, despite my protestations that I don't need any drugs.

She is the last person I see for two and a half hours. So much for being under observation!

I'm just attempting gingerly to get out of bed, with the idea that I could discharge myself if I know that I can actually walk, when there is a knock on the door so quiet that I almost don't hear it.

'Hello?' I venture uncertainly.

The door slides open a few inches, and a small blonde head peers around.

'Cas?'

'It's all right, she's on her own,' I hear her whisper to someone in the corridor.

The door swings open and Cassie inches into the room. I can see Luke just behind her; he raises a hand but doesn't step into the room, staying in the corridor, his head swinging from left to right like a spectator at Wimbledon.

'What's going on?' I ask.

'We've come to rescue you,' she whispers, her face bright with mischief and determination. Luke disappears from view as the door swings shut and Cas slips across the room, grinning broadly.

'Laura told us the old bastard wouldn't let you come home, even though you wanted to, even though you told him that you're okay. You *are* okay, aren't you?'

I nod, pleased that I now appear to be able to move my head without aggravating the headache.

'Then let's go. Come on – let's go home.'

We both jump as the door opens again, but it's only Luke. He's pushing a wheelchair.

'I don't need one of those!' I protest.

'It'll be easier for what we have in mind, trust me.'

They both help me from the bed, then Luke is sent into the corridor to stand watch whilst I change out of the green hospital nightgown into the clothes that Cas has brought me in a carrier bag, hidden under a large paper bag of fruit. My legs feel a bit wobbly, and my chest is tight and sore, but the feeling of elation that I'm going to get out of the hospital is better than any painkiller for me. I even sit down in the wheelchair without complaint, and let Cas wheel me out of the room, chuckling softly as she begins to whistle the theme tune to *The Great Escape*.

As we reach the end of the corridor we hear a harsh voice call my name. It is unmistakably the voice of Dr McCardale. Cas doesn't stop, she simply begins to whistle even louder, her grin increasing in breadth as she does so, her pace increasing also as she runs full pelt toward the double swing doors at the end of the corridor.

Laughing and breathless, we career dangerously through the hospital grounds, finally reaching the main car park, and they tip me as gently as possible into the back seat of my own car. Cas gets in beside me, whilst Luke shoves the wheelchair hastily toward the grass verge at the side of the car park, and then sprints round to the driver's seat.

'Home, James!' Cas cries, taking my hand and squeezing it gently.

449

Luke looks confused.

'Just step on it, Luke, before someone catches us up.'

'What on earth have you done?' Laura is trying to look angry but failing dismally.

'We sprang Nattie out of Colditz,' Cas beams. 'You said she wanted to come home, so we stole her while the doctor wasn't looking.'

'I don't approve of your methods, young lady,' she tells Cassie, trying to look stern, 'but I have to admit the motives were admirable.'

'Does that mean we can keep her?' Cas asks hopefully as though she's just brought home a stray puppy.

'We'll have to see about that. I'd better phone the hospital.'

'You can't!' Cas cries indignantly.

'I have to.'

We wait breathlessly while Laura goes to the study and places a call to Alan McCardale. She comes back ten minutes later looking grave.

'They want you to go back.'

'Oh.' Three faces fall simultaneously.

'So I told them that you've discharged yourself.' She breaks into a smile. 'They weren't very happy about it, but there's not an awful lot they can do, is there? I've got to keep an eye on you though. A very close eye,' she jokes, coming up to me and pressing her forehead against mine, so that our eyes meet from an inch apart. 'I love you,' she mouths, so that only I can see, then she places a kiss on my cheek and holds me gently before letting go. 'Happy New Year, darling.'

'Is it New Year?'

'New Year's Day,' Cas confirms solemnly.

'I missed it?'

'What – New Year's Eve in a hospital waiting room full of drunks? You didn't miss much, trust me. Now before I send you to your room, is there anything I can get you?'

'Yeah, a bottle of champagne.'

'Champagne?'

'That's what I said. Have we got any?'

'There's one of Petra's left in the fridge, yes, but Nat . . .'

'Then fetch it for me, Mum, please. I want to toast the New Year.'

'Can you have alcohol with those painkillers?'

'Probably not, but I'd rather have a glass of champagne than a Diazepam any day. And besides . . .'

'Dad always used to toast the New Year,' Cas finishes for me, coming to my side and taking my hand.

'Exactly, and I think we should start this year as he would want us to go on.'

Luke is sent home, and I am sent to bed, ostensibly to get some rest, but seeing as how everybody has decamped to my room with me, this is only a vague possibility. The portable television has been carried up from the kitchen and put on the chest of drawers opposite the end of the bed, and is now on and showing an old Ealing Studios comedy with the sound turned low. The open fire is lit for the first time, and the dogs are parked firmly in front of it. Laura is in a chair at the side of the bed, and Cas is curled up at my feet at the end of the bed, chattering away to me about Luke.

'It was my idea to get you out but I couldn't have done it without his help, because of course I can't drive. I hope you don't mind us taking your car without asking first, but this did kind of classify as an emergency, didn't it? Do you think I could start to learn to drive soon? I know I won't be seventeen for almost another year, but Luke's offered to take me up and down the track in the Landy if Laura will let us. It's perfectly legal apparently, as long as I'm on private land.'

I watch her, smiling like an idiot. I'm struggling to assimilate this girl with the Cassie I thought I knew. I've

451

seen a glimpse of her over the past few weeks, but I thought I'd lost her again.

'He's not the brightest light bulb in the box,' she chatters on, 'but he's kind and fun, and don't you think he's seriously gorgeous?'

'Oh yes, seriously,' I reply with a straight face.

'And besides, that's all I need at the moment. I'm far too young to even contemplate settling into a steady relationship, but that doesn't mean we can't have fun together, does it?'

She sounds so old and wise it makes me smile to hear her. She suddenly stops and looks over at Laura to make sure that she cannot hear her. Noting that Laura is asleep in her chair, she leans closer to me. 'Nat, about you and Connor . . .'

'Oh Cas, I'm so sorry. I tried to explain to you. I'm so sorry you found out like that. I wasn't lying when I said we weren't together – we weren't then. It wasn't until that afternoon that we . . . I knew I should have talked to you about it, but I couldn't find the courage.'

She cuts into my breathless attempt at explanations with a question that stops me completely in my tracks.

'Can I ask you something about Daddy?'

I nod slowly.

'You really loved him, didn't you?'

I nod again, biting my bottom lip so hard it hurts. 'I still do.'

She ponders this for a moment. 'I'm glad. I'm sorry I refused to see that when he was still alive. I do see it now, I promise, but I'm sorry it's too late to make a difference.'

'But it's not,' I laugh with relief. 'It's never too late. My love for Rob didn't just die when he did. It lives on inside me and it's as strong now as the day that I married him. Don't you understand how good it feels to finally know that you believe that this is true?'

She ingests this for a moment, and then her eyes,

which were full of earnest apology, flood with a different emotion that I find hard to read.

'Do you think you and Connor ... maybe some-day ... that you could love someone else as much?'

'Maybe, some day,' I reply carefully, watching her face as I speak for any signs of distress. 'I never thought that I could, but ...' I trail off. Is it fear I see in those clear blue eyes – insecurity? I'm not quite sure, but I remember what Cassie said to me the night that Luke brought her home when she was so drunk she couldn't stand.

She thinks that if I want Connor then I can't want her.

I *do* want Connor – that I cannot deny. He has filled my life and my heart with new hope, with the promise of a happy future, but I see now that I have another heart to heal before I can even think about the happiness of my own. I have failed Cas so far; I will not let her down again.

'Perhaps one day Connor and I could ...' I pause, to try to think of words that she will understand, 'have a relationship, go out, date sometimes ... but it's probably not the right time at the moment. There are too many things in my life that I need to deal with.' I stop, aware that I haven't chosen the words as well as I would have.

She lapses into a thoughtful silence yet again, but it's only momentary. When she speaks, it is to change the subject.

'Oh, by the way, Granny called for the eightieth time to see how you were. I told her your condition hadn't changed a jot in the ten minutes since her last phone call.' Her voice is too bright.

'She's worried,' I reply.

'We all were,' she whispers, turning away from me.

'Cas?'

She reluctantly turns back to face me. The smile has slipped and she is struggling hard not to cry.

'Cas, what's the matter?' I try to sit up but move too

quickly, catching myself with the sharp pain of my bruised rib.

Cas hears my intake of breath and turns back to me. 'Nattie, are you okay?'

'Yeah.'

'Are you sure?' Then all I can hear is the sound of muffled sobbing. She is crying as if her heart were breaking.

'Oh Nat, when I thought I was going to lose you too . . .' Her hand reaches back and I can feel her fingers slip between my own, lacing tightly, holding on as hard as when I was trying to stop her from falling.

'It's okay, Cassie, honestly. I'm not going anywhere. You're never going to lose me. You'll probably end up wishing that you could, but you're stuck with me now – all right?'

I feel her hand grip more tightly onto mine.

'For as long as you need me, I'll be here, and that's a promise.'

I wake the next morning with the sun streaming through the window as my eyes open slowly to focus on a blur of green and blue on the wall opposite my bed. I know that I'm awake, but surely I must still be dreaming. As the haze of sleep disperses, I finally realise what I am looking at.

It's the painting of the waterfall. Laura is asleep in the chair beside me. She has stayed in that chair since I came back from the hospital, refusing to leave me other than briefly to fetch meals and drinks. She stirs as I sit up to take a closer look.

'The painting. You got it back.'

Laura rubs her eyes and smiles slightly. 'Yeah. When I sold it, I was lucky – I sold it to Charles. I think he only bought it to help me out, not because he liked it particularly. No gun dogs or pheasants,' she explains as I widen my eyes in disbelief that anybody could not like such a beautiful painting. 'It was therefore fairly easy to persuade him to let me have it back. It's only there temporarily though.'

'Oh, he lent it to you, did he, to cheer me up? You have to give it back?'

She shakes her head. 'No, darling, I bought it back, but it's a gift, a gift for you, so that you can wake up to it wherever you are.'

'Then it stays here.'

She looks at me in puzzlement. 'But you're going back home in a couple of days' time.'

I don't answer her straight away.

'I never knew what you found here that made you stay,' I begin eventually, 'but I see it now. When Rob died, Cas and I lost an awful lot, including our home. I'm not talking bricks and mortar. Connor once said to me that home isn't where you're born, it's where you feel you belong. We lost our home, and now you, and Hank, and Orlaithe, and Luke, and Connor have given that back to us. London isn't home. Whitsunday is – *you* are – and it doesn't matter where we are from now on, we'll never be very far away.'

My room is full of flowers. Orlaithe and Hank came to visit after breakfast, Hank hidden behind the largest bunch of daffodils I have ever seen in my entire life.

'We did a ram raid on the Eden project, so we did,' Orlaithe told me laughingly. 'Can you just imagine that great pink car bursting through Eden's bubble and making off with a rake of their best blooms?'

A massive bunch of orchids arrives from Petra, along with a Get Well Soon card of a doctor getting a touch too friendly with his buxom patient. There is a card from Louisa-May, and another from Morwenna the post lady, a bunch of winter roses from Charles, and a surprisingly sober Daveth delivers a card signed by all the regulars at the Ship. Even Luke comes back to visit clutching a bunch of Michaelmas Daisies, although I think it's more of an excuse to see Cas than a desire to enquire about my health. They don't stay long, choosing instead to take a walk down to the field where Chance has been turned out to run his fetlocks off as Cas hasn't ridden him since New Year's Eve morning.

There is only one person conspicuous by his absence. Cassie told me it was Connor who rescued me, who climbed down the cliff edge with no thought for himself, and lifted me to safety.

By the afternoon I've had enough of being confined to my room.

'I'm getting up, despite what you say,' I tell Laura, as she begins to protest. 'I may have a bruised rib, and a bruised ego, but I feel better now than I have done for a long, long time.'

I take a long soak in a lavender-scented bath, scrubbing away the smell of the hospital, which still lingers on me like a cheap and sickly perfume. I'm back in my room and just changing into some comfortable clothes, when Laura's head appears around the door.

'You have a visitor.'

'Another one? Would it be awfully rude to make them wait while I get dressed?' I joke, gingerly pulling a sweater over my head, my chest burning with pain as I lift my arms.

'Well, the first time I met you I saw your naked arse, so I don't think you've got much left to worry about now, do you?'

I look up at the sound of his voice, embarrassed by the alacrity of the smile that has slipped so easily onto my face, surprised by the flood of pleasure at finally seeing him again . . . and yet not surprised at all.

I have tried so hard not to think about Connor too much and yet along with Cassie, he has been on my mind pretty much constantly the whole time I've been confined to my bed.

I realise now how selfish I have been – using Cassie's hostility as an excuse not to be there for her when she so obviously needed me. This time I cannot and will not put myself first. I know now exactly how I feel about Connor. And yet I'd rather hurt myself than hurt Cassie ever again.

Connor hasn't brought me flowers, he's brought me a painting of flowers.

'They last longer,' he explains, 'and you don't have to rush around the house trying to find an empty vase.' He looks around the room. 'It's like the Lost Gardens of Heligan in here.'

'I find I have a lot of friends.'

'How are you doing?' He sits down on the bed next to me. Laura has discreetly left us.

'I'm okay.'

'You're probably wondering why I haven't been to see you before now?' I realise that he looks uneasy. His gaze, which is normally steady, holding my own, is darting around the room like a honey bee, unsure which flower to land upon first.

'I'd be lying if I said that thought hadn't crossed my mind.'

'And you wouldn't want to lie to me now, Natalie, would you? Just like I couldn't lie to you even if I wanted to.'

I look at him in puzzlement. 'I don't understand.'

He finally looks at me, the usually honest and open blue-green eyes wary and uncertain. 'I haven't been to see you because I wasn't sure whether you'd want me here or not. Believe me, I wanted to be here. I waited at the hospital until that damn doctor sent us all home. Hell, if Cassie hadn't sprung you I'd have probably been there myself with a ladder at your bedroom window. I wanted to beat a path straight to your door as soon as

Laura phoned and told me you were home, but . . . but something held me back. I have to be honest with you . . .' He pauses, looks away from me for a moment and then turns back to me, his face determined, yet still so vulnerable. 'I have to admit I'm scared, Nat. I don't think I've ever felt like this about anyone before. I know in my heart that what I feel for you isn't fleeting or imagined, but I don't know exactly what this is . . . what *I* am, to you. I know you've been through hell in the past two years. I know you're frightened, too. The same fear that has made you and Cas hold each other at arm's length. Fear of feeling that pain again – the pain of losing someone you'd gladly die for. Of having someone in your life who you love so much that if you lost them, it would be the end of the world all over again. I know from what you've said, and from what Laura's told me, that you *have* loved someone this strongly, that in a way you still do and always will. But I also know from what I feel in here,' he presses a fist to his heart, 'that you do care about me.'

'Of course I do.' I reach out and clasp my own hand around his balled fist, feel his hand relax, our fingers slide together momentarily and then apart. 'More than you know – I can't deny that. I don't want to deny it, but I can't help feeling guilty that I do feel this way.'

Connor places my palm against his lips; he brushes a gentle kiss in its centre. 'Do you believe Rob loved you any the less for having loved someone else before you – enough to marry her and have a child with her?'

'No.'

'And if it had been the other way round, if it had been you who were in that accident, would you have wanted him to spend the rest of his life on his own, unhappy and miserable without you?'

'No,' I whisper.

'Natalie,' he says, so softly I can barely hear him, 'I think I could love you, if only I dared to let myself feel it, if only you would let me . . .'

For a moment I almost lose my resolve, but then I think of Cas and how much she needs me, of the pain in her face when I tried to talk to her about me and Connor.

'It's not Rob,' I say cautiously, drawing back so that his hand falls away. 'At least, not any more. I've realised that he would want me to get on with my life, to *have* a life, to love even, and if I'm completely honest with myself I've known that all along, it's just taken me a while to accept it. And it's not you, Connor, not us. I need to know that you understand how I feel about you, that I feel the same way as you, but you must also see that I have to put Cassie first now. She couldn't cope with it at the moment, with us. It would be wrong of me. She needs me and I haven't been there for her. She needs to know that for the moment at least she's my first priority.' I draw breath, look up at him, praying that he will understand. 'Maybe given time, you and me . . .'

*Given time*. I know all too well that time is an unpredictable animal, that it can be taken away in a single exhalation of breath. I reach out to him, my hands drawn by the longing that is stirring so strongly inside of me like the tide pulling the sea to shore. I cradle his face, feel him sigh as my fingertips touch his flesh and I allow my heart to speak to him instead of my head.

'I don't want to let you go,' I say.

'Then don't.'

'But I need to be with Cas. I need her to know . . .'

'And she will know, she does . . . we'll both be there for her, Nat, together.'

'I can't let her get hurt again, Connor. What if this didn't work out? It would hurt her just as badly as either one of us.'

'We could take it very slowly.'

'Slowly?' I let my hands fall to his shoulders, reluctant to break the contact.

'Yes, we could arrange our first definite date. What do you say? I could take you to the Treloars' next Christmas party.'

I exhale in relief at his words, smile up at him gratefully. 'Well, that gives me a year to decide what I'm going to wear.'

'So it is a date then?'

'Definitely.'

He smiles, but the smile is wistful.

'I'm sorry, Connor.'

'Don't be. There's nothing to be sorry about, not yet anyway. There's still the future, Nat. We both have one, you know, and at some point, at the *right* point, I feel certain that they'll run together.'

'You're a good friend, Connor.'

'And I'm truly glad to be given the gift of your friendship, Nattie.' He takes my hand, lacing our fingers tightly together, and I lean against him, taking comfort from him, my head resting against his shoulder. And we both know that for now at least, this has to be enough.

# *Epilogue*

On what is supposed to be our final full day at Whitsunday, Cas and I rise early and take a walk along the cliff top. We walk all the way to the bottom of Mile Meadow together, quiet in a comfortable way, silent in camaraderie. It is a new feeling, a good feeling; the animosity that burned so fiercely between us is no longer, and we are friends. More than that, we are together. The self-inflicted isolation born of insecurity is gone, the thorny wall of shattered feelings blown away on the breeze. We walk almost to the Huer's hut before Cas actually begins to speak. When she does, what she says gives me a shock.

'Nattie, I want to quit Cheal.'

'You do?' My eyes widen in surprise.

'Yes,' she states firmly. 'I don't want to go back there, ever.'

'But what about your friends?'

'I'll still see Emily.'

'And your dancing?'

'That's the thing. Don't you see? It's not *my* dancing – I've finally realised that. I'm not doing it for me. I've never danced for me, and that's how it should be – I should want it more than anything in life, but I don't.' She speaks slowly, as though only just allowing herself to recognise the full implications of her words. 'Yes, it was a passion, but not *my* passion. I just wanted to follow in my mother's footsteps. In fact, do you know something? I don't *love* dancing at all. As a matter of

461

fact, I *hate* it. I *hate* dancing.'

She lets out a long breath, then laughs loudly, a though relieved.

'There — I've said it. I've finally said it. I hat dancing. I HATE DANCING!' she suddenly screams throwing her arms into the air, and bellowing th words into the endless sky above. As though finall throwing off a heavy weight, she spins dizzily, whirlin around with her arms flung out. When she finally stop spinning she is standing in front of me, her eyes bright her cheeks red with the wind and with the flush of a eager excitement.

'You're not angry with me, are you?'

'Of course I'm not.'

'Then it's okay? I can leave?'

'Do you think I'd send you back there knowing how unhappy it would make you?'

She shakes her head. 'No, you wouldn't, would you? she replies, her eyes narrowing as though she has onl just let herself realise that I do honestly care about her.

'It's not straightforward though, Cas. What about you exams?'

'Well, I haven't exactly been working as hard as should since Dad died. I want to do my best in my GCSE and if I take them this year then I'm not going to do ver well at all. I was thinking, I was wondering if perhaps could take some time out? You know, get myself straight Maybe find another school in September.'

'I think that's a good idea.'

'You do?'

'Yeah.' I put an arm around her shoulder and w continue walking. 'It's a great idea.'

Just beyond the Huer's hut sits the cluster of rock: that gather protectively around my special place, my little hideaway, and while Cas is exploring, I slip quickly and quietly through the rocks and post my last postcard to Rob. My final farewell, so that I can lay him to res

462

peacefully within myself, a memory linked only to happiness, and look toward a brighter future.

The message is short and simple, and yet I know that it is the one, the only thing that Rob would be waiting to hear from me.

*Although we have lost you, we have finally found each other.*

At lunchtime we drive back down to Sennen Cove and take a walk along the beach. We eat fresh mussels at an old coaching inn, mopping up the wine and garlic sauce with hunks of hot, home-made bread. We sit outside to eat, our faces warmed by the weak yet determined sun, fingers numbed by the actual cold of the day which is belied by its summer-like brightness. We are watching out for the dolphins that Cas has yet to see, but is determined to find one day.

And we talk.

We talk as though we have just learnt a new language, hesitant at first, careful to enunciate and communicate exactly what we mean so that no misunderstanding can come between us again.

And we make decisions.

About us. Our life. Our future. For we finally recognise that our futures lie together, intertwined. And that our future is here. We're going to stay. We're going to renovate Smuggler's Cottage, so that we are close to Laura and, Cassie announces, Louisa-May will come to visit us whenever she is well enough.

Us. Cassie and I.

And even if it doesn't happen quite the way we plan it, we're both safe and happy in the knowledge that we are planning a future, together, as a family. They say that blood is thicker than water. Cas and I aren't related by blood, but we know now that our bond is greater even than that. We were brought together by one man who loved us both, neither taking anything away from the other within his heart, and we are both so grateful that we can now finally understand and recognise this, and the fact that he has left us an important legacy.

His love.

Our love.

Each other.

Last night I dreamt that I was at my waterfall again. Only this time I was alone and I was lying in the water. Naked in the water. And it was cool and cleansing, washing over me, as though it were washing away my sins, washing away my heartache. I felt safe and happy, as though the water were cradling me, filling me with a sense of peace and of love. And although I was alone, I could feel someone watching over me, smiling down on me.

I wake up the next morning for the first time in ten months with warm feet. Cassie has slipped downstairs from the attic in the middle of the night and is now nestled into my back, like a small delicate silver christening spoon, cosying up to an old everyday teaspoon in the cutlery drawer, her arm about my waist, her small feet resting parallel against mine. Like her father's used to. I lie and listen to the soft regular sigh of her sleeping breath, my tears steadily soaking the white linen of my pillowcase, sliding like rain down my face into the corners of my smile so that I can finally taste the salt of them.

Our cases are packed and placed in the boot of my car, unusual in so far as at the end of a journey they are normally fuller than at the beginning and yet this time they are far lighter, for most of mine and Cassie's belongings have been left exactly where they belong, at Whitsunday.

Despite this fact, Mum is struggling not to cry. I throw my arms around her, hug her tightly, let her wipe away her tears on the shoulder of my jumper like a child.

'It's not like we're going away for ever,' I reassure her. 'It's only going to be a few weeks. As soon as we've got everything tied up in London, we're coming straight back.'

'I know, I know,' she sniffs, throwing her hands in the air as I let her go. 'Mad, isn't it? I'm just being a daft old bat . . . I know you're both coming back soon, but I'm going to miss you so much whilst you're gone.'

'We'll keep in touch, I promise. I'll be on the phone to you every five minutes trying to sort out the sale of the cottage. In fact, that phone will be ringing so often it'll drive you round the bend. You'll start pretending that you're out so you don't have to answer it.'

It works. The smile has returned. The handkerchief goes back in the pocket of her slacks.

'Now – has Luke gone yet?'

Mum nods. 'At last. Anyone would think the pair of them were never going to see each other again, the way they were carrying on this morning.' She sniffs.

I throw her an arch look, which she accepts with a slightly foolish smile.

'Okay, so we're all going to miss you. I know, I know,' she holds up her hands in her own defence, 'you're coming back soon.'

Cas is sitting on the gate at the end of the long passage, looking out across Mile Meadow, watching Chance high-tail it round the field in the sunshine. She turns as she hears my footsteps behind her and smiles broadly in greeting, jumping down from the fence to stand beside me.

'Are you ready then?' I ask.

'As I'll ever be,' she replies, a trace of sadness in her voice.

'It's not goodbye. We're coming back, remember, very soon.'

'I know.'

'He'll be okay.' I nod toward Chance. 'Mum'll look after him for you until we come back.'

'I know,' she repeats, still staring out into the field. She is obviously troubled by something.

Stu is sitting at Cassie's feet. Concerned that he will come to harm in London, having been used to roaming freely around the farmyard, he is to stay here with Laura until we return. Perhaps this is what is bothering her. I bend to stroke him.

'If you're worried about leaving Stu, we could always take him with us. He'll just have to get used to going on the lead a bit more often,' I offer.

Drawn back from her reverie by my voice, Cas looks down at me, hearing but obviously not digesting what I have. 'Nat, can we talk? I need to talk to you.'

I stop stroking Stu's silken head and look at her flushed face curiously.

'Are you okay?' I ask in concern.

She nods vigorously, but says nothing, simply turns once more to stare out into the distance. I go to stand beside her, and she steps closer to me, so that our shoulders are touching. I squeeze the hand that she has instinctively placed in mine.

'So what did you want to talk to me about?' I prompt as she stays silent.

She hesitates for a moment, biting the bottom corner of her lip as though worried as to how I will take whatever it is she's about to confide in me.

'Do you feel like a walk?' she finally asks. 'Have we got time?'

'Yes, all the time you want. We're both free agents now, remember? No work, no school.'

Her smile returns briefly at this last.

We walk across the top of Mile Meadow and the fields beyond, heading down toward Smuggler's Cottage. Perhaps she is anxious for another look at the house that is soon to become our new home. But when the house is in view, Cassie cuts to our right and I follow her across to the edge of the land, where she comes to a stumbling halt, looking out where the land falls softly away to the beach below, a tumbling mix of winter-weary bracken and pale-green sea grass.

'What is it, Cas? There's something wrong, isn't there? If you've changed your mind it's not a problem, we don't have to move. We don't have to do anything you don't want to.'

'No, no, that's not it.'

'Are you sure?'

'Definitely. I can't wait to come back. What about you?'

'I feel the same.'

'And your job?' Cas queries, not quite convinced that I can so easily give up the job she has seen me devote my entire life to.

'I can't deny that I'll miss it a little. I'm not used to having so much free time, but I'm going to sort out the houses, which will take a lot of time I'm sure, and then I'll probably start to write again . . . but for myself this time.' I think of the copy of the manuscript I have been so lovingly and carefully updating, tucked safely away in a drawer in the bedroom, ready for me to start work on once more when the time is right.

'It's what I want to do, honestly,' I reassure her, as she continues to frown in concern.

Cas nods slowly, as still a little sore from the accident, I sit down upon the grassy bank that marks the edge of the field, holding a hand against my chest to nurse the sharp pain that nags me like a persistent toothache.

'And you?' I ask her. 'What do *you* want to do with your time off? It's a long time until you start at the new school in Truro. You've got a whole seven months until September.'

'I know,' she replies, her smile widening massively at

the thought. 'And do you know what I want to do? I'm going to ride.' She pauses and looks at me sideways, watching my face closely. 'And I want to paint. In fact, I LOVE to paint. I think I might become an artist. Connor says I'm good enough. He says I have a good eye.'

'He told me the same.' I smile at her.

She kneels in the grass beside me, and taking hold of both my hands leans forward so that she is looking directly into my face.

'He's a great guy, Nat. Connor – he's lovely.'

'I know.'

So this is what was troubling her. I knew there was something.

'You don't have to worry about Connor, Cassie,' I begin but she interrupts me breathlessly.

'If you were ever to find someone else, I'd like it to be someone like Connor.'

Surprised into silence I meet her gaze for a moment, and I see something in her eyes that has been missing for such a long time. Hope. And something else, something that makes my heart feel infinitely stronger. Concern. A concern, for me.

'Do you mean that?'

'I've not been fair to you, Nattie, never, at all. I've been awful, and you . . . well, you've done everything you could to make me happy. No matter how badly I've behaved or what a total cow I've been, you've always put up with me. And now I want *you* to be happy.'

'With Connor?' I probe gently.

'Yes, with Connor. I think I'd like that. No, I *know* I'd like that. He's lovely, Nat. He's kind and funny, and gorgeous. He'd make you happy.'

'He'd make *us* happy,' I reply, reaching out to touch her face. 'You and me, Cas, we come as a package now, you know.'

'You mean I'm excess baggage?'

I start to reassure her, then realise that she is making a joke.

'Please, Nat, I mean I know you don't need my permission for anything, but if it's me that's stopping you, that's holding you back then I don't want it to be.'

'But I—'

She pushes a finger against my lips to silence me. 'No buts. I know what you're going to say, you want us to spend some time together. Well, I'd like that too, I really would, and we will, I promise, but it doesn't mean you have to shut Connor out of your life to do it. I mean, I've got other things too, haven't I, like Laura and Chance, and then there's Luke . . .' The smile turns mischievous. 'We could always double date.'

She stops speaking and grins at me, hopeful and optimistic, the trust in her eyes reaching out to me, connecting with me, reassuring me.

'I really want you to do this, Nattie, if it's what *you* want.'

'Are you sure?'

'Absolutely. This is what you want, isn't it?'

I nod slowly.

'Then what are you waiting for? For heaven's sake go and sort it out before someone else snaps him up – because they will, you know, if you don't. There's a queue, I know. Even Laura's in it.'

Reaching across I kiss her gently on the forehead. 'Thank you,' I whisper.

I feel her wrap her arms tightly about my waist, and we hug.

We hug for so long that the clouds speed above us like cars on a motorway, the wind for once turns to go around us, instead of trying to creep through us, we hug for so long that the night turns to day, and the dawn comes.

A new dawn.

I find Connor on the white sand beach at Sennen.

I knew instinctively he would be there, drawn to him by the thread that connects my heart to his, my thoughts to his own. He is standing at the water's edge looking out across the deep grey mass of sea curling languorously toward him along the sand, like fingers stretching out to caress his bare feet. The sun hangs low in a red sky, its golden light gilding and permeating the pale grey bellies of the vaporous clouds that languish there.

Although he cannot hear me coming, my footfalls cushioned by the soft pale sand, Connor turns to face me as though drawn by the same thread that brought me to him.

And as he calls out to me in surprise and recognition, starts to move hurriedly and joyously over the sand. I suddenly find that I am no longer treading slowly and cautiously toward him. I am running.

Now you can buy any of these other bestselling
Headline books from your bookshop or
*direct from the publisher*.

FREE P&P AND UK DELIVERY
(Overseas and Ireland £3.50 per book)

| A Married Man | Catherine Alliott | £6.9 |
| Olivia's Luck | Catherine Alliott | £6.9 |
| Baggage | Emily Barr | £6.9 |
| Backpack | Emily Barr | £6.9 |
| Expecting Emily | Clare Dowling | £5.9 |
| Country Loving | Julie Highmore | £6.9 |
| Fame Fatale | Wendy Holden | £5.9 |
| Pastures Nouveaux | Wendy Holden | £5.9 |
| Staying at Daisy's | Jill Mansell | £5.9 |
| Millie's Fling | Jill Mansell | £5.9 |
| A Compromising Position | Carole Matthews | £5.9 |
| A Minor Indiscretion | Carole Matthews | £5.9 |
| Better than a Rest | Pauline McLynn | £5.9 |
| My Favourite Goodbye | Sheila O'Flanagan | £5.9 |
| Isobel's Wedding | Sheila O'Flanagan | £5.9 |

TO ORDER SIMPLY CALL THIS NUMBER

**01235 400 414**

or visit our website: www.madaboutbooks.com

Prices and availability subject to change without notic